friction 4

friction 4

best gay erotic fiction

edited by jesse grant
and austin foxxe

alyson books
los angeles | new york

©2001 BY ALYSON PUBLICATIONS. AUTHORS RETAIN COPYRIGHT TO THEIR
INDIVIDUAL ARTICLES. ALL RIGHTS RESERVED.

MANUFACTURED IN THE UNITED STATES OF AMERICA.

THIS TRADE PAPERBACK ORIGINAL IS PUBLISHED BY ALYSON PUBLICATIONS,
P.O. BOX 4371, LOS ANGELES, CALIFORNIA 90078-4371.
DISTRIBUTION IN THE UNITED KINGDOM BY
TURNAROUND PUBLISHER SERVICES LTD.,
UNIT 3, OLYMPIA TRADING ESTATE, COBURG ROAD, WOOD GREEN,
LONDON N22 6TZ ENGLAND.

FIRST EDITION: FEBRUARY 2001

01 02 03 04 05 **a** 10 9 8 7 6 5 4 3 2 1

ISBN 1-55583-593-7

COVER PHOTOGRAPHY BY MAXX STUDIOS.

Contents

Preface

Wow, it's that time of year again. Time for another *Friction: Best Gay Erotic Fiction* anthology. Avid readers of this series will probably notice that this year's volume, containing a mere 29 stories, is slightly less chunky than its predecessors. (Last year's mammoth work contained more than 40 tales of debauched man-on-man revelry.) This reduction in content isn't because the publisher was too cheap to spring for the extra paper; it's because Austin and I decided to be unusually selective this year. And, after all, 29 stories is still pretty long. Longer than you can last, I'll bet.

Despite reducing the number of stories, we did, once again, strive for diversity in content, structure, and authorial voice. As a result, perhaps not all of the stories will be your cup of joe. But rest assured, more will than won't. Austin and I will swear to that on a stack of Falcon videos.

One last thing: We would like to thank Scott Jacobs for his tireless work in helping to assemble this collection. Without him we'd have missed our deadline, and you'd be jerking off to some other, lesser book of erotica. Heaven forbid!

Jesse Grant
Los Angeles
December 2000

Immersion
Bob Vickery

Nick's sister called him that afternoon crying so hard that Nick could hardly understand the words she gulped out. He didn't have to. He'd been expecting this call for some time now, and he comforted her absently, letting himself be distracted by the various street scenes outside his window: a couple laughing; teenagers skateboarding by; two drivers arguing over a parking space. He ended the conversation promising to fly back to New Jersey the next day on the earliest flight he could get. After he hung up he remained sitting in the chair, staring blankly at the telephone. *I should call the airlines,* he thought, *and make a reservation.* But he didn't move.

After a while he picked up a pack of cigarettes, shook one out, and lit it. He smoked the cigarette calmly, flicking the ashes out the window because he didn't feel like walking across the room and fetching the ashtray. Late afternoon turned into evening; the streetlights blinked on, and he still remained in the chair.

The phone rang on two different occasions, but he ignored it each time. He had long since finished the pack, which he had crumpled and thrown out the window, so he just remained in the chair, in the dark, his mind blank.

The only thing he could see in the darkness was the green glow of the VCR's clock. He didn't stir until it said it was almost midnight. When he finally did climb out of his chair and walk across to the kitchen's light switch, it felt like he was wading through water. He flicked on the switch, wincing at the sudden burst of light, and looked around the room. The kitchen sink was full of dirty dishes, there were open cartons of Chinese takeout on the counter, and the garbage can was overflowing. *I should clean this place up,* he thought. *It looks like a dump.* He went over instead to the kitchen table and picked up the gay newspaper that he had left there earlier. He turned the pages slowly, his eyes scanning up and down each one until he finally stopped toward the back. He tore out an ad and stuffed it in his back pocket.

He walked into his bedroom, flicking on the light. The expression on his face was calm except for his eyes, which seemed to focus with an heightened intensity on the objects around him. He took off his shirt, opened his dresser drawer, and pulled on a T-shirt that hugged his muscular torso like a second skin. He grabbed his car keys and walked out the door. He had never been to this particular sex club before; in fact, he hadn't been to any sex club or bathhouse in years, and the address in the gay newspaper ad was for a street unfamiliar to him. He finally found the right street, then the right block, then the right building, and parked his car. Other men were streaming down the dark street and into the unobtrusive entrance lit by a single bulb overhead. Nick walked in, paid the requested fee, and climbed the flight of linoleum stairs that led into the club.

The place was dim, with pools of light strategically placed so that prowlers could check out the action. Music pumped out of the speakers, the beat pulsing and intense. Men walked silently down the twisting corridors, their eyes hungry or hooded. Or both. Nick was a handsome man: Greek-American with crisp, black curls, dark eyes, and a wide, sensual mouth, and many of the men he passed stared into his face in open invitation. Nick returned every stare—his expression unreadable but not set in the hard lines of rejection, at least. A few of the men turned and followed, their eyes trained on Nick's wide shoulders and tight haunches. Nick wandered down the corridors, into the mazes, and out the other end, into the dimly lit orgy room. He leaned against the far wall and waited.

Men slipped into the room one by one and hovered uncertainly in an irregular ring around him. After a while one of them approached him and tentatively laid his hand on Nick's chest. Nick stared at him, not moving. Emboldened, the man slipped his hand underneath

Nick's T-shirt, the fingertips sliding against the smooth, hard muscles. He grasped Nick's left nipple and gently squeezed. Nick's eyes never left the man's face, and he nodded his head slightly. The man's other hand rubbed up and down Nick's crotch, pressing through the thick denim against the bulge underneath. Nick stirred, pushing his hips away from the wall, and the man undid Nick's belt, pulled down his fly, and with two quick jerks pulled Nick's jeans down around his thighs. Nick wore no underwear, and his dick flopped half hard against his thigh. He hooked his thumbs under his T-shirt and pulled it off, letting it drop to the floor.

The circle of men closed around him—half predatory, half worshipful. Nick was standing directly beneath one of the covered bulbs, and light spilled down on his naked flesh—shadows catching in the curves and contours of his muscles, the hollows of his eye sockets, the underside of his chin. To the men who surrounded him he looked like an apparition. Another one approached, then a third, then all of them—crowding around him, jockeying for space, for some access, however limited, to Nick's hard flesh. Their hands were all over Nick, tugging at his skin, stroking it, playing with his nipples, his dick, his balls. The mouths followed soon afterward, moist, hungry; the tongues sliding across Nick's skin, leaving long, wet trails behind like the paths of slugs.

Nick accepted them all, shifting his gaze from face to hungry face, even letting his mouth curl up in an encouraging smile whenever a given stroke seemed hesitant and nervous. He rejected no one, regardless of age or body type or degree of beauty. One of the mouths found its way to his dick, and Nick sighed as he felt the lips nibble down his shaft. He began pumping his hips, sliding his dick in and out of the wet, warm confines of the stranger's mouth. The man was a skillful cocksucker, twisting his head from side to side as his lips descended the shaft, sucking hard as his lips ascended again. Another man crawled down between Nick's legs and, craning his neck, bathed the loose folds of Nick's ball sac with his tongue.

Nick pushed away from the wall and into the center of the dark room. Now the men had access to every inch of his flesh. Tongues licked him everywhere: over his nipples, into his armpits, into the crack of his ass...licking his asshole as if it were a puckered ice cream cone. Lips moved up his neck and finally planted themselves on Nick's mouth. Nick felt a tongue snake into his mouth, and he frenched the kisser back enthusiastically. He kissed one mouth, and then another, and then others after that. Some of the men were skillful kissers, some were clumsy, but Nick paid them all equal attention.

The tongue up his asshole was replaced by a finger that massaged the pucker of flesh without penetrating inside. Nick exhaled slowly, relaxing the muscles of his body, opening himself up to the sensations that tingled through his body. He spread his legs farther apart and bent over slightly. The finger pushed inside him tentatively at first, and then with greater assurance, knuckle by slow knuckle, corkscrewing up until it pressed against Nick's prostate. Nick groaned. The finger up his ass began to fuck him slowly, sliding up and down in a twisting spiral. He closed his eyes, feeling the finger up his ass as another mouth worked his dick. His dick was stiff and urgent, but the orgasm eluded him and his mind still buzzed with thoughts no matter how much the mouths and hands worked him over. *This isn't working,* he thought. *I can't drown myself in this.*

He pulled his dick out of the latest cocksucker's mouth. "Let me fuck you," he said. The man looked up at him, his face a pale oval in the dim light. He cleared his throat uncertainly. "There's no fucking allowed in this club," he said, his voice apologetic. "If you try, the monitors will kick us both out."

Nick didn't say anything, and after a while the man went back to sucking him off. Nick pulled out again. "I really need to fuck some ass," he said, his voice taking on an edge. The man looked up at him again but said nothing. "Look," Nick said. "Is there some place around here where I can fuck ass?"

The man rose to his feet. Now Nick could see that he was young, late 20s maybe—short and wiry with a square, blunt face. He didn't speak for a long time. "Yeah," he finally said. "I could take you to a place."

Nick gently shook off the hands and mouths that were still feeling and tasting his body. He bent down and pulled up his jeans, and then found his T-shirt and slid it back on. "Let's go," he said.

The two of them stopped outside the club's entrance. "Do we need to drive?" Nick asked.

The man shook his head. "No," he said. "This place is only a couple of blocks away. We can walk." He was at least a head shorter than Nick, but his body was solid and compact. He looked up at Nick, his eyes hard and curious. "What's your name, man?" he asked.

"Nick."

The man still stood in front of Nick as if waiting for something. After a few beats he cleared his throat. "I'm Tim," he said finally. "In case you're interested."

"OK," Nick said.

Tim still didn't move. "We could go back to my place," he said. "You could fuck me there." He ran his hand through his shaggy hair and looked up into Nick's face. His voice was hard, even belligerent. "In fact, I'd fuckin' love it if you did."

Nick seemed to consider this. "How long could you take a pounding?" he asked. "Would you let me fuck you all night?"

Tim laughed uncertainly. "Well, eventually I'd like to get some sleep."

Nick shook his head. "I'm not going to be sleeping tonight."

Tim stared at him. *Fucking tweaker,* he thought, not saying anything.

Nick zipped up his jacket. "It's cold. Why don't you take me to this place you know about?"

After a couple of beats Tim nodded. "OK."

It was a beat-up leather bar over on Harrison Street; the door, a black leather curtain tacked onto the frame with corroded chrome studs. The space inside seemed to suck up light, and Nick could just dimly make out the forms of men lined against the wall or bellied up to the bar. The only illumination came from a monitor mounted over the bar, showing a fisting video.

Tim turned to Nick. "Do you want a drink first?" he asked. "Or should we get right to the action?"

"I don't need a drink," Nick said.

Tim gave a snort of laughter and shook his head. "OK, man," he said, "then follow me."

They threaded their way through the length of the bar. The air vibrated with hip-hop and the buzz of conversation, with occasional laughter. Nick's eyes slowly adjusted to the dim light, and the features of the men around him came into some kind of shadowy focus. It was a rough crowd, with weather-beaten faces and hard eyes like black glass marbles. The crowd thickened the farther back they went, until they were surrounded by a crush of bodies. By the light of a few shaded bulbs Nick could make out men with their pants down around their knees, stroking their dicks, being sucked by dark figures kneeling before them or fucking the asses of men crouched in front of them. The air was thick with stale cigarette smoke and the smell of poppers. A hand groped Nick's basket while another squeezed his ass.

"This is it," Tim said. "Just about anything goes here."

The place was stifling hot from the heat of the bodies and the poor ventilation. Nick could feel beads of sweat form along his forehead, trickle down from his armpits, soak his T-shirt. The beat of the hip-hop music throbbed in the air like something tangible, and the darkness pressed down on him like a heavy cloth. Nothing felt real. *Yeah,* Nick thought. *This is more like it.* "Do you still want to get fucked?" he asked.

"Yeah," Tim said. "Sure." He shot a hard look at Nick. "That is, if you're still up for it."

"I'm still up for it," Nick said. He unbuckled his belt and pulled down his zipper. The hip-hop song ended, and the Talking Heads started singing "Take Me to the River." Nick pulled Tim to him and kissed him, pressing his body tight against him, grinding his hips. Tim snaked his tongue into Nick's mouth and slid his hands over Nick's torso, tweaking his nipples with a sharp pinch.

"Yeah," Nick said, "oh, yeah. I like it like that."

Tim pulled back and fished a small square of cardboard out of his jeans pocket, pressing it into Nick's hand. It was a condom packet. "If you don't mind," he said.

"No," Nick said. "I don't mind." He tugged his jeans down, and his hard dick sprung up. He let Tim slide the condom down his shaft.

"I have lube too," Tim said.

"You're just a regular Boy Scout, aren't you?" Nick said. "Prepared for everything."

Tim gave a brief laugh. "I'm prepared at least for Friday nights." He unzipped his pants and let them fall. Nick squirted a dollop of lube onto his hand and burrowed it between Tim's ass cheeks, then stroked his sheathed dick with his lube-smeared hand and wrapped his arms around Tim in a tight bear hug. Tim pressed against him, and Nick rubbed his hard dick up and down the length of Tim's ass crack. Other hands stretched out from the darkness and caressed Nick's own naked ass, squeezing and pulling on the muscular cheeks, sliding up his back. Nick ignored them as he poked his dick head against Tim's asshole, then slowly skewered him.

Tim gave a long, drawn-out sigh, and Nick paused, his dick full in, his body pressed tight to Tim's. Slowly, almost imperceptibly, he began pumping his hips, timing his strokes to the throbbing beat of the Talking Heads. Tim moved his body in response to him, meeting him thrust for thrust. Nick sped up his strokes, his arms still folded around Tim's chest, his hips squirming against Tim's ass in deep, grinding motions.

He could feel himself slipping away into the act of fucking, all the thinking in his head dissolving into sensation. He closed his eyes in relief, welcoming the cocoon of darkness that enveloped them both, the invisible hands that stroked his body, the dark shapes that hovered around him, the music that drowned him in its volume. *Yes,* he thought. *This is what I need.* He slid his dick in all the way and churned his hips. Tim groaned again louder. After a few seconds Nick slowly pulled out. Tim squeezed his ass muscles tight against Nick's shaft, and Nick's legs trembled from the sensations this caused. He pulled Tim up and buried his face in Tim's neck, now slick and salty from sweat. Tim twisted his head around, and they kissed awkwardly, his lips fumbling against Tim's. He reached down and wrapped his fingers around Tim's dick. It felt thick in his hand, and its heat flooded into his palm. He stroked the fleshy tube in sync with each thrust of his dick up Tim's ass, and Tim's body writhed and pushed against him.

The hands were all over them both now, stroking them from all sides, pulling at their flesh. One man leaned his naked body against Nick, dry-humping Nick's back. Nick reached behind him and tugged on the man's balls, and after a while, groaning, the man ejaculated. Sluggish drops of come slid down Nick's back into the crack of his ass and down his leg. The man bent down and dragged his tongue against Nick's skin, eating the load he had just deposited.

Tim had taken over stroking his dick, and he was jacking off furiously now. "I'm getting close," he gasped. "I could shoot anytime."

"Let me do it for you," Nick growled in his ear. He slid his lube-slicked hand down the length of Tim's shaft just as he thrust his own cock up Tim's ass, hard. Tim cried out, and his dick pulsed in Nick's hand, sperm spurting out and down the shaft like white lava. One pulse, a second, another, and another still: Tim's load gushed out as his body shook violently against Nick's.

"Yeah," someone growled. "All fuckin' right!"

Nick felt another load splatter against his back from one of the men behind him. And another after that. Tim was standing with his weight against Nick, breathing heavily, his chest rising and falling. "Damn!" he said.

Nick slowly pulled out of him and peeled the rubber off his still-hard cock. He turned toward the dark shapes beside him. "Who's next?" he said.

As the next man bent over in front of Nick, Tim pulled up his jeans, reached into his pocket, and pulled out a handful of condoms. He thrust them into Nick's hand. "Here," he said. "I'm done for the night. You'll need these more than I will."

Nick said nothing, but he closed his hand around the packets. Tim leaned over and gave him a kiss on his mouth, then disappeared into the darkness. Nick tore open one of the packets and sheathed his dick. A minute later he was slamming the ass of the stranger in front of him, his strokes hard and savage. Once again he let the darkness and the heat and the stroking hands around him strip him of everything except raw sensation. *Finally!* he thought, before he stopped thinking altogether.

He fucked ass all night, one after the other——the dark forms bending down before him and taking his hard dick that refused to shoot. It wasn't long before he was regarded as something of a phenomenon, even to this jaded backroom crowd. His beauty was wasted in the dark, but the men's fingers could feel his muscular body and appraise him, and his relentless dick won an eager admiration. He fucked indiscriminately without pause, triggering orgasms in one partner after another even while his own eluded him. He fucked until gray light filtered in around the edges of the leather curtain draped over the front entrance. Now, every time someone left or entered pushing the curtain aside, a pale, feeble light washed in, even as far as the back room where he fucked. He would catch quick glimpses of his partners, of the men who still surrounded him, waiting their turn before the light was once more extinguished by the drop of the curtain. "You are fuckin' amazing, man," someone growled in his ear, but Nick ignored him, hell-bent on skewering the ass of the man in front of him.

He fucked until the bartender turned them all out, telling them he had to get some sleep and they should too. Outside, the early-morning light dazzled Nick's eyes. He had lost his T-shirt somewhere back in the mass of churning bodies, and he drove home shirtless, his mind bruised and sluggish.

He waited at the airport terminal on standby all that morning and afternoon before he finally snagged a seat to Newark on an early-evening flight. A couple of hours later he got out of his seat and walked down the aisle to the lavatory. It was almost midnight, and the passengers were huddled in the dim light into every possible sleeping pose. One man, however, was awake, sitting in an aisle seat toward the rear of the plane. He looked like a businessman, early 40s, dark suit and red power tie. As Nick passed they locked eyes. Nick paced up and down the aisle a couple of times, to make sure—and each time the man's eyes fixed on him in a hard stare.

They fucked in the lavatory, the man hoisted up on the small chrome sink, his legs wrapped around Nick as Nick slammed into him with one savage thrust after another. The man started groaning, and Nick kissed him roughly, more to shut him up than out of passion. It was late at night, and despite the crowded plane they had the lavatory to themselves. They didn't exit from it until the plane was preparing for its descent into Newark. The man had shot two loads, but Nick's orgasm still eluded him, even though his dick had never been stiffer.

He had telephoned his sister in the San Francisco airport just before his flight's departure, and she was waiting for him at the terminal. The sky outside the terminal window was still black, but there was a streak of gray in the eastern horizon. This was Nick's second night without sleep. He walked over and hugged his sister as a sleepwalker would.

"You look terrible," she said.

"I feel worse," he replied.

They didn't say anything else until they were in his sister's car.

"She was in a lot of pain, Nick. It's better this way."

"Yeah," he said. He leaned back and closed his eyes. It started to rain, and his sister turned on the windshield wipers. He wedged himself into the corner made by the seat and the car door, but sleep still shunned him. He lay there, eyes shut, exhausted, and listened to the rain pelt the roof of the car, comforted in some small part that the sky could shed the tears he was still unable to find.

Holding the Ladder
Xavier Texeira

S on of a bitch! Looks like T.J. forgot his drawers today. I wish he'd
be more careful. Monday through Friday, when the rest of the
crew's here, he's all business: starched jeans, long-sleeved work shirt,
hard hat, and safety boots. With his square jaw, clear complexion,
broad shoulders, and strawberry-blond crew cut, he looks like Ralph
Lauren–meets-OSHA. But Saturdays? There's no telling what he'll
show up in.

Still, he's a good kid. Polite as hell too. At first he made me nervous with all his "Yes, Mr. Texeira" and "No, sir, Mr. Texeira" stuff.
After all, I'm only 27 to his 19, but it's a habit for him. T.J. just finished his plebe year at Alabama Military Institute up in Birmingham.

Some of the employees resent T.J. because he's a "little college-kid
know-it-all punk," but I don't. I can't help liking him. He has this
puppy-dog quality. He grins a lot, and when he does his emerald eyes
light up like Christmas bulbs. T.J.'s good company too. Time flies
when we work together. He knows more about baseball than anybody
I've ever met, and I'm a fanatic. I grew up in Pawtucket, R.I., right
down the block from the Pawtucket Whalers' field. When I was young
I memorized every baseball card that I could steal from 7-Eleven.

Thomas Jefferson Wright Sr., the owner of the company I work
for, South Coast Fire Suppression, founded the company here in Fort
Myers, Fla., when he got back from 'Nam. Now it's the biggest sprin-
kler company in the Southeast. When he decided to let a college kid
intern with us over the summer, Tommy asked me to show the kid
the ropes and keep an eye on him. Truth is, sometimes I can't take
my eyes off him.

Like today. The two of us frequently work Saturdays, knocking out some of the light work that Tommy hates to pay a full crew for. Since lunch we've been installing 165-degree fixed-temperature heads in the apartments that the crews piped this week.

We're taking turns on the ladder because this job gets you in the back of the neck. T.J.'s installing, and I'm doping heads and handing him tools. My most important job, though, is steadying him on the slippery tile floor.

T.J.'s in fantastic shape, and that's important; pipe fitters need a lot of physical strength. I guess nine months of "Drop and give me 50 push-ups" didn't hurt him any, because he looks like an anatomy chart. Every sharply defined muscle in his back and chest is reflected over and over by the mirrored walls surrounding the vanity in the bathroom of the unit we're working in. As he works, his thighs twist and flex, his ass cheeks moving and sliding under my hands like small animals fighting to escape their denim cage.

T.J.'s a different kid on Saturday. Relaxed. No "sir"s. I'm just Tex, and you wouldn't believe how unmilitary he looks. Today he showed up half naked, dressed like the lead singer for the Village People. All he has on is an unfastened pair of Nike Alpha Projects, a Marlins baseball cap, a titanium dive watch, and a pair of baggy cutoff cargo pants faded to almost white. They're so torn and shredded that every time he moves I get a venetian-blind peep at his muscular young butt. They're so loose I could see all the way up to…but I'm not looking, of course.

I mean, I'm 27 years old, and he's only a kid. Anyhow, I don't fool around like that. I'm as straight as an arrow. I've got a wife and two daughters up in Rhode Island. Or at least I did until Beth ran off with her boss last year. A real fuckin' prize she left me for—the housewares manager of the Kmart in Fall River, Mass.

She said I was "just a pipe fitter, not a professional like Bruce." Oh, and Bruce has blond hair and blue eyes. He's a fantastic catch in Pawtucket, where everybody looks down on us Portuguese. People like me, with curly black hair, brown eyes, and a Mediterranean complexion, are as popular as Nelson Mandela at a Klan rally. Beth never loved me. She just married me to spite her mom, and because she loved my dick. It's not very long, but it's super thick, with a size XXXL head.

After she threw me out last fall I drifted south until I ended up in Florida. I rented one of those little cinder-block cabins they built for tourists right after the war. The next day I bought the Sunday want ads, and by Monday noon I was the new man for South Coast. Tommy couldn't believe his luck: a master pipe fitter for Florida peon wages.

That's how I came to be here, holding a stepladder for a half-nude teenager in the unfinished bathroom of a condo in Bonita Springs, Fla. South Coast has the contract for three of the waterfront pigeon coops they throw up for retirees from Terre Haute, Ind. I hate them. They block the beach for a hundred miles like an endless row of decaying teeth. But a job's a job.

"Yo, Tex. I said 'Hand me the Stilson.' I can't screw these things in with my teeth."

T.J.'s voice jerks me back to reality. I mean, I'm really not interested in the kid. It's just that as I steady him, his ass only inches from my face, I'm getting this sticky, uncomfortable feeling in my crotch. I realize that he's young enough to be my kid brother, but from this angle T.J. looks real grown-up. His stumpy, muscular thighs are covered with fine red hairs, the same shade as his crew cut and long, thick eyelashes.

When he leans down to grab the wrench, the baggy shorts gape open, giving me a quick flash of his wrinkled sac and the slate-blue head of a man-size cock. After a second it's gone, and he doesn't even know what I've seen. The problem is that it keeps happening. Every damn time he bends down I get another peep.

I guess I could say something, but T.J.'s just a kid. I know he doesn't realize how horny grown men can get sometimes, and I don't want to embarrass him. He looks so innocent up there.

I know the crazy feelings will pass. I can't be turned on by another guy. It's just that I've been lonely as hell since I came to Florida. I arrived dreaming of steamy nights with tanned blond beach bunnies.

Instead, every woman I meet seems to have blue hair and support stockings. Wanna know what girls in a Fort Myers pickup bar look like? Think Vicki Lawrence in *Mama's Family.*

I've been having a little trouble concentrating. My hands are wandering all over. It's like they're hypnotized by T.J.'s handsome body. Every time he moves they creep up a fraction of an inch all by themselves. By now they're actually in his shorts and almost out of sight. No wonder my balls hurt like a toothache.

After making sure T.J.'s looking the other way, I reach down in my jeans and adjust my hard-on, trying to find a way to relieve the pressure. What a mess. My drawers feel like somebody dumped a cup of Karo syrup down there.

But it doesn't matter. Even if I weren't 100% straight, I know better than to fuck around at work. It's just that it's so hot I'm having trouble concentrating. After all, it is July in Florida. That's why I'm sweating like this. Fuckin' humidity. It's not my hands on the boy's thighs or the way the weight of his tool belt has pulled his shorts down, exposing the top two inches of the most beautiful crack that God ever created.

It's not the way that each little hair on his spine has trapped a tiny droplet of sweat that glitters like a diamond in the sun. It's not even the way they make a V like an arrowhead pointing down to someplace that I'd give my left nut to…

No, it's just me. I'm tired of being alone, of spending every night with a six-pack, jerking off to the Spice channel.

It can't be his smell that's fucking with my head, can it? The fragrance of a youthful body like incense in the steamy air? I thought it might be the odor of his leather belt or his deodorant or even the detergent in his shorts, but it's not. It's something else. Something sending frantic signals deep into my brain stem. It's something earthier, more primitive.

It's lust. The murky pheromone of raw sex. It's a mixture of funk from his crack, sweat from his full, heavy balls, and the perfume of his crimson pubic hair.

I'm really out there, not paying a damn bit of attention, when T.J.

suddenly strains hard against the wrench. His foot slips, his hand slams against the ladder, and the wrench flies past my left ear, taking a chunk out of someone's new genuine fiberglass tub.

"Son of a bitch!" Sucking on a busted knuckle, T.J. clambers down the ladder to stand just inches from my face. His cheeks are flushed, and he's trembling with rage. "That's it. I'm not putting up with this shit anymore. Let's do it."

I can't believe it. I have a decent job, and now I'm gonna have a fistfight with some kid and end up getting fired.

"I'm sorry…" I begin, but he cuts me off.

"Fuck that. Do you want to do it or not?"

"Do it?"

"My ass. Do you want to fuck my ass? You've been staring at it all day. Rubbing yourself and licking your lips."

"I…I don't know what you're talking about," I stammered. "I'm not gay."

"Yeah…sure. That's why your hands keep sneaking up inside my shorts while you're supposed to be steadying me."

"Hey. That's not my fault. They're so baggy."

"Of course they are. I've been trying to get your attention for a month. If nothing happened this week, I was gonna buy a fuckin' kilt."

"You don't mean you planned this?"

"Well, duh! I'm lucky I don't have killer hemorrhoids, the way I've been sticking my ass out in your face."

"Man, T.J. I don't know about all this. You're still a kid. What do you know about sex?"

"Yeah. Right," he answers, his voice brittle with anger. "A 19-year-old kid who just spent nine months up at AMI. I don't think there's much I don't know about it."

"You mean…"

"Come on, Tex. Don't get stupid on me. Haven't you ever read stories about military colleges? You never saw *Lords of Discipline*?"

"Yeah, but I thought they were mostly that. Stories."

"Well, you were wrong, at least for AMI. It started the very first night. More fuckin' and suckin' than a *Melrose Place* reunion. Our parents kissed their precious babies good-bye at 4 o'clock. At 9 o'clock there were 350 stark naked freshmen lined up in the gym for inspection."

"You're kidding," I whisper, shocked. Not because I haven't heard of stuff like that. I watch *20/20*. What I'm having trouble with is how turned-on I'm getting as I listen to the boy's story. I mean, I'm as straight as an arrow, but the image of those hundreds of young dudes, all naked and vulnerable, all those big cocks and sweet young asses, is messing with my head.

"Like fuck I am. It was crazy. The upperclassmen strolled up and down the ranks shopping—jacking a dick here, handling a pair of balls or finger-poppin' a virgin rectum there. Picking out a bed partner for the night. Nobody thought to move. It was like we were all overwhelmed.

"It was the same thing every night after that. They checked us out like paperback novels, tried us, and either kept us or dumped us back onto the pile. Cadets got passed around until somebody picked up their option. You either got paired off or you left in disgrace."

"Did you...uh..." I mumble, avoiding his eyes.

He holds up his left arm, the one with the watch. "Tag Heuer. Twelve hundred bucks. Kind of an engagement present from Shane Campbell. He's gonna be a junior. We're rooming together in the fall. Not everybody was as lucky as I was. Almost a third left the first semester. Some had academic problems, and some just couldn't get with the program. Maybe they refused to swallow some senior's come or couldn't take a hard one up the old poop chute."

The grin returns for a second, and I smile back at him. I'm beginning to look at T.J. and the idea of gay sex in a different light. My crotch seems to have taken over my brain. They say a hard cock doesn't have a conscience, but I still have enough left to ask, "Doesn't it hurt you to...uh...do that?"

"Hurt? The first time I wasn't sure I could take it. Five sophomores took turns with me. I guess they might have resented their plebe year, because they wore me out. But you get used to it. The first couple times are hell; the next couple times are OK; after that it's heaven. It's all you want to do. So what's up?"

"What's up?" I echo, confused by the sudden switch.

"Do you want to do me or not?" he persists, grabbing the rigid pole in the front of my jeans. "Guess that answers that."

Sitting down on the bottom step of the ladder, he unzips me and fishes it out through the fly of my boxers. "Nice," he smiles, sliding the loose foreskin back. "Oh, yeah. That'll do the job." Leaning forward, he takes my shaft completely into the silky heat of his mouth. Thought and control melt away, leaving me with feelings so intense that I can't catch my breath. The stroke of his tongue, caressing of his lips, and abrasion of his teeth are killing me.

Standing up, he kicks off his shoes and unsnaps his shorts. They drop to the floor. Stepping out of them, he turns in a circle like a dancer, chin up and arms held out to the sides. It's a hell of a show: His balls large and tight, his youthful penis circumcised and so hard, it almost touches his navel. While his body and legs are toasted brown by the Florida sun, his thighs and gently rounded ass are milky white, almost translucent. The purple veins of his erection are as distinct as a road map.

"Well?" The way he's looking at me, it's obvious that he's waiting for a compliment. I struggle to find the right word, but I don't seem to have a vocabulary to admire male bodies. I settle for "beautiful," and he beams.

Leaning against the edge of the countertop, T.J. unbuttons my jeans. He pushes them and my boxers down into a bunch around my knees. Too late to stop now. I'm already half crazy with need, seven months of stored-up juice boiling in my aching nuts. Reaching into his tool pouch, T.J. holds up a ribbed Trojan.

"Boy Scout?" I ask.

"American Express," he quips back. The rubber is followed by a tube of the water-based silicone lubricant that we use on O-rings. "Industrial strength K-Y," he winks, using his teeth to tear the foil package open. Handing me the tube, he rolls the condom carefully down my waiting shaft.

"Glad I got the big ones," he mumbles, sliding his hips back onto the countertop. Bracing his shoulders against the mirror wall, he props his heels on the edge. When he drops his knees apart, his boy pussy blooms open just inches from my throbbing cock.

I squirt a big dollop of grease on my fingertips and begin to gently smear it around the corrugated pink pucker. "It's so small," I whisper, thinking out loud.

"Don't worry about that," he laughs, grabbing me by the wrist and jamming two of my fingers into the silky heat. "It doesn't bite."

I guess I catch on pretty quickly, because as I work my hand in and out he leans back against the mirror. Squeezing his eyes closed, he gives a low moan and begins to fuck himself against my hand.

"Now," he orders suddenly, knocking my hand away and pulling my erection down until it's centered on the vertical slit, now slick and inviting. The head is congested with blood, a dark lance inside the white latex. "Do it now!"

I push with my hips, but his sphincter tightens. I hesitate, afraid of hurting him, but he isn't having that. He arches into me, lifting his hips up off the marble countertop. Slowly he begins to slide down on me, inch by inch. As my rod drives into him, filling him, his breath leaks out in a long, slow hiss, like steam. "Ye-e-es."

It's unbelievable how fuckin' great it feels. So tight and muscular. Beth was cold raw liver compared to T.J.'s love chamber. It's hot as hell. It actually feels like something's smoldering deep inside his young body. I immediately try to force myself all the way in, but T.J. stops me.

"Slow down," he pants. "Just let me get used to it." Seconds later he's ready. "OK...now...fuck the hell out of me."

I begin again, much slower this time—pushing in an inch, then pulling out a fraction. Finally, cradling his thighs for leverage, I spear in until I hit his hard, round prostate. It's a hot coal attacking the nerves on the bottom of my dick. I know it's good for the kid too by the way he's moaning and grinding his hips under me.

"Jerk me off," he pleads. "I want to come when you do." I look down at his erection. It's flat on his muscled abdomen, leaking a stream of precome. Grasping him in my palm, I begin to milk his beautiful young tool. It feels weird touching another man, but it's way too late to get shy now. A dozen shining images accuse me from the mirrored walls.

I'm getting the rhythm now, thrusting all the way in, then sliding out to rub against the now-stretched open lips. It feels so damn good that I know I can't last much longer. I jerk him even faster, his narrow rod bumping across my fingers, his balls bouncing as they draw up against his belly.

I try to coordinate my humping with the hand job to give him the maximum possible pleasure. It must be working, because the kid is rolling his head from side to side, his fingers digging into my shoulders.

Suddenly he screams "I'm coming" so loud that it should have shattered the mirrors. His rectum jerks and spasms around me as a stream of thick, pearly boy juice shoots across his flat brown chest to run down the mirror.

"Yeah…yeah…God…that's it," he moans. "Fuck faster…don't stop." Dropping his feet from the counter, he locks his ankles around my back. Trapped in the heat of his embrace, I burst inside him, my scalding semen filling the latex sheath.

His legs pin me immobile until my climax passes and I begin to soften. Only then does he put his heels back on the counter and allow my deflating organ to slip out of him.

Bam! As soon as T.J. releases me, guilt smacks me in the face. I can't believe what I did. Tommy trusted me with this impressionable young man, and here he is lying naked on a sink top, his ass still dilated from our lovemaking.

As I peel off the condom and wipe myself on a rag, I try not to look at T.J., but I can't help it. I've never seen another man in such a revealing position, but he obviously isn't embarrassed. My eyes keep going back to the beautiful boy pussy that just pleased me so well. Minutes ago I was assaulting it like an enemy. Now it's relaxed and so damn pretty, the pink pucker divided by the still-gaping slit, shiny with grease. Shit! My cock's starting to harden again.

Sitting up, T.J. grins at me like we're sharing some deep, dark secret. Maybe we are. I reach down to pull up my shorts and jeans, but T.J. puts his hand on my wrist and shakes his head. "No," he says, "why not just take them off?"

I'm confused, and I guess it shows on my face. "How come?"

This time his boyish grin flashes wider than ever. "Simple. It's my turn to hold the ladder."

In Love and War
Wendy Fries

"—and if you'd stop thinking," here Ranger Jacob St. John's voice dropped to a whisper as he leaned over the tiny café table, "with your hormones," he discreetly pushed a hand away from his leg, "you'd realize I'm right." The blue-eyed man leaned back, satisfied he'd made his point with the surgical precision of his tablemate.

Dr. Ben Nushi smiled, withdrew his hand just as discreetly, and said nothing.

It took barely a dozen seconds before Jacob began fidgeting, self-satisfaction crumbling. "You do know I'm right, don't you?"

The doctor shook his head, dark eyes clouding, his black skin hiding the forming of a frustrated flush. "Dear God, Jacob, what better time for love than war? What better time to shout that I'm head-over-heels for hyperactive beauty with the cheekbones of an archangel? What better time to love?"

The ranger fought a lopsided grin and, to avoid answering, turned to stare out the dusty café window. There was nothing to see out there but a few men and women, many of them probably Kosovarians who'd fled here to Macedonia to escape the bombing, the poisoned wells, the land mines waiting patiently for them at home. Escaping Kosovo's ruined body perhaps, they brought with them Kosovo's bleeding soul.

The ranger looked back at his tablemate, blue eyes full of sorrow for the wounded people and for the two of them. "I'm sorry, Ben, I just can't."

They'd had this talk before. For many reasons, not the least of which was his mantle of ancient British reserve, Jacob did not want anyone knowing about his relationship with the tall, dark doctor. "I'm here to help," he'd said the first time they'd argued the subject. "How can I justify us, amongst so many people who have nothing left?"

Without the war they'd never have met, yet it was the war—in some ways—keeping them apart.

Tired from too many hours shuttling between refugee camps, the doctor stood up, staring for a long time at this strange and wondrous thing—his lover. In a few months Jason might go home to his bountiful life. Ben would stay awhile and try and find his grandfather; contact between them severed when the bombing started. Then maybe he too would leave, go back to New Zealand, where he'd grown up and lived before the war had prompted him to come. In the meantime he'd do as Jacob wished, pretending only the most platonic of friendships between them. After all, there was still the nights, and the times they could find alone…

Ben Nushi felt a grin forming and his ever ready humor dispelling the spiritual gloom. Just before turning away he bent close to his tablemate's ear. "Don't worry, Jacob, I'll keep my promise," he whispered, breath disconcertingly hot. "I won't say a word about us to anyone. I especially won't tell 'them'—whoever 'they' are—that the last time we fucked, I thought I'd *come* for a week." Jason's eyes remained fixed on dusty window glass, but he bit his lips. Ben continued gleefully. "And I won't tell them that right now I have a hard-on you could dig to China with." The ranger's whimper escaped. "No, though I love you and am currently fantasizing about coming deep inside your mouth, I won't say a single word to anyone about us."

The doctor straightened and, in the normal tones of a man chatting with an acquaintance, said, "So, I'll see you at Miriam's birthday party tomorrow night."

The ranger sat alone at the little table for another 10 minutes, waiting for his blush—and erection—to go away.

Alone in the midnight quiet of the Kempos refugee camp medical clinic—really, just a string of tents clustered together—Ben sat at his desk, updating the night's last medical record. He looked at the date he had just entered and felt his jaw slowly drop. He'd come here as part of Doctors Without Borders only...*five weeks ago?* It seemed so much longer since he'd entered Gllogovc to find all the medical supplies burned to ash; so much longer since he'd driven with the mobile clinic two days straight, immunizing people in villages throughout Decan; so much longer since a volunteer group of ex-rangers had come to help the doctors, the refugees...anyone who was simply trying to live through what was unlivable.

Only five weeks?

Ben rubbed his eyes, shook his head. Eternity must be made up of days like this.

Today had been a double-shift day but quiet, with the camp receiving no new refugees, and he responsible for nothing more than a stream of physical checkups. Looking at his watch, he smiled, surprised at the early hour. Could it be he'd actually make it to Miriam's birthday party? Logistician for the doctors—and miracle worker who found them beds, IVs, medicine, even cars when they needed them—she had turned a mere 26 last week. Only now had they found the time for celebrating.

With a tired sigh Ben stood, lacing his fingers together and stretching. Turning around, he was startled to see that Jacob had come in silently and was sitting on the clinic's one high surgery bed, looking at a pile of shrink-wrapped bandages and needles as if they were alien and wondrous, as indeed it sometimes seemed they were. The ranger, prone to insomnia, looked awake, curious, and slightly bored all at once. He looked like an overlarge and beautiful child.

Suddenly, Ben had no desire to go to Miriam's party. He had no desire to leave this room.

"Jacob." It was a whisper, light as a dawn breeze, soft as the warmth of a faraway sun.

Jacob looked up, smiling. Seeing the look in Ben's dark eyes, the pale man's smile went away.

The doctor pursed his lips and moved forward. Jacob sat stock-still, hands gripping the edges of the bed, legs dangling motionless over its high side.

Ben came to a stop between the ranger's knees, his belly pressed to the bed edge. He leaned forward a little, holding the pale man's eyes, his warm breath curling over Jacob's lips…and waited.

The ranger hesitated. Here and now was not the place for this, even as late as it was; anyone could come through the clinic's doors.

A corner of Ben's mouth quirked up in a grin. The look in the ranger's eyes was solemn and sexy as hell. The dark beard silking the angles of his jaw made his lips a prize to reach for. Ben leaned forward, captured the lower lip between his teeth, sucked gently, then a little insistently. "I like sucking," he murmured. "I love…sucking."

Jacob's hands gripped the edges of the bed harder. "Not here." And yet, he couldn't help himself from kissing back as Ben's tongue slid into his mouth. Just as he leaned forward, more deeply into the kiss, the doctor broke it and melted…

To his knees and to the floor.

Jacob's nails dug into the bedside.

Ben pulled off the ranger's calf-high boots, tossing them to the floor, careless of the noise. He wrapped his hands around Jacob's bared feet, smiling at his chestnut-dark fingers over Jacob's light flesh.

"We look like a candy cane," he murmured, lifting the ranger's foot until it was mouth-level. The doctor smiled like a boy who knows he is about to be very bad. "And I like candy." He leaned forward, his tongue probing between the ranger's toes, squirming around each one, waiting for the response he knew would come.

"Oh, God, Ben…" It was the voice of a devout man resigned to sinning; Jacob could not have pulled himself away from this seduction if the bed had suddenly begun smoking. Gratified, the doctor bit gently, was further pleased by a small moan, and then he sucked.

Ben Nushi was not an especially oral man. Or hadn't been until he'd met Jacob. The ranger had been the first lover Ben had ever had who made everything clear as glass: Bite Jacob gently at the back of the neck and his body would be covered in gooseflesh in seconds; run your fingers along his bare ass and he would arch his back with a groan and thrust toward you; suck on his toes with a good deal of hot-mouthed passion and he would soon have an erection even a celibate would love.

Ben stood and held his hands out until the ranger joined him upright beside the bed. Holding his lover's gaze, Ben reached down and undid the belt at the ranger's waist.

"Not here, Ben, we can't."

The doctor undid five buttons and went down with the ranger's pants. After a moment Jacob lifted his feet and the doctor removed pants and underwear. And came eye-to-eye with a perfect cock.

Ben's lips pressed just to the side of it. "Not—" he exhaled, hot breath pooling across Jacob's skin, "—here?"

Jacob's eyes were closed tight. Each brush of Ben's fingertips, every brief touch of lips on his fevered skin, felt like the center of the universe. A tongue probed wetly between his legs, and Jacob groaned raggedly.

"No—" Jacob whispered as Ben licked him again, "—n-not here."

Ben pressed against Jacob's thighs, mouth nipping at skin, warm breath leaving a tiny trail of moisture.

"I can't—"

Ben's palms slid slowly along the backs of Jacob's legs until his dark hands cupped the ranger's ass.

"—be silent—"

Fingernails drew light trails down again, along the skin of the ranger's legs, raising gooseflesh.

"—I don't know how."

It took only a few silent moments for Ben to slide a condom onto the ranger. "So?" he said, nipping carefully at the head of Jacob's covered cock.

"Y-y-you'll get in trouble, Ben."

A slick tongue flicked around Jacob's erection.

"S-s-s-s-someone will hear."

Ben sucked along the underside of the ranger's cock until he heard a guttural moan. He pulled back a little, murmured huskily, "Good."

The ranger's neck arched, his eyes glazed and staring at the multi-colored canvas ceiling, at shadows and doubts. He opened his mouth for air, a thin trail of sweat dripping from his hair and along his temple. He barely moved. Instead, Ben moved: his teeth, sharp and tormenting along hypersensitive skin; his hands, their touch light as they squeezed the tight package of Jason's sac or spread his legs wider; his body, pressing against the pale man's legs and radiating far more than body heat against his skin.

Heart pounding, the ranger felt the fire began to come up like lasers along the back of his legs. He moaned harshly, groped for Ben, his hand sliding across the black man's cheek until his palm and fingers pressed hard against the doctor's head.

One of Ben's hands slid tightly along the shaft of the ranger's cock while the other reached between his legs, fingers massaging Jason's perineum until the man moaned and stepped wider. Then, hand sliding further back, exploring, finding, two of the doctor's fingers pushed inside.

The ranger dug his nails into the doctor's shoulder, eyes clamped shut as the sensations of dual penetration grew and the fire line fanned out across his lower back, wrapped around his thrusting hips, and then dove between his legs.

Some part of Jason wanted to stop, truly fearing this mixing of Ben's business and their pleasure would cost the doctor. Some part drawing farther and farther away. Some part of him as quiet as another part of him was not.

Moaning loudly, he pumped harder in the doctor's mouth, the fire burning all over the surface of his skin, rushing to extinguish itself in his cock. But he stayed on the precipice, fear of discovery fighting the final release.

And then Ben pulled away.

"Pleasepleaseplease..." the ranger keened, shaking with the need to come, thrusting at nothing, his eyes full of begging. Ben's mouth and hands were on him again then, and Jacob's back arched as he began to come in the doctor's mouth.

It was the dark of 3 A.M., with no moon to light the path as Jason picked his way toward the front gate. As he reached it, along with another ranger, a diesel bus lumbered into the camp, slowed, and then stopped. As soon as its doors opened, a slow-moving tide of refugees emerged down the squeaky bus steps. Some took the helping hand

Jason offered; others moved right past him, looking through the tiny crowd that had awoken to the sound of the bus and now surrounded its doors. The new people and the old moved amongst one another, refraining from touching anything, even themselves. Hands hanging empty, or floating near their chests as if weightless, each side looked for mother, friend, or sister thought dead, but in the end, no one claimed another. Jason knew it happened rarely, but when it did, the sense of relief within himself—who had lost nothing—of pleasure so intense it made him almost hysterical, was worth anything he had to give.

Two hours later, his insomnia filling him like a surging current, Jason stood staring at the silhouette of the camp gates as the black around them turned into a beautiful pinkish-dark—a lovely light for bombing. He was searching again for the words to describe the savage joy of merely witnessing reunion when a movement just outside the gate caught his eye. Quietly he moved closer.

Just outside the camp two men stood, arms wrapped around each other, holding one another so tightly Jason couldn't see where the one began and the other ended. The reunion—of brothers, lovers, old friends, Jason never knew—was as silent as the camp that slept unawares: just the one man's hand stroking the hair of the other as they rocked together in their silent embrace. For 15 minutes Jacob watched them.

For 15 minutes they held on.

Ben sat alone at the camp's gate late the next day, staring at his reflection in a gray rain puddle. Another shift had ended 45 minutes earlier, and along with the slowly setting sun, the good doctor was settling down for the night and daydreaming, using recent memory to do so.

It had taken mere minutes before Jason had insisted on payback last night, albeit more discretely, moving them from the clinic's bed to the doctor's tiny canvas-walled office. It had been a tight fit in there, Ben remembered, and it wasn't the office he was talking about. Murmuring something about "your Chinese digging tool," Jason had arched his back like a bird's wing, and to the doctor the sweet curve just above the ranger's ass had looked like something awaiting a saucerful of cream. Metaphorically speaking ,that's what it soon got, or rather, parts somewhat further south. Ben's sound effects when he came were, by his nature, far more inclined to low sighs, but the sensations were in every way just as fine. By the time they left that cramped little space, Ben knew he'd be a week finding the things they'd pushed off his desk, and he also knew he'd relish each little reminder as he found it.

And in a rewarding of the wicked that was almost unfair, the pair even caught the best part of Miriam's birthday party.

Idly toeing the dirt, twinning his fingers together, the doctor smiled dreamily. *And then what happened after the party?*

"You're mooning at that puddle like Narcissus."

Miriam Minsky materialized by the battered stool at the doctor's left about the time Jacob approached from the right. At the site of Miriam—who had an unnamed grudge against all the rangers—Jacob hung back unnoticed, half a dozen feet further along the fence.

"Just glad to finish another long day, my friend."

Minsky tapped herself out a cigarette, the one vice even a war couldn't eradicate, and turned to look at her brown-eyed friend. "Me too, babe. I tell you, I sure can do without all this life-death-and-bedpans thing."

Minsky struck a match, touched it to her cigarette, inhaled with gusto. After a moment she raised the thin burning cylinder in the air in silent toast. "To life after death, babe," she said, and then sucked on the cigarette with the sensuous pleasure of a healthy 26-year-old. Then, "Speaking of death, there was some god-awful moaning come from the clinic late last night. Sounded like someone giving birth, dying, or having sex."

If Ben was blushing beneath brown skin, Jacob couldn't see it. The ranger's cheeks, however, were red beacons. He moved a little farther away.

The doctor fought against a grin and won, solemnly replying, "A patient. Really suffering. I was doing all I could to put an end to his misery. I hate to see someone in pain, don't you?" Ben carefully pretended not to see Jacob's shuffling retreat.

Miriam's face scrunched up, "I'd go nuts, people moaning and groaning at me all day."

"Groaning," the doctor agreed, "begging, pleading…"

Eight feet further along the fence, Jacob whimpered. A young Kosovarian, passing by and smoking with the same youthful abandon as Miriam, glanced at him curiously.

"It gets…*hard*, Miri, it sure does, but somehow I manage."

The logistician frowned, offered her cigarette to the doctor. "You deserve this more than I do."

Once again Ben smiled dreamily, staring into the distance. "Yeah, it gets *very hard*, but somehow I get a *grip* on things, and the *moaning* and the groaning stops."

The ranger's knees buckled. He grabbed the cool metal of the fence. No one noticed.

"What was wrong with the guy, anyway?"

Ben's mouth was a little dry. He sucked on Miriam's cigarette, choked, and chanced a look at Jacob. The ranger was staring out into the dusk light, tongue pressed against teeth, his chest rising and falling too fast.

"Well, ah…" the doctor turned toward Minsky. "It wasn't anything physical, actually. A young man with an overdeveloped sense of personal responsibility. Feels guilty over pleasures the rest of us enjoy."

Minsky swiped back her cigarette, took a puff. "That's ridiculous. But what's he doing with you? You're no headshrinker."

Ben smiled. "Uh, yeah, I know. But I'm not bad in that department either."

Can you say "double entendre"?

"Or at least that's what he told me. It was sort of primal regression therapy. Lots of…*coming out* with one's feelings, you know."

Ben chanced another look at Jacob. The ranger's eyes were closed now, his breathing shorter, shallower.

"Boy, I'd never do what you do."

Ben's grin grew. "You'd be surprised how easy it is to do things like that, Miri. It takes little skill really, just lots of human feeling. Joy in your work."

Jacob moved a little closer.

Miriam stomped out her smoke, turned to the doctor, "Want a little ultrasecret, hidden-where-you'll-never-find-it vodka, babe? My treat."

"No."

Ben and Miriam turned.

"I'd say it's my turn to be kind to the doctor. Isn't it, Ben?"

The doctor smiled, pleased that his lover had finally joined them. "Yeah, I think it is."

Some time in the pink morning of yesterday Jacob had watched those two men and finally realized that hiding his love for this brown-eyed beauty was his own pointless war. No more. He leaned toward the lovely doctor, his lips pressing against the other man's.

Miriam Minsky lifted an eyebrow, understanding Ben's word games not five minutes earlier. She looked at Jacob with something almost like respect. If he could turn the overworked doctor's head and sound off like that during sex...well, maybe he was...no, such thoughts wouldn't do.

Miriam Minsky stood up, tapped out another cigarette, and wondered where Carlos was and if he was busy.

Ben and Jacob continued about the business of being nice to one another. They used a lot of tongue to do it.

Little Leather Boy
Alan Mills

1

I think it was his eyes, and when I write that, I don't mean it was his eyes that were the first thing I noticed; I mean it was his eyes that made me curious about him. There was something, I don't know, deep about them, innocent but not innocent, reflective and entrapping at the same time.

Maybe this description is too abstract, but looking into his eyes made me feel something really strange, understand? Something twisted in my gut. See, they were a dull-blue, kind of like faded denim or like the overcast sky above Laguna Beach. I've seen his eyes at other times. Sometimes they were brighter. Sometimes more olive. Sometimes more gray. That's another thing about him that caught my attention. He always seemed to change. He was cute too, with spiky, light-brown hair, and I just kept staring him down. He finally stretched out his hand and said, "Hi, I'm…"

"Hey," I said, "I don't give a fuck what your name is."

Back at my place, he looked up at me with something like hurt in his eyes. Most people think that hurt looks like tears or a watery glaze, but it doesn't. It's a shaking in the eyes that precedes emotion.

He sat there, on my bed, staring up at me, looking all hurt, but he was breathing heavy, and I could tell he was enjoying it. That's important. Make them enjoy it.

"Listen up," I said flatly with neither anger nor kindness. "You're gonna take off all your clothes...now."

He stood up and opened his shirt. I watched as he provocatively undid one...two buttons...three. He touched the fourth and stopped to sort of tease me.

I grabbed his belt, spun him around, and pushed him chest-first onto the bed. I sunk my fingers in his spiky hair and pulled his head back. "Goddamn it, when I tell you to do something, you fucking do it!" With one hand I reached under his stomach and ripped his shirt open. He let out a bit of grunt as I let go of his hair and harshly pulled his shirt off. Caressing his back, I pushed down hard on his muscles. Grappling my arm around his neck, I growled, "Get the rest of this shit off."

When I let go of his neck, he got up and pulled his shoes...socks...pants...even his watch...off in a hurry.

I pointed to a lighter on my nightstand. "I want you to light all these candles. When you're done," I pointed to the hardwood floor at my feet, "I want you to kneel right here and clasp your hands behind your back." I stroked his cheek gently. "Can you do that for me?" He nodded, and I touched his lips. "Good. Get started."

I walked out into my living room, looking for something. I looked his way, but he wasn't moving fast enough, taking his time. But still, there was an aura of eagerness about him. He'll do nicely, I thought.

When I walked back into the bedroom, he was just going down on his knees. I walked up to him, glaring down as if about to punish him. He looked up at me, worried. I liked that. He knew what he was doing.

I stroked his hair, bent down and kissed his mouth, pushing my tongue in deep, trying to lick his throat. He moaned, and I pulled out, pulling his face onto my crotch, his wet lips vibrating as he groaned.

I kicked his knees apart and stepped back, still holding his head against my crotch. I backed up more until he was angled forward as much as he could be without losing his balance. It was a struggle, but he loved it.

"You want that cock, don't you?"

"Yes, sir." I felt him straining.

"You want it real bad, huh?"

"Yes, sir." I could sense the fear.

I eased back until his weight was back over his knees. He looked up at me, excited—almost too excited, like his heart was beating out of control.

"What the fuck you lookin' at, boy?"

He lowered his eyes. "Sorry, sir."

I undid my belt. "Know what?" His gaze was fixed on my crotch. "You need somethin' in that smart-ass mouth."

I freed my cock, and he stared at it, hungry, almost drooling. I held it in a strong fist, my piss hole pointed at him, my shaved nuts bursting from between my fingers.

"Yes, sir. Shut me up with it, sir."

I took a step forward so that his lips kissed my nuts; my cock pointed up, pressed to his face. "Yeah, boy, smell that fuckin' crotch!"

He moaned against my nads, trying to get a lick, but I squeezed his neck. "Knock that shit off, boy! Just get used to my scent. This is gonna be in your face a lot tonight."

Without warning I stepped back a bit, and just before he fell forward I grabbed his jaw and forced his mouth open. Suddenly my cock was down his throat, and he was balanced precariously on it.

This was the test. I wanted to see if he'd be a good boy. I wanted to see if he'd reach for my cock or the ground to steady himself and stop from gagging. But he was a good boy. He kept his hands behind his back. "Good boy," I said appreciatively. "Good boy."

I pushed forward until his center of gravity was returned a spot between his legs. I slid my cock out, then back in, pumping his face. Sometimes I just pushed the head in. Maybe a bit of the shaft. Other times I rammed the entire length and width down his gaping throat.

"Stroke your dick," I ordered, and he did, bringing his right hand to his cock and stroking it for me. He was already wet, and I knew he loved my prick in his mouth, his breath hot and fast. "Stroke that fucking cock, boy!"

He beat it furiously, my cock pounding in his mouth. He could barely keep me down his throat—shaking, eyes watering, snot dripping from his nose.

I looked down at him and watched him struggle. It felt so good. He choked and coughed. Before he could I shouted, "Don't you come, boy!"

He let go of his dick in a hurry. I grabbed his head and jackhammered my cock all the way deep down his throat. He shook as if he were crying, like he had a vibrator in his heart, his prick bobbing, about to shoot. And still, I fucked his sloppy lips, keeping us both on the brink. When I pulled my cock away from him his face was red and wet, and I shouted, "You almost made me come, you little fuck!"

"I'm sorry, sir." He looked so scared.

"You're gonna be."

I pushed him down on my bed facefirst. "Get your ass up." He raised his butt, exposing his hole. I grabbed his arms, pulled them behind his back, and wrapped a red handkerchief around his wrists. "That OK, boy?"

"Yes, sir."

I tightened it more; he winced in pain—what an actor. It wasn't like he couldn't pull his wrists free.

I stood next to the bed, where he could see, and took off my boots, socks, jeans. He didn't move but watched me like he might die of lust.

I took up a position behind him, pressing my thumb to his sphincter, letting my fingers play with his nuts.

I licked his hole roughly, and a shudder ripped through him. "I normally wouldn't fuck a slut like you, but you've been good."

"Thank you, sir," he said proudly.

"I'm not gonna finger you, though. If you want my cock, you're gonna hafta take it fresh."

"But...your cock's so big, sir."

"That's your fuckin' problem, boy." I stroked some lube down my cock and licked my boy's ass again. He shook, like he was afraid the sudden pressure might be my cock going in.

I rolled latex on while I rubbed cold, slick lube against his wrinkled iris, feeling the fluid warm between my fingers and his ass. I poured more on his hole. It dripped down his balls. I reached between his legs and slicked his cock. His ass twitched as I pulled his dick back and gave it a few strokes.

I dripped more lube on my cock. Hard and ready, I pressed it to his ass. "Oh, fuck, sir!" was the first thing he said.

I shoved the head in slowly, letting his sphincter open to swallow it. "Push out, boy," I commanded.

"Yes, sir…fuck…" My dick went in, just a bit, his anus opening like a flower. When my glans disappeared and his sphincter closed around my ridge, I whispered, "You like that, huh?"

"Yes—" (I jammed the rest of my cock in) "—fuck! Goddamn it, sir!"

I was buried to my nuts. "Oh, fuck!" he shouted. "Shit! sir! I'm gonna—"

"You better not fuckin' come, boy!"

I pulled an inch out of his ass and pushed back in. "Fuck, sir!" I pulled two inches out, then sent them back into his guts. "God! Man! Fuck, sir!"

"Yeah, you love that cock, huh?"

I buried it in him. "Yes, sir." I pulled it all out, touched his gaping hole with my reservoir tip. Buried the whole motherfucker in him again. "Fuck, sir, you're gonna make me come!"

"No!" I shouted, fucking him hard.

"Oh, God, sir!"

I pulled all the way out. "Ever been fucked by a bigger cock, boy?!"

Then I just started fucking him, bashing his guts without mercy.

When I knew he'd had all the pounding he could take, I withdrew and pulled my condom off. "Thank you, sir," he panted with forced breaths.

"Boy, I'm not done with you yet."

"Please…sir…" I reached under my bed, grabbed a black dildo, and rubbed it on his chest, letting him know what I planned on doing next. "Gotta make sure you get your money's worth."

I lubed it up, put it in his hands, and dripped more lube onto his worked-over asshole.

"That's going up your ass," I said, letting his fingers feel the girth.

"No, sir, I'm really satisfied, honest."

I put the dildo to his hole and pushed it in slowly. "What was that, boy? Are you complaining?"

"No, sir!"

His sphincter opened like a starving mouth. "That's right. Push out."

"Yes, sir!" he grunted. The head became enveloped in flesh, and then the whole dildo disappeared, its synthetic nuts touching his real ones.

I fucked the dildo in and out of his hole, watching his sphincter kiss the rubber as it moved through his guts.

I knew he loved it even though he kept begging me to stop. Deciding to prove what I thought to him, I pushed my crotch against the fake nads, trapping my toy inside him, and undid his mock binding. "Reach back and hold that fucker." He stretched to reach it. "Now, roll over and fuck yourself."

"Yes, sir!" He rolled onto his back, keeping himself impaled. I watched as he pulled it out and drove it in. "Oh, fuck," he moaned, his legs dangling in the air as he did himself harder.

I grabbed his cock and jacked myself at the same time. He fucked himself even faster as I pumped our cocks in unison. "Oh, fuck, sir, I'm gonna—"

"Go ahead," I grunted, pumping him, watching my toy sink into his ass as jizz shot from my cock, hitting his chest first, then his face. "Yeah, boy!" I shouted, as come erupted from his slit and poured down my hand like white water from a hot spring.

He rubbed his wrists, attempting to get feeling back in his hands. "At first I couldn't imagine that it would be worth it," he said, "but I was wrong." His face was still dripping spunk, but I looked past that and listened. "I'm not in the habit of doing this sort of thing." He wiped his chin.

"Really?" I said, sitting next to him. "You were pretty convincing."

"I mean, being with a…you know. But…it was great. I've seen you so often, and I finally got to have you."

I smiled, honestly happy for him, honestly understanding that this was simply the way my life was.

"That guy over there." He pointed to my dresser and a photo of me and my first L.A. boyfriend. "Is that…"

"No. Not anymore."

"Did something happen?"

"People change." I changed.

"Are you seeing anyone now?"

"Boyfriends don't really fit in my life these days." The truth was, he was hard to replace. The truth was, some things happen only once.

"I'm really sorry to hear that."

I stood at the sink, washing spunk from my cock while he got dressed. My dick felt warm and sensitive as I stroked water up and down it. I returned with a towel wrapped around my waist. He was putting on his shoes. My towel was white. Alex and I stole it from a Radisson in Dallas before I dumped him. "That was hot," he said.

"You're hot," I said, kissing his smile.

"It's all there," he said, looking at my dresser. The cash sat in front of the picture of me and Alex. I missed being 19, not much else.

"Plus a little extra." He kissed me back. "For being so nasty. God, I'm happy I met you tonight."

"Thanks," I said, feeling strange inside. "I'm dead tired now."

"See ya," he said. The door shut, and I stared at the photo, remembering how one boyfriend used to look at me.

2

I think it was his eyes I noticed first, but that's only because he was staring at me blatantly—well, more than blatantly; he was staring at me coldly, intently, like he was hungry or something. He was

handsome and buff—you know, the really big-daddy kind of buff—
the kind of buff that most guys fantasize about.

And his eyes were blue, the same kind of clear blue that most mil-
itary-type blonds have, the same kind of blue that I have—hell, the
same kind of blue that every fucking blond in California has. I wasn't
really impressed.

But, it was a party and everything, so I thought, What the fuck,
and went over to him to introduce myself.

He was wearing a leather harness and a cap made from leather that
he had pulled down so that the brim almost covered his eyes. He was
wearing leather chaps and looked pretty fucking outrageous. Leather
retro, at the very least. It was a Tom of Finland thing. He was sexy,
though, and I walked up to him slowly but with strength, and started giving him my line.

"Shut up!" he said. "I don't give a fuck about your name!"

I was shocked. I just stood there, you know, with my mouth open.
I realize that this reaction isn't too surprising, but I really didn't know
what the fuck to do. I was standing in a leather party, so instead of
starting a fight, I decided to just accept that this is how these kind of
parties were.

"And I don't want to know your fucking sign either," he continued, "or where you live, or what you do. Well, I already know what
you do, you little fuck-dog, little fucking whore…"

I swallowed hard, and I could feel my lower lip start to tremble. I
was pissed, and I tried to stop my lip from moving. I didn't want to
let him get to me.

"What?! You gonna fuckin' cry?"

I wasn't going to, but I must have looked it. I couldn't believe what
I was hearing, but I didn't know what to say back. He was bigger than
me, but I didn't feel overwhelmed by his size. There was something
else, something in his voice.

"I'm sorry, baby," he whispered. "Want me to make it better? Tell
you what I'll do. I'm gonna shove my cock up that sloppy little ass,
OK, baby?" His voice turned cruel. "You think you're crying now,
baby? Just wait till I shove my cock into your mouth, you fucking

slut. Just wait till I'm buried in your ass...then you'll fucking be crying, boy."

That's when I did it. I walked away from the freak without saying a word. But he grabbed the collar of my tight T-shirt and pulled me back, one of his arms wrapping around my left pec. "Where the fuck you goin', boy?" My skin went hot, and I was sure he could feel it. He must have, because his hand dropped down to my crotch as he held on to my collar. Fuck, I was already hard as a rock, but I pushed him away regardless. Men who are executed get hard too. No matter how exciting, I knew what was happening just wasn't right.

I walked away. This time he didn't stop me. I would have slugged him if he had. Directly across from me, another guy stared as I walked toward him. His outfit was more discreet—just jeans, a white T-shirt, a thick leather band around his left bicep. He relaxed against the wall, but in my mind he blocked my escape. Before I knew it I was staring at him defiantly as if I didn't know why he was there. "You OK?" he asked softly. I kept glaring. "Doug comes on strong, huh?"

I felt my defenses lowering slowly. "Yeah," I said, "I guess."

"I'm Alex."

I smiled despite myself. "Jeff."

"You're new to this?" His eyes were brown, sympathetic.

I looked down shyly. "I'm new to a lot of things."

He shut his door, and his dog came running up. Alex stepped behind and put his arm around my shoulders and chest. His forearm looked like power. He kissed my neck. "How ya doin'?"

"OK." He was big. I felt enveloped.

"How old are you, Jeff?"

"Nineteen."

"You didn't drink tonight, did you?"

"A little."

"Oh. Are you a bad boy, then?"

"Yeah. A bit."

"Really? Well, I'm just gonna call you 'Boy.' Is that OK?"

"I guess so."

"Good." He stepped around me and stood close, his crotch touching my leg. "Feel that?" I breathed heavy but didn't answer. "Yes or no, boy?"

"Yes."

"Yes, what?" He gripped my neck.

"Yes, sir…"

"Yeah, that's good." He stroked my hair. "Yeah, you want that cock, huh?"

"Yes, sir."

His kissed me deep. Stubble burned my lips. "You want it real bad, huh?"

I couldn't think straight. "Yes, sir."

"Would you like a beer?" He pulled away from me and walked into his kitchen. It was clean with old yellow tiles on the counters. The kind from the '40s.

"Yeah, sure."

He glared back at me.

"Yes, sir. Thank you, sir."

"Kick off your boots." I did as I was told while he pulled two beers from the fridge, opened them, and walked back to me. He handed me one: "Here, drink up."

I took a big swig. It was Bud. He smiled. I took another swig. Still grinning, he placed his own bottle to my lips and poured some of his beer down my throat. Just as I was about to choke, he pulled the bottle away. Beer dripped down the sides of my mouth. He kissed me and took his own swig of beer. He kissed me again. Our mouths were wet and tasted of beer. It dripped down my shirt.

After a few Buds he had both of our dicks out. He only let me touch his lovingly…gently…he wouldn't let me grip it or jack it off. He treated me the same way. His dog was quiet, watching us lackadaisically from the couch.

When I finished my third bottle and half of his, he asked me if I wanted another.

"No, sir. I need to use the bathroom, sir."

"You need to piss?"

"Yes, sir."

"Bathroom's over there."

I put myself away and walked down the hall. His apartment was quiet, and his bathroom had dark-green towels, and an antique decoy sitting on the counter. It had been painted like a mallard, but now it was faded and was mostly just wood.

I stood there before a mirror, making the pressure go away, my head spinning, my reflection making me feel sexy, the cock in my hand swollen and warm.

As I shook the drops of beer away, I heard music start playing. It was rugged and rough, like punk, only the guy singing was screaming things about movie stars, running away, and sin.

When I came back to the living room Alex was lighting a cigar. He sat in a large, leather smoking chair—the kind you'd see in a gentleman's study. But I couldn't see Alex as a gentleman. His cock jutted straight up out of the fly of his jeans, and he stroked it provocatively while he puffed on his cigar, letting go of himself as he breathed out the smoke.

"Come over here, boy."

I stepped up to him, standing before him for a moment. He glared up at me until I gave in and dropped to my knees.

His cock was large, slightly curved, and as I leaned forward to lick it, tentatively, I could see precome collecting in the slit. When I touched the drop with my tongue, it tasted clean and almost sweet, and the pheromones swimming around in it and steaming off his crotch made me dizzy, like my body had drifted off the earth.

I pressed my tongue more firmly to him and let my lips wrap around the fat crown, and as I slipped my mouth over his cock like a warm, wet sock, I could feel his body shift; I could hear him moan.

And then he was in my throat, and I felt filled by him, fulfilled by him; I felt like he belonged to me. "You're one sweet fuckin' cocksucker," he said, "aren't you, boy?"

I didn't answer, concentrating on the cock sliding over my tongue, the ridge of his crown scraping the back of my throat. Then I felt his hand on my jaw, his cigar hot near my ear. He lifted my face up off him until our eyes met. "I asked you a question. You're my sweet cocksucker, aren't you, boy?"

I could feel spit dripping down my chin from my precome-coated lips. "Yes, sir," I said proudly, "I'm your cocksucker, sir."

He made me take off my clothes. He made me stand in front of him and take off my clothes—my shoes first, my socks, my shirt, my jeans. My underwear. He said, "I want to watch you take off your clothes. Take that shit off for me now!"

I stood a few feet away, shivering slightly in the chill of the room. Alex just in his chair, stroking his cock while he watched my dick swell. "Turn around," he said, and I did as I was told, giving him a good look at my muscular flank.

I started to look over my shoulder, but Alex was already walking up behind me. "Don't move," he said. "You're too beautiful the way you are." He pressed himself against my back, and I shut my eyes, feeling his hands trace the shallow trenches of my stomach. The cigar was still clenched between his fingers, and though he never brought it too close to me, I could feel its heat everywhere he touched. And I trusted him, letting myself get lost in his arms, the smoke from his cigar warming my skin, the dark air from his lungs blowing gently across my face.

"Come with me," he said.

"Yes, sir," I said.

"Do you mind if I fuck you?" he asked.

"Do I have any choice, sir?" I said.

"Shut up, boy! I ask the questions."

I stood next to his bed as he took his clothes off. When he stood before me naked, I went down on my knees again. "No," he said, "come here." He positioned me so that I faced the wall and, gripping my wrists behind my back, he pushed me forward. "Don't do anything I don't tell you to!" He gave my ass a hard smack while holding my wrists with one hand.

"Sorry, sir."

"Put your hands on the wall!"

I did as ordered, but he kicked my legs further apart and gave my ass another good smack. Then his hands moved up my back, and his hard cock slid up my crack.

I felt kisses travel down my spine, felt fingers pry my ass apart. His tongue flicked at my hole. My cock was pulled back and sucked, my asshole rubbed with a thumb.

I couldn't see what he was doing, but I needed to push back against him. I was close, but I didn't dare move. So close to blowing my load, I didn't dare. I felt it coming on. I felt it. I stopped breathing, and he stopped sucking just before the point of no return.

Alex knelt between my legs. With gentle fingers he reached up and rubbed lube on my nads and cock. "Yeah, boy," he said, "look at those clean-shaven nuts." I felt something cold and metallic wrap around one of my balls. It was a cock ring. "Don't move," he said, and one of my nuts got pushed through the unforgiving circle. My other nad followed. Then he started pushing my cock through.

Soon the ring slid over my shaft, just as I was about to get too hard to fit through it. Alex gave my cock a few wet strokes. "Good boy. Now, stand over here." He got up and led me to his bed. A leather harness was laid out on top of it. He put the thing on me and attached the center strap to the shiny ring that held my nads. "That's better," he said, pulling on the center strap and forcing me onto the bed by threatening to rip my nuts off.

I don't know how he did it, but in moments he was on his back on the bed, and I was on my knees, sitting on his lap. He kept his grip on the strap. "You see that condom right there?" he said. "Put that on my cock and get your ass ready."

He lined his cock up with my ass and pulled me down on it by tugging on my harness. His cock sank into me slowly.

"Your ass is one tight motherfucker!" he groaned. I had trouble breathing. It hurt and felt good—felt great. I wanted to cry. "Sit on that fucker, boy!" I sat all the way down, grinding my ass on his nuts. "Oh, yeah! That's good cock, huh?"

"Yes, sir," I whispered.

He thrust up fast, hard. "What, boy?"

"Yes, sir!" I shouted.

He pounded his whole body up into my hole. "Give me that fuckin' ass!"

"Yes, sir!" My ass felt open. My whole body felt vulnerable. He tugged on the strap to pull me down, relaxing to let me back up.

I felt like a toy, a thing, an object to be fucked, and I liked it. "Hot damn!" he grunted, fucking my burning ass, pounding my exploding prostate. "Get on your feet, fucker. I want to be deep inside your fuckin' asshole."

I struggled to get one foot out from under me. I got the other one on the bed, and my hole was his. He pummeled up into it. "Jack your cock, boy!" I gripped it, ready to release.

Jizz fired from my cock. It went up into the air, hitting my nose and falling in an arc down to his chest. "Yes!" he grunted, filling me with his cock and his come.

"Oh, fuck!" I shouted as the come kept pouring out of my cock. I collapsed on top of him, my dick still pumping out jizz.

His cock pushed into me still. My whole body felt overheated. His body felt on fire too. I never wanted to let go.

He wrapped an arm around me and pulled me to him. With his other hand he gripped the base of his rubber and pulled his dick from my ass. "That was—"

"Ssssh," he said, holding me.

I kissed his shoulder. Our bodies were drenched with sweat. "I think I could love you forever," I said.

He cupped my tongue and lower lip inside his mouth, stroking my hair, kissing my ear. "Ssssh," he whispered, letting me lose myself in his sleepy gaze.

Side Effect
R.W. Clinger

L et us sit back and critique this subject for a moment. Do not rub anything more than the side of your head in deep thought. Keep your analogies and subject matter as straight as possible. Focus now and listen…

I'm very good at critiquing, because I have to be. I teach freshman composition at an all-musky male school, and I'm forced to use a red pen to correct vital errors, produce young and charming writing spirits out of unessential, moderately unbound boy-minds. My victims are usually 18 or 19 years old. I prey on them, adore them, feed off their errors with ease. I stay up late-late into darkening, emotionless hours and read their every fiery written passion. I'm a wordy slave, if the truth be known: Professor Lethargic. No kidding.

This story isn't about now, though; it's about a young man who was adorably Black in every sense of the word, was not very keen on word usage, and came to me for help. And this story is about critiquing. The beginning starts about five years ago, when springtime caught up to the end of the semester, when young men began to run around shirtless and nipple-hard on campus. They wore those skimpy see-all shorts that were about as snug as the African-male lovemaking gods, Nika and Sulu, who can be found pressed together in the warming, come-covered jungles.

The young gent that I speak of was named Emanuel Faulk. A delicious and supine creature with intimate, caring blue eyes. Manny, as I reluctantly named him, was not the genius or carver of great words. He was only 17 when we first met and when he spawned interest in passing my class, since he had a solid D. The D, of course, meant determination to succeed in my vast, worldly mind—or delectable, dainty, and distinct.

Our visits were utterly too short, but dreamy for me. I had spotted him at the beginning of the semester. My thoughts craved the need to touch his dark skin within my brown dancing fingers. I wanted to suckle a virgin nipple on him, press his young head into my splendid crop of Kenya fineness, and have Manny gobble up every inch and morsel of Professor Lethargic's immaculate beauty. But this never occurred. Yes, all throughout the heated semester Manny left me perplexed and disgruntled as I sat with my balls tightly pressed inside sweaty inner thighs, clamping my eight-inch erection against my solid, lined, cocoa-colored chest, listening to his words of hope and need to pass my so-called excruciating(!) class.

Our last visit came just before school let out. He sat bare-chested across from my reddish-brown desk. A football rested in a firm hand. His pecs were wide and solid, slick with glazed, edible sweat. I counted his abs with meticulous care. Our glances clung together for a few seconds. Then he directed his view at my...own chest, maybe looking at my tie, maybe comprehending that Professor Lethargic had a woody building inside his Jockeys. I pulled my glance away, desiring immediately to pinch his nips with teacher's ease. He had been running, and his flat chest rose and fell, rose and fell, like the visions of our bodies clinging in my shameful mind.

I couldn't bare to see him struggle with words, I confess now. I wanted to be unbiased and give the dashing God something wholesome, a real chance to *(plunge his long, red, slithery man-tongue into the back of my bookish throat?)* survive.

"I'll pass you, dear thing," I uttered with simple enchantment, one hand pressed against my sweaty, frivolous brow. I felt his blue mesmerizing eyes tickle the base of my nervous spine and workable buttocks. I felt his smile against the nape of my back—large and beaming-white, thin-lipped and kissable—making a professional like me...succumb to grace him with a generous C.

"Thank you," he uttered, smiling, pressing his firm, football-tossing, breast-holding hand into mine. Manny naïvely said, "I'll repay you some day. I promise."

As he left, I wondered if I would see him again. He would never make it in college. The world was tough. Not everyone was generous like P. Lethargic. I hoped he wouldn't get eaten up. And if anyone was going to eat him up, devour him, I wished it were me.

"Good-bye, Manny." I found it easy to blow a gentle kiss in his direction, but he was already gone.

Let's critique for a second.
There are four rules in teaching young, hot guys:

1. Be fair.
2. Never look a stud(ent) directly in the eyes.
3. Do not be touched by a stud(ent).
4. Do not touch a stud(ent).

I was fair with Manny, I think. I broke rule number 2 with ease, though, because I looked him in the eyes on that last united day, leaving me want to slip over his 10-inch of coal-colored niceness and have him squeeze some of his ivory-white student juice into my...

And, of course, I broke rules number 3 and 4 too.
Shame on me!
B-a-a-ad Mr. Lethargic!
Listen more...

Three summers had passed rapidly. I woke one early morning from a dream about Manny Faulk sucking my cock head dry, repeating with come spilling out of the corners of his mouth, "C, C , C, C, C, C, C." I ran that dream off, enjoying a fine sweat on my well-toned biceps and dark chest. Naked, I swam privately in my pool, long strokes, continuously for hours, having my dangling brown balls glide with me underneath a watery world. Usually those wet moments of slick aloneness made me grow hard and harder, enticing a teacher like me to come into the pool with chlorine-colored explosion, but that didn't happen on this day. It seemed as if I wanted to carry the dream out (like foreshadowing in a composition paper). I wanted to save my precious white, hot spew for a certain time later—and a certain handsome someone.

By evening I ate alone and drank a single glass of red wine underneath the June, July, August stars that I had named after all of my most handsome, exuberant male students: Marco, Lamont, Tanglo. Manny was one of those stars too. I became the silent professor, diligent in my quiet. I was happy and unchanged by time...until another visit aspired with Emanuel Faulk.

It was unintended, this second visit. I did not search the now 21-year-old boy-man down, investigating his every intricate move. I did not stalk Manny, hunt him down, threaten him with my lined cock dangling before his shivering mouth. What transpired was spontaneous—out of the African god's hands, even. Simple actions in a perhaps needy sexually frigid time. It occurred a few evenings after I had dreamed of Manny and his delicious cock. It had happened...

There is this larger-than-large bookstore across town that I frequent often. Barnie's Books. It's made up of three levels (of course, constructed in an old, refurbished barn). The third level is designed with narrow, book-lined passageways and is a dusty tomb of male-on-male books and had the privacy to match. While visiting up there, if you are lucky, you may retrieve a pretty boy's phone number or smile. These narrow passageways permit one to glide a richly masculine back against that of a stranger's. Elbows could bump in some type of literal dance. Lips may sometimes caress luxurious, brilliant skin, like a shoulder or cheek or neck. It's not a dirty place, but rather romantically kind to the silent fag or peaceful queen.

Yes, I was involved in the pages of a delicious piece of fiction inside the attic room. James Baldwin was tucked away up there inside my craving hands, and I was totally immersed with a charming, ancient copy of *Giovanni's Room*.

Usually I stand still, consumed by the literature around me. After reviewing titles and copies of some unpopular, naughty fiction and gay-toned classics, I pick a book off the shelf, browse through it, see its worth, become interrupted by a moving, handsome body beside me (about six inches away from me), and say hello to the six-foot African god. I maybe wink at him or allow his nice hands to travel up and down one of my muscularly built shoulder blades. We share generous hellos, and then I pass along with wanted purchases, happily.

I was hooked into *Room* when I heard Manny's familiar voice beside me, looked up, and saw his dark, unchanged, and splendid face again. He simply said, "Professor Lethargic, is that you?"

I blushed. Of course, blushing on a dark man isn't that easy to see, but I did blush, and I think Manny knew I turned a different, beautiful shade of cocoa.

It was the last place I believed to run into him. I couldn't possibly imagine how a football-playing hunk was interested in literature. These thoughts became easily erased, though, because my inquisitive eyes began to scan Manny. He was still delectable, dainty, and distinct. Manny's smile was broad and all teeth; I've always liked men with large smiles. His caring blue eyes twinkled like the night stars that I had named. His chin was dotted with the familiar dimple that I had so wanted to press my tongue into and utter chants like something out of Mali in Africa. His shoulders were broad and massive-looking, tucked nicely into a skin-tight white T-shirt. My eyes passed over every bump and line on his well-formed chest. I counted his abs again, like only months before; unintentionally licked my lips. My eyes darted quickly down to the man's massive lower torso. Manny's blue shorts were too tight, sporting a well-defined package that allowed me to think for a brief moment: He pushes some kind of side effect into me.

I was at first surprised to see him in the upstairs part of Barnie's Books, but that willowy sort of feeling vanished easily. "What brings you here, Manny?" I asked.

I wanted him to say "man sex," "cock-craving," or "rim job." I wanted Manny to become dirty and intentionally undignified. I wanted to watch him strip off all his sexy, needed-no-more clothes, and dance meticulously with our chests pressed together in Brotherly fineness. I wanted him to push me against one of the bookshelves, facefirst, and have my moistened, tender lips drag across a well-used, tiny paperback called *Do Me More Favors* as Manny did his man-job from behind me with every scheme to hurt and please P. Lethargic.

The side effect offered dribbles of saliva to caress the edges of my lips. I licked the upper one first, then the lower. I listened to Manny's delicious answer: "Rumor has it that a boy like me can find something fun up here."

He was making my solitary place dirty...but I didn't mind. Manny just corrupted a sweet, pleasant place in an upstairs attic room with slim books and passageways. I answered softly, closing *Room,* "And what kind of fun did you have in mind, Manny?"

I should have never asked that question for two reasons. One: I was still his former teacher and easily stepped over my boundaries as a professional. And two: Manny, I realized for a brief moment, was too pretty for me, too model-perfect. His eyes connected with mine, but that was the only connection I believed or told myself that we would share. Granted, I worked out. I had the chiseled-perfect chest and biceps. I looked good for my educated age. But Manny...he was divine in every way. He was richly masculine in all the right places, destined to bed the hottest brown dudes in the world. He was out of the teacher's league, I figured. And I was OK with that.

"Don't I owe you something?" Manny whispered, blinked.

Side effect–ness again. I felt woozy. I felt as if I could lean into him, because I would eventually fall and strap my thin arms around his cord-lined neck, plunge my tongue down his red throat and suck face with Manny for the next half hour. Instead I swallowed Lethargic juice, sighed heavily, smiled back, kept my eyes tucked away into some kind of boy-man or student-teacher package with him. I simply answered, despite feeling completely flushed and out of place–out of mind, in a pompous, arrogant, rather domineering tone, "You owe me everything, Manny."

Then...he smiled back, giggled slightly. I didn't think he would have ever giggled like that with a female companion. I didn't think that sissy-slippery giggle would have exited his fine lips with his football-tossing pals. It was a teacher-student giggle that uttered playful need all through it. Lethargic need.

After that smile and questioning giggle was shared, rule number 3 got broken. Manny quickly moved forward, tilted his head slightly, dove for the arch of my neck, and placed one firm, intended kiss to the fragile nape. His right hand clamped on to my left hip as he whispered, "I followed you here, Lethargic. Keeping my eyes on you. I always keep my promises."

He dashed away before I could say anything. I still felt his untamable lips on my neck. I felt his breath inside my ear, teasing me. My legs wobbled, and it was then, immediately after I watched his large, splayed back vanish into the day, that I fell into one of the shelves of books. I sat with my legs spread apart on the floor. One knee bumped a book called *Ready for You Now*. Shaking all over, breathing in a quick shift of motion, I thought how appropriate the title of the book was. Maybe I was willed to lead Manny into a sense of being dirty with me. Maybe I was ready for Manny to cash in his promise. I breathed quietly, and patiently I waited for him to return and to begin a long, enchanting process of African queer love, with Manny Faulk sucking on my hard, popping knob in my vulnerable khakis.

I had other errands to run. I didn't return home until later that evening. It was too hot, sticky, and unclean. Every inch of my colored skin was limp and malleable. I thought of Manny all afternoon, that sudden, heart-pulling kiss. It was probably one of the better kisses I have ever shared with a man. Manny seemed so innocent but so experienced at the same time; that's what that single, delectable kiss produced in my stimulated mind.

Once at home, tucked away from the city, I put Black Jazz on the stereo, showered, shaved again. Tucked away in a summer robe, evening allowed me to reach for a single wine glass, and evening also allowed me to spot something large and beautifully Black floating in my outside pool. I snatched up two wine glasses instead of one and walked out to greet Manny Faulk.

Of course, he was naked. I saw his long stems, his flat stomach and chest. I noticed (almost immediately) his long cock, which was stiff and looked generous. I listened to him add to the sensual, sexual scene, "I've been watching you for a long time."

I wanted to tell him that he didn't have to talk, that I was all ready for his payback. I was no longer soft and malleable. Every muscle on my body was tense and hard. My heart pounded within my chest with unstable nervousness.

"Bring the wine, come in, and join me."

A dream come true. I listened, dropped the robe to the side of the pool. He said I was handsome and looked ready to handle a student like he. I poured two glasses of wine, carried them into the pool, handed him one. He gulped it down quickly, kissed my lips before I could even touch them to the glass I was holding. He pulled at one of my nipples with his free hand and chanted, "Why don't I show you some of the literature I know?"

I didn't argue with him, breaking rule number 4.

The wine glasses were somewhere. My robe was lost. We stood in aqua-blue pool water up to our waists. Manny shoved his tongue down into my throat, pulled on nipples, cupped my luscious balls in his hands. He whispered, "This is what I owe you, isn't it?"

I said "Yes" because he did owe me.

"I won't stop until you get enough."

I pulled away, felt dizzy from the wine or Manny's intrusive touching. I whispered with a lethargic, beaded smile, "I hope you don't." Then I touched his countable abs and nips, sucked on Manny flesh with the greatest potential. I felt my hard rod slip against his. I felt the two of them dance and linger for the longest moments, gliding together with warm, summery water wrapped around their extended, fleshy bodies.

"Follow me."

I did. I wasn't about to argue or contemplate or meander in deep thought about right or wrong. All the rules for teaching had been broken with this singular, divine student. Everything from that moment on was going to be nasty and dirty, completely unprofessional…but fine too.

We waded through the water to the edge of the pool. As Manny collected protection, I sat on the side of the pool with a rock-hard cock touching the top of my naval. I peered restlessly into the glimmering, dreamy pool and thought: Manny's a legal drug.

He came back to my side, kissed both nipples, touched the head of my mushroom-shaped man probe and whispered, "Time to be dirty, professor."

I thought: Time to be dirty, roll around, back pressing against concrete and swimmer's towel…time to *Ready for You Now* and *Do Me More Favors* and tongue down my throat again, something finding my nips and my own delicious abs, my mind splitting into two equal halves as my dark ass splits into two halves with the same tongue that was just down my throat…time to dance to Black Jazz, have Manny's fingers inside me, spreading Prof. Me wider and wider and wider…

His words: "Breathe now…one big breath."

Our eyes snagged onto each other's.

I thought: He's between my legs, and I can see his fine body above me, willing itself to enter me. Manny is a god that I have adored. He is every man that I have loved, swept up into one body. He is my stalker, my student, my lover, my friend, my new companion. He whispered for me to close my eyes and listen to him, move with him, feel his hot steel rod enter me, leaving me in deep, penetrating thoughts, critiquing this direct moment in masculine time:

The African god, Tika, has bumped into Me, cock inside hole, international literature being accomplished here, promises being kept by the summer pool, nipples touching, swollen hearts and cocks beating, men doing one of those naughty-dirty tribe dances together, push and grind, all the Black Gods in Africa dancing together, Tribesmen of the jungles in love, Baldwin witch doctors, Giovanni's Wet-Dew-Come–Covered Room, lost in Africa, inside Africa, red, yellow, green…

"Please," Manny moaned from atop his own plateau of gay erotica, pumping and pushing inside literary me.

I opened my eyes and watched glistening sweat dribble down his perfect cheeks and defined chest. I listened to Manny huff and pump and grunt like some unknown jungle animal along the Senegal River in French west Africa. I felt Manny blasting into me, pushing student meat into me, holding my thighs apart and then touching my slick, moistened, erect jism rod with both hands.

As he spread me apart, I whispered in delight, "I should have given you an A in my class."

He chanted back in his methodical, reassuring measure, "I'm the teacher now…you'll pay for errors," pushing harder, willing my cock with his free hands, spreading Professor Lethargic apart.

Then, both of us dizzy and confused, he pulled out of me, ripped the condom off and tossed it aside. Manny leaned into me further, pressed his slick ass stabber against my shaft. Kissing African cocks. With his right hand, he grabbed my left hand and placed the two hands against the two kissing cocks. Pump, rush, pump; hips moved uncontrollably and 10 fingers mixed with the flesh of the student-teacher cocks.

I imagined we were in the jungle again. I saw tropical plants with unfamiliar names. I saw tribesmen naked and surrounding us. It was one giant, Black circle jerk. All of us were coming together, stroking and chanting, jungle music playing, drums and wood being beaten by worthy hands, pounding and pushing, a tribesmen orgy in my mind. I thought of one of the books I might have found in Barnie's attic, *Witchdoctor's Circle,* and couldn't hold back anymore, couldn't keep my eyes open anymore, couldn't help from pumping and thrusting my body into Manny's hand.

"Comi," I thought he whispered, some African word that I didn't understand, but it was really "come" that he said. Again I listened, feeling African rain splatter over my fingers and on my chest as Manny chanted in his ancestral manner, spewing on me, spewing with me, covering my dark skin with white bubbles of majestic tribal ooze. Dancing together. We arched backs and thrust one last time together. Spew flowed like white, creamy rivers in my mind that I had imagined. We pumped jism wildly, allowing it to mix over our hands and in our dark pubic hair. We huffed and flinched, pumped and moaned. Man love. Divinity. Sex-end.

With promises kept and shared, all the rules of the teacher broken, I was exhausted and spent. I watched Manny write his tribal name on my chest with our mixed spew: TIKA. He kissed my lips and my neck and whispered, "Will you swim with me now?"

As he backstroked out into the pool, I sat up with international, white come dripping over fingers, stomach, chest, and stiff rod, feeling compassionate and dizzy, bonded to him. I felt out of my pink mind and perfectly content. Softly I whispered, watching him, adoring my Black Tika and young scholar, "Absolutely," as I slipped into summery water.

Headlock
Greg Herren

I was nervous when the doorbell rang. It was understandable, I suppose. I had met people online before, and the reality was rarely what had been promised through instant messages, profiles, and traded pictures. Yet Phil and I had been talking online for months. We had talked on the telephone, and he seemed like a nice guy. We'd first met in the wrestling chat room, sharing a mutual interest in working out and wrestling. We liked the same holds and we liked the idea of hard competition that we both found arousing, and so we decided finally to meet and actually wrestle. My experiences with other wrestlers had been disappointing thus far. I wanted to compete. I wanted someone who wanted to actually wrestle as opposed to simply roll around as a prelude to sex. That was what was arousing to me, and Phil seemed to feel the same way.

I opened the door. "Brad?" he asked. He was taller than me, about 6 foot 3. He was almost completely bald on top, with the rest of his hair clipped very short. He was wearing a gray sweater that stretched tightly across his chest and shoulders. His black jeans were tight. His voice was deep, almost rough-sounding.

I held out my hand, and he shook it. His grip was tight, strong. The sleeves of the sweater he wore were pushed up, revealing hard forearms with protruding veins. "Come in," I said, trying to keep my voice from shaking. Physically, he was exactly what he had said, and now I was worried that I was disappointing to him.

"Nice legs," he said, smiling. I was wearing Lycra shorts and a white ribbed tank top.

Relief coursed through me. Our favorite hold was scissors, and we were both into strong legs. I knew I had good legs—I'd been told on more than one occasion that my legs were my best feature, but there was still that sense of self-consciousness, that I wouldn't measure up. Phil had made gay wrestling videos, and while I knew I had a good body, I knew I wasn't beat-off material.

"Thanks," I said, adding, "You look pretty good yourself."

He winked at me. "Where's the bathroom?"

I showed it to him, and he disappeared inside with his gym bag. I walked into the spare bedroom. I had put down two mattresses on the floor, wedging them into place in the corners of the room. It was a primitive setup for someone who was used to wrestling on mats or in a ring. There was the problem of crashing into the walls, but there was still room. I pulled off my tank top and my shorts and slipped a red thong on, adding a red-and-blue-striped bikini over it.

My hands were clammy with nervousness. We had been talking trash to each other on the computer and over the phone for months. I wasn't nearly as experienced as he was, and in wrestling I knew that experience and practice were the keys to success on the mat. Weight and strength could prove an advantage, but a more knowledgeable wrestler could easily defeat a bigger opponent. I had 10 pounds on Phil, but that wouldn't be enough.

I heard the bathroom door shut, and Phil walked in. He was wearing a black bikini, high cut on the thighs. His abs were sliced with muscle. His pecs were thick and hard. A scattering of clipped hair covered them. The cleavage between his pecs was deep. His legs were solid and defined. My legs were bigger, but his looked strong. He walked up to me and tweaked a nipple.

"Very nice," he said, "but I'm gonna kick your ass."

He dropped down to the mattress and began stretching. I did the same, occasionally glancing over at him. His ass was round, tight, and hard. Muscles rippled in his back. *What the hell was I thinking?* I wondered, remembering all the trash I had talked to him. *Stop thinking like that,* I admonished myself. *He's just another opponent. So what if you don't beat him? Focus on fighting back and not being an easy win for him. Remember: It's all about the fight, not winning or losing.* I took a deep breath and got up onto my knees.

He did the same, facing me. "Now is when you pay for all the shit you've been talking."

I felt my cock stirring. His body was beautiful. "Bring it on, you old fuck."

He pounced at me, and we tangled, arms trying to get some kind of advantage with leverage. I managed to get my right arm around his head and pushed with my legs. Off-balance, he fell to the right. I moved my weight on top of him. He fell up against the wall on his upper back. I positioned myself so that he couldn't move. His face began to redden. He struggled and pushed, but I held firm. I looked down. His abs were exposed. *Why not?* I thought to myself, reaching down with my right hand as I curled my fingers. I had seen this done on televised matches and never really understood it. With the cut muscles of his abs there, it clicked in my head. I grabbed hold of one of the washboards with my fingers in the cut and my thumb below and pinched the muscle—hard.

"Fuck!" Phil half shouted, moaning at the same time.

Delighted, I lessened the pressure, then reapplied it. Again, he moaned in pain. "Give?" I asked quietly.

"Fuck you. You're not getting the first submission!"

I squeezed again. "Give?"

He moaned. "No way!"

I brought my left hand to another one of his washboards. I squeezed both of them, clenching my forearms. His back arched. "OK, OK, OK!"

I moved back and sat on my haunches. He sat up, taking deep breaths. Beads of sweat were forming in the valley between his pecs. Damn, but he was hot.

"Good move," he growled, rubbing his abs.

"I've never tried that before," I replied. "I've seen it on TV, but that's it."

"You catch on fast." He got back up. "But now you're gonna suffer."

"Come on then."

He rushed me, and his momentum carried me onto my back. I quickly twisted over onto my stomach, bringing my arms in tight to my sides, denying him the chance to get his arms through for leverage. Instead, he slipped his hands underneath my chin and began pulling upward. Squatting on my back, he pulled my head. I strained my neck muscles, but he was too strong. My back started to arch as he pulled up and back. "Won't work." I grunted. "My back's limber. I was a gymnast, remember?"

Someone with a less flexible back would have been screaming by that point. Silently I thanked God for those gymnastics classes when I was a teenager. But then he started twisting my head. He sat up a little, and I turned to relieve the pressure on my neck. He was going to turn me over. I knew I was going to be vulnerable, but I had no choice. I turned but squirmed my legs out from under him. His long legs went around my waist and locked behind my back. Damn it! He fell backward, tightening his grip with his legs. I was now on top of him, but he was smiling as he started squeezing tighter.

I looked down at his face. I smiled. "Oh, ouch." I taunted him.

His face reddened. "You fuck!" He arched his back up and tightened his legs.

That hurt.

I started taking shallower breaths. He would lessen the pressure, I would draw in breath, and then he would squeeze again. The muscle cords in his legs rippled. Finally, the pain became too intense. "OK, OK, OK," I groaned, tapping his right leg. "I give."

He relaxed and let go, sitting up with a smile. "How'd you like that, boy?"

"Nice." I shook my head, twisting my torso from side to side. He was smiling. My hair was slick with sweat. Damn, but he was hot.

We got up and looked at each other. This time I got the advantage and managed to get my legs around his head. "How you like that, tough guy?" I asked, squeezing. My ass contracted. "Give?"

"No way," he grunted. He swung his legs around and tried to get them around my head. I countered this by batting them away with my arms. He tried again, and this time I managed to grab hold of one of them. I twisted it slightly, tightening my legs around his head. His face was turning red. "Come on, big guy," I taunted, feeling my cock stiffening. He tried to buck me off and get his leg free. Smelling a submission, I tightened my grip on his leg and squeezed his head again, and with my free hand I punched his abs, three times in a row.

"Fuck, OK, OK." I let his leg go, but squeezed his head one more time and got one last punch into his abs before letting go. He rolled over onto his stomach, breathing in air. I slapped his hard ass and sat back.

"That's two out of three," I said.

"You think this is over?" He was twisting his head from side to side. "Is that all you got in you?"

"I'm not even breathing hard," I shrugged. "I can go all day." I could see that his dick was hard too.

"You ready?"

"Bring it on."

The next two submissions went to him. The first time he managed to get me flat on my back, his legs around my head, squeezing until my ears rang and I was forced to give up. For added humiliation, he kept grabbing my head by the hair and pulling it into his crotch, rubbing my face on his hard cock, making me smell the musty scent of his mixed sweat and arousal. The next time he worked me down with a combination headlock and body scissors. With his free hand he was pinching my nipples. I fought it as long as I could, but there was no chance of getting out of it, and his damned legs were just too strong for me to keep holding out. I gave.

We took a break while I went to get us each a glass of water. When I came back, he'd pulled his bikini off and was there in just a black thong. His bare ass, with just the Lycra triangle at the top in the crevice, was one of the most beautiful ones I had ever seen. I handed him his water and pulled my trunks off. My hard-on, which kept coming and going, came back. He drank his water and set the glass down. Both of our bodies were slick with sweat.

This time I wasn't going to lose, and I didn't. After neither of us could get an advantage, I managed to get him on his back. I was on top and locked a full nelson on him. My hard-on was on top of his hard ass. He strained his arms, trying to break the nelson. I struggled to hold on. His ass just felt so good to my erection; I wanted to hold him there forever. I could feel that I was losing my grip. His strength and my own sweat were working to beat me. I held on and weighed my options. I pulled my own legs up underneath me and quickly let go of the nelson. In that split second when he was too surprised to move, I slipped my hands under his chin and pulled him up.

"No!"

I laughed. I held his chin up with one hand while I reached back and slapped his ass. "Give?"

"No way!"

"I'll break your fucking back!"

"No way!"

I stopped slapping his reddening ass and reached down and twisted a nipple. "I swear, I'll break it."

I slipped my legs around his waist and applied pressure there. That was it. He gave. I let go but didn't get off his back. I reached down and shoved his head into the mattress. "Not so tough now, are you, stud?" I taunted. I moved my legs up and around his head and contracted the muscles. He moaned again. "Give it up, stud, or I'll crack your head."

"OK, OK, OK!"

This time I let him up, watching him warily. The tip of his cock was poking out of the top of the thong. I let him catch his breath for a moment and then attacked again. I forced him over backward, cradling his head between my legs, squeezing and pulling his head up into my aching hard-on. "You're gonna pay," he muttered between moans. "You are gonna pay...OK, OK, let me up, you son of a bitch!"

Again I released him. My balls ached from the pressure of the almost constant arousal.

He got up, smiling. "You're pretty tough."

"Thanks." I was gulping in air myself. "You too."

I shook my head, and that was it. While I wasn't looking he

jumped me. My head was trapped between his legs. He was on his back, and I was on my knees. I grabbed his legs, trying to pry them apart. Through the ringing in my ears I could hear him laughing and taunting me. I opened my eyes, and there was his cock: long, thick, red, and hard. He pushed it up toward my face and said "Suck it."

I opened up and took it into my mouth. He leaned back and moaned. I started tonguing the head and swallowed it down into my throat. I tasted sweat and musk. I worked it with my tongue as I slid it in and out of my mouth. As I thought he might, he let go with his legs as the pleasure heightened, but not completely. He held on to my head, just lightly enough to cause a little pressure but not enough to make me give in to it. I reached around his legs and started pinching his nipples. He started bucking a little bit, his tight ass contracting and loosening.

I pulled my head back from his cock just as it shot its load, spraying my face and hair. He shuddered and moaned until the last drops dribbled from the head.

His legs relaxed, and I pulled my head out from in between them. He lay there panting. I pulled back a little bit.

"Oh, man," he said. "You give great head."

I moved around him. He was still lying on his back, eyes half closed in the aftermath of his explosive orgasm. I straddled him and wrapped my legs around his head, rolling over onto my side, wrenching him over onto his.

"You fucker!"

"Payback," I said, and pulled his face up into my crotch. He began lapping my cock, sucking it down. I reached down to his ass with my free hand, grabbing those hard cheeks and squeezing, keeping my legs in position. It felt so damned good. He was a master. It didn't take me long. I felt the come moving up my shaft and shoved his head back just in time to spray his face with my load. I moaned as my body convulsed and bucked with each long, pent-up shot.

Spent, I lay back, releasing his head. "Damn, that was hot," I mumbled, every muscle in my body aching and sore.

He laughed. "That was one of the hottest matches I've ever had."

High praise from a video star. "Thanks." I collapsed on my back. Eyes closed, I sensed him lying next to me. He put an arm around me. I turned my head and we kissed, deep and wet and long.

While he showered, I wiped myself down with a towel. Just thinking about the match made my cock start to stir again. When he came out of the bathroom, he was dressed. I walked him to the door. We kissed again at the door. "Let's have a rematch soon, OK?"

"Anytime."

I watched him walk down my steps, his tight jeans caressing the legs that had made me scream out submissions.

"Anytime."

The Foreman and the Grunt
Derek Adams

I zeroed in on the guy the minute he stepped onto the site. Here at Norris Construction we get assigned a crew of greenhorns every summer. Most of them are young, dumb, and full of come, and I generally steer clear of them. This particular guy probably wasn't much over the company's minimum hiring age of 18, and he was no doubt up to his eyebrows in jizz, but there was something about him that stuck in my mind like a burr, refusing to be shaken loose.

For one thing, he pretty much conformed to my idea of what a wet dream looked like. He was about a head shorter than me, built solid, with broad shoulders and narrow hips. His shirt sleeves were rolled up high enough to show the full curve of his biceps, and his lower body was giving a faded pair of Levi's a real workout. I mean to say, he was stretching those pants in all the right directions—side-to-side and front-to-back. His skin was burnished dark-brown by the sun, his eyes were blue as the summer sky, and his thick mane of hair was the color of wheat.

As luck would have it, the guy ended up working for me. My crew is responsible for getting supplies distributed to wherever they're needed on the site. The new guy was naturally gonna end up being the grunt—doing all the shit work that the rest of the crew foisted off on him. I sort of felt sorry for him, but he looked strong enough to handle it. Besides, the work wasn't gonna do him any harm.

"You're all done," old man Norris told the guy as he turned over the last of the employment forms he'd been filling out. "This here's Harry Andrews. He tells you to jump, you jump." Norris waved at me then walked off across the site.

"Morning, Mr. Andrews." The guy was a baritone but just getting used to the fact. He spoke softly, like he was afraid his voice might break if he shouted.

"Harry," I corrected him. "Just call me Harry. I'm the foreman, you're the grunt. The work ain't glamorous, but the pay's better than you'd get leaning on the counter in a convenience store. Basically, you do anything anyone on the crew asks you to do unless it's against the law or just plain stupid. You put in a good day's work, we'll get along just fine." I looked into his impossibly blue eyes and felt a tingling in my balls. I'd have to be careful around this one. "What's your name?" I barked gruffly.

"Sonny," he replied. "Sonny Regis."

"Come on, Sonny. I clapped my hand on his shoulder. Muscle jumped against my palm. "Let's get you a hard hat and some decent gloves."

I got him outfitted then sent him over to my crew. Every time I walked by to check on the guys, Sonny was in the thick of things, fetching and carrying. I knew my crew—they'd ride his butt hard, and he'd be sore as a boil for a few days, but they wouldn't let him get hurt. I went on about my business, checking inventory and ordering supplies.

At noon I stepped into the wire cage of the elevator and rode it up to the top. My boys liked to eat their lunch out in the sun, so they were always at the highest level that had been floored in. When the elevator shuddered to a stop, I opened the door and stepped out into the brilliant sunshine. Matt Preston, a practical joker from way back, turned around from where he was kneeling and motioned for me to be quiet. The boys were up to something—that much was clear from the wicked gleam in Matt's eye.

"We're doing us some initiating," he whispered, after he had crept silently over to my side. "The new guy is joining me and the boys in a little circle jerk."

"The hell you say," I muttered, shaking my head. It was such an old trick it had grandkids, but Sonny seemed to have fallen for it in a big way. I stepped over to where my guys were huddled in the center of the floored area, unable to resist the temptation to watch the proceedings.

Sonny was already blindfolded, a red bandanna bound tightly around his head. He'd taken his shirt off to soak up some rays, and I got a chance to study his body at close range. His pecs were squared; the small nipples capping them were burned just a shade darker than his skin. His belly was flat and hairless, ridged like a washboard. A few silvery hairs peeked out from under his arms, but for the rest, he was slick as a whistle. As I watched he slowly unbuttoned his fly, encouraged by the loud groans all around him.

When he pulled his whanger out of his pants, I damn near groaned out loud. It was nice and thick, the fat head covered with skin. A finger-thick vein ran up the middle of the shaft, pulsing slightly. His nuts were hanging low and loose in a bag that was damn near as hairless as his chest. Most of the hair on his body was concentrated in the dense curls that clustered around the base of his meat. They spilled out around the edges of his fly, gleaming like spun gold in the noonday sun.

After about five quick pulls Sonny's prick jutted out stiff as a poker. Nobody would ever tease him about the size of his business, that was for damned sure. It was a double handful, and Sonny's hands weren't small. He squeezed it, and a glistening drop of goo oozed out the slit in the tip. I licked my lips, knowing I'd be dreaming about this for days to come.

All the guys were groaning and moaning, pretending they were beating off, so Sonny got busy, determined to win the bet. You know how these things are supposed to work—first dude who comes up with a handful of scum wins. Thing is, there's usually only one dude doing the jacking, so the guy with the sticky palm is the goat. Anyhow, Sonny started off nice and slow, squeezing his piece from the base, right out to the hooded tip. By the third pull he was drooling juice. Once he had a skinful it oozed out, hung in the air, suspended by a glistening thread, then broke off and splashed onto the floor.

You could judge Sonny's progress by watching his body. His nipples were standing out on his squared pecs, delicate nubs of flesh that I longed to mash flat with my tongue. A couple of minutes into it, the veins on his biceps popped out like cords, slowly extending till they bulged from his shoulders to his wrists. A flush of red crept up from his belly and spread over his chest and neck. Within minutes his face glowed crimson and beads of sweat glistened on his forehead and upper lip.

"Shit, guys, here it comes," he gasped, his shoulders hunching as he raised up onto his knees and started fisting his prick so fast, it was a flesh-colored blur. "Oh, fuck, man, I'm coming. Better stand back!" His hands dropped to his sides and his hips shot forward, his cock vibrating like a tuning fork. A big glob pushed out the come hole and started to drool down onto the floor. Then Sonny's muscles flexed, and he grunted.

I saw the sun glinting off the end of his knob, but I didn't see the arc of his first shot till it splattered against my forearm. The spicy, pungent smell of his juice damn near did me in. His second shot sailed past me and splattered on a girder. He pumped a couple onto the floor in the middle of the circle, then spit one onto the toe of my left boot.

"I win!" he shouted triumphantly, reaching up and taking off his blindfold. The expression on his face when he got a look at the other guys was priceless. "I'll be damned," he croaked as he took it all in. Then he started to laugh, his voice ringing out on the summer air. The other guys joined him, all of them cracking wise. Sonny had definitely passed the test and had been accepted as a regular part of the crew.

"Harry!" I turned and saw Sonny waving at me as I left the job site that evening. I waved back and he ran over to me.

"Survived your first day with flying colors," I remarked.

"Yeah." He blushed scarlet under his tan. "I'm really sorry about...about...well, you know."

"Don't worry about it, Sonny. It wiped right off." I chuckled and gave him a conspiratorial wink. "I don't even think it's gonna leave a scar. Hey, can I give you a ride someplace?" We had reached the parking lot, and Sonny was still following me. I liked having him walking along beside me, his shoulder occasionally brushing my arm. Every time I took a breath I could smell him, a heady mixture of sweat and pent-up spunk. My fingers ached to reach out and caress his skin, just to see if it felt as soft as it looked. Damn it, the guy was driving me right around the bend. "Where you headed?"

"Well, if you can give me a ride over to the bus terminal, that'll be OK."

"The bus terminal?" I stopped beside my old Chevy pickup and shot him a puzzled look. "You figuring on doing some traveling?"

"No, nothing like that. It's just that I'm sorta between places to live right now. The guy I was bunking with moved this weekend, and I couldn't afford the apartment by myself. I'll find something after I get my first paycheck. In the meantime, I've got my gear stashed at the bus depot. I was gonna wash up down there, then I figured I'd camp out in the park."

"That's pretty damned dangerous, Sonny."

"Hey, I can take care of myself." He squared his shoulders, and his handsome features settled into a scowl that wouldn't have scared an old lady.

"I don't doubt that you can take care of yourself," I assured him. "However, I don't figure a couple of weeks in a public park is going to do anything for your job performance. This is pretty hard work, just in case you haven't noticed. You'll be needing a good night's sleep."

"I'm sorry, Harry, but I don't have any options." He shrugged his broad shoulders and smiled a sad little smile.

"You can come and stay with me." When the words were out of my mouth I stood there, dumbfounded. With the brief exception of a disastrous marriage right out of high school, I hadn't lived with any-one for almost 18 years. I had a small one-bedroom apartment that was barely big enough for me. I don't know what the hell came over me, but I'd said it, and I'd stand by it. Besides, the grin that spread over Sonny's face would have melted a stone.

"That'd be great, Harry!" he enthused. "I'll be real quiet, and I'll pick up after myself. Hell, you won't even know I'm there."

Well, he was quiet and neat, but I sure as hell knew he was there. He sat beside me in the evening while we watched TV, he was across from me when we ate, and he was always slipping in and out of the bathroom while I was getting ready for work in the mornings. The worst thing was that he was always touching me. It was always real casual and natural, but it was driving me up the fucking wall. I saw him all day long, and after I went to bed he was etched on my eyelids as I tried to get to sleep.

Today was Saturday, so I had to face the prospect of a whole day with him. I got up early, did a few stretches, then took off for a run, hoping that maybe a few miles would take the edge off the dull throbbing in my groin. I'd had a hard-on for days now. I beat off in the shower in the morning and after I went to bed at night, but I still popped a rod every time I thought about Sonny.

When I got back to the apartment, he was just getting up. He got up off the couch and gave me a sleepy grin. He was stark naked, his perfect prick hanging down between his perfect thighs. "Good morning," I said, fighting to keep my eyes off his butt. The cheeks of his ass were like two melons—firm, smooth and golden. They flexed with every step, a dimple in the left cheek winking at me teasingly. I stepped past him and headed for the bathroom, intent on a shower and maybe a quick hand job. Sonny followed along after me, obviously ready to talk.

"You've really got a great build, Harry," he said, leaning against the door frame, idly rubbing his belly. "Ever since I was a little kid, I always hoped I'd grow up to look like you."

"What?" I turned and looked at him curiously.

"Oh, you know, big and muscular with a hairy chest. Man, have you ever got great arms!" Suddenly he grabbed my arm, squeezing my biceps appraisingly. I flexed as his fingers dug into the muscle. He stood there, his hand on my arm, looking up at me with those big blue eyes. "Could I touch your chest, Harry?"

My throat muscles worked violently but no sound came out. I nodded my head slightly, too overcome by lust to remember any of my ironclad rules for living. His hand hovered over my left pec, brushing against the tangle of fur that grew there. He gradually pressed down till he made firm contact, his palm hot against my swollen nipple. Our eyes locked, recognition of our need sparking both ways. I put my hands around his narrow waist, my fingers burning as I finally touched him. He laid his head against my chest, and I was lost.

"Let's do it, Harry," he whispered. I picked him up and lifted him high in the air. He grabbed the shower curtain rod and threw his legs over my shoulders. I burrowed between his legs, snuffling hungrily at his prick and balls, taking in the heady mixture of sweat, jizz, and funk he exuded.

Sonny yelped when my tongue made contact with the tender rosebud of flesh tucked behind his big balls. I licked and teased, then thrust my middle finger deep, forcing my way past his tight ass ring and into the steamy heat of his fuck hole. Sonny squirmed and moaned, struggling to reach out and grab his meat so he could start jacking himself while I finger-fucked him. I refused to cooperate, purposely keeping him off-balance so he had to hang onto the bar with both hands.

"I wanna touch my prick, Harry. Come on, man, I really need to touch my prick!"

"Not a chance," I grunted. I drove my finger deeper up his hot hole, and his thighs tightened against the sides of my head. I licked his asshole and balls while I poked at his prostate. Sonny howled, and his asshole spasmed. With my free hand I reached into the medicine cabinet and grabbed a rubber. Opening it one-handed wasn't easy, but I managed. I plopped the lubed latex on the end of my meat and rolled it down the shaft.

After I'd licked and fingered him till his asshole gaped, I shrugged my shoulders roughly, dislodging him from his perch. The backs of his thighs slid down my sweaty chest, his asshole tugging at the hairs on my belly as it spasmed and throbbed. My aim was perfect—my swollen meat jammed right up Sonny's twitching hole as his butt slipped down to my crotch. There was a moment of resistance, then his eyes opened wide as I breached him and sheathed my fat piece in his hot, silky hole.

I dropped to my knees and fell forward onto him, pinning him to the floor, my dick buried deep. His smooth chest rubbed against my hairy one as he grabbed my arms and ground himself against me. His cock and balls mashed against my belly, the honey flowing out of him hot and thick. I'd only pumped him a few times when he closed his eyes and let fly with one of his high-powered loads. The first blast caught me under the chin, splattering on my throat and drizzling down over my pecs. I reared back and stirred my cock around in him slow and easy, watching him score his abs with creamy white streamers of jism.

After he was drained, I braced my hands on either side of his blond head and started fucking him, my prick sliding in and out of his unresisting ass channel. He was hard again in seconds. I nibbled his succulent tits, and his asshole spasmed tight around my prick. Then I licked him, neck to navel, continuing down till I got the head of his piece in my mouth. I nipped the silky foreskin between my teeth and pulled it up tight over the fat knob. His balls rose up against the sides of the shaft, jiggling as I relentlessly pounded his ass.

"Fuck me," he squealed, grabbing his hard-on and jacking it furiously. I pummeled him, my balls slapping against his back. My orgasm began with a heat that permeated my skin and set all my nerve endings to throbbing. The sensation intensified as it swirled around my belly and coursed through my loins. I stopped humping when my groin muscles spasmed and my balls knotted tight between my legs. My cock flexed, and I began to shoot, flooding the rubber with my thick cream. Sonny's eyes rolled back in his head as he blasted my chest and belly with his second load.

I humped him till my balls were drained, then collapsed on top of him, my whole damn body tingling in the aftermath of the best screw I'd had in years. Sonny kissed me, his lips hot against my neck. When my dick slid out of him I rolled over on my side and looked down at him. "You just made me break every rule I ever managed to devise about keeping work and pleasure separate," I told him, tracing the curve of his chest with my fingertips.

"Hey, Harry, that's what rules are for, right?" He winked at me and sat up, stretching lazily. "Would the foreman like to shower with the grunt? Maybe we can come up with a whole new set of rules for you to live by."

"Yeah," I chuckled, getting to my feet. Sonny jumped up, slipped his arms around me, and began nuzzling my chest. "Maybe we could."

Family Affair
Bob Vickery

Nick and Maria ride up front in Maria's beat-up '74 Buick convertible, Maria driving like a lunatic, weaving in and out of the traffic, me wedged in the backseat with all the beach gear tumbling over me. The radio is turned on full blast, set to an oldies station belting out a Beach Boys tune. "I wish they all could be California girls," Nick sings along. He buries his face into Maria's neck and makes loud farting noises. Maria screams with laughter, and it's only by the grace of God that she avoids plowing us all into the highway's concrete median.

"Jesus Christ!" I cry out in terror.

Nick and Maria crack up—Nick wheezing, Maria's shoulders shaking spasmodically. "What the hell is wrong with you guys!" I shout. "You been sniffing airplane glue?"

"No," Nick says. "Drano." Maria breaks up again, laughing until she starts hiccuping.

"You two are fucking crazy," I say, shouting over the wind and the radio. "You're going to kill us all."

Nick turns his head and looks at me, grinning. "Lighten up, Robbie," he says. "We're supposed to be having a good time." I glare at him. He turns back to Maria. "I didn't know your little brother was such a tight-ass," he laughs.

"Oh, Robbie's OK," she says. She glances back at me in the rearview mirror and widens her eyes in comic exaggeration. I turn my head away sulkily and stare over on my left toward the ocean, which stretches out as flat and shiny as a metal plate.

We ride together for a few minutes in silence, then Nick reaches over and turns down the radio. He turns his head toward me. "So, Robbie," he says affably. "I hear you're gay."

"Jesus, Maria!" I exclaim.

Maria isn't laughing now. At least she has the decency to look embarrassed. "I didn't think you'd mind me telling him, Robbie," she says. But her guilty tone makes it clear she knew damn well I'd mind. She shoots a poisonous look at Nick. "You've got a big mouth," she hisses.

"He's not the only one," I say.

Nick's eyes shift back and forth between Maria and me. "Oops," he says. He laughs, unfazed. "It's no big deal. I'm cool. It's not like I'm a born-again Christian or anything." He looks at me. "So, are you just coming out or what?"

"I don't want to talk about it," I say frostily. Maria flashes me an apologetic glance in the mirror, but I just glower back at her. We ride the rest of the distance to the beach in silence.

It's still early: The sun has just started climbing high, and there are only a scattering of cars in the dirt parking lot. We start the trek to the beach—Nick and Maria leading the way, me lagging behind with the cooler. Nick leans over and says something to Maria, and she laughs again, her previous embarrassment all forgotten now, which makes my mood even pissier. At the top of the dunes the two of them wait for me to catch up. The sea stretches out before us, sparkling in the bright sun, the waves hissing as they break upon the sandy beach. "Bitchin'!" Nick says. He reaches over and squeezes the back of my neck. "You having a good time, Robbie?" he asks, smiling.

Though I hardly know the guy, I know that this is as close to an apology as I'll ever get. A breeze whips over the dunes, smelling of the sea; the sun beams down benevolently, and I see nothing but good humor in Nick's wide blue eyes. In spite of myself I smile.

"Attaboy," Nick laughs. "I knew you had it in you!" He lets go, and we start climbing down the dunes to find a stretch of beach isolated from everyone else.

After we've laid the blanket out Maria and Nick start taking off their clothes. I hurriedly pull my bathing suit out of my knapsack. "I'm going to change behind the dune," I say.

Nick has one leg raised, about to pull off a sneaker. "I'll go with you," he says abruptly.

I have mixed feelings about this but don't know how I can dissuade him. We circle the nearest dune, leaving Maria behind on the broad expanse of beach. Nick peels off his shirt, and I can't help noticing the sleek leanness of his torso, the blond dusting of hair across his chest. My throat tightens, and I turn my attention to my fingers fumbling with the buttons of my jeans. Nick kicks off his shoes and shucks his shorts and Calvins. The honey-brown of his skin ends abruptly at his tan line, and his hips are pale-cream. Nick turns his back to me and stretches lazily like a jungle cat, arms bent. His ass is smooth and milky, downed with a light fuzz that gleams gold in the sun's rays. Nick turns around and smiles at me. His dick, half hard, sways heavily against his thighs.

I turn away and quickly pull my jeans off. When I look back at Nick, he's still standing there naked, only this time his dick is jutting out fully hard, twitching slightly in the light breeze. He sees my surprise and shrugs helplessly. "Sorry," he grins, his eyes wide and guileless. "Open air always makes me hard."

"This isn't a nude beach," I say, trying to sound casual. "You have to wear a suit."

"In a minute," Nick says. "I like feeling the breeze on my skin." His smile turns sly, and his eyes lose some of their innocence. He wraps his hand around his dick and strokes it slowly. "You like it, Robbie?" he asks. "Maria calls it my 'love club.' "

"What the hell are you trying to prove?" I ask.

Nick affects surprise. "I'm not trying to prove anything," he says, his tone all injured innocence. "I'm just making conversation." I quickly pull on my suit and walk back to the blanket. Nick joins us a couple of minutes later.

Nick and Maria race out into the waves. She pushes him into the path of a crashing breaker, laughing as he comes up sputtering. They horseplay in the surf line for a while and then swim out to deeper water. Eventually, they're just specks in the shiny, gun-metal blue. I close my eyes and feel the sun beat down on me. Rivulets of sweat begin to trickle down my torso.

Suddenly I'm in shade. I open my eyes and see Nick standing over me, the sun behind him so that I can't make out his features—just an outline of broad shoulders tapering down. He shakes his head and water spills down on me. "Hey!" I protest.

He sits down beside me on the blanket. "The water feels great," he says. "You should go out in it."

"In a little while," I say. "Where's Maria?"

Nick gestures vaguely. "Out there somewhere. She didn't want to come in yet." He stretches out next to me, propped up on his elbows. "So why are you so upset about me knowing you're gay? You think I'll disapprove or something?"

"Jeez, what's with you! Will you just drop the subject?"

"I've gotten it on with guys," Nick goes on, as if he hadn't heard me. "It's no big deal." He grins. "You want to hear about the last time I did?"

"No," I lie.

"It was in Hawaii. Oahu, to be exact." Nick turns on his side and faces me, his head on his hand. "I was there on spring break last year. I started hanging out with this dude I'd met in a Waikiki bar, a surfer named Joe." He laughs. "Surfer Joe, just like in the song. Ah, sweet Jesus, was he ever beautiful! Part Polynesian, part Japanese, part German. Smooth brown skin; tight, ripped body; and these fuckin' dark, soulful eyes." He smiles. "Like yours, Robbie. Like Maria's too, for that matter," he adds, as if it was an afterthought.

"Anyway, I had a rented car, and we took a drive to the North Shore. Somehow we wound up lost on this little piss-ass road—nothing but sugarcane fields on both sides. It'd been raining, but the sun was just breaking out, and all of a sudden, wham! This huge technicolored rainbow comes blazing out right in front of us." Nick sits up, getting excited. "It was fuckin' awesome! The motherfucker just arced overhead like some kind of neon bridge and ended not far off in this little grassy patch beyond the cane. Well, Joe leaps out of the car—I tell you, he was one crazy bastard—and he races across the field toward the rainbow, and because I couldn't think of anything better to do, I do the same."

Nick's eyes are wide, and he's talking faster now. "Joe makes it to where the rainbow hits the ground, he pulls off his board shorts, and he just stands there naked, his arms stretched out, the colors pouring down on him. Blue! Green! Red! Orange! I strip off my shorts too and jump right in."

Nick laughs, but his eyes drill into me. "It was the strangest damn sensation—standing in that rainbow, my skin tingling like a low-voltage current was passing through me." He blinks. "Joe wrestles me to the ground, one thing leads to another, and we wind up fucking right there with all the colors washing over us—me plowing Joe's ass, Joe's head red, his chest orange, his belly yellow, his legs green and blue. When I finally came, I pulled out of Joe's ass, raining my jizz down on him, the drops like colored jewels." Nick gazes down at me, his eyes laughing. "Like I said: fucking awesome!"

"You are so full of shit," I say.

Nick adopts an expression of deep hurt. "It's true. I swear it."

"Fuck you. You can't stand in a rainbow, for chrissakes. It's against the laws of optics."

" 'The laws of optics,' " Nick snorts. "What are you, an optician?"

"You mean a physicist. An optician prescribes glasses. Jesus, you're an ignorant fuck."

But Nick refuses to be insulted. He laughs and picks up my tube of sunblock. "Here," he says, "let me oil you up again. You've sweat-ed off your first layer." Nick smears the goop on my chest and starts stroking my torso. His hand wanders down my belly and lies there motionless. I can feel the heat of his hand sink into my skin. The tips of his fingers slide under the elastic band of my suit. He looks at me, eyebrows raised. When I don't say anything, Nick slips his hand under my suit and wraps it around my dick. "Do the same to me," he urges.

"Maria…" I say.

Nick scans the ocean. "She's way out there," he says. "She can't see anything." His hand, still greased with sunblock, starts sliding up and down my dick. I close my eyes. "Come on," he whispers. "Do it to me too. Please."

My hand seems to have a mind of its own. It slides inside Nick's suit and wraps around his fat, hard dick. His love club. "Yeah, Robbie, that's good," Nick sighs. "Now stroke it."

We beat each other off as the sun blasts down on us, the ocean shimmering off in the distance like a desert mirage. After a few moments we pull our suits down to our knees. Nick smears his hand with a fresh batch of lotion and then slides it down my dick. I groan. "Yeah, baby," he laughs. "You like that, don't you?" I groan again louder, arching my back as the orgasm sweeps over me. Nick takes my dick in his mouth and swallows my load as I pump it down his throat. Even after I'm done he keeps sucking on my dick, rolling his tongue around it, playing with my balls. He replaces my hand with his and with a few quick strokes brings himself to climax, shuddering as his load splatters against his chest and belly.

Maria staggers out of the surf a few minutes later and races to the blanket, squealing from the heat of the sand on her soles. Nick and I are chastely reading our summer novels under the umbrella. She flings herself down on the blanket, grabs a towel, and vigorously rubs her hair. "You guys enjoying yourselves?" she asks.

"Yeah, sure," Nick says, his mouth curling up into an easy grin. "Except your degenerate little brother can't keep his hands off me." He winks. Maria laughs, but she shoots me a worried look, checking to see if I'm offended. I shrug and smile back. I feel like shit.

Nick stops by my place a week later. It's the first time I've seen him since the beach. "Is Maria here?" he asks. "I swung by her apartment, but she wasn't home." He's dressed in a tank top and cutoffs, and he carries a summer glow with him that makes him shine like a small sun.

"No," I say, my heart beating furiously. "I haven't seen her all day." Nick peers over my shoulder. "You alone?"

"Yeah," I say. My mouth has suddenly gone desert-dry. Nick regards me calmly, waiting. "You want to come in for a while?" I finally ask.

Nick smiles and gives a slight shrug. "Why not?"

As soon as I close the door behind us he's on me, pushing me against the wall, his hard dick dry-humping me through the denim of his shorts, his mouth pressed against mine. After the initial shock passes I kiss him back, thrusting my tongue deep into his mouth. Nick's hands are all over me, pulling at my shirt, undoing the buttons, tugging down my zipper. He slides his hands under my jeans and cups my ass, pulling my crotch against his.

I push him away, gasping. "This isn't going to happen," I say.

Nick looks at me with bright eyes, his face flushed, his expression half annoyed, half amused. "Now, Robbie," he says, smiling his old smile. "You're not going to be a cocktease, are you?"

I zip my pants up again and rebutton my shirt. I feel the anger rising up in me. "You're such an asshole," I say. I push past him and walk into the living room.

Nick remains in the hallway. I sit on the couch, glaring at him. He slowly walks into the room until he's standing in front of me. He looks out the window and then back at me again. "Why am I an asshole?" he asks. "Because I think you're fuckin' beautiful?"

"You may not give a shit," I say, "but Maria's crazy about you."

Nick sits down beside me on the couch. "Ah," he says quietly. A silence hangs between us for a couple of beats. "What if I told you I'm just as crazy about Maria?" he finally asks.

"You sure have a funny way of showing it."

Nick leans back against the arm of the couch and regards me with his steady blue gaze. He gives a low laugh. " 'Now, next on *Jerry Springer*!' " he says. " 'My sister's boyfriend is putting the moves on me!' " I look at him hostilely, not saying anything. He returns my stare calmly. "You know," he says, "lately every time I fuck your sister I think of you. It's getting to be a real problem."

"Will you knock it off!"

Nick acts like he hasn't heard me. "It's no reflection on Maria, believe me. She's a knockout. Great personality, beautiful…" He leaves the sentence hanging in the air, lost in thought. His eyes suddenly focus on me. "But there are things I want that she just can't give me."

I wait awhile before I finally respond. "What things?" I ask sullenly.

Nick's smile is uncharacteristically wistful. "You, Robbie. That's 'what things.' " I don't say anything. Nick lays his hand on my knee. "It's fuckin' amazing how much you look like Maria sometimes. The same dark eyes, the same mouth, the same way you tilt your head. It's like the excitement of meeting Maria all over again." He leans forward, his eyes bright. "Only...you have a man's body, Robby. That's what Maria can't give me." His hand slides up my thigh. "She can't give me a man's muscles, a man's way of walking and talking." His hand slides up and squeezes my crotch. "A man's dick. I swear to God, if I had the two of you in bed together, I wouldn't ask for another thing for the rest of my motherfuckin' life!" He looks at me and laughs. "You should see your face now, Robbie. You look like you just sucked a lemon."

I feel my throat tightening. "You're fucking crazy if you think that's ever going to happen."

"Maybe I am crazy," Nick sighs. His eyes dart up to mine. "But I'm not stupid." His fingers begin rubbing the crotch of my jeans, lazily sliding back and forth. He grins slyly. "If I can't have you and Maria together, I'll settle for you both one at a time." He leans his face close to mine, his hand squeezing my dick. "Come on, Robbie, don't tell me I don't turn you on. Not after our little session on the beach."

I don't say anything. Nick's other hand begins lightly stroking my chest, fumbling with the buttons of my shirt.

"You want monogamy, Robbie?" he croons softly. "I promise I'll stay true to you and Maria. I'll never look at another family."

"Everything's a joke with you," I say. But I feel my dick twitch as his hand slides under my shirt and squeezes my left nipple.

"No, Robbie," Nick says softly. "Not everything." He cups his hand around the back of my neck and pulls me toward him. I resist but not enough to break his grip, and we kiss, Nick's tongue pushing apart my lips and thrusting deep inside my mouth. He reaches down and squeezes my dick again. "Hard as the proverbial rock!" he laughs.

"Just shut up," I say. We kiss again, and this time I let Nick unbutton my shirt. His hands slide over my bare chest, tugging at the muscles in my torso. He unbuckles my belt and pulls my zipper down. His hand slides under my briefs and wraps around my dick.

"We're going to do it nice and slow this time," Nick says. He tugs my jeans down, and I lift my hips to help him. It doesn't take long before Nick has pulled off all my clothes. He sits back, his eyes slowly sliding down my body. "So beautiful…" he murmurs. He stands up and shucks off his shirt and shorts, kicking them away. He falls on top of me, his mouth burrowing against my neck, his body stretched out fully against mine.

I kiss him again—gently this time, our mouths barely touching. His lips work their way over my face, pressing lightly against my nose, my eyes. His tongue probes into my ear, and his breath sounds like the sea in a conch shell. I feel his lips move across my skin, down my torso. He gently bites each nipple, swirling his tongue around them, sucking on them. I can see only the top of his head, the shock of blond hair, and I reach down and entwine my fingers in it, twisting his head from side to side. Nick sits up, his legs straddling my hips, his thick cock pointing up toward the ceiling. He wraps his hand around both our dicks and squeezes them together tightly. "Feel that, Robbie," he says. "Dick flesh against dick flesh." He begins stroking them, sliding his hand up and down the twin shafts: his, pink and fat; mine, dark and veined. Some precome leaks from his dick, and Nick slicks our dicks up with it. I breathe deeply, and Nick grins.

Nick bends down and tongues my belly button, his hands sliding under my ass. He lifts my hips up and takes my cock in his mouth, sliding his lips down my shaft until his nose is pressed against my pubes. He sits motionless like that—my dick fully down his throat, his tongue working against the shaft. Slowly, inch by inch, his lips slide back up to my cock head. He wraps his hand around my dick and strokes it as he raises his head and his eyes meet mine, laughing. "You like that, Robbie?" he asks. "Does that feel good?"

"Turn around," I say urgently. "Fuck my face while you do that to me."

I don't have to tell Nick twice. He pivots his body around, and his dick thrusts above my face: red, thick, the cock head pushing out of the foreskin and leaking precome. His balls hang low and heavy above my mouth, furred with light-blond hairs. I raise my head and bathe them with my tongue and then suck them into my mouth. I roll my tongue around the meaty pouch. "Ah, yeah," Nick groans. I slide my tongue up the shaft of his dick. Nick shifts his position and plunges his dick deep down my throat. He starts pumping his hips, sliding his dick in and out of my mouth as he continues sucking me off. I feel his torso squirm against mine, skin against skin, the warmth of his flesh pouring into my body. Nick takes my dick out of his mouth, and I feel his tongue slide over my balls and burrow into the warmth beneath them. He pulls apart my ass cheeks, and soon I feel his mouth on my asshole, his tongue lapping against the puckered flesh.

"Damn!" I groan.

Nick alternately licks and blows against my asshole. I arch my back and push up with my hips, giving him greater access. No one has ever done this to me before, and it's fucking driving me wild. Nick comes up for air, and soon I feel his finger pushing against my asshole and then entering me, knuckle by knuckle. I groan again, louder. Nick looks at me over his shoulder as he finger-fucks me into a slow-building frenzy. "Yeah, Robbie," he croons. "Just lie there and let me play you. Let's see what songs I can make you sing." He adds another finger inside me and pushes up in a corkscrew twist. I cry out, and Nick laughs.

He climbs off me and reaches for his shorts. "OK, Robbie," he says. "Enough with the fuckin' foreplay. Let's get this show on the road." He pulls a condom packet and a small tube of lube out of his back pocket and tosses the shorts back onto the floor.

I feel a twinge of irritation. "You had this all planned out, didn't you?"

Nick straddles my torso again, his stiff cock jutting out inches from my face. I trace one blue vein snaking up the shaft. "Let's just say I was open to the possibility," he grins. He unrolls the condom down his prick, his blue eyes never leaving mine. He smears his hand with lube, reaches back, and liberally greases up my asshole. Nick hooks his arms under my knees and hoists my legs up and around his torso. His gaze still boring into me, he slowly impales me.

I push my head back against the cushion, eyes closed. Nick leans forward, fully in. "You OK, baby?" he asks. His eyes are wide and solicitous.

I open my eyes and nod. Slowly, almost imperceptibly, Nick begins pumping his hips, grinding his pelvis against mine. He deepens his thrusts, speeding up the tempo. I reach up and twist his nipples, and Nick grins widely. A wolfish gleam lights up his eyes. He pulls his hips back until his cock head is just barely in my asshole, then plunges back in. "Fuckin' A," I groan.

"Fuckin' A is right," Nick laughs. He props himself up with his arms and fucks me good and hard—his balls slapping heavily against me with each thrust, his eyes staring into mine, his hot breath against my face. I cup my hand around the back of his neck and pull his face down to mine, frenching him hard as he pounds my ass. Nick leaves his dick fully up there, grinding his hips against mine in a slow circle before returning to the old in-and-out. He wraps a hand around my stiff dick and starts beating me off, timing his strokes with each thrust of his hips.

We settle into our rhythm: Nick slamming my ass, his hand sliding up and down my dick as I thrust up to meet him stroke for stroke. There's nothing playful or cocky about Nick now: His breath comes out in ragged gasps through his open mouth, sweat trickles down his face, and his eyes burn with the hard, bright light of a man working up to shoot a serious load.

I wrap my arms tight around his body and push up, squeezing my asshole tight around his dick at the same time. I look up at Nick's face and laugh; it's the first time I've ever seen him startled.

"Jesus," he gasps. "Did you learn that in college?"

I don't say anything—I just repeat the motion, squeezing my ass muscles hard as I push up to meet his thrust. Nick's body spasms as he moans strongly. "You ought to talk to Maria," he pants. "She could learn some things from you." The third time I do this pushes Nick over the edge, making him groan loudly and his body tremble violently. He plants his mouth on mine, kissing me hard as he squirts his load into the condom, up my ass. I wrap my arms around him in a bear hug, and we thrash around on the couch, finally spilling onto the carpet below—me on top, Nick sprawled with his arms wide out.

After a while he opens his eyes. "Sit on me," he says. "And shoot your load on my face."

I straddle him, dropping my balls into Nick's open mouth. He sucks on them noisily, slurping audibly as I beat off. Nick reaches up and squeezes my nipple, and that's all it takes for me. I give a deep groan, arching my back as my load splatters in thick drops onto Nick's face, creaming his nose and cheeks, dripping into his open mouth. "Yeah," Nick says, "that's right, baby." When the last spasm passes through me I bend down and lick Nick's face clean.

I roll over and lie next to Nick on the thick carpet. He slides his arm under me and pulls me to him. I burrow against his body and close my eyes, feeling his chest rise and fall against the side of my head. Without meaning to, I drift off into sleep.

When I wake up, the clock on the mantle says it's almost 1 in the morning. Nick is gone, but he's covered me with a quilt from my bed. I'm too sleepy to get up, so I just drift back into sleep again.

Nick, Maria, and I are all sitting on Maria's couch watching *Night of the Living Dead* on her TV. Maria sits between us, nestling against Nick. We're at the scene where the little girl has turned into a ghoul and is nibbling on her mother's arm like it was a hoagie sandwich. "Gross!" Maria says.

Nick grins. "You're so damn judgmental, Maria," he says. "I don't put you down when you eat those Spam-and-mayonnaise sandwiches of yours."

Maria laughs and burrows deeper against Nick. As we continue watching the movie I feel Nick's fingers playing with my hair, and I brush them away with a brusque jerk that I make sure Maria doesn't notice. After a while, though, he's doing it again. When I don't do anything this time, Nick entwines his fingers in my hair and tugs gently. From where she's sitting, Maria can't see any of this. The ghouls are surrounding the farmhouse now, closing in on the victims inside. Eventually I lean back and sink into the feel of Nick's fingers in my hair.

Wild on the River
Jay Starre

Kevin and I negotiated the rapids of the Snake River fairly well that August afternoon. Our canoeing experience was extensive, yet part of the thrill of riding these wild rivers was the chance of disaster. It struck on the torturous bend of the Idaho river without warning. Suddenly we were in the water, our canoe ahead of us, our gear floating away. We struggled against the white water and swift current, thankful for our swimming skills.

The current slowed; an isolated pool was abruptly before us. We crawled from the water, dragging our canoe and the wrapped bundles of our waterproofed supplies to the safety of a narrow, rocky beach.

"Goddamn! That was close, but we fucking made it!" Kevin groaned with relief, collapsing on a large, flat boulder.

I stared down at him, breathing heavily from our exertions, soaking wet and still shaking. He was on his belly, his arms spread wide, his tanned and muscular back dripping moisture. Kevin was a hunk, with short blond hair and soft-brown eyes, a sweet smile and a beefy build. At that moment, with the afterglow of excitement from our crash, I was still pumped with adrenaline and gazing at the blond stud's body precipitated a sudden erection throbbing beneath my wet shorts.

My eyes focused on Kevin's chunky butt, outlined by the equally wet trunks he wore. Sprawled out with his thighs apart, each big butt mound protruded beneath the clinging swimming shorts. The material disappeared into the deep ass crack—hiding what delights, I could only imagine.

"We were lucky, that's for sure," I mumbled, my eyes still glued to those magnificent ass cheeks. Standing over him, my cock pulsing with aching lust, my legs trembling, the relief of our escape, all combined to cause my next actions. At least, that was my excuse.

I ripped off my bulky life jacket, which Kevin had already done, and without so much as a second's hesitation, I dropped down on my hands and knees on the hard stone, shoved Kevin's beefy thighs apart, and ripped at the waistband of his shorts.

"What the hell, " he began, but my hands were already squeezing his naked ass cheeks and yanking them apart to dig into the cold wet butt crevice between them.

"Oh, goddamn!" He grunted, lifting his ass, shoving it upward into my exploring palms.

With one hand already poking at his tight and cold asshole, I removed the other from his butt and dragged down my own soaking shorts. My hard cock leaped out like a hungry snake purple with lust. I dropped down over Kevin, ramming that dick right into the wet butt crack.

"Are you going to fuck me right here!" he squealed, that deep manly voice of his having raised up an octave or two as he squirmed beneath me.

My exhaustion and excitement were intertwined in a bizarre mixture of surreal lust. The feel of that cold flesh against my heated dick, with the small asshole quivering tightly across the dripping head, was enough to make me squeal as well. I rubbed my cock in the deep crevice frantically, humping his butt crack like an eager rabbit.

Kevin and I were friends, but nothing like this had ever happened between us. He was straight, at least I had thought that he was, being the captain of our college soccer team and all. But it was only a few days earlier that a pal of mine had confided that the blond jock was actually homo. He had spotted him at a gay bar in the city.

So the thought of just such an impromptu outdoor butt fuck as this occurring on our canoe trip had been at the forefront of my devious mind even before we started out that morning. It had taken our spill in the icy river to bring that wish to fruition. Now I prayed he would not turn over and belt me one.

"Go ahead, you big Greek stud, fuck me then!" Kevin groaned, his face buried in his own folded arms. My mind was a chaos of lust and sensation, and his words did not immediately penetrate the tiny portion that was coherent. But the feeling of his ass rising up to shove back against my dick spoke plainly enough.

Both of us had our trunks around our knees, restricting our movements, yet we managed to get pretty wild, writhing and humping over that hard stone like the horny 20-year-olds we were. I was sliding my dick up and down Kevin's smooth butt crack, pulling the big cheeks apart with shaking hands and gasping out a steady litany of "oh fuck yeah"s. Kevin had stopped speaking, only a mewling sound coming from his muffled face.

I was suddenly aware of the hot sun beating down on us as my activity began to warm up my icy skin. Some measure of sanity began to return. I realized with amazement what was happening: I had the stud college hunk at my mercy, his ass bare, my dick humping his crack. I decided I was going to enjoy the moment and that I just had to get into the tight little asshole my dick head was rubbing across.

I rose up, stripping my shorts off entirely, now butt naked. This isolated portion of the river was remote, although some other idiots might attempt to negotiate the rapids we had failed to. I didn't care at that moment. I sat over Kevin, staring down at his deeply tanned body, his white ass with swirling blond hair outlining the hefty cheeks, the large thighs spread apart with the orange trunks around his knees. I reached down and stripped them off, then attacked his butt. With both hands I yanked them apart, staring down at the crinkled butt hole, a wisp of hair surrounding the tight rim.

"God, what an ass—I gotta get inside you!" I grunted.

"Spit on it, lube it up!" Kevin answered, his face still buried, his butt writhing beneath my hands, apparently as eager for it as I was.

I drooled a generous gob of spittle down into that crack and rubbed it into the quivering butt maw. He groaned as my fingers tickled his anal ring, teasing it apart, stroking the clamped entrance.

With a finger on that clenched button, massaging slippery spit into the entrance, I crawled up to Kevin's head and with my free hand grasped his short blond hair and pulled up his head, forcing his face to the right so that it was in my lap.

"Open up," I grunted.

He did. Those big sweet lips of his gaped, his soft eyes looked up into mine, and his tongue flopped out. That fat appendage was lying there waiting for my dick. I placed the hard head right on it, stroking his open mouth and that protruding tongue. At the other end of his big body my finger dug into his muscled ass ring, suddenly slipping past the first knuckle into tight heat. Kevin gasped, clamping his mouth over my cock head.

The sight of those bowed lips wrapped around my fat joint had me gasping. He sucked while shoving his butt back over my finger. Incredible!

My hard body contrasted with his lush muscularity. A dark Greek-American, I was tanned nearly black. My crotch was paler but still amber compared to his pink cheeks. I hovered over him like a dark devil, my fat cock a swollen purple invader disappearing between those small, pursed lips. I leaned over his face, feeding him my dick, grunting and moaning. He sucked me inside, half my cock shaft buried there.

Meanwhile, his tight asshole began to open up for my exploring finger. I held his head with one hand and stretched his asshole with the other. I had my finger past the second knuckle, twisting it around in circles while his butt squirmed up and down around it. The sun grew warmer, the water drying on our bodies, sweat beginning to break out.

Kevin pulled his head back and looked up at me. His eyes stared right into mine. He opened his mouth wide, sticking his fat tongue out once more. I rubbed my cock head back and forth over it, gazing down at his wide-open mouth. It was so hot…his handsome face a hole for my fat Greek sausage. He held that lush mouth open, passive and accepting. I stroked the lolling tongue and lips with the purple head of my cannon, his drool coating it to a glistening sheen. Then he slowly closed his lips over it, again sucking it deep into his hot face cavern.

There was no way I could keep from coming. It had all happened so abruptly and unexpectedly. I was on the edge of orgasm from the first minute I had stared down at his sprawled body and big hard ass. Now with those sucking lips vacuuming my dick and his tight bung hole accepting a deep finger-fuck, I exploded. I shot come right up his throat.

He gagged but then swallowed, his lips clamping over my cock shaft. I screamed. I leaned over him and unloaded, my entire body shaking. My finger was planted far up his butt hole, and I kept it there.

"Come on, get me off too!" he gasped, his mouth finally sliding off my dripping cock. I looked down at him, his lips wet, his eyes boring into mine.

I got up, my finger still inside him. Although I was breathing like a spent racehorse, I managed to crawl behind him. He got up on his hands and knees, wiggling that big butt around my buried finger and moaning. He looked back at me, his mouth still open, his amber eyes half lidded and full of heat.

"Come on, you big stud, finger my butt till I come!"

Although my dick was flopping at my waist, half hard and satiated, his hot words and his hot asshole were stimulation enough. I got right in behind him, planting my own hard thighs between his spread legs and began to work on his offered anal slot.

I dug into it with the finger already there and gobbed another good supply of spit over the sweaty crack. I worked it in good with my finger, the ass ring opening up enough so that I could just begin to insert another finger.

"Oh, man, yeah, stick two fingers up me!" he grunted.

The sun was intense on my back, the sound of the river loud directly behind us. Although I was spent with all that had happened, Kevin offering up his asshole was enough to have me getting hard all over again.

I reached under his stretched thighs and found his hard pecker fat and slapping up against his belly. I felt his stomach too, hairless and lush. He wasn't lean like I was, so his belly was soft and warm. I stroked it and squeezed his fat cock and swollen nut sac at the same time.

"Yeah, play with my dick, do anything you want to me! I've been wanting your hard body for so long!"

Music to my ears—I really got into it. The blond soccer player was mine for the taking. The edge of my lust had been satisfied—now I took my time. I stroked his dick and stomach slowly, agonizingly. He thrust his hips forward to take advantage of my teasing hand, then shoved his big butt backward to feel the two fingers digging into him better. He didn't know which way to go.

I strummed his dick with a maddening hand, fingering his cock head and the drooling slit, then rolling his fat balls in my hand, then gripping his shaft in a harsh squeeze, keeping him on edge and off-balance. Two of my fingers brutalized his fuck hole, stretching the tight lips apart, turning the ass passage into a yawning cavern that I eventually managed to insert three fingers into. I spit continually into that fingered hole, staring down at the pale ass crack as it glistened with sweat and drool, the reddened anus stretched wide by three of my dark Greek fingers.

I would sense him approaching his climax and I would back off, releasing his dick and squeezing his nuts. My fingers would stop their marauding momentarily. He would moan for me not to stop, for me to finger him harder. I would laugh and continue, managing to bring him to the brink at least a half-dozen times.

Eventually his stamina was exhausted. Writhing on his hands and knees with three fingers far up his bung hole, a hand stroking his hard dick, and the open air caressing his naked body, he finally shot.

"OH, MAN! OH, FUCK!" he shouted.

I felt jism rocket out of his fat dick. I chose that moment to yank my fingers out of his spasming asshole, shove him down on his belly, and ram my own hard bone right up that spit-wet anus. While he was shooting come all over the hard boulder beneath us, I had him flat on his belly and my dick jammed all the way up his stretched asshole.

"Oh, God, don't…oh, man, it's too much, you're killing me, your dick is tearing me in half," he moaned, his body convulsing around my rapidly plowing shaft.

I didn't care. I had to fuck him. I lay on top of him and went to work. His protests petered out as I laid the pipe to his exhausted body. His asshole was spit-slick, gaping open and slack enough for the entire fat length of my dick. He was feeling no pain—in fact, he was groaning "Fuck me, yeah, fuck my butt" even before his own dick had finished draining.

His warm body was a lush bed. I lay on him, kissing his neck, slobbering over his ears, whispering incoherent words of pleasure as my dick went in and out of his heated ass passage. The sun seemed to melt us together in one mass of warm, writhing flesh. My fucking became a continuous deep plugging, his body a slack and welcoming hole beneath me.

If anyone swept past us on the river, we never knew, or cared. The sun beat down on us relentlessly while we fucked, the river continued its uncaring flow, our gear dried out on the sun-baked rocks beside us. I moaned how beautiful his ass was; he begged me to fill him with dick.

What brought me to my second coming was the realization that he was blubbering beneath me in the throes of his own second eruption. His slack body did not tense up: The big muscles merely grew more languid, the warm asshole gaping even wider, his ass lifting up slightly to accept my dick to the balls.

"You're fucking the come right out of me with your hard cock!" He grunted between whimpers.

That was enough to send me over. I pulled my cock out of his butt hole and lay the spewing shaft in the sweaty crack between his big butt mounds. Cum drooled down over both our balls.

We lay together for a while, our energy completely spent. The sun had moved around so that we were half in shadow. I never wanted to move again.

"Get off me, you weigh a ton," Kevin eventually murmured. But he moved his ass around my sticky dick, which was still planted between his lush butt cheeks provocatively at the same time. If I hadn't been utterly spent, I would have started all over again.

We laughed as our eyes met. "Pretty wild!" he murmured.

We splashed in the icy water to rinse off our come and sweat. There was a reserve between us. What had happened was so out of the blue, we both didn't quite know how to react.

But then Kevin grinned and made it all fine. "Let's camp here for the night." His eyes twinkled.

"It's pretty early," I said, thinking I was an idiot as soon as the words were out of my mouth.

"I think we can find something to do to pass the time."

Enough said. We spent a wild night on that wild river, that wild jock butt giving it up to my Greek meat another couple of wild times before the sun rose again.

Vietnam Siesta
Victor Ho

We left for lunch a few minutes early. I was starving. Till today, this Vietnam trip was a big disaster. After days of running to the toilet, my stomach finally settled. I was actually looking forward to food.

We mounted James's rental moped and headed toward Phuong Rose, a neighborhood restaurant the concierge recommended. We rode through the lunch traffic drunkenly. Schoolchildren held hands in twos and threes, staying on the dirt path away from the paved street. Shadows fell from lush banana trees to give a little relief from the heat.

My body leaned forward every time James slowed abruptly to avoid a collision with a bike or a stray child. I planted my hands firmly on his thighs to keep from falling. I rested my chest against his back to catch my balance. My nipples felt raw against the sweaty T-shirt. It was too hot. I wanted to take off both our shirts so I could feel his sweaty skin against mine.

We rode past a mother chasing after her youngest son with a spoonful of porridge. The toddler ran pantsless into the street, his short, chubby legs chasing one after another. She was always a step behind, dropping her spoon in resignation. The toddler caught my eyes and screeched in laughter. James swerved violently, causing my hand to fall between his legs. I blushed and hesitated about leaving it there. I couldn't believe that after so many months of yearning to touch that sacred spot, it actually happened. I wanted to wrap my fingers around his mound and squeeze until a moan escaped from his lips, begging me not to stop. But, alas, I removed my hand reluctantly.

I met James in my Japanese Art History class, one of the general electives that fulfilled both my non-Western and my art requirements. I had a horrible time remembering the Japanese names and had an even harder time trying to spell them. In class we always said hello but never really talked. One afternoon I ran into him at the gym. His workout partner didn't show, so he asked me if I would spot him. I was only too happy to oblige. I watched him pump the dumbbells up and down, grunting with each exertion. My eyes drooled over his bulging biceps and his washboard stomach. His hips thrust up from the bench as he heaved the bar back onto the holder. He shook out his arms and threw me a grateful smile. I was so in lust.

When he offered to spot me, I couldn't refuse. After about six repetitions my arms were giving out. To help me leverage the weight, he straddled closer to my face, allowing me to look up his shorts. I inhaled deeply, letting his musk travel into my bloodstream, effusing through all my pores. It was like pure energy, giving me the strength to push the bar back up again. Every so often I faltered and he straddled me. Bending his knees, he lowered himself until he was a few inches from my mouth. I wanted to engulf his sweaty balls, but I was afraid that he would drop the weight and crush my ribs. I was dying to take a bite of the forbidden fruit.

James and I became gym buddies and study partners. My body showed drastic improvement after teaming up with him. I couldn't believe the striation as my pecs harden and my arms grew thicker. My body started to look like the male models that everyone was lusting after. Amazing what lust can do.

James parked the moped on the sidewalk in front of the restaurant. The dust took awhile to settle. Chickens chattered loudly, perturbed by our loud entrance. The ripe smell of squid and alcohol perfumed the hot air. Synthesized pop music blared from the oversize speakers. The conversations paused momentarily when we entered. I guessed that not many white tourists had visited these neighborhood dives.

Two waitresses rushed over to help us be seated. They were pretty the way restaurant food was good: colors and taste heightened, glossy lipstick drawn outside the edge of the mouth, eyes circled with dark pencil.

"Hi," one said as she poured sweaty beers into icy mugs. "You Vietnamese?" she addressed James. "I can tell you Vietnamese." She smiled seductively. The other girl hovered over me quietly, probably not sure what to do or say. I didn't really mind, since she wasn't particularly my type. James laughed and answered her in Vietnamese. She looked over at me and giggled. The other waitress blushed crimson.

"Fred," James said. "She thinks you're hot." He punched me in the arm and laughed loudly. She covered her mouth and giggled.

The waitresses took the menu and disappeared into the backroom. I surveyed the room and watched other waitresses drape their arms over the patrons. "What kind of place is this?" I asked James.

"Just your local hangouts," he responded. "These guys are taking a break and having lunch. Vietnamese usually rest at noon, when it's too hot to work. They go to places like these where pretty women serve them lunch."

"They sure drink a lot during lunch," I said, pointing to a table next to us with at least 10 empty bottles of beer.

"Yeah," James added. "Beer is their favorite pastime."

"So, what happens when they're too drunk to return to work?"

"They just sleep in the rooms out back until the siesta's over."

"Oh," I said. It finally dawned upon me what type of place this was. James's waitress returned to the table with a plate of fried calamari and two more bottles of beer. She bent over the table precariously and opened each bottle with great difficulty. She giggled as foam splattered on the table. I watched her, draped seductively on James's shoulder, as she picked a piece of fried squid with her chopsticks and fed it to him. The other waitress brought a plate of salad and two beers and sat timidly beside me. I saw James's waitress giggle and dab the thin film of sweat on her cleavage line. She glared at my waitress, who sat meekly beside me in uncomfortable silence.

She caught my eyes and smiled demurely. We ate and James translated the saucy flirtations. I blushed after a few more rounds of beers.

James suggested that we take a siesta before heading out. He stretched his arms and yawned as his waitress helped him from the table to the backroom.

I watched him leave and wished that it were me who accompanied him. I sighed and took another swig from the glass. It tasted bitter. The vinyl tabletop was littered with empty bottles and greasy plates of squid and shrimp. The back of my neck was sticky, hot, and sore. My eyes felt tired. The heat and the beer were making my eyes lazy.

The restaurant grew quiet. The cracked concrete floor was strewn with bits and pieces of food. Most of the patrons were either buying something else in the back of the room or had returned home to rest. I wanted to go back to the hotel and take a short nap before James returned. There wasn't much here for me.

My waitress took my hand and led me to the backroom, but I shook my head no. "Sleep," she smiled shyly, pleadingly. Reluctantly I followed. A bush of flowers was in bloom—bright-red in the heat. The rest of the yard was filled with garbage; two chickens pecked at the rubble with great care. How could I make her understand that it was James whom I wanted to cuddle with and strip naked? I sat on the wooden bed, and she smiled coyly at me. "More beer, please," I asked, refusing her advances as kindly as I knew how. "More beer," I mimed with my hand.

She left me in the cool dark room and disappeared to the kitchen. I could hear her yelling in the kitchen, probably telling her boss that I wasn't interested and that she wasn't going to make any tips from me. Damn American, she probably cursed.

I closed my eyes and waited. I tried to listen for James's voice, to hear whether he was a moaner as he slid his erection inside of her. I imagined my hands caressing his ass, tracing his back as he plunged deep inside of me. I wanted him to whisper into my ear, "Oh, Fred, you're such a great fuck."

I didn't hear the door close until the beer glasses were set down on the table. I opened my eyes and withdrew my hand. James stared at the tent in my jeans and locked the door. He slowly took off his Gap

T-shirt and draped it at the end of the bed. His dark eyes watched me as he poured me a glass.

"It's so hot here." He fanned his hand against his chest. I stared at him with my mouth ajar. The same smooth skin covered his muscled and fluid body. His brown nipples stood erect. The curve of his back was soft, like a hand had sculpted it. His belly button was a black hole in the middle of the washboard. He watched my expression and smiled softly. "Aren't you hot," he repeated as he took off his pants.

James stood naked in the middle of the tiny room. My eyes ran up and down his body, hairless but for the thick, unruly patch over his soft, dark penis. The curve between the small of his back and the round buttocks was a perfect fit for a face. He ran his hand over his chest, then mussed his pubes.

He sipped from the glass and fed me the beer. As I swallowed wordlessly, his fragile fingers unbuttoned my shirt and his soft lips found my left nipple. His tongue circled the areola before bathing the nipple. He inhaled, and cool air tingled my nipple, sending chills through my spine. "James," I moaned, as his mouth covered mine.

"You're so cute when you're excited," he whispered. He traced his fingers around my face, rubbing his thumb gently across my lips. He cradled my chin in his hand and lifted my face up for another kiss. Pressure built up in my lungs. When his lips finally traveled down to my neck, I gasped desperately for air. I felt like I had been swimming underwater for miles, and finally I was able to poke my head above water to fill my lungs.

"I've been dying to do this," I whispered, as I rolled on top of him and nibbled lightly on his neck. My kisses trailed down his clavicle to his left nipple while my fingers found his right. I rolled his man tit in my tongue and twisted the other between two fingers. I bit down on his nipple softly to make it more sensitive. I felt his body shutter as his fingers tightened around my arms. He closed his eyes and moaned. Satisfied with the results, my lips proceeded downward. "I've been wanting to kiss these abs for such a long time." He giggled as my tongue tickled his belly button.

James was perfect beneath his clothes, as I had always expected.

His boner stood straight up from a fine bush of curly pubes. The head of his penis was barely covered by his foreskin. I stretched it back and uncovered a beautiful mushroom head, all glistening and moist. I milked the foreskin back and forth a few strokes to make sure the precome coated the entire head. "You're so beautiful," I whispered, as I bent down and kissed the tip. I slipped my tongue between the head and the skin and circled it clockwise and then counterclockwise. I savored the salty taste on the tip of my tongue. He moaned softly.

"So beautiful," I whispered, as his dick slipped deep inside my mouth. James arched his back and grunted, surprised as his penis touched the back of my throat. He ran his hand along the side of my face and laced his fingers through my hair. My tongue slid under the belly of his penis, feeling the pulsating veins rubbing against my taste buds. I traced the neck of his cock where his foreskin gathered, licking the ridge in circular strokes. My fingers massaged his ball sacs gently, cupping them, pulling on them, rolling them in my palms. James arched his back urgently.

I held his butt and felt his glutes flex and shiver as he thrust deeper inside of me. I could feel his love muscle flexing inside my mouth, the warmth pulsating from the head as it expanded and expanded deep within my throat. He dug his heels into the bed, his calves tensing, his breathing heavy and panting, but I wasn't ready to let him explode. I wanted to keep him begging. I let it pop out of my mouth. I kissed his inner thighs, rubbing my stubble against his smooth skin. He opened his legs wider as I lifted them to his chest.

My nose nuzzled against his heavy balls as my tongue licked his perineum before trailing down to his puckering lips. His body shivered with anticipation. I wanted him to feel and understand everything I experienced this last semester while daydreaming about him. I wanted him to experience the longing and desperate emptiness of needing to be filled that traveled from your renal canal up your back to the very center of your being. I wanted him to want me the way I was desperate to have him.

My tongue lapped around his opening, darting back and forth. I kissed it, smelling the deep musk of sweat imbuing throughout my body and soul. My fingers rubbed the wetness, massaging the entrance, applying a light pressure, teasing it till it opened up to breathe, till it quivered in wait of being touched.

I knew then he was ready to be explored, as I stuck a finger slowly inside. I felt the vacuum built up inside of him, a vortex that sucked and squeezed. God, he was tight. I waited for his breathing to slow and for his ring to adjust. Then I wiggled my finger a bit, moved deep in, and withdrew briefly. I couldn't tell whether he was in pain or pleasure as he held his breath and bit down on his lower lip. Sweat beaded on his forehead, his hair matted against his side. I curled my finger toward his perineum and massaged his love spot.

I watched his eyes opened in shock as he inhaled sharply. I tapped it again to watch his breathing burdened and his penis flexing. In and out one finger slithered, then joined by one more. In and out they wormed their ways. Just when his muscles started to relax, I wrapped my mouth around his tool and took it deep within my mouth. I glided up and down on it in rhythm to my probing fingers.

James clawed at the bed as he threw back his head and grunted. "Please" was all he could muster as a loud groan again escaped from his throat. He was begging me to take him. I was in love. I pulled out my finger and prepared my dripping member for entrance. I quickly slipped on a condom and lubed up.

I shivered as the head slipped through his lips. I leaned forward slowly, letting my shaft push through inch by inch until his mouth wrapped tightly around the hilt. I felt him shuddered as his body tried to accommodate my niner. I was amazed how warm and velvety soft his hole was. His muscles contracted, squeezing me inside.

"Relax, baby," I whispered, as I bent over to kiss him. His tongue tangoed with mine. My heart pounded harder than my thrusts. I was in heaven, if heaven could be so lucky. His hands cupped my face, brushing aside my bangs. He threw back his head and lifted his chin as my shaft rubbed against his G spot. "Uggghhhh," he cried, as his legs embraced me.

I tweaked his nipples, rolling them in between my fingers. James inhaled deeply, and I felt his muscles starting to vibrate. I withdrew slowly until only my head was lodged, before pushing all the way back in. I kissed the sweat that was forming around his lips. He opened his mouth to moan and to receive my tongue. His breathing accelerated when my thrusts became more regular. James pulled me toward him, his hands cupping my back, drawing me closer so that our bodies meshed against each other.

With a few more deep thrusts his body shook. All the muscles of his rectum went as if into cardiac arrest, clenching down tightly on my penis, squeezing me so tightly. Warm come squirted onto our stomachs. I could not resist anymore when his body clenched and unclenched, alternating the pressure. My penis head expanded, pushing against the wet walls before all my energy washed over me. Air burst from my lungs and shot out my urethra. I pumped as hard as I could as come sloshed and dripped out.

I kissed him again, my heart pounding to escape, my lungs desperately sucking as much air as I could. He smiled up at me as my body collapsed on top of him with one last shudder.

"I never thought it would happen," I whispered, as he nibbled softly on my earlobe.

"Me neither," he laughed. James held me and whispered sweet nothings as sleep washed over me. I could get used to this tropical heat, I thought, smiling as I imagined what we were having for dinner.

Hard
R.J. March

He kept his shorts up, dick out the fly, big and pink, making Billy Clark swallow his gum. It had a tiny pink head, his cock a lot like a thimble capping off a log. Kind of pretty, Billy was thinking. He squinted up at Bam Richards, who was looking down at himself, hands on his hips, his smile crookedly smuglike.

"Well?" he said.

Billy Clark shook his head. He didn't care much for Bam Richards, hadn't since high school, when Bam had said some unkind things—unkind and untrue—about Billy and Jose Ortiz, which was just about fucking stupid, Billy was thinking now. *Imagine me and Ortiz,* he was thinking, looking at the thick droop of Bam's cock. *Imagine me and Ortiz.*

Bam made his dick sway. His boxers were blue, the same color as the vein that meandered the length of Bam's swinging member. "Patch'll be through soon," Billy said, and it was true. Patch was on his rounds, and he would hit the head like clockwork in just a couple of minutes. Bam understood. He bent over and hauled up his pants, tucking his prick away, and they heard Patch's footfalls down the hall. Bam stepped up to the sink where he washed his hands, big raw-looking paws that wrestled one another in the suds.

Patch came into the bathroom, keys ringing like a tambourine against his hip. Billy Clark was pretending to piss, having stepped up fast to one of the urinals, leaning close to hide his erection.

"You still here?" Patch said, startled, his white hair wild over his head. He touched the front of his pants, and Billy pushed his engorged prick back into his pants, hitting the flush. The rush of water drowned out Bam's easy reply.

"I thought that'd be done by now," Billy heard Patch say, referring to the packing machine they'd been working on for the past two months. Bam said, "Well, you know how fucked up it is around here."

"Cluster fuck," Billy said. "I'm thinking of going to Campbell's. Buddy of mine's there. Better benefits, and he gets a case of soup each month."

Bam gave him a look. He smiled like he smiled when he was looking at himself and his big joint.

"You boys leaving soon?" Patch asked.

"Soon," Billy said, and Bam nodded. Patch checked his watch. "Almost 9 o'clock—where'd the time go?" He looked from Bam to Billy and answered his own question. "Damned if I know."

When Patch was gone Bam reissued his initial proposition. "I'm not wrong about you," he said. "I never was."

Billy lifted his shoulders, running both his hands through his short blond hair, wiry as a terrier's. He groped the whole front of Bam Richards with his blue eyes. In high school he'd sucked the bent, uncut dick of Bam's best friend—not Ortiz, for chrissake—who was now singing country-western songs on the radio in a played-up hayseed twang. Billy was being offered Bam's prime choice cut, the long drop of it apparent even through his green work pants, which Bam hitched up, further accentuating his pants-bound prize.

"Fuck you," Billy said anyway. "You know I got a wife and little girl at home, Richards. And you don't know fuck about me."

Bam slipped his thumbs through his empty belt loops, puffing up his chest in faded blue. He grinned at Billy as though he just couldn't help himself, sticking the tip of his tongue into the not-so-tight space between his two front teeth.

"Well, OK then," he said graciously, his eyes dropping to the fattened front of Billy Clark's pants. "My bad, Billy boy. No offense, no harm done. Our little secret, though, OK? Just between me and you? Nothing to talk about, right?" He stuck out his right hand, and Billy regarded it, wondering what was with the easy give. He took Bam's hand and shook it anyway.

"You got a big hand there, Billy," Bam said, holding on longer than he needed. "And a nice firm grip too." Billy broke the lingering shake, his palm sweating, feeling the fuzzy buzz of desire redden his ears. He still had his tools to put away, the Blakely machine to clean up, and a cold dinner waiting at home for him. And what did Bam have to look forward to? Billy wondered. Bam was married too, to a little hottie cunt he'd met Senior Weekend at Ocean City and knocked up. Billy was there for that, at the same underage house party, fucked-up himself, but not so much he didn't take note of the half dressed Bam Richards, his bared torso bearing the cuts and definition of maniacal workouts and a brief stint with steroids, escorting out of the house the little U. of D. freshman, her hair in blond corn-rows that ended with bent beer caps, her T-shirt tied up to harness her enormous tits.

Must be as happy as me, Billy was thinking as he watched Bam turn and head out of the john, ass twitching lazily.

Billy did not go home directly. Instead, he drove to the county park, headlights spotlighting strung-down deer, the coming headlights of other cars blinding Billy. He parked in a pine-enclosed cul-de-sac between a newish BMW and an old wood-sided Jeep. He'd been here before, sitting in his Camry, playing with the radio, ignoring the other men who'd come there to peer into his open window, asking him for the time, fingering the fronts of their pants. The time, Billy wondered, what was it about the time that made guys so horny?

Lights out. He felt blind and a small rush—a gut flutter, a pulse rise he blamed Bam Richards for. It was Bam's fault he was here at all, detouring to this place because he didn't know where else to go, where else to take the dull ache of his hard-on. Where else but here? He turned on the radio, missing the noise of it. He turned the volume low and waited, but not for long.

"What time do you have?" he was asked, a rough whisper through his open passenger-side window. Billy told him.

The lights of the BMW went on, and Billy saw the driver standing outside his car now, bending in to study Billy before reaching back into his own car and turning the lights off again. Billy rushed to remember what he'd seen: a short, suited man, early 30s, thick-lipped, straight brown side-parted hair.

"Do you hunt?" he heard the man ask.

"Hunt?" Billy said. He leaned toward the voice.

"Deer," the man said. "Have you ever seen so many?"

Billy tried to blink the man back into detail. The sky was black and moonless, and his eyes wouldn't adjust to that kind of darkness. He tried to envision what he'd seen—what color were his eyes? His suit? Billy saw the pale ghosts of the man's hands on his door and said, "Come in."

Bam stripped in the locker room. "Fuck the overtime. I'm going home." He stood in front of his locker in the same blue boxers he wore last week. He looked over at Billy. "You want a beer?"

Billy shrugged. "Where at?" he asked.

"My place," Bam said, reaching into his locker for his jeans. The fly of his boxers winked, and Billy caught a glimpse of Bam's pale tool, its white heavy head.

"Darlene out of town?" Billy asked, thinking he'd gotten it, what Bam was up to. He hadn't mentioned the night he'd offered himself to Billy, nor had he offered again.

Bam stepped into his jeans, pulling them up his big, gold-haired thighs. "No such luck," he said, zipping up his fly, looking over at Billy again with a shadow of a smile on his face, and Billy, embarrassed, wrong, got out of his work pants. He felt ridiculous in the green bikini briefs his wife had bought him for Father's Day this year. His crotch, bound in its pouch, bulged obscenely, he was thinking while looking down at himself.

"Run out of shorts?" Bam said. "You gotta wear the old lady's?"

"Fuck you." Billy shrugged off his shirt, aware of Bam's lingering stare. He pulled his wife-beater up over his head.

"What do you bench?" Bam asked.

Billy shrugged. He knew, but he didn't want to say.

"You don't know?"

Billy shook his head.

The two were quiet as they finished dressing. Billy tied the laces of his new Adidases.

"We could go to the Canteen," Billy heard Bam say, grabbing his lunch cooler and slamming his locker shut.

"Blue Marsh?" Billy said, watching Bam comb his hair at the sinks. He had a big ass—not fat; just big—and his T-shirt covered his back like skin.

"You coming?" Bam asked, using the mirrors to look at him, and Billy said, "Yeah, I'm coming."

"I'm done," Bam said, pushing his glass away from him. It was crowded for a Tuesday, and Billy recognized a bunch of guys who worked at Carpenter. Bam was mostly quiet, and what little talking he did was about the packing machine they'd been working on and then about how fucked-up management was. Other than that, though, he stared straight ahead, giving off little sighs every now and then that lifted and dropped his big shoulders. Billy swallowed the last of his beer. "Me too," he said.

Out in the parking lot Bam lingered, leaning against the fender of his pickup. "Saw Donny Krause last week at Sam's."

"How's he doing," Billy asked, remembering the tall and skinny kid they'd gone to school with.

Bam shrugged his shoulders. "Who the fuck cares?" he said. He took a couple of steps toward the lake, passing Billy with a glance. He kept walking to the edge of the parking lot, out of the light, through the trees, disappearing. Billy watched him go, staying where he was for a moment, wanting to stay, to get into his car and drive away. "Shit," he said, feeling something like a pull from the darkened edge of the lot where Bam emerged, spotlit by the moon, his arms crossed, waiting.

"You don't say shit, Clark. You just stand there looking." Bam turned away, the wind off the water coming between them. "What are you looking at, Billy?"

Billy looked past Bam, his profile, out at the dark water of Blue Marsh Lake. "I'm not," he said. "I'm not looking."

"You are, though," Bam said, turning to face Billy again. He let out a low belch that Billy eventually caught wind of—beery, sour. Bam hitched up his jeans.

"Why are you here?" he asked quietly.

Billy listened for the water to make a sound, but it was silent. The moon glowed through a haze of sheer clouds. Then there was a splash in the distance—a jumping fish, Billy guessed—and then there were more, more and more, and the lake seemed to be catching a pouring-down of water from the sky, its surface frothy with white water.

"Jesus," Bam said, barely heard.

They couldn't see the fish, but they could hear them, their collective noise, the air rushing through gills, perhaps, or the mass fluttering of fins. It went on for a minute, a minute and a half maybe, the lake appearing to boil, and then it stopped, and the air was quiet save for the settling of the waters, a low, sissing hiss.

"What the fuck was that?" Bam asked.

Billy shook his head. "Holy crap," he said finally. Bam stepped backward and Billy forward, and they collided this way, and Bam turned fast, his arms going around Billy's waist. "There you go," he said, lips brushing Billy's ear, nosing in to the hair behind it, making him feel like a little boy. He kept his arms at his sides, letting Bam do it all, hands all over Billy's back, finding the end of Billy's shirt untucked, discovering bare skin. He breathed again into Billy's ear, digging into Billy's tight jeans, grabbing up his ass cheeks and squeezing them hard.

Bam got his mouth on Billy's, opening it wide, his tongue all over Billy's lips, drooling spit down their chins. He pulled his hand free of Billy's jeans and held his head instead, pulling back and coming into focus, moonlit. He looked astonished, his eyes wide and staring. "Stop it," Billy said, and Bam kissed him again, holding him tightly. Billy felt the press of Bam's cock between them as well as his own, and then Bam's hand fumbling with the fastenings of Billy's jeans, pulling and tugging, struggling to get at what was inside. Once freed, Billy's cock stiffened thickly, throbbing in the night air. Bam gripped it, groaning into Billy's mouth. He fisted Billy's cock tightly, squeezing up precome.

Bending at the waist, Bam lapped the ooze that smeared Billy's cock head, and then he took the whole prick into his mouth. Billy gasped at the heat that engulfed him, the tender drag of teeth, snorts of breath into his pubes. Bam touched his belly, up under Billy's shirt. He ruffled Billy's nipples with his thumbs and then reached around and uncovered his ass, grabbing his cheeks again, letting air get to the moist crack.

Billy leaned into the hot hole of Bam's mouth. He hit the back of the man's throat and stayed there, making Bam gulp and sputter and grip Billy's butt harder. Billy pulled out and looked at Bam's lips, full and wet, wanting, and he smacked his dripping dick against them.

"Son of a bitch," Bam said, shaking his head, kissing the sticky cock head, standing up fast and undoing his own jeans, getting them down his thick thighs. His cock poked stiffly out of his bush of curly pubes. He licked his palm and took hold of himself, jacking the long shaft, pinching the little pink head with each cuff. He lifted each leg in a cocky strut, turning himself around, showing off his bright-white ass. Billy played with himself, regarding the twin globes, the way they glowed. He touched them, the skin of them cool, and they tensed, turning to stone under his fingertips. Bam pushed it back at him, pressing his fanny against Billy's dick, getting it in between his cheeks, riding the length of him slowly.

"Put your hands on me, man," Billy heard Bam whisper as he pulled off his shirt, putting his palms on his thighs and crouching in front of Billy. Billy stroked Bam's long back, kneading the tensed muscles across his shoulders. He reached around Bam's waist, looking for his prick, and pushing his own downward so that it rode over the tight ring of muscle around Bam's asshole. He dropped a gob of spit between them—it landed in Bam's split and drooled down onto Billy's cock.

He sucked on his thumb, wetting it before sticking it up into the hard bloom of Bam's anus, the inside of him hot and silky, his sphincter gnawing on Billy's digit. *Now this is something*, Billy was thinking, being new to it—*butt sex*. The closest he'd ever gotten to ass fucking was with his wife on their honeymoon when she'd gotten really horny after too many Alabama Slammers; no further than this, though: His thumb went up her ass as he fucked her pussy. He fucked Bam this way, fingering him, making him moan and look over his shoulder, winking at Billy, whose own cock dripped needfully, stringy jizz hanging off the tip of it.

Bam dropped his ass, riding the thumb inside him, working it. He asked for the real thing. "Give it to me," he said, begging, making Billy smile.

"You're fucking cute," Billy told him. "Anyone ever tell you that?"

"I hear it all the time," Bam said back, bobbing his butt. "Just fuck me, Billy—you can tell me how pretty I am later."

He pushed his dick into the small aperture, and Bam yelped. "Christ," he said. "It looked easy in that movie."

"What movie?" Billy asked.

"Never the fuck mind," Bam said. "Just do it, will you?"

Billy got himself inside the burning hole and stayed there, feeling the race of Bam's heartbeat down there. He started to fuck the man slowly, holding on to his hips and pulling the ass on and off his aching throb. He fucked him gently, holding him tight, putting his lips on Bam's back and kissing him there, licking his shoulder blades. His balls swung heavily between their thighs, bouncing against Bam's nuts.

"How you doing there," Billy asked, and he saw Bam nod, heard him whisper, "Fine and dandy, pal, fine and dandy. Your dick feels like a fucking fist, though."

"Hurt?" Billy wanted to know. He couldn't imagine it, really, couldn't imagine taking Bam's huge slug, but the thought made his dick whimper in the hot sleeve of Bam's bung hole, and he felt himself sliding closer to the edge of a big bang. He pulled out, and Bam's hole farted out air.

"You can't fucking stop now," Bam said, pumping himself wildly. Billy used his thumb again, rubbing the hardening bulb of Bam's prostate. The man's ass cheeks shivered, clamping tight on Billy's hand. "Oh, what the fuck," Billy heard Bam say, in a normal but agitated tone Billy heard heard often enough at work when he felt pressed for time or came up against something that did not yield to him. He stood up straight, banging his cock in his fist, bringing up veins in his neck, muscles rippling coltlike under the skin of his back. He looked over his shoulder at Billy. "You," he said, and Billy smiled, using his free hand to tickle Bam's swaying bag of balls.

He unthumbed himself and got up close to Billy, using his belly, knuckling against it, his dick in a stranglehold. He was looking down at himself, but then he looked up, his eyes almost doelike, moist and unguarded, and he licked his lips, about to speak, but he stayed quiet and he looked down again, and Billy looked too, and thick ropes of come leapt out of the milky split head, laying themselves across Billy's chest like wet ribbon.

"Now you," he said, getting on his knees, taking Billy's solid prick in his hands. He jerked it clumsily, licking the end of it, panting still from his own recent exertion. Billy played with his short-cut hair, thumbing the man's eyebrows, feeling each of Bam's tugs in his gut until he was once again toeing up to a precipice, about to jump in. The feeling of falling rushed over him, wind in his ears, and he let Bam pull warm squirts of semen out of him, pushing himself into Bam's slicked grip, splashing his come across Bam's fat lips.

It was quiet then, save for the pound of heartbeat in Billy's ears. Bam wiped his mouth with the back of his hand and stood up with a soft groan. He looked at Billy. "It wasn't so hard, though," Bam said, his hand on Billy's shoulder. And Billy said, "No, it wasn't so very hard. Just hard enough."

"We're bad, you know," Bam said, grinning wickedly, and Billy laughed, remembering the fish, the flying fish, and he looked out across the lake, waiting for something, anything, to present itself as a sign, anything at all, as Bam's come cooled on his chest.

Plaza del Sol
Sean Wolfe

I had been in Guadalajara, Mexico, for nine months. I had a good job teaching English at a private school. Made lots of money, had lots of friends, gotten lots of sun. Being 25 years old, with blond hair and blue eyes made me more than a little popular with the cute Mexican boys down there and, to my horror, even with the girls. I did my best to put the girls off as much as possible—and to get it on with as many of the cute boys as possible. It wasn't hard. I never dated a student of mine, but once I was no longer their teacher, it was open territory, and never a shortage of volunteers. The clubs there were always packed with lines way out the doors, and I never went home alone unless I wanted to.

Not that it was all about sex. I did make a lot of really good friends. Coworkers, straight and gay friends from the theater and dance groups I went to see often, friends from clubs.

But after nine months I began to become a little bored. That, and I was a little homesick. I worked 10 hours a day during the week and five on Saturdays. Though I loved my job, I was getting a little burned-out and started thinking about returning to the States.

We had two-hour lunch breaks at the school. There were a number of fast-food restaurants right around the school that I visited every once in a while. But I usually went to a little family-owned restaurant located in Plaza del Sol, a shopping mall three blocks from the school. Every day they had three homemade meals you could choose from as entrées. They were all cheap, delicious, and served with fresh homemade tortillas and endless glasses of "agua frescas," delicious drinks made with water and fresh fruits. After eating lunch

I would take a book and sit in the open courtyard and read for an hour or so until it was time to return to the school.

I was always so engrossed in my books that I never realized the intense cruising that went on in that open-air mall. On this sweltering day in July, however, I finished my book very early after lunch and contented myself with watching the action and scenery around me. Sitting on one of the park benches that surrounded a fountain at the main crossroad in the mall, I was given a fantastic view of the goings-on around me. Mall employees rushing back to or leaving leisurely from work; high school kids and working moms getting in some shopping; little old ladies sipping lemonade.

And then there were "the boys." It amazed me how many young men, anywhere from 15 or so to about 30, roamed aimlessly up and down the sidewalk, staring each other down. There was nothing subtle about their movements at all. They nodded their heads at one another, raised their eyebrows, licked their lips, and groped their crotches. Several of them cruised me very openly, some of them even daring to sit at one of the benches next to mine and flirt with me there. I was amused but had no place to take them, since I lived quite a ways from the mall, so I pretty much ignored most of them. I watched with fascination, as they performed their mating rituals in front of me, and thought about returning to San Francisco.

Then Javier sat down right next to me. I'd seen him a couple of times before, eating lunch at the same little restaurant. He was always wearing a name tag that tattled he was a sales clerk at Suburbia, a Mexican equivalent to Montgomery Wards. He was tall and very solidly built, with straight black hair and hazel eyes accented by long curly eyelashes. Twin dimples pierced each cheek that was braced by a strong jawline and a clefted chin. He was young, probably about 19 or 20, and adorable. I'd stared shamelessly at him when I saw him, trying to get his attention, but whenever I looked at him he was either not looking at me or he'd look away suddenly. I never pursued it more than that.

But now here he was, sitting right next to me. He was reading a book and finishing his lemonade. I nodded at him as he sat down, and he nodded back before he began reading. No smile, no licking of the lips or groping of the groin. So I went back to my people-watching, trying hard not to think about Javier.

I wasn't very successful. I kept sneaking a peek at him through the corners of my eyes. I could smell his sweet cologne, and after a while I swear I could distinguish his body heat from the 98-degree humid heat of Mexican summer. I'd sat there for about 15 minutes when I suddenly felt his knee brush mine. The first time, it was just a quick brush, and he pretended to reposition his feet. The next time, he let it rest there for a few minutes before moving it. The third time, it rested against mine for a moment and then began applying pressure against my leg.

I looked over at him. He continued reading his book as his leg pushed harder against mine. I looked away quickly and kinda gave my head a quick little shake. I looked back at Javier, and this time he looked me right in the eyes and smiled. His beautiful pink lips parted to reveal perfect, pearl-white teeth and those drop-dead gorgeous dimples. My heart did a triple beat, and I quickly looked away. With just the batting of his eyelashes and the dimple display, he was causing my dick to stir in my jeans.

When I looked back at him, he marked his place in the book he was reading and closed it as he got up to leave. I panicked. My heart dropped to my stomach, I stopped breathing, and I felt my face flush hotly. Where was he going? Why didn't I talk to him when I had the chance? Why couldn't I live much closer?

He brushed my leg again as he deliberately walked in front of me rather than going around his side of the bench. I watched him leave, and saw that after a few steps he turned back around to look at me. He smiled that lethal smile again and nodded for me to follow him.

I couldn't breathe. This was one of the most gorgeous men I'd seen while in Mexico. He seemed shy and sweet and sexy and mysterious, all at once. And now he was motioning for me to follow him. I turned to see which direction he was heading. He stopped right outside a door marking the men's room, made sure I saw where he'd gone, and then disappeared into the door.

I stood up slowly and took a couple of deep breaths before forcing my feet to move one in front of the other. When I reached the restroom door, I saw it was a stairway that went up a narrow hallway, winding around one corner before opening up into the rest room. I took the steps two at a time and walked into the rest room before I could chicken out. Once inside, I had to stop and catch my breath. It was a fairly large bathroom: eight urinals on either side of the room at the far end, with six stalls between the door, and the beginning of the urinal section on one side and a bank of sinks and paper towel dispensers across from them.

The doors to each of the stalls were locked, and I could hear slurping noises coming from behind them. Javier stood alone at the wall of urinals on one side, and two young guys stood next to each other on the other side. They'd moved their hands back to their own tools when I walked in, but it took them only a few seconds to size me up and move back to jerking each other off in their urinals.

Javier smiled when he saw me walk in, and then moved the shy smile down to his cock. He was standing a few inches from the urinal, showing me his cock. It was still soft but already long and thick, with a soft sheath of foreskin covering its head. He watched it himself as he shook it a couple of times and then looked up at me, still smiling, as he began moving his foreskin slowly back and forth over the shaft.

He nodded at me to take the urinal next to him. I gulped deeply as I noticed his cock hardening in front of my eyes, then walked dazedly to the pisser next to him. I pulled out my half hard dick and pointed it into the urinal, looking straight ahead and pretending to pee.

Javier gave a quiet "psst," and when I looked up he winked at me and motioned his eyebrows toward his cock. I ventured a look down there, and my knees almost buckled beneath me. His cock was fully hard now, and a drop of precome hung loosely at the head. It was long, maybe nine inches or so, and very thick. When he pulled the foreskin back I saw a long throbbing vein run the length of the top of his dick. My mouth was dry as cotton, and I forced my eyes back to the wall in front of me.

I heard some of the stall doors open, and their occupants began to meander out one by one. I was getting nervous and started to put my cock back into my jeans when I heard Javier cough conspicuously. I looked over at him, and he shook his head no and nodded toward my dick. Another man, about 40, came into the rest room and took the last urinal on our side of the room. He peed quietly as I leaned as far as I could into the urinal so he couldn't see my shriveling dick. Javier didn't seem to care one way or the other and remained where he was. The older man finished relieving himself and left the rest room along with the last of the stall occupants.

The two boys behind us were still there. The shorter of the two was on his knees sucking his friend, who was leaning against the stall next to him. The sucker kept darting his eyes toward the door, watching out for anyone coming in. They apparently did not think of Javier or myself as a threat.

Javier turned away from me and, with his dick still hard and sticking out of his jeans, walked to the restroom door. He pulled a piece of paper from his back pocket and used a piece of gum from his mouth to stick it to the door. Then he shut the door and stuck the chair which was occupied by a lavatory attendant except during lunch under the handle.

I watched this with stunned silence and listened to my heart pounding in my chest as Javier walked smoothly back toward me, his huge, uncut dick leading the way. When he reached me, he put his hands on either of my shoulders and slowly pushed me back until I was leaning against the wall.

My cock was fully hard now and throbbing uncontrollably in front of me. Javier looked me directly in the eyes, smiled, and leaned forward to kiss me. His lips were soft and warm. I parted my lips slowly as he licked them and slid his tongue into my mouth. The room grew very hot, and I felt a little dizzy as he kissed me passionately. I don't usually precome, but I felt a drop slithering out of my cock head. I was afraid I'd come just from Javier's kiss, but he broke it before I did.

The two kids behind us were moaning and groaning, and Javier and I looked over at them. The kid on his knees was shooting his load onto the floor as he continued to suck his friend furiously. The taller guy let out a loud grunt and pulled his dick out of the shorter guy's mouth. He yanked on it twice, and we saw him shoot a huge load onto his friend's face. Spurt after spurt of thick, white come covered the kid's face. He turned his face away after three or four sprays, and the jism shot past his ear and onto the floor.

Watching this turned Javier on more than I could ever have imagined, and before I knew what was happening, Javier pushed my shoulders down, forcing me to the floor. Before I could stand back up or figure out what was going on, I felt a shot of hot sticky come land between my nose and my mouth. I looked up at Javier's dick. He wasn't even touching it at all, yet it was shooting a load almost equal to the tall guy across from us, all onto my face. He moaned loudly and just let it shoot onto me without touching his dick. I didn't turn my head away; I loved the feel of the hot wet come as it hit my face.

Javier hooked his hands under my arms and pulled me up to my feet again. He kissed me on the lips, licking his own come from my face and sliding his tongue covered with his cooling jizz back into my mouth. I sucked on his tongue hungrily, swallowing his come and making my own cock throb spastically.

The two guys who'd shot their loads just a minute earlier walked over to us and began undressing us both. I looked around nervously, and the younger and shorter of the two boys took my chin in his hand and kissed me strongly, letting me know we were safe and wouldn't be bothered. When we were completely naked, our two new friends dropped to their knees and began sucking us at the same time.

I can't vouch for the kid sucking on Javier's huge dick, but the one with his lips wrapped around mine must have had a Ph.D. in cock sucking. He swallowed my thick cock in one move and somehow had eight or 10 tongues licking the head, the shaft, the balls, all while he moved his mouth up and down the length of it.

Javier leaned over and kissed me while we fucked the boys' mouths in front of us. It didn't take long before I felt the come boiling in my balls. I moaned softly and sucked harder on Javier's tongue as the kid on his knees in front of me sucked and swallowed my dick like it had never been sucked before. Javier sensed that I was close and broke our kiss as he pulled the young guy off my dick and onto his feet.

He turned me around so that my back was to him and pushed me gently up against the wall. He told our friends to do the same, and they did as they were told; the older and taller boy against the wall as the younger guy moved behind him. He and Javier bent down and played follow-the-leader.

Javier began kissing behind my right knee, nibbling and licking his way up the back of my legs until he got to my ass. He kissed and licked my ass cheeks one by one, then gently spread them apart. I was so hot by then, I could barely breathe. I wanted him to fuck me so badly, but when I pushed my ass closer to his face, he just licked it again and blew a cool breath on the exposed hole.

I looked over and saw the short kid was playing the same cat-and-mouse game with his partner, who was as delirious as I was. His eyes were closed, and he was moaning loudly as he pushed his tight, smooth ass closer to his partner's teasing mouth.

Javier reached between my legs and pulled gently on my hard cock as his fingers spread my ass cheeks and teased my hole. I grunted my delight, and he finally decided to reward me with what I wanted. I felt his nose press against the small of my back and a second later felt his hot tongue tickling the outside ring of my sphincter. I almost shot my load right then, but tensed up my body and counted to 10 to avoid it. Javier moved his left hand from my cock so he could use both hands to keep my cheeks spread open. He slowly worked his tongue around the outside of my ass for a couple of minutes, and then slid it very slowly inside, snaking it in, then out, then back in a little deeper each time. I was going nuts, and noticed the guy next to me was too.

The younger of our new friends was really getting into licking his friend's ass. I looked down and saw his cock was rock-hard and dancing wildly between his legs. He had a nice cock, about my size, but uncut. Huge amounts of precome dripped from the head of his dick, enough to make me wonder if he'd come again.

Javier and his counterpart stood up simultaneously. They must have had some secret code, because they moved together as one from the moment Javier turned me around. The younger kid turned his partner around just as Javier did the same to me and directed me and my counterpart to kiss. We did, very deeply and passionately, as Javier and our other friend dug through their jeans pockets for condoms. As we kissed, the guy in front of me reached for my hand and placed it on his cock. It was huge, almost as large as Javier's. I wrapped my hand around his dick and began sliding his foreskin up and down his thick pole.

He moaned and gyrated his hips, grinding his cock into and out of my fist. His dick was hot and throbbing strongly. My mouth watered with desire. I wanted to suck him so badly, I could almost taste him in my mouth, even as my hand pumped him gently closer to orgasm.

Javier leaned forward across my back and kissed my ear.

"Que quieres, papi?" he whispered huskily in my ear. He had his nerve—asking me what I wanted as he gently pressed his huge dick against my ass.

I shuddered as my response and pressed my ass harder against his hot cock. He gave me a tiny laugh and bit my ear softly to let me know he'd gotten the message. Then he moved his head back down to my ass and licked the hole some more, lubing it up to take his mammoth dick. As he stood up again and positioned the huge head of his cock against my twitching hole, he bent me over, indicating he wanted me to suck the guy next to me.

Never one to argue with authority, I leaned over and licked the head of the cock of the guy next to me. It was covered with precome as well, salty and sweet at the same time, and slick as silk. I'd never been with anyone in the States who precame very much at all, but decided at that very moment I was quite fond of the sweet, sticky stuff. I licked the guy's head until it was clean from stickiness, then took a deep breath as I swallowed his cock all the way to his balls.

On my second time swallowing the giant cock I felt Javier shove the head of his big dick just inside my ass. I tensed up and knew the boys in front of me were doing exactly the same thing, by the deep animal groan escaping my suckee's throat. It took me a moment to relax with Javier's throbbing pole up my ass, but I finally did, and resumed the task of sucking my new friend dry.

I think it may have been a little awkward for the kid fucking the guy next to me, since my guy had to stand up straight so I could suck and swallow his dick. The kid fucking him kept pulling out of his ass and trying to find better positions to fuck him in. He must have signaled Javier, because after only a couple of minutes Javier pulled me into a standing position. He had absolutely no problem whatsoever staying inside me. My ass wrapped itself around his long, thick pole and sucked it further inside. He slid into me in long, slow strides, as the shorter guy to my side smiled gratefully and bent his friend down toward my cock.

I closed my eyes as I felt Javier's cock slide into my hungry ass and a hot, wet mouth envelop my dick. I'd never been fucked and sucked at the same time, but it took no time whatsoever to realize it was my new favorite position. The kid getting fucked while sucking me was every bit the expert cocksucker his friend was. He and Javier found their rhythm with me almost instantly: Javier's thick cock sliding into my ass just as the guy sucking me slid off my cock.

I looked over at the guy with his dick inside my cocksucker's ass. He was pumping wildly, sweat dripping from his brow. He closed his eyes and moaned loudly, just as Javier was doing. I could tell they were both close. I was too, and trying desperately to hold back my orgasm.

I was up to about eight in my silent counting game when the guy fucking my cocksucker pulled out suddenly. He ripped the condom from his cock and pointed it at his friend's back. The first shot rushed past his friend's head and landed on Javier's chest. Javier grunted loudly, and I felt his cock grow unbelievably thicker inside my ass. It started contracting wildly inside me, and I knew that he was shooting a huge load into my ass as the kid across from me shot his hot load all over his friend's back and ass.

Javier kept his cock inside my ass as he came. That, and seeing the other kid shoot, was all it took for me. I pulled my cock from the other guy's reluctant mouth, shooting my own load in every direction. Some of it landed on the guy's face, some on the floor, some in the air, and some even on the kid fucking my cocksucker. I'd never shot such a large, wild load, and I laughed a little as it just kept pouring out of my dick. When I laughed, my ass muscles squeezed Javier's cock and sent shocks of pleasant pain up my ass and back.

The guy who had been sucking my dick suddenly stood up and tensed his entire body. He cried out loudly as wave after wave of thick white come shot out of his dick and splattered against the wall in front of him. We all just watched in amazement as it kept coming and coming. It seemed there was enough to fill a glass.

I started laughing first, which caused me so much pain, I had to pull Javier's cock out of my ass. Unbelievably, he was still hard. Then the others started laughing as well. We all leaned against a wall or sink and caught our breath. There was come everywhere; on the wall, the floor, a sink, all of us. The air smelled strongly of it. Pity the next people who came in here to actually use the rest room!

Javier removed his condom carefully and laid it on the sink next to the paper towel holder. It was almost completely filled with his load, and as he laid it on the sink, a good amount spilled out onto the counter. All four of us looked at it and began to giggle again as we got dressed.

We all kissed one another and walked out the door together. As I passed through the door I pulled off the note Javier had placed there earlier. I wanted a memento of the best fuck of my life. I stuck it in my pocket and watched as Javier ran back to his work and the other two friends departed in separate directions. I started walking back to school and pulled the paper out to read it on my way.

TEMPORARILY OUT OF SERVICE

I smiled to myself, doubting the rest room had seen that much service in quite a while.

Scandinavian Sex Ed
Aaron Krach

"On the left is where the royal family lives, and over on the right is the gay park," said the busy-haired driver, as if I'd asked for a guided tour so soon after a 10-hour transatlantic flight.

"Really?" I asked, just loud enough to not be a total asshole.

"It's a park where the gays go to meet," the driver continued, with extra emphasis on 'the gays.' "It's very famous for that in Copenhagen. Don't you have parks like that in the United States?"

"I don't think so. The gays," with my own emphasis now, "can go to any park they want in America."

Less than an hour inside the country, and already I was being picked up. Or was I being subjected to American-style machismo? So much for getting way from the ol' U.S. of A. What the fuck was this all about? This was Denmark, after all. I didn't come here for this. Certain people think I came here "to study abroad," and I did. But I also came here to be as far away from America as possible. I wanted to be as "European" as possible, and by that I mean European like in the movies, where everyone drinks and smokes and falls madly in love with whomever they damn well please, at least until the movie is over.

European also meant *gay*, at least in my 21-year-old head.

Having spent the first 18 years in SoCal suburbia, my sexual experience was limited to horny sons of boring pastors and closeted men I met at the mall. College life was a little better but not much. Without a car, sexual liaisons were limited to horny grad students cruising in the library and frisky beach bums more interested in making eye contact that catching rays. Not that I'm complaining. If it hadn't been for that nearby beach, I would have started jumping my roommate in the middle of the night. And let me tell you, that wouldn't have been pretty.

Which brings me back to Denmark, the smallest-fucking English-speaking beautiful-in-the-summer-but-damn-cold-and-dark-in-the-winter country on the planet. I arrived in June and was going to be here until the next June, so I'd better not let crabby cab drivers get me down.

We finished our drive through the center streets of downtown Copenhagen—wonderful, wonderful Copenhagen, as they say. He dropped me off at my new home, an absolutely hideous example of why the '60s will not go down as architecture's great decade. But this is the boring stuff; let me jump ahead.

Two weeks later things started looking up, or down, which was actually the case. It's just that in my case, looking down—at a large Danish cock—meant things were starting to look up. I was leaving a particularly boring cocktail party at some professor's house when I decided to walk home. My path took me directly through Orsted's Park. Yes, the aforementioned gay park. Honestly, I'd never been one for park bathrooms or parking lots—too smelly, too dirty—but I didn't let that stop me.

The park was a lot smaller than I'd expected. Damn thing was less than a full city block long. Before I realized it I was out on the other side and hadn't noticed a single gay thing. I turned right back around and took a curling path to the left that went over a small bridge. I could see there were a few trees and bushes, and I assumed because it was somewhat private that it would make good cover for tawdry bushwhacking sessions even though that wasn't what I was looking for. I prefer my sex in at least some light so I can see what I'm working with.

Just when I was about to give up on this country's so-called gay park, a young man walked up and kept pace with me. Without saying a word he just kind of looked over and kept walking, parallel to myself.

"Hi," I said.

"You are not Danish," he said back quickly.

"No, American."

"Oh," he muttered to himself before sidling up much closer.

(Note: The increased interest in my American blood inspired during my year abroad instilled the most patriotic feeling I ever had. God Bless America.)

He was a handsome guy. He was young, maybe 20-something, very pale, and somewhat tall. Basically, he looked like a typical Dane. Me being six feet, and he being a bit shorter—I'd put him at 5 foot 10 or so. Unsure exactly how this whole gay-park thing was supposed to work, I didn't say much.

"Do you know about this park?" he asked.

"Yeah" was the only reply I could think of.

"Do you want to come to my house? It's only two blocks from here," he said. "We could walk in five minutes."

I was beginning to like this gay-park thing. So quick and easy.

"Yeah" was all I could say, again.

It wasn't that I was tongue-tied or stupid, I just couldn't think of anything to say to this person who I didn't know anything about. Maybe he thought I was nervous. He was obviously a bit uncomfortable too. After a little more small talk (how long I'd been here, etc.) we arrived at a typical Danish building: four or five stories, slate-gray, box windows punched out at standard intervals. He lived in a pretty big studio, with a large mattress thrown on the floor in one corner, a table and two chairs in the other. There was a desk on the other side with a pretty fancy computer on it. Maybe he was a big-time computer hacker—I'll never know.

After even less conversation than that in the park, he grabbed me and kissed me. He had a sloppy wet tongue that wriggled its way inside my mouth. He was moving quickly—maybe too quickly. The Uncle Sam in me firmly wrestled control. He was like a dog, lapping away, kissing me. It was gross, but the underlying horniness was intriguing. I wondered when the last time he had sex was.

Quickly I relaxed and got into it. We ripped our shirts off and rubbed each other's chests. His was very pale, and there were little tufts of black hair around each nipple. I rubbed his crotch while he undid my pants. He dropped to his knees and started sucking me off. I fucked his mouth slowly and then faster and harder. He was a total animal, sucking and slobbering all over my meat like a thirsty dog.

He stopped and pulled me down to his mattress. He kicked off his shoes and tore off his pants before settling down next to me. Maybe I was just less horny than he was, but I undid my shoes a bit more cautiously. Then I saw his wanker.

(Note: My friend David and I have a few different names for male genitalia. A cock is a nasty man's piece of meat: not too big, not too small, and always hard. A prick is actually an asshole, as in "He's a total prick for not calling me back." A dick is an average penis, usually soft and decent-looking. A wanker is a very big dick that can turn into a cock when it's hard but overall is just so juicy, so tumescent, and so plump, it can only be called a wanker. Mr. Denmark had a wanker.)

I scooped his uncut wanker into my mouth. Swished my tongue around his foreskin and nibbled on his head with my teeth. I grabbed his shaft with my hands and sucked like a drunk on a bottle of booze. He started hollering and shaking and pulled away. I thought, Uh-oh. I must have bit something a little too hard. But no. He grabbed hold of his shaking cock and...ka-boom. He shot a thick white creamy load. Mr. Denmark must not have shot his wad in days, because the cream kept pouring out.

Up on my knees, overlooking his spooge-covered stomach, I jacked my own self off. By the time my jizz was mixing with his, you could barely see his stomach for the trees, I mean the splooge.

Ever the conversationalist, he jumped up, gave me a towel, and before I could wipe up, he was dressed again. I took that as a subtle hint that my presence there was no longer needed—and I blew the joint. But at the door he gave me his number and said I should call him.

Which is exactly what my horny foreign ass did only a week later—call him. *We* met up a pseudo-classy gay bar in the middle of town called Sebastian. We were trying to chat—about what, I have no recollection—when my wandering eye spied a rather handsome man dressed a little fancier than the average Sebastian fag. He was talking to an equally well-dressed (but shorter and bigger) man. Cruising ensued, which just goes to show how clueless Mr. Gay Park was. He didn't notice a thing. I wasn't sure how to proceed, so I hit the john to strategize. Then on my way out Mr. Well-Dressed stopped me.

"I know you are with that man, but here is my card. You are very handsome. Call me," he said.

"OK," and I left, slipping the card into my pocket with an overly confident flick of my wrist.

I have to admit, I was pretty thrilled by the situation. What a cool guy he was to not only pick me up so discreetly but to have noticed I was American and *not* said anything about it. I was definitely calling him tomorrow.

"Hi, this is Aaron. We met yesterday at Sebastian."

"Oh, yes. How are you? I'm so glad you called."

"I'm good. Is this a bad time?"

"No. I just got home from the store and was about to cook some dinner. Would you like to come over and eat?"

"Sure."

"Well, the only thing you should know is that the man with me last night was my boyfriend," he said sheepishly.

"Oh," I said, unsure what that was supposed to mean.

"He'll be here for dinner as well. So as long as you don't mind eating with the both of us"—accent on the "both of us"—"then come over."

I figured what the hell. This is the European adventure I came here for. Right?

"What's your address?" I asked.

It was embarrassing how excited I was to get over to this guy's house. I think his name was Caspar, and I don't remember his boyfriend's name, even though I ended up liking him a lot more than Caspar. Three-ways were never that easy to come by in the States.

Getting one person to come home with me was always more than enough work.

Their house was rather nice: a lot of Danish (surprise) modern furniture and walls lined with books. One of them was a professor somewhere, and I don't think the other one worked. Or at least he didn't tell me what he did. They met me at the door with an open beer (Danes really are always drinking) and led me into a plush living room. We talked a bit. They were thoroughly intrigued to find out what an American was doing spending a year in their cold, dark, and boring corner of the world.

Having psychotic experiences like this, thank you very much.

Then Caspar leaned over and started kissing me. He put one hand on my crotch while tonguing me gently. He was a smooth kisser, and his boyfriend didn't seem bothered in the least. In fact, he swept down on my drink and rescued it from my hand. After setting it down—on a leather coaster, of course—he came and sat on the other side of me. He began massaging my shoulders, kissing the back of my neck casually, warmly, and very comfortingly.

Caspar was apparently just getting warmed up. He grabbed my head with both hands and started kissing me quite aggressively, forcing his tongue into the corners of my mouth. My dick was hard as a rock, and the boyfriend's hands were kneading it under my jeans. They must have done this several times before, because without a word Caspar focused on my face and the boyfriend undid my pants. He pulled out my cock and started sucking on it. All I had to do was sit back and enjoy.

I felt for Caspar's nipples. His chest was firm and sexy. I lifted his shirt and felt his hot skin, ran my hand down to his navel and felt his leather belt. I didn't bother to undo it. I just reached in. He sucked in his already thin stomach and let me find his raging hard-on tangled inside layers of cotton underwear. I grabbed my hand around it and felt it harden even more. I slid my hand along the shaft, found the head, and felt drips of precome oozing out.

At this time Caspar shuddered and stood up. In front of me, with his boyfriend's lips firmly locked around my cock, he undressed.

What a specimen of Danish manhood: blond hair and fair skin, a firmly built torso but not overly so. His frame was well-designed to hang a nine-inch piece of cock from the center of. He reached out and grabbed my hand. I got up and followed him into the bedroom. The boyfriend stayed and went to the kitchen, I think.

In the bedroom, simply appointed with wood and warm white paint, he undressed me and pushed me down to the bed. I fought back. I wasn't this much of a bottom, but I was horny and in the mood to get fucked, especially by his big Danish Lincoln Log. In a haze of sexual wrestling he managed to slip a condom onto his cock and slide it in. Once inside he set about like a rabid dog, humping my ass till he let out a guttural sigh, shooting his load into the condom. (What was it about these Danish guys that sent them into hyperactive overdrive whenever they got right down to the nitty-gritty?)

I was so into getting plowed that I lost most of my hard-on without noticing. *No* matter. As he pulled out, I noticed Mr. Boyfriend standing on the side of the bed stretching a condom over his considerable piece of Danish meat. He stroked his cock like a man—underhanded. As Caspar left the room My Boyfriend jumped down and sucked my soft cock hard again. (Which took all of about, oh, two minutes.) Then he slipped a condom on me and straddled my American ass. After a few minutes of fucking, he got up and ripped off the condom, tossing it to the floor with masculine nonchalance. He scooted up to my face and shoved his cock in my mouth. Uncut, like most Danes, his dick slapped my lips a few times before throwing his head back and shooting all over my face. Only most of it didn't land on my face. Horny bastard shot all of his worn-leather headboard and white pillows.

Without missing a beat he got off me and went to town on my now near-busting cock. After a few nibbles and slurping licks I shot a huge load of jizz all over my stomach. Caspar was back in the room holding a warm wet towel. He used his other hand to pull on my balls while his boyfriend milked my cock for all it was worth.

I stayed for dinner, and we talked about having a round of international diplomacy, so to speak, later. They were going to Egypt for vacation and wanted to see me when they came back. I got a post-card from them, but I never called—figured it would never be as good as the first time...so why bother.

Constantine's Cats
Dominic Santi

I didn't lose my wallet to the pickpockets at Termini station, but I was still marked as a tourist the minute I caught my backpack in the door of the Rome Metro. Even a whistle shrieking as the door opened and closed again didn't cover the snickers in the packed-to-the-gills coach. I was used to disdainful sniffs at Americans. I flushed to the roots of my hair, though, when I realized the slender young Roman god standing next to me—I mean, the most gorgeous hunk of man I'd ever seen in my entire fucking life—was laughing so hard, his eyes were watering.

"New backpack," I muttered, reaching up to grab the overhead railing next to the godling's hand. I wasn't fast enough. The train lurched forward, and I tipped nosefirst into the armpit of hunk boy's leather jacket. As I groped his waist, trying to find my balance, my nostrils filled with the heavenly scent of warm, healthy male sweat, my hands gripped washboard abs that made my dick twitch, and I figured my short life in macho het-boy Rome was over. I was stunned when a surprisingly strong arm reached down and pulled me to my feet.

"Hold the pole, like this."

My Roman wet dream's voice was buttery smooth. So were his deep-brown and, fortunately, still smiling eyes. I felt myself falling into them as he firmly lifted my arm up beside his on the railing. I grabbed hold automatically, bracing myself next to him as I mumbled my thanks.

Even when he looked away my greedy photographer's eye soaked in his aristocratic features—the warm Mediterranean gold of his

Italian skin and the thick brown hair that fell to his shoulders. My eyes kept traveling all the way down to the firm, perfectly rounded ass that showed how God had meant a man to wear jeans.

Dreamboat's face now held the same emotionless mask of his fellow travelers, but his eyes twinkled as they swept over my crotch, obviously aware of what I'd been doing.

"American?" he asked.

"Yeah," I coughed, trying to regain my composure. "Photographer."

He nodded, and the hand on the railing pressed gently against mine.

"You like Italy?"

"Very much," I smiled, letting my quick glance downward show what I liked best.

This time a smile cracked the edges of his lips. While I basked in the glow, the train jolted and I bumped against him again as we slid into Cavour station. This time he didn't move away. Instead, he pressed against me as the door opened and the additional incoming passengers crowded us closer together. When we jerked forward I felt a hard dick press against my leg. I decided that if my Roman idol was a pickpocket, he was welcome to whatever he found, so long as he took his time searching.

"What do you photograph?" His conversation was light, but the bulge brushing my thigh had my shaft bending uncomfortably against my buttons.

"Cats."

He stared at me blankly.

"*Il gatos.*" I knew I was mangling the plural, but my Italian sucked. I'd been taking advantage of the fact that most of the locals in the tourist areas spoke at least a smattering of English. "I'm on assignment for *International Feline.* I'm going to take pictures of the cats by Constantine's arch."

He quietly pressed against me. "I did not think such was your interest."

I turned and resituated slightly. This time it was my hard dick pressing against the side of that firm, shapely ass. I locked my eyes on his. "Lots of people like pussies." I was still looking at him as the train again ground to a stop and the doors opened. I jumped when he pushed me toward the door.

"Colosseo—this is your exit."

"Thanks!" Without thinking I pushed my way into the crowd streaming through the door. When the whistle blew I turned to catch a final glimpse of my Roman wet dream—and someone plowed into the back of me.

"Excuse me," I started, then I saw who it was and laughed. "I didn't know you were there." His grin lit his face all the way to his warm, sexy, velvety brown eyes, and my dick throbbed so badly it hurt. As the throng pushed forward around me, he grabbed my shoulder and pulled me toward the exit.

"Come on, American. I will show you the cats."

"I'm Steve," I said, smiling back at him.

"Tonio," he laughed. "Now walk and pay attention."

We stepped out of the station, and I almost stopped breathing. The Colosseum rose above me to the left, the afternoon light casting eerie shadows in the archways of the age-darkened stone. A full third of the building was swathed in scaffolding, but the view was still breathtaking. I drank in the site of the ancient ruins, sharply contrasted against the bright-green grass and the darkly wet streets slick from a passing spring rain. I didn't even notice when the sidewalk ended. A firm hand yanked me back as a bus zoomed by my nose.

"Are Americans blind?" Tonio's gorgeous locks swirled in the sunlight as he shook his head. "Come. It is late. The Colosseum is dangerous after dark, and you do not pay attention so well."

"Sorry," I blushed. "I was just admiring the scenery." I again looked pointedly down his body. "Hope you don't mind."

He grinned lecherously at me. "I like your artist's eye." He nodded toward the huge arch next to the Colosseum. "This way." Constantine's arch was directly in front of us, the lower half of one of the stone legs also covered with scaffolding. I followed the sexy sway of Tonio's ass up the short stone walkway, past the few tourists the rain hadn't chased away. I didn't know what kind of shots I'd get in this light, but my job was rapidly taking a backseat to my cock as we reached the excavations at the base of the monument.

"Gladiator quarters." Tonio pointed down into the maze of ruins, toward the newly uncovered walls, shoulder-high amid the steel supports and plastic sheeting.

I forced myself not to think about naked men living and training in those trenches. Fat pigeons and fatter-still cats strolled the paths and lounged in the damp grass at the edge of the dig. I pulled out my camera and started shooting—orange tigers, golden-yellow tabbies, panther-black tomcats. They were everywhere, stretching and preening, obviously wild, but with no fear of the human intruders.

I shot three rolls, including several pictures of Tonio pointing out particularly photogenic specimens. I focused on his ass, especially on the profile of his succulent round globes against the Colosseum. His grin told me he knew exactly what I was doing. Tonio had been right, though. We didn't have much time. The light faded, it started to rain again, and suddenly it was dark.

"We could go in there," I said, nodding toward the Colosseum as I shoved my camera back in its case. Tonio shook his head.

"Too many guards and drug dealers." He grabbed my arm as I slipped on the slick stone path. "Come." With a quick tug he jumped down into the excavations and dragged me under a low sheet of corrugated plastic. As we knelt on the wooden work plank, he wrapped his arms around me and his hot tongue swept into my mouth. I kissed him back hard, sliding my hands under his jacket and holding him close in the darkness. Surrounded by the sound of the rain, I cupped his ass in my hands and pulled his cheeks as far apart as those skintight jeans would allow. "I want to fuck you."

Tonio wiggled against me, still kissing me, his dick hard against my crotch. His mouth was hot and wet and sweet. I wanted to tongue his lips, wanted to tongue his ass lips as well.

"All Italian men are tops." Tonio's breath was warm against my face as he wiggled his ass back into my hands.

"I won't tell," I growled. I reached down and yanked the front of his jeans open. His gasp caressed my ear as I skinned his long, beautiful cock and leaned over to take the salty, slippery head between my lips.

"Mmmmmm. You taste good."

It was hard to see in the shadows. I closed my eyes and ground my nose into his pubes, inhaling the clean, heavy man scent emanating up from his balls. My dick was so hard I couldn't stand it anymore. I tore my jeans open and pulled out my throbbing, leaking cock.

"Bello," Tonio gasped, thrusting up into my throat. "So good." He put his hands on my head and started pumping. I felt his dick getting stiffer, and I didn't want what we were doing to end too soon. I pulled off, saliva dripping from my tongue, and sat back, yanking Tonio's jeans down to his knees.

"Turn around and bend over."

He didn't argue. I lifted his jacket and shirt, licking up his warm, smooth butt as I worked my own pants down over my hips. Then I grabbed Tonio's firm mounds, pulled them apart, and buried my face in his crack. He squirmed right away, moaning softly, his talented ass lips kissing me back as I feasted on his "virgin" hole.

"I like rimming Italian pussy," I growled, sucking softly on his loose, receptive pucker as he arched his ass at me. "You sure all Italians are tops?" I poked in hard and tongued him ferociously, pulling his ass cheeks even wider as I dug in deep.

"Fuck me," he gasped. "Now!"

I indulged in one final taste, then leaned back and dug a rubber out of my jacket. As soon as I was sheathed, I grabbed his hips and shoved in, hard. Tonio's ass lips slid down my dick like they were swallowing a sword. My groans were as loud as his as I sank in all the way to the hilt.

"Nice ass," I gasped, pumping into him, my hands gripping his hips. Tonio's shoulder moved as he took his weight on one arm and started stroking himself. I reached down and pulled him upright, gasping as loudly as he did when my dick slid over his joy spot. Tonio shook in my arms. I sank my teeth into the back of his neck and slammed my shaft up into him. "Come for me, pussy boy. Take me deep and make your dick spurt." It was a quick, hot fuck—too hot to last. Tonio's body tensed around me, and I thrust my hungry dick into him hard and fast.

"Americano!" he cried out softly as his body tensed and his asshole clenched hard around me. His hot Italian pussy spasmed over my shaft. I buried my cock up his ass, grinding against him as his asshole sucked me deep and my guts clenched. The smell of his jism filled my nostrils, and I was gone. I shook as I emptied my balls up Tonio's quivering ass.

We didn't stay around to see if any of the local guards had noticed us. I tossed the rubber in a trash box, and we yanked up our pants and scrambled back onto the walkway. Nobody was there but a fat tabby strolling nonchalantly by with a few loose feathers in its mouth. Tonio and I innocently made our way back to the well-lit Metro station and the last of the tourists and commuters heading home.

When we reached the entrance Tonio stopped and smiled at me. "Are you hungry, American? There is a good pizzeria a short bus ride from here." He paused, looking at me deliberately as I once more melted into his soft-brown eyes. "By my apartment."

I licked my lips before I realized what I was doing, then all I could do was laugh. We were still laughing as I followed him onto the bus and the shadows of the Colosseum disappeared into the distance.

Adam On
Jett Simpson

I picked up the damp washcloth and wiped up the gob of spunk that had landed splat on my knee. Then I turned the cloth over to clean up the come that had seeped onto my leg from my subsiding cock. I milked the last bit out and, satisfied that I had cleaned myself up, tossed the washcloth into the hamper.

The computer still hummed with a faintly static sound. My most recently invoked Adam had reverted to screen-saver mode. The nude figure walked back and forth across the room-size screen, waiting to be clicked on again.

The Y2K scare had just been that. The world did not come to an end, computers did not crash, banks did not go bankrupt, and the fanatic fringes had, for the most part, annihilated one another. By 2015, computer technology had advanced far beyond man's 20th-century vision.

My holographic imager and screen were new toys for me. I could feel my dick getting hard again as I considered the endless possibilities they offered.

I watched the male image traverse the length of the room. His superbly sculpted body glowed with the slightest film of perspiration as he paced. At the end of the room he turned and stopped, his aqua blue eyes looking at me as if to say, *Turn me on again.*

I walked over to the wall and walked beside Adam as if we were "taking a turn" about the room. I could have put his action on pause, but I enjoyed watching the rhythm of his sinewy muscles, the slight sway of his cock, the movement of his ass.

As he reached the end of the wall and turned, I commanded, "Stop."

His action stopped, but I could still see the heaving of his chest as he breathed and the tiny pulse of his heart beat in the slight throbbing of his massive neck. His piercing eyes blinked through long black lashes eagerly.

"Begin," I said.

He resumed his pacing, and I watched as he moved along the length of the wall.

Although nearly every command was voice activated, the imager also had a palm-size remote-control panel, where additional commands could be entered or the image altered.

I pressed COLOR and was given options: eyes, skin, hair. I chose HAIR and was given a new set of options from a color bar. I clicked on the various colors offered, watching Adam's hair color change.

Finally satisfied with the various changes I had made, I said, "Adam on."

What was two-dimensional became a three-dimensional form. The beauty of the 21st-century hologram was that it was an image that could be touched, an image that I could feel, an image that responded—but also an image that could be adjusted according to whim.

Adam stopped his pacing and looked across the room to where I was standing.

"Aah," he said, beginning a slow series of stretches. I watched, fascinated, as his skin became more supple and his muscles gained strength. Even the girth of his cock responded, becoming thicker, heavier.

My cock responded in kind, growing heavy as it began a languid extension.

It was as if he had read my mind and no longer needed prompting. He came to where I stood and placed his hand on my dick, caressing it gently while reaching down with his other hand to cup my balls. He placed his full lips on mine, and his tongue darted in and out playfully.

I placed my hands on the muscular globes of his ass and drew him to me so that his cock pressed against mine. We ground against one another, cock to cock, feeling the rush of man-sex adrenaline.

Adam's dick was a model of porn magazine manhood: eight thick inches with a fat, uncut head. A single blue vein cut down the center of his cock and seemed to pulse as his dick grew. With each pulse it grew more erect until his cock stood out in front of him like a proud soldier.

I fell to my knees and sucked his dick slowly into my mouth. My tongue danced around the massive head and worked its way under the supple foreskin. I continued on down his stiff tool while my hands massaged his amazing ass. A soft layer of down covered his pale buns, and I felt goose pimples crawl over his skin as I kneaded.

With my middle finger I probed and prodded my way around the tight pucker of his asshole. His soft moan let me know he was ready, and I inserted my finger slowly, marveling at the velvety softness of his interior. I probed deeper and inserted a second finger.

I felt his cock stiffen in my mouth as I continued to penetrate him. By now I had inserted three fingers, and Adam had begun to fuck my mouth as if he was ready to come.

I pulled my fingers out of his ass and stood up to look at my toy. His smooth, unwrinkled face looked at me with eyes that brimmed with life.

"I'm ready for you," he said, bending down to suck my cock. His soft lips encircled the head of my dick and moved down the shaft. His saliva was slick, wet, and hot as he moved his mouth expertly over my rod. He spit into his hand and rubbed the lubricant onto his ass. He then turned and bent over again so that his ass replaced his mouth.

My rigid cock quivered in anticipation as I began the slow entry into Adam's central core. Then I felt the tight cherry of his ass pop as I quickly thrust, pulled out, and then thrust again. His sexual instincts began to take over, and his holographic hole sucked me into the vortex of his being.

Suddenly I was transported into the world of the unreal; I felt myself floating through a universe of electrons and flashing neurons that throbbed and pulsed like a giant sex organ.

Adam's slick, wet hole clamped around my cock like a vise grip. I heard him moan and reached down to grab his throbbing rod, pumping it with each thrust I made up his ass.

I knew I was going to come and couldn't stop myself.

"Ah! O-o-oh!" I cried.

I shoved my cock deep into his body, unloading gobs of spunk with each thrust, forcing us both to the floor.

Adam shuddered and began to buck under me like a bronco as he reached his climax. I wanked his cock and continued to pump him until his load began to spurt out in unison with his thrusts. Spent, we both moaned and I lay flat on him, my dick softening in his ass.

I finally pulled out of Adam and let my semihard cock rest in his crack. As we lay there I could feel his breathing slowly returning to normal.

I stood up finally and reached down to help Adam to his feet. With two words I ended our encounter.

"Adam off," I said.

His eyes looked imploringly at me for a moment and then seemed to glaze over slightly before he walked back to the screen, reentered it, and began pacing back and forth, his body again a two-dimensional form.

I slept fitfully that night. Dreams of Adam kept entering my subconsciousness. Exasperated, I finally got out of bed and made my way to the video chamber.

Adam, my faithful sentry, was making his paces across the wall. I felt as if he looked over at me when I entered the room but knew it was just my nighttime imagination.

I grabbed the remote and studied my specimen carefully.

Although the Adam holographic imager I had purchased could be altered to look like almost any male form, his unaltered image was that of a California surfer: blond, blue-eyed, and tan, with sinewy muscles built from surfing and swimming.

Not that I was bored with this image. But just knowing that I could alter him so easily...

I began pressing buttons on the remote, watching Adam change with each touch. Now tall, now short, fair-skinned, dark, longhaired, cropped, cut, uncut.

The image that finally traversed the room was tall, with long, dark hair, olive skin, and shiny black eyes.

Under his lips I installed a goatee, and on his swarthy torso I added a thin dark line of hair that ran from his chest down to his pubic area.

His cut cock, now semierect, swung unabashedly with Adam's every step.

"Adam on," I said.

I watched as he came to life, leaving the confinement of the screen behind and expanding to a three-dimensional form. I could almost hear the sound of the change from two to three dimensions, like a balloon getting the breath of life.

With surprising directness he came over to where I stood and wrapped his arms around me tightly. The soft hair of his goatee brushed against my chin, and his full lips pressed against mine. I felt my cock fill and rise up again as his hot tongue darted teasingly in and out of my mouth and he began to fondle my balls.

He got on his knees and sucked my cock into the soft wetness of his mouth. His hot tongue played over my prick.

"Oh, fuck," I said. "That feels so good."

I felt his finger pressing on my anus. Then he dipped into my hole gently, slipping the finger in and out rhythmically. I closed my eyes and relaxed, letting Adam continue his anal probe.

Suddenly he was behind me. He bent me forward, exposing my ass to the light, and I felt his lusty tongue pierce me, then disengage, only to explore the rim of my ass and penetrate me again.

He stood, placed his stiff cock in the crack of my ass, and began to move slowly up and down, stopping momentarily to let the head of his throbbing dick press against my horny hole.

He inserted the tip of his swollen head, just the tip at first, then he pulled out and returned again to insert his cock a little deeper, teasing my fuck chute and bringing me to the brink.

"Aah," I moaned. "Fuck me, Adam."

He sensed my urgency. Without hesitation he plunged his stiff prick deep into my ass.

"Oh-oh-o-o-oh!" I cried.

Adam began to pummel me with a hard and steady beat. Each thrust seemed to go deeper and deeper until he finally settled into a steady rhythm that allowed me to feel his thick tool as it glided in and out.

I reached for the remote and pressed the plus sign. I felt his cock expand in my ass and pressed the plus sign again. His dick was now almost bigger than I could bear, but he was relentless and kept up his steady pace.

He reached around me and with one hand lightly pinched my nipple. With his other hand he grabbed my cock and began to jack on it while slowly increasing the tempo of his pounding dick in my ass again.

I could feel Adam's dick growing even stiffer in my ass as he neared orgasm. I reached back to feel his giant ramrod as it plunged into me.

Adam began to pump my cock with light, quick strokes. I tightened my asshole as he rammed his cock home, intent on shooting my load simultaneously with his.

"I'm going to come," he shouted hoarsely in my ear.

I felt his load shoot like a rocket in my ass, splintering off into a relay of electrical impulses that touched every erogenous nerve in my body.

I don't know what happened next—I lost track. I felt the come shoot out of my ass, and I felt our bodies merge. But I was defenseless. The last gush of come shot out of my dick, and that's the last thing I remember.

I was completely disoriented when I came to. I looked for Adam and, from the corner of my eye, could see him comfortably sprawled on the chaise, his legs spread apart, his cock soft. Seeing that I was awake, he looked at me with a mischievous grin as he grabbed the remote and said, "Adam on."

On the Dotted Line
Trevor J. Callahan Jr.

For Christmas during my junior year of college, my sister bought me an exercise video.

Frankly, I was surprised at her gift. I'd always been a very athletic person—always playing sports and working out. In college I didn't have as much time to work out as I used to, but I was always playing a pickup game of basketball or softball; I hardly thought I needed a low-impact aerobics tape.

"Come off it," I told her. "So what if I've gained the 'freshman 15'?"

"It isn't the 'freshman 15' I'm worried about," she said matter-of-factly, "but, rather, the junior jiggle I'm starting to notice in your gut." Then she showed me my football picture from my senior year of high school.

I went on a diet the next day.

I began to work out in earnest, first using the aerobics tape she gave me to reclaim my cardiovascular fitness and then moving on to weights. Soon I had outgrown the simple exercises on the tape and added roadwork and serious lifting to my workout.

By the time I started grad school I was in better shape than I had ever been. My almost six-foot frame was toned and hard, my chest broad and defined, my abs cut into a rigid six-pack of muscle. Still, on rainy days or on a busy weekday, I sometimes worked out to that old aerobics tape my sister had given me two years earlier. Was this a sentimental decision on my part? Hardly. You see, on the tape, in the third row, all the way on the left, was this guy. His body was toned, of course—broad shoulders; a smooth, muscular chest; strong pecs and delts; thick, firm thighs and calf muscles. He had wavy brown hair, a strong, square jaw, and deep-green eyes. Every time he lifted his arms I could see the dark tangle of his underarm air. The guy drove me wild. Every time I worked out with this tape I had to jerk off afterward. His name was Matthew Michaelson. And let me tell you, he motivated me to get fit.

It was a rainy weekday, one of those dreary New England fall days that come all too often for my taste. I didn't have classes until late in the afternoon, but I always woke up early to do some reading or clean my apartment. It was definitely too wet to go jogging, so I figured I might as well spend some quality time with my favorite aerobics instructor. I popped in my trusty tape for a quick workout, followed by a leisurely hot shower with a long, slow jerk-off session.

I was halfway through the lunges when I heard a knock at the door. Though I had been working out steadily for 20 minutes, I had hardly broken a sweat, so I just wiped my forehead on my sleeve, hit PAUSE on the tape, and answered the door. It was the UPS man with a care package from home. My usual UPS man was a big hairy guy with a thick beard and mustache—very cute but very married. This one was new to me.

"Hi," he said when I answered the door. There was something vaguely familiar about him. "Got a package for ya."

"Thanks," I said, taking the package and placing it on the couch.

"You just need to sign this." He handed me a pen, but it was out of ink.

"Don't worry about it," I said, "I'll get one from my desk." I crossed to my desk, which was so cluttered with papers and books I could hardly see my computer, and began to search for a pen. I could not shake the feeling that I had seen this guy somewhere. Probably on campus, I reasoned. "Where's Louis?" I asked, referring to my regular UPS man.

"Vacation," the man answered.

"Oh, did he finally get to take his family to Florida? I know the missus has been wanting to go for a while."

"Yeah, he did." I still couldn't find a pen. "From a girlfriend?" the delivery man asked me, indicating the package.

I shook my head. "Mother," I said. I found the pen, signed the form and gave it to him, along with the pen. "Keep it," I said, noticing that his name tag read MATT.

"Thanks," he said, turning to go.

Suddenly the connection clicked in my head. "Oh, my God," I said, amazed. "You're Matthew Michaelson!"

The guy looked at me quizzically. "That's right," he said. "Have we met?"

All I could do to reply was point at my television.

Matthew stared at it for a moment, then his face brightened and he laughed. "That's funny," he said. "But how did you remember me? Most people have probably never even seen the credits."

I felt my cheeks turn red. "That's a long story," I said. "Let's just say I find you very motivating."

"I'll say," he murmured, checking me over. "You're in great shape." Was it my imagination, or was he flirting with me?

"How did you get here?" I asked. "I mean, why aren't you still making workout tapes? You're still in great shape." And he was. He filled out that UPS uniform just right.

His green eyes sparkled. "Thanks. I only did it for a quick buck, though. Things in California didn't work out, so I came back here, and now I'm in your apartment."

"I can't believe you're here. Will you sign my tape?"

Matthew looked at me self-consciously. "Are you serious? Now I know how celebrities feel." But he took the pen and signed the tape.

As I sat there and stared at him, all of the dirty sexual fantasies I had had about him flooded through me. I could feel my cock growing in my loose shorts. *Down!* I thought as he handed me back the tape. "Here you go."

Even his signature was sexy. "Wow. Thanks."

We just stared at each other for a moment in silence. Finally, he laughed nervously. "This is kind of weird," he said, "but nice."

His words shook me from my fantasy. "Can I get you something to drink?"

He shrugged. "I'm not supposed to, but, yeah, thanks." He sat down on my couch. "I've been on my feet all morning. It's nice to sit."

I took a towel and wiped my still-glistening brow. I went to the kitchen and poured two glasses of iced tea. When I returned I found Matthew looking at the pictures on my desk.

"Girlfriend?" he asked, pointing to a picture of a young, blue-eyed blond in a bikini. I shook my head. "Twin sister," I replied. "She makes me keep it there in case any potential husbands come through."

Matthew smiled at my joke. "Brother, then?" he said, pointing to a picture of a good-looking redhead in formal wear.

I shook my head ruefully. "Ex-boyfriend," I answered. There was an uncomfortable silence for a moment. *Now I've done it,* I thought. Desperate for a distraction, I opened the package my mother had sent me. Clean underwear, warm socks, homemade cookies, and a brief letter. No cash. *Figures,* I thought.

I handed Matthew a cookie and quickly perused the letter. "Does your mom have anything interesting to say?" he asked.

"Read it yourself," I said, tossing him the note.

Dear Trevor,

I'm sending you some clean underwear because I am sure you haven't done your laundry in weeks. Please remember to wear them in case you get in an accident and have to go to the hospital. If they should cut off your pants and see you in dirty underwear, what kind of mother would they think you have? Are you dating anyone new? I wish you would find some nice man and settle down. Between your sister's fear of stretch marks and your fear of commitment, I don't think I'll ever have any grandchildren! Meet a nice man and adopt one soon, OK honey? Your father and sister send their best.

Love, Mom

Matthew smiled as he read the letter. "Your mom sounds great. My mother never wants to hear about the guys I date."

Yes! "And are you dating anyone?" I asked, feeling weak in the knees and smiling all over.

Matthew gave me a sexy look. "Nope." *Thank God!* "Are you?"

I shook my head eagerly. "Absolutely not!" We both smiled, peering deeply into each other's eyes. His were even more green than they appeared on the tape. "I've got to be honest about something," I said, possessed by the spirit of confession. "I kept that tape because of you. I just always thought you were the hottest stud I had ever seen." I lowered my voice. I had no clue why I was saying any of this. "Every time I watch the tape I always have to jerk off in the shower afterward. Every time."

"Wow. That may be, like, the nicest compliment I ever got."

I was amazed. "Really?" In response Matthew reached over and clasped my hand firmly in his. I looked down, loving the sight of our two strong hands clasped together. I looked back up just in time for him to kiss me.

That kiss! In my fantasies I had always imagined our first kiss to be soft and gentle, him shy and me the aggressor, our two selves finally melting into one giant embrace. I couldn't have been further from the truth. Matthew's lips were pressed hard against mine, his hands reaching around me—one clasping at the back of my neck, the other on the small of my back. His tongue parted my lips before it forcefully entered my mouth and thrust itself deep down my throat. I was taken completely off-guard, and as I leaned back to relieve the pressure he put on me, he followed, leaning more solidly on my lips and body until he covered me. His hard body pressed against mine, his mouth wide and open, his tongue ravenously exploring my own mouth, his hands busily moving all over my body, up my shirt, across my back, finally burrowing between the couch cushions and my firm ass cheeks. When he finished he pulled back, exultant, while I gasped for breath and realized happily that I had a straining, full-fledged, rock-solid hard-on.

I had barely a moment to realize what had happened when Matthew was on me again, his lips nibbling furiously on my neck and ears. One of his meaty hands wrapped itself around my hard shaft, and I gasped as he gave it a tug. He squeezed my cock even harder, then slipped his hand down the front of my shorts, under my jock, and to the base of my shaft, where he began to roughly squeeze and stroke my red-hot cock. Gasping for air, I could hardly believe how good this was all making me feel.

Matthew pulled my shorts and jockstrap down, and my cock stood out straight and hard from my body. He bent and began to tongue the shaft, his lips moving up and down my hot tool as his tongue slicked up my cock. With a sudden motion he thrust it into his mouth and immediately swallowed the whole seven inches; I could feel the head of my shaft go down his throat while his nose buried itself deeply in my thick blond pubic hair. He began to move his head up and down on my rod, his tongue constantly flicking all over my cock, his ravenous moans interrupted only by the gasps coming from my mouth.

He stopped abruptly, standing in front of me, tall and masterful, his crotch bulging before my eyes. "Undress me," he said. I stood carefully, my shorts and jockstrap wrapped around my ankles, my T-shirt falling onto my stiff rod. I unbuttoned the shirt of his uniform and slid it off him. I pulled off his white T-shirt and marveled at his chest. It looked as if it had been carved out of marble. Eagerly I began to lick the space between his pecs, kissing and nibbling on his rock-hard flesh while slowly moving over to one of his pointy nipples. I bit down hard, and the sharp intake of his breath told me he liked this. I bit down harder, and he moaned, using his brawny hand to push my mouth against his chest. I continued torturing his nips, moving from left to right, eventually biting with force on both of them. They grew red and engorged, but it had an effect: I could feel his cock stirring beneath his brown pants.

With a hand on each of my shoulders he pushed me to my knees. I could see his huge rod outlined against his pants and began to stroke it. I put my mouth against it and began to chew lightly on his cock through the rough fabric of his UPS uniform. While I was doing this I unbuckled his belt and undid the button of his pants. Hooking my fingers under the band of his underwear, I looked up at his face and stared into his eyes, as if awaiting permission to pull his trousers down. He nodded once, quickly and eagerly, and I yanked his pants down to his ankles.

His cock was huge—it must have been nine inches long. It was so thick I could hardly get my mouth around the head. It was definitely the biggest cock I had ever seen. But the biggest surprise was his fore-skin. Even hard, I could see he had a nice thick bit of foreskin to cover his long, hot shaft.

I had never been with an uncircumcised guy before. Fascinated, I wrapped my hand around his shaft and tugged forward. The skin moved with my hand, wrinkling up until quite a bit covered his bulbous head. I moved forward cautiously; when my mouth was right next to the overhang, I gently stuck out my tongue and licked it. It tasted fleshy, slightly salty, like a crinkly extension of cock. I thrust my mouth around his entire shaft and stuck my tongue between his cock head and the foreskin. I began to move my tongue in circles around the head, feeling the loose skin move around my tongue and tasting the musky scent of good cock. Matthew's moans indicated that he liked this, so I went faster, moving my tongue wildly, pausing sometimes to gently bite the entire head and other times just the overhang. I sucked as much of the foreskin as I could into my mouth and let it slide back as his cock thrust into me. I enjoyed the feeling of his cock amply filling the skin and my mouth. I did this several times—slowly at first, then more rapidly, and I was soon rewarded with a sweet drop of Matthew's precome. "Yeah," he said, grabbing my hair and pushing me deeper on his shaft. Placing my fist firmly at the base of his huge shaft, I was soon being face-fucked by his huge rod, feeling that delicious foreskin move perfectly over his engorged prick while it penetrated my mouth again and again.

Matthew placed one of his legs on the arm of the couch to afford me a good view of his balls and the underside of his crotch. Making the most of this, I began to lick and suck his large, heavy nuts, plac-ing first one and then the other in my mouth before licking and sucking the area behind his ball sac. With a strong hand Matthew pushed me on my back; as I lay flat on the ground, he first stepped over me and then crouched until his hole was directly over my mouth. I gently probed his hole with my tongue, but Matthew was having none of that; he promptly sat right on my face, forcing me to shove my eager tongue up his hot asshole. "Yeah, eat that ass!" he said, grinding his whole hard ass into my face. "Mmmmph!" I moaned, feasting heartily on the meal he had given me.

Matthew flipped around and soon replaced his ass with his cock. He resumed fucking my face almost savagely, pumping his shaft down my throat. I could feel him pulling up my T-shirt to get at my cock, and I felt his hot, wet lips wrap around my shaft. Grunts filled the air as he eagerly sucked me and fucked my throat, his cock filling me before he would pull completely out, the head and piss slit dangling millimeters above my lips before he plunged them back in. He grabbed my balls and squeezed them hard, as if forcing precome to ooze from my piss slit. He eagerly lapped it up as he sucked on my rock-hard prick.

Just when I thought I was going to shoot down his throat, he rolled off me, removing my shorts and jockstrap from my ankles and sitting up. He indicated that I should join him. He kissed me hard; I could feel his tongue, coated with my own precome, enter my mouth and examine the area he had just fucked. I reached between his legs and grabbed his slick, hard shaft; I watched as I moved the foreskin back and forth over his cock. "I've never been with a guy with such a huge cock before," I said. "Or with a foreskin, for that matter."

"Yeah?" he asked, pulling my T-shirt off of me. "What do you think?"

"It's the hottest fucking cock I've ever seen."

Matthew smiled at me. "Funny you should say 'fucking'…stand up. Now turn around and put your hands by your sides." I obediently did as I was told. "March," he ordered, guiding me toward my bedroom. He pushed me facefirst on my bed. "Stick that ass up!" he bellowed, and I did. "Where do you keep the condoms and stuff?"

"Nightstand," I answered, indicating the table by the bed. He pulled the drawer open and took out a condom and tube of lubricant. "You have one sweet ass," he said, rubbing it vigorously and slapping it gently. "This is gonna be fun." I thought he would just start to fuck me, but instead I felt his tongue slowly lick my crack, his teeth nibbling the flesh of my ass before his tongue found its hot center. "Oh, man, that's so fucking hot," I groaned, as he continued to probe my hole with his tongue, forcing the whole muscle into my ass. "Oh, you definitely have a hot piece of ass here," he said, sliding his large middle finger straight up my hole. "A-a-aw," I said, as he moved it around my ass. "Feel good?" he asked. "Oh, yeah," I said. He added another finger, and I began to writhe in pleasure. "Yeah, yeah!" I said, horny as shit.

"Oh, you like that, huh?" he asked.

"Yeah, man, you're so fucking hot, you know that?"

"You are too, Trevor," he said, moving his fingers inside me again. "Fuck!" I exclaimed, as he shoved a third finger up my hole. "Got to stretch you out," he said, wiggling his fingers up my hole. "Oh, shit!" I gasped, but I meant *Oh, yes!* It felt great. After one more twist of his hand, he withdrew his fingers. My ass burned as he removed them, but I wiggled it in anticipation of what was to come.

"Ready for some hot, uncut cock?" he asked.

Damn straight I was. "Just be gentle with me," I said.

I could feel the head of his cock at my hole. "I don't do gentle," he said, right before shoving his whole cock up my tight little hole.

I saw stars. I felt all the air in my body leave me. "O-o-oh," Matthew moaned as his cock slid all the way up my hole. "Ughhh!" I said, as he pushed his cock up to my prostate. It felt as though my ass was being invaded, but as Matthew began to move his cock in and out of my hole, a warm, full feeling took over my ass. "Yeah!" I said, as I could feel Matthew's heavy balls slapping against my ass. "Fuck me, man!" "You got it, boy. I'm gonna fuck you hard!" And he did; I could hear the *thwup thwup* of his groin against my ass. Between his thrusts and my movement, he fucked me harder than anyone ever had. In and out his cock moved, filling me before he withdrew almost completely, only the head in, then thrusting, filling my hole again. In and out he went, in and out, slowly getting faster until the room was filled with the sounds of grunting and the smacking of our two bodies.

Still he fucked me; I lost track of all sensation except that between my legs at the parting of my thighs; my ass was on fire with his huge, uncut cock. One of his brawny hands reached around to stroke my throbbing tool. He squeezed my dripping member and began to jerk me in rhythm to his rocking hips. "I'm gonna come!" I shouted, feeling my legs tensing and my cock tingling. He pulled me up until I was perpendicular to the bed; with his arms wrapped around me, both hands grabbing my cock, his hips thrusting into me, I heard him shout, "Yeah, come, boy! I'm gonna shoot too!" Just then my cock shot its huge load all over the bed; glob after glob of shiny white come spilled out of my dick. "Ah, ah, ah!" I shouted in pure pleasure. "I'm coming, Trevor, I'm gonna shoot—here it comes!" With one great thrust he shot his load. I could feel his cock quivering up my asshole as he unleashed load after load of hot, sticky come.

He held me like that for a long while, our chests heaving, his head nestled against my shoulder, one of his hands wrapped around my chest while the other still held on to my cock. Finally, he released his hold on me; I fell to the bed in utter exhaustion. He fell beside me. We stared at each other. "That was some workout," I said, and we both laughed.

Matthew took a shower before going back to work. I sat in the living room in my large robe, my bed sheets tucked in my laundry bin, wondering what had just happened. One of my biggest fantasies had just come true; I never thought it could happen. Now that it had, I didn't want it to be over. Matthew had said nothing as he went into the bathroom for a shower. I guess I knew where I stood. Hey, there's nothing like a good fuck session, right?

He came out of the bathroom refreshed and handsome, his face still flushed from sex and his hair ruffled by my hair dryer. He grabbed his shoes, put them on, and headed for the door. I stood in front of him inspecting my feet. "Don't forget to write your mother back," he said, indicating the package that sat on one end of my couch. As he gave me a quick peck on the cheek, he whispered in my ear, "You can tell her you've met a really nice guy." Giving me a wink and a broad smile that matched my own, he left; I watched from my window and waved him off as he continued his delivery route.

The Guy From the Circle-X
Gen Aris

I could see it grow and lengthen down his leg, right before my eyes. Or was it only my libido and a little imagination—wishful thinking even? "It" was the cock of the tough but good-looking stud standing in front of the convenience store, insolently slouched, his strong back and shoulders supporting him against the rough concrete facade. He had a hard, indifferent look on his face, but as I waited for my brother to get his nicotine fix inside the Circle-X, I watched the hunk, and it seemed to me that he was aware of my scrutiny—and was posing for me. Was he just waiting, as I had first assumed, for a callback on the pay phone beside him, or was this dangerous-looking guy offering himself up to the night and whatever anonymous pleasure it would yield?

The old white jeans he wore emphasized his well-muscled legs and seemed to gift-wrap his crotch. I was convinced that his cock was swelling, maybe on command, to entice some action, or maybe he was that horny. By the time my brother made it back to the car, my own cock was strangling itself in my jeans, from my looking at him and wondering about what could happen.

I thought about him, regretfully, for the rest of the evening spent with my family celebrating my sister's birthday. Later that night when I drove home, my eyes were drawn as if by magnets to the front of the Circle-X—but he was long gone.

Just the thought of him, so arrogant and tough, calling up a hard-on in those tight-wrapped white jeans in front of a convenience store on a busy road, just a scant few feet beyond my windshield, was enough to bring me to immediate attention. My rod was so hurtfully hard in my jeans, I could barely stand it until I made it home and up the stairs to my second-story apartment. I fell back onto my bed without even taking my clothes off, slowing only long enough to unsnap and unzip my pants and free my tormented cock.

It was already purple-red, oozing, and mean-looking—and I hadn't even worked it yet. As I stroked it furiously, my free hand wildly explored my balls, ass, and up under my shirt to my chest and nipples. Behind my closed eyes I could see him leaning against the storefront, heatedly rubbing the front of his tight white jeans, conjuring up the demon snake within, his eyes challenging and hard, looking right into mine.

Oblivious to the nighttime traffic on Ulmerton Road, only 20 or 30 yards beyond the gas pump island, he popped the zipper down and wrestled the snake out of the confinement of its lair, boldly stroking its hard, pulsing length. I could see the head swell even more, and the vein stood out clearly along the thick member as his strong hand ran up and down his meat. He ran his other hand down under the pounding meat—cupping, scratching, and caressing his nut sac and the exposed skin of his muscular thighs.

His eyes never left mine as he pounded his swollen cock, already glistening with precome in the light of the parking lot and streetlamps overhead. He moaned and bucked violently, beating his meat even more fiercely, and heavy jets of come splattered my windshield as he came explosively.

I came at the same instant, triggered by the fantasy of him in the throes of a fierce orgasm, his throbbing cock blasting off. As I pumped out my own release, I saw his hard eyes still locked on mine as the vision faded, and I opened my eyes to the sight of my still-pulsing meat and my hands and body bathed in come. I lay there on the bed as I recovered, sticky everywhere from my prodigious shooting, still hot from the afterglow of my imagined encounter with the nameless exhibitionist stud from the Circle-X.

The next day at work, my mind wandered with images of the stud and my fantasy of the previous night. That next night, after unsuccessfully trying to keep occupied and resist the temptation, I got in the car and made the pilgrimage to the shrine—in this case, the Circle-X. He wasn't there, but I did get this month's copy of *Men's Fitness* magazine while I was out, so it wasn't a completely wasted trip. The next night I picked up the current issue of *Car and Driver,* and the next night *Motor Trend.* After a couple more nights spent picking up new magazines, instead of the good-looking hunk I really wanted to pick up, I was beginning to realize that seeing him there that one time had apparently been a fluke and that I probably wasn't going to see him again. I was let down, but my memory is good—real good—and with my eyes closed he looked as good as the first time, time after time, night after night. Again I flogged my straining dick, hot as a firecracker, looking into his arrogant, hard eyes.

Over the next two or three weeks I made an occasional random run by the Circle-X, hoping to get religion and have another vision, but he was never there. Much as I hated to accept it, it seemed that he was a one-time treat, at least in the flesh. At night, though, I worked as hard at keeping his image fresh in my mind as I did at satisfying my hungry cock.

One night, more than a month after I had given up casing the Circle-X, I found myself out of beer, and on the way to the Pick-Me-Up store less than a minute from my apartment, I suddenly had an urge to drive 10 minutes the other way, to the Circle-X. OK, so it didn't make sense, but once I thought about him, I just had to go see.

And there he was: shirtless in the hot, humid August Florida night air, in the tight white jeans of my memory, bare shoulders thrust back against the rough wall of the Circle-X. My pulse put the pedal down, and I felt the blood stirring in my groin. I pulled up in front of him and parked, staring at him. I decided to actually go into the store and buy something, anything, then try to talk to him on my way out. I nodded at him as I went by. His hard look never wavered, but he watched as I went past him, and I felt his eyes on me, behind me, as I reached the door and went in. I was so heated up, so nervous about what might happen, I could barely think. I grabbed a bottle of Coke and a six-pack of Coors as I tried to get control of both my wits and my dick. I thought to myself, *This guy could be really fun or real trouble. I wish I had some kind of clue which it was going to be.*

I work out regularly, and I'm proud of my body, but I still wouldn't want to have to get into it with some stud if he wasn't receptive to me making a pass. At 5 feet 9 inches and about 160 pounds, I'm filled out real nice and I'm solid, but this guy not only looked a hell of a lot meaner and tougher, he was about 6 foot 1 and probably outweighed me by 30 or more pounds.

When I came out of the store he looked at me with the expressionless, unwavering stare of a carnivorous predator, but my instincts, sharpened from hunting of my own, insisted that there was sexual tension there—that that was what he was hunting. So I ignored my doubts and nodded, looking him straight in the eye.

"How's it going?" I asked with feigned nonchalance.

"It's not going, at least not around here." He looked disgusted, glanced around the empty parking lot of the Circle-X, past the traffic out on the road beyond the lot, and straight into my eyes. He didn't smile or in any way show any interest, but his eyes, by then locked on mine, said that he wanted something. Or, at least, that's what I thought they said.

He nodded at the six-pack in my hand. "I was thinking about getting a beer myself. It's so fucking hot." He shrugged and waved his outstretched elbows, hands anchored in his pockets, and my eyes dropped his to follow the ripple and play of his chest and stomach muscles. He couldn't be naïve or stupid enough to miss my interest in him, but still showed no response. It was going to be up to me; I threw the dice and took the gamble.

"Sitting in this heat and drinking alone sucks, man. I got great A.C. at my apartment. How 'bout it?" I waved the six-pack in the general direction of the car.

"OK," he said without inflection, pushed off from the wall, and walked around the car to the passenger side.

In the car I was torn between heady, heated lust and twisting doubt and apprehension. In the dim light from the instrument panel and from the flickering streetlamp, he was beautiful. Thick, dark hair; well-defined, striking features; gracefully muscled arms; and big, sexy hands—and so very close. I was electrically aware of how close his arm was to mine as I shifted up through the gears.

"Air feels great," he said, breaking the tense silence. "The compressor went out at my house. I got to make up my mind to fix it or replace it. It's a bitch on nights like this. Sure can't sleep in the truck with the motor running all night to keep cool." His voice suited him. It was rough, sexy, and confident, assured. It was stirring music to my crotch. I could feel my cock shifting in my jeans.

"What's your name?" I finally remembered to ask. "Mine's Gen."

"Jack."

At my place he wordlessly followed me up the stairs and into the apartment. I flipped on the CD player. Too distracted to want to think about what to listen to, I hit PLAY and the U2 disc that was in the machine from earlier came to life. Mood music...

"Good tunes. I have that on cassette," he said, and nodded, taking the beer I was offering.

I sat down on the couch beside him but not too close yet. I still wasn't completely sure what I had brewing here—maybe one helluva wild night, or one helluva fight and a beating. I tipped up my beer, winced as I felt the pull of my sore muscles. I had been really pushing my workouts lately and had added even more weight to my upper-body routines the day before.

He watched me stretching. "You work out," he said—more a statement than a question.

"Yeah," I agreed, and told him about my progress.

He flexed his arms, pantomiming lifting. "I work out at home, but I just have free weights and a bench with a rack and leg tackle," he said, kicking out his feet as if he was doing leg extensions.

"I have a decent starter machine in my bedroom," I continued, glad that we had found some conversational ground to stand on that loosened us both up and that he clearly was interested in. "It has the butterfly attachment, leg tackle, steppers, and lat bar, so it pretty much covers the ground for now. I can do lat pull-downs, military and bench press, curls, squats, extensions, dead lifts, chins and shrugs, and more—so it's pretty decent."

He was attentive and starting to look downright enthused; his previous hard, blank expression had been replaced by his interest in the conversation and was a lot friendlier.

"Let me check it out. You mind? I wouldn't mind getting one myself, if it fits me right."

I shrugged, agreeing. "Sure, come on. I'll show you."

I led him out of the living room and down the hall into my bedroom. I'm not much for making my bed, exactly, but I do habitually at least pull the bedspread up over the mess each morning, so it wasn't too gross for unexpected company. The landfill of dirty clothes wasn't even evident, since I always pile that stuff up on the closet floor. As bachelor digs go, not bad at all, if I do say so myself.

"OK if I change stuff around?" he asked. "I want to try some pull-downs."

"Sure, go for it."

I showed him how to release the main arm to raise or lower it. He changed the bands and did sets of pull-downs, and I watched his muscles ripple seductively under his smooth, supple flesh. He swiveled around on the bench and tried out the leg tackle with some extensions. I showed him the manual that came with the machine detailing the adjustments, features, and accessories. When I ran down, I looked up to find him looking over my shoulder intently, but he dropped his eyes to meet mine. I could feel my blood boil.

"You're gay," he said, a flat statement.

I held his gaze and was silent for a long moment. I considered; his tone had been even with no obvious hostility behind it. "Yes."

His eyes wavered between mine and somewhere behind me, not like avoiding my eyes, but looking at something. I turned around and spotted the magazine thrown on the floor over on that side of my bed—the full-color centerfold man displaying his assets proudly. I turned back to him, a little embarrassed, but at least it was out in the open. *Now, what was going to come of it?* I wondered.

I looked at him, and he stared back, intensely. He seemed still as a statue, but in the back of my mind I could see, almost feel, the pulse in the side of his neck, the breath in his chest, and I could sure as hell feel my own pulse racing through my cock. Slowly, deliberately, I reached out and put my hand on his chest, feeling his heat and the solidity of him like a shock. Something flickered briefly in his eyes, though I couldn't guess what he was thinking. But he didn't pull away or draw back to punch me. I ran my hand over his chest, feeling the hard muscle and soft, smooth satin of his skin, and used my other hand to grab the back of his neck to pull him closer. I looked him in the eye and kissed him deliberately but gently. I licked his lips, and he broke from his unresponsiveness, met my kiss and more. I felt his strong arms grip me, and I felt his hands running wild up and down my hot back. My prick was engulfed in flash fire. This hot man was at last in my arms, under my hands.

I pulled him down onto the floor with me, and we rolled and thrashed around like animals in heat, as we tried to rub, stroke, grab, or fondle every part of each other's body. I could feel his hard cock through his jeans, grinding against my firm body. I was suddenly afraid I would blow my wad even before we got our clothes off. I started working on getting his Nikes off of him, and he worked on my shirt buttons, but honestly, I think a couple of them lost out to his rough enthusiasm.

Fuck 'em, I thought. That's what vacuum cleaners are for. I think I heard seams giving way too, but I was beyond caring about dumb shit like that. I unsnapped his jeans and worked the zipper, and he obligingly raised his hips and ass to let me work the tight denim down his beautiful thighs and off over his feet.

He ripped off my sneaks and then aggressively pulled my jeans open and down. When he had me free of them, Jack surprised me by hefting me up off the floor and putting me down on the bed.

I grabbed his hard shaft, pulled it, tested the weight and feel of it, and then I couldn't wait any longer. I licked the big, distended head, the pearls of precome drooling down the crown, as he bucked and reared like a bronco. I ran my tongue down the length of his meat, laved his furry ball sac, and then nipped the inside of his bulging thighs.

He moaned and thrashed as though possessed by demons. His hands were roving, exploring all over my body, grabbing, rubbing, stroking me. He fisted my throbber enthusiastically. His other hand wandered up across my shoulders to the back of my head, his hips and cock thrusting up, wanting, begging to feel my mouth on his succulent meat.

I took his cock in my mouth and swallowed his thick, hard slab down my throat hungrily and bobbed back up to the head. I sank on his shaft again, deeper each time I bobbed on it, taking time to lick and nibble the head and the juicy underside each time on the way up.

Jack was getting louder and more frenzied with each stroke, and his rhythm on my cock was getting more intense by the second. He started cranking my meat so hard, fast, and furious that I thought he was going to rip it off. But it felt so damned good, I knew I was getting right to the edge.

I sped up working on his crank, down to the root—his pubes against my face—back to the swollen head, and then back deep down to the root. I could feel the tremors in my gut and balls, and knew I was going to heaven. I could tell by his groaning and seizures that Jack was getting there with me. I went deep as Jack blasted off, uncorking a monster load down my deep throat as I shot off all over him, his hand, and me. We collapsed in a limp tangle on the bed.

After a quiet recovery he ran a hand down my shoulder and side, and sat up, silent, on the side of the bed. I sat up beside him, not touching, wondering what he was thinking afterward. I looked at him intently, and he finally turned to meet my eyes.

He wasn't embarrassed or ashamed, from what I could tell. I didn't get the impression that he felt compelled to bolt because of what he had done with me. But he sat there silently—almost, I thought, as if wanting to see what was going to happen or what I was going to say. "Stay," I said, meaning it—and hoping he would.

"OK," he answered gravely, nodding. His expression was unreadable, but I felt somehow that he was glad that I had asked, that he had wanted to stay the night, but also that he had wanted me to ask him.

"Take a shower with me?" I asked him hopefully. The thought of us, hard bodies and hard cocks together in the small shower, soaked in the warm caress of the water, was an immediate turn-on.

He nodded mutely and rose with me, and we made our unsteady way into the bathroom, where I got the water running. The warm water definitely felt good—and suggestive. Jack ran his hands through my long blond hair and down my back as we got drenched under the spray. I could feel his cock behind me, rising to the occasion already.

We ran the soap over each other's body until he grabbed me hard against him and kissed me roughly, panting with lust. I was squeezing him in my arms and could feel his powerful hands on the mounds of my ass, kneading the muscled globes like bread dough. I usually want to ride, not be ridden, but I'm flexible at times, and I sure wanted to have him, to feel him pound my ass with his meat club and to show him how good it could be. I turned my back on him and leaned against the cool tile of the shower wall, offering up my muscled ass invitingly.

He grabbed me in a rush, and I felt his fingers urgently exploring, opening and teasing my hot hole. I reached back to stroke his rock-hard prick. I was so hot for him and his fingers were pushing my buttons so hard, I wanted it now—right now.

"Put it to me, Jack," I panted. "Now," I urged him, as I danced to his finger music.

I felt the swollen cock head at my suddenly emptied hole, and he held me tightly and thrust the length of his engorged rod into my hungry butt, slowly but determinedly. I caught fire as his meat spread me open, and his lusty moans of pleasure told me it was good for him too. I could feel my hole greedily swallow it up as he bottomed out in my guts. I could feel him against my back, and his balls and pubes against my plugged butt hole.

He worked it around, stirring up my fire even more, and began working it out, sliding the length of his meat out my craving tunnel and back in, slamming home with a satisfying thump as our bodies met and merged.

Every time he banged my butt hard and bottomed out, my

drooling cock jumped and throbbed wildly. I reached one hand down under us to feel his balls and ass and the root of his prod as it withdrew and thrust again, in and out of my tortured hole. Jack was loudly groaning and carrying on, and I felt his excited bites and kisses on the back of my neck and shoulders as he rode me like a stallion in heat.

"Let's go to the bed," he said.

Withdrawing slowly and sensuously, he left my heaving, twitching hole hungry and unsatisfied. I felt empty to my guts and was gasping for breath. We managed to get out of the shower without falling or tripping over each other, and we even remembered to turn off the water. He tackled me down on the bed and grabbed my arms, wrestling them up over my head, working his well-muscled body atop me. His knees spread my legs open, and I raised my legs willingly, eagerly, up over his back.

Jack jammed his man meat back into my greedy hole, and my ass rose up to meet his strokes, hot for his fuck pole. I grabbed his hard ass cheeks and pulled him into me as hard as I could. In response he thrust furiously, hollering and moaning like crazy.

"Oh, man, oh, yeah! Your ass is so fucking good, so tight and hot," he rasped.

"Fuck me, Jack, pound me, ride my ass till you can't take it, man. Just let go and ride," I urged, uncontrollably thrashing and moaning like the lowest, cheapest slut.

Each thrust, each time he rammed his meat home in my heaving guts, I could feel the echo in my own throbbing prick, and the breath left me in a shuddering rush.

"That's it, baby. Back up on it, take it," he grunted, as he sank his shaft again into my overworked hole. He shouted and thrust frantically, powerfully driving his savage fuck tool as far up my abused ass as he could get it without climbing in after it. He was rocked in shuddering spasms as he flooded my hot hole with his geyser of come.

His last bottoming thrust had set me off, and as his hose pumped me full, I showered both our chests with my spurting jism. Creamy wad after wad splattered on us, erupting from my pulsing cock as his thrusting wound down, and he fell down on top of me, drained and exhausted. I was dazed and more fucked-out than I could ever remember being in my young life. I felt Jack's hands run through my hair affectionately, and I smiled drowsily, totally sated.

When I woke up we were wrapped up in each other's arms, and one of his heavy legs was thrown possessively over mine. The digital alarm clock showed 1:20 A.M. Jack stirred sleepily and broke out in a shy smile. It was the first time he had smiled all night, and he was a heart-stopping sight. His smile was like spring sunshine after a long, hard winter.

"What time do I need to have you home this morning?" I asked him, as I reached for the alarm clock.

He considered a moment. "Home by 6:30 or 7 should be OK, I think." He looked down, then added, "I live about four blocks from the Circle-X."

I set the alarm and put it back on the nightstand.

His strong hands were already running over my body, and my dick sprang to life almost instantly, like a switch had been thrown. He pushed me flat out on my back with a hand on my chest and looked me in the eye, while his other hand roamed down to find and catch my waking cock.

I knew what was coming, and I was a bit surprised, but at the same time immensely turned-on.

He lowered his head—shining black hair unruly from sleep, our shower, and wild sex. Jack ran his lips and tongue down my chest, tasting and teasing my nipples, down across my flat abdomen, tickling my sides. He went further down, licking, nipping, and tasting the sensitive skin of my groin and inner thighs.

I went wild at the feel and sight of him over me and on me. My meat was twitching and bobbing, calling for his attention.

He tentatively licked up the side of it, and I panted encouragement. He licked the head, and my cock danced.

He seemed to be a little shy about it but willing to try.

I was pretty sure that he had never eaten another man's meat before, and that in itself was a roaring turn-on.

He opened his mouth and started feeding on my cock, and it felt so good, I had to keep myself from grabbing his head and burying my rod in his face. He got into it as he found out how good it felt and tasted, then began to really eat it like a hungry man. I gave in to the pleasure, feeling his strong throat wrapping my cock, watching this stud sucking my dick—his first.

Watching Jack's dick throbbing and twitching without any help gave me other ideas, and I reached for him and pulled him around so I could eat his meat while I fed him mine. As soon as his cock sank into my hot mouth, his feeding frenzy on my cock meat increased tempo, and I could both feel and hear his moans around my meat stuffing his mouth.

He was jamming his crank down my throat eagerly, and I was doing a good job of trying to choke him too, but he sure as hell wasn't complaining. As the heat of our suckfest warmed his lust, his throat opened wider and deeper, and just like that, I was bottoming out my hard, throbbing meat down his throat. He had me to the root, my bush sanding his face. He took it like a real man and grabbed my ass and pulled me harder against him, at the same time hammering his shuddering shaft down the back of my throat so hard, I felt like his groin was going to bust my nose when he hit bottom.

At that, I blew uncontrollably, like a volcano, firing my load down his virgin throat, and he rewarded me with a fierce jet of cream down my own throat as he pumped away like a madman. When he pulled off my wilted cock, my dessert was trickling down his chin, and we kissed, each tasting his own cream on the other's raw lips.

"Was it like you thought it would be?" I asked him, when I had my breath back.

He looked at me, looking somewhere between surprised and disappointed. "That bad, huh? You could tell it was my first time?"

"I could tell by how you acted about it that it was your first time, but I sure couldn't have ever guessed that by how it felt," I told him, smiling, very satisfied. I looked into his eyes and held him warmly. "It was great, really—you were fantastic."

We got comfortable and went to sleep for the little bit of time left before he had to go.

The alarm brought us back to the real world abruptly. I wondered briefly how he would act this morning, as I reached for the snooze bar. The friendly hand on my shoulder pulling me close told me that Jack was still OK with the events of the night in the harsh light of day. The bad news was that we didn't have time to be more than just a little bit friendly.

In the car, I drove and he navigated. As I pulled up into his driveway I noticed that the house, not overly large or new, was very neat and well-kept. The big pickup truck in the drive was rigged out with scaffolds and toolboxes. On the side, I read the magnetic sign that told me Jack Hamilton was an independent subcontractor and builder.

I looked at Jack and waited to see what he would say. I knew right then that I really didn't want to let him get out of the car and walk away—not for too long, anyway. I also knew that he was either new to this or not completely reconciled with the idea of man and man. No matter how eagerly he had enjoyed the pleasures of that idea in the night, I realized you can't push people. It just doesn't work out in the end.

He watched me reading the truck sign and gestured to it. "That's my truck," he said evenly. "The sign's for my business; the phone numbers are for my house and for the truck phone," he added just as evenly, as if merely relating facts.

I laughed as I suddenly understood. I read the numbers off the sign and fumbled around for a pen from the map pocket.

He smiled—it was like spring sunshine after a hard winter—and squeezed my hand before he got out of the car. At the front door, he turned and waved once before putting his key into the lock.

I put the scrap with his phone numbers on the seat beside me, smiling. Next time I would see about opening up his other end. Maybe in time something else would open up—like maybe our future.

Hot Prudes
Roddy Martin

TYLER:

"So," I asked. "What's your opinion of gays in the military?"

"There aren't any."

"Huh."

I was meeting my sister at the farm, riding with her husband, the marine. "Gum?" My glance fell to the pecs that filled out his black T-shirt.

"No, thanks."

Nick was 28, blond, and tense. He hated being alone with me. Note the scrunched-up shoulders, the grip on the steering wheel. The handsome forearms.

"Fabulous landscape!" I lisped, to make him squirm.

"You should see it in May."

"Can't wait. Why are we stopping?"

"Gotta stretch my legs."

I watched Nick's jeans flex as he strode behind a tree. Glancing back, he strode behind a farther tree. What a stick! As if I needed to ogle his critical mass. We'd soon see about that.

When he returned, my fingers were laced on top of my head. My shirt was gone and my fly unbuttoned. The car keys dangled from my teeth. "Cute," he said. "Give me those."

I slid the key ring down my 20-year-old abs into my pants. "Get them yourself."

"Think I won't?"

Yeah, I thought he wouldn't...

"Figures," he muttered, groping stoically. He discovered I don't wear undershorts, that I get dense and real sticky. "Shit." Nick's hand stopped. Cupped my goods.

Began to knead. I couldn't breathe.

Nick stepped back. He pulled his T-shirt out, up, and off. I said, "Er."

"Shut it."

Coppery hair covered his chest from throat hollow to nipples, which were the same virile pink as his mouth. His hands dropped to his belt. They opened it. They opened the first fly button, and the second, and the third. Cotton briefs glowed against his skin.

He turned and pulled down the briefs. His ass was round, ripe, and brushed with fluff. I reached for it. He knocked my hand away.

We stood, naked to the knees. Nick's half hard-on bobbed above a ball sac the size of a peach. His gaze was hot on my torso. He started to stroke.

I looked him in the eye. "Let me hold it."

"No way."

"Let me suck it."

"This is wrong enough."

Having doubled in length, Nick's shaft pointed up 90 shell-white degrees. The crown was red, angry; the foreskin looked like a tourniquet. Nick was taking deep breaths, holding them high in his chest.

You could smell the precome.

I fell against the car, fucked my folded hands. "Yeah?" I puffed.

"Yeah. Happy now—"

"Fuck!"

"—Queerbait?"

Nick threw back his head. "Ugh!" He splattered on my arm, my stomach, my hip. It was hot. It was thick and I shot. I shot.

We stared at our accomplishments. I felt like shredded beef. Nick drooped without shrinking. His crown stayed red. It was pearly with spunk.

"Queerbait?" I said, cocking a brow.

Nick pulled up his pants, grabbed his shirt. "Give me the keys." We rode in silence.

DARRIN:

I'd arranged to meet with Mr. Zwick, the real estate agent. We talked about the house. Our lips got closer and closer. I fled to the bedroom.

"What's wrong?" he asked.

"My glasses. They're fogged."

"I'll wipe them for you." He advanced with predatory grace.

"Listen—"

"Oh, you are a challenge." He slithered off his tie. "I like that in a man."

Zwick had a dimple on his chin; smart hangdog eyes that caught you and pulled. He started to unbutton his shirt. Suddenly it became imperative for me to grab his face, to breathe his breath and taste his tongue.

"Ummm. Ummm." Zwick threw off the shirt, ripped open his slacks. "Ummm!" I sank to my knees, clutching his waist and pressing my cheek to the wonderful, wonderful skin.

"Whew," he said, "If you feel this way, why'd you sign with the competition?"

How to answer? Zwick's fly revealed underwear molded so tightly to the pipelike base of his erection, you could see the come tube. "Please believe," I said, licking the fabric, "I didn't call you for this."

"No problem."

"I just...what's that noise?"

"Nothing, baby." Zwick pressed my head to his crotch.

"That's not nothing, that's Gary! Hide!"

I found my husband with a washed-out couple and Onna McGloan, the rival agent. "You're home," said Gary. "You're flushed. Is anything wrong?"

"No, I—"

"We want to see the house," announced the washed-out wife.

"Of course, I—"

I was in a panic, besides which, my loins blazed. "Sure you're OK?" Gary asked, crinkling his forehead. I loved his face—so handsome, so true. Our bond was one in ten thousand. I'd never betray it for the sake of a common lay.

Like I did those other times, which were mistakes.

After five endless minutes I broke away and fixed my hair, bow tie, and tortoiseshells. I rushed to the bedroom. Was anything unfortunate in sight? Blazer? Briefcase? I rapped on the closet door. "Mr. Zwick?"

"Present."

He was completely naked and more beautiful than you can conceive—the bad-puppy gaze, the jutting pink cock with dew in the slit.

Oooh, the cock tasted wonderful. A couple gulps and it filled my throat. I felt the familiar thrill. I loved big cocks. I knew it was bad, but I wanted to be bad.

Fellatio.

I grabbed Zwick's butt cheeks. He grabbed my head and tried to pump. I didn't let him. Who cared about the in and out? I'd suck the whole damn thing.

"Uh," Zwick groaned. "I'm—"

"Dare?" It was Gary calling from down the hall. You can't say I didn't hit crossroads.

"Your assistant," Gary explained, handing me the cell phone.

"What?" I barked into it. "Hold tight, I'll see you in an hour. No, we're showing the house. Right, bye…right, bye!"

Gary eyed my hair, my complexion. "Are you sure you shouldn't take the afternoon off?"

The washed-out wife appeared. "We want to see the bedroom."

"They came all the way from Flying Hills," said Onna. My cell phone jangled.

I waited for them to visit another room. "They're almost gone," I told Zwick. "Fuck me."

"Yeah."

"Shhh. Hurry."

"Yeah." He knelt behind me. "Shit, it broke."

Another crossroad. Well…Zwick pried my cheeks apart. I whimpered. I bit my hand, but those lips, that tongue!

"God," said Zwick. "A Trojan."

"Put it on, put it on!"

The thrust was hard and fast. I screamed for joy. Then, nothing. Looking over, I saw Onna and the washed-out couple. And behind them, Gary.

ANDREW:

"Bods in the Buff will Buff your Stuff."

Incredible, but this was in the Sunday paper. Seemed the gay student union at the university was offering "Naked Maid Service" as a fund-raiser for Flood Relief.

Sure.

Liberals stop at nothing to infiltrate decent homes, but two could play the Trojan Horse game. I called the next day.

"Hey!" cackled a tenor voice.

"Hey. Is this Bods Opposed to Flood Famine?"

"Yeah, this is BOFF!"

"Do you, uh, serve straight men?"

"Sir, the only thing we care about is the green on your greenback dollar!"

I made an appointment. I had nightmares all week about a punk in leather pants who ejaculated on my foot and knelt to lick it up.

Come Saturday morning I stuck my fiancé's picture in a drawer. I paced and paced and paced, feeling too big for the room. Long and lanky due to my celibacy regimen. The Bod was due at 10 o'clock. What would he look like? Not that it mattered. All I needed was dirt for my magazine exposé on the gay agenda.

The bell rang. I took a breath, opened the door, and found myself staring at a white cotton tank suspended from two healthy shoulders.

"Hi," said its owner. "I'm Kyle, your Bod."

Kyle had neat, tawny hair. He had a sparkly grin and an warm handshake. Big, innocent eyes. He could have stepped off the cover of a gospel magazine. Or a teen rag—that tank top showed a lot.

"Mr. Martin?"

"Oh, come in, come in."

Was I confused? I didn't know the half. "You too?" the young man asked.

"Me too, what?" Kyle was holding up my Bible. I said, "Uh, yeah."

"Praise the Lord!" Beaming, he clapped me on the back. "What work wants doing?" He started to pull up his shirttail. His stomach was flat, his skin peachy and smooth.

"Care for coffee?" I stalled. "Soda? Lemonade?"

Mercifully, the shirttail fell. "Water, please." He downed it in one gulp and proceeded to chatter about religion and housework. More and more confusing.

"So, got a girlfriend?" I asked stupidly.

"Lord, no! Here's my sweetie." He flashed a snapshot. "Isn't he the most beautiful man you've ever seen?"

I said, "He's nice." And realized I'd given approval to an ungodly relationship.

Kyle set down the glass. "Well, better get busy."

Off came the shirt. For real this time. Wow. His torso was…three-dimensional, with broad latissimus dorsi in back and fingerlike muscles south of the pecs. Who'd have anticipated…my guest opened his drawstring, dropped his sweatpants.

"Moment of truth," he said, turning demurely. "Here goes." He hesitated, thumbs hooked under his briefs. "Ha," he said. "Ha ha. I don't know if I can—"

He did. I gaped at his buttocks.

And then at his penis, which curved out and down a good eight inches and was starting to inflate. Kyle blushed prettily all over. He said, "Whew, this isn't so bad.

"Now what did you say you wanted done?"

HE MAY SEEM INNOCENT…I typed these words and froze. Kyle was in the kitchen. He'd finished the dishes and was on a stepladder, wiping woodwork without being asked. *He may seem innocent*, I thought.

His butt seems innocent. Oh, my God.

Well, it did!

It seemed both firm and cuddly. His lower back dimples formed an arrow that pointed to the cleft, and you could see that really well because he pulled his knee up.

"Mr. Martin?"

"Huh?"

He stood over me. My gaze fell on the plane between his pelvic bones. "I forgot to give you these pamphlets," he said, Sunday-school earnest. "They tell about Famine Relief, which is so important."

"Thanks."

He returned to the sink, bent, and touched his toes. Suddenly I felt like the impure one. What was wrong with Kyle showing beautiful skin? With his being young, sun-kissed, 6 foot 1, and happy, happy, happy?

I got a problem below the belt.

Just went to show. If nude virility had such an effect on a journalist, think what it would do to some unsuspecting young husband and father. I meant, wife and mother. Why was I thinking in male terms?

A one-minute shower helped.

I had most of the dirt my article needed. Or at least I would once I cleared my brain. I'd send Kyle away now. I'd do it nicely.

I found him on his back with his head under the kitchen sink. He had about one third of a typical male response. It was flopped by his navel. There were streaks of seminal fluid.

I asked, "What are you doing?"

"Fixing the leak. Give me a hand, will you?"

I gave it to him. My arm hair brushed his stomach. I smelled his deodorant, studied his thigh. It was so smooth, I had an urge to stroke it. I kind of knew how it would feel. Dry and hard and soft.

Kyle sat up. "What else do you want done? I still owe you an hour."

"Um." Maybe I did need to probe deeper. "Want some tea?"

"Tea?"

"I would offer a beer, but considering your beliefs…"

"Beer's fine."

I'd purchased a six-pack especially to loosen his tongue, besides which, I was dying to know how the manly brew tasted.

I choked on the first sip.

"You OK?"

"Yeah," I said, "Why do you—"

"Why do I care about Flood Relief? Rafe. He's my lover, I showed you. His name's actually spelled Ralph, but it's pronounced…"

I'd prepared a lot of questions that would expose the BOFF axis, but knee-to-knee with Kyle, I couldn't call any to mind. Amazing. His abs stayed taut in any posture.

I noticed my beer can was half empty.

"Anyway, Rafe cares about Flood Relief, and I care about Rafe, so…"

"Why shave your pubic hair?"

Kyle shrugged, rubbed the stubble absently. "It makes me feel big."

In that case, shaving probably wasn't necessary. There was a full inch between head and circumcision scar. "Sorry," I said. "I didn't mean to stare."

"No…sweat."

A second later his organ was in my mouth. It jerked. I tasted something thick and salty.

"Ughn!" Kyle gasped, grabbed my head.

Another jerk, another shot, and another and another. His virile thighs squeezed my face. I fell back, intoxicated. Then…

"Oh! I'm going to be sick."

Kyle knocked on the bathroom door. "Mr. Martin?"

I answered through mouthwash. I was recovered more or less, stripped down to my skivvies. Kyle stepped in behind me, put his hands on my shoulders. "Don't worry. These things happen." He sounded doubtful.

I was looking at my chest. I'd almost forgotten I had one. It…wasn't bad.

"I didn't mean it to…" Kyle went on. "I'll give you your money back."

"That's not necessary."

"No, really, I'll go. I'll go."

He didn't go. He grabbed my underwear. He yanked it down and sank his teeth into my butt.

"Ahhh!"

"God, you've got a good ass." He was squeezing it, kissing it. He pulled it open, buried his face...what was he doing, and how could he do it?

I bit my lip.

Next thing, his mouth—his hot, hot mouth-was pulling my penis. I never knew such pleasure. We were rolling around the throw rug. I had one hand in his hair and the other on his damn drawstring.

"Condom," Kyle panted. His erection sprang free.

"Medicine chest."

He knelt between my legs. I felt the huge knob trying to...*yeow!* It was in. That...that shaft didn't quit. It hurt. It hurt beautifully. I reached for Kyle's torso.

"Shouldn't," he puffed, pumping hard. "Shouldn't do this. But you closet cases. So fucking hot!"

"Fuck!" I hollered. I was corrupted in every way.

After Kyle left I sat and stared. Closet case. Closet case? I went to the computer, wrote for hours. Lies of the Gay Agenda.

Roped and Steered
The Hitman

Reaching the house on Wentworth Mountain from Boston took me three hours by car—and another 10 minutes on foot after a heavy spring downpour had turned the long driveway to my friend's house into one big, sloppy mud puddle. That afternoon, I'd trudged with my bags up to the two-story passive-solar wood-frame house at the cleared center of the 80-acre mountaintop spread, sure it would all be worth it, sure I would sleep better here and return from the weekend relaxed and recharged. By 6 o'clock that Friday night I'd showered, shucked myself down to a comfortable pair of blue jeans, a T-shirt and wool socks, and had my big feet propped up on a chair in front of the woodstove, convinced my high-stress, pain-in-the-ass city job was a million miles away. A good mystery novel half read on my lap, I stared out the big bay window at the one other light on Wentworth Mountain—a house in the distance, I'd figured—then closed my eyes.

"Perfect," I sighed.

When I opened my eyes a few minutes later, the light I'd seen through the trees, mistaking it for a distant neighbor's house, had somehow gotten brighter and was jiggling its way now in the trees just beyond the slope of the property. A wave of paranoia bolted through my insides, along with flashes of scenes from that popular TV show about alien cover-ups and government conspiracies. I had just kicked my fire-warmed feet down from the chair when what sounded like a freight train roared past the bay window. I caught a glimpse of something big and heard the sloshing clunk-clunk sound of footsteps in the mud outside. By the time I'd hiked on my boots to see what the hell it was, the cold white beam of the jiggling flashlight had almost reached the house. I zipped up my coat and unbolted the house's front door.

A chill had come up over the mountain. The air was cold and raw, a mix of early spring and wood smoke from my fire. As I stood there waiting for the guy sloshing up the driveway to reach the front patio, all sorts of things filled my mind. The freight train could have been a bear, the man with the flashlight, a hunter. I mean, this was mountain country. A bear, or a moose, or hell—I thought with a chuckle—Bigfoot.

The crunch of gravel beneath work boots crew louder. With only a night sky full of stars and the beam of the flashlight, I focused on the figure.

"Hey," I shouted in a friendly voice.

The flashlight strobed from its jiggling course and homed in on me. "Hey, yourself," a deep, youthful growl answered. The man it belonged to slowed his steps and approached. "Sorry to disturb you like this, but you seen Babe?"

"You mean that movie about the talking pig?" I joked, extending a hand. The man, standing maybe a little taller than me (somewhere over six feet), met my offer and shook. His bare fingers, bearing no wedding ring, were rough and strong.

"Very funny, but in this case, she's a heifer."

"That locomotive that ran past my living room window a few minutes ago was a cow?" He nodded, and I pointed toward the level hilltop meadow surrounding the house. "I think I heard her go that way."

"Shit," the man sighed, tapping the heel of one boot against the ankle of the other. "She bolted on me when I was putting her in for the night. She's in heat. They get funny like that. I'm sorry for charging up your property like this."

"It's not mine," I said. "This place belongs to a friend on mine. I'm just here to bust some stress. Name's Craig Harper—"

"Ben Wentworth," he offered. "My friends call me Benjy." Now that my eyes had adjusted, I could see he was wearing a heavy flannel shirt and jeans, and an old ball cap over what looked to be, in the poor light, like a set of decent sideburns, neatly trimmed.

"Wentworth, like the mountain?" I asked.

"Yeah, like a jillion years ago. My great-great-something-something staked out a claim to it. All we got left now is the name and that dairy farm two miles down the hill, and even that's on the verge of bankruptcy." He took a deep breath and huffed it out. "And we'll be one cow less if I don't rope the horny bitch."

Like Benjy, I sucked in a hit of the cold, dark air. The night now smelled even rawer, like sweat, pine, flannel, and leather—the smell of Benjy Wentworth. I couldn't be sure how old he was—late 20s, I figured. But I knew I liked him immediately.

"Tell you what, neighbor," I said. "How 'bout I grab a flashlight and help you?"

Benjy smiled in the shadows. "That would be much appreciated, bro," he answered. "And like I said, my friends call me Benjy."

"Cool, Benjy," I stressed, doubling back to the house for the aforementioned flashlight. I thought I'd remembered seeing one in the mudroom when I'd first arrived, and I wasn't wrong. When I turned back, standing just outside the door now in clear view of the house's light was Benjy. The image of just how handsome he was momentarily robbed me of my breath.

His face, not shaved that day, was covered in prickly brown fuzz from the base of his nose all the way around his hard, square jaw. Two deep blue eyes met mine. I'd been right about his age—no older than 27, 28: a solid, perfect body toughened by the life of a farmer.

"You're sure you don't mind?" he asked.

Ten minutes later we were both out stalking the beast, and the real fun that night began.

"How 'bout this," I whispered after our third attempt to get the rope around Babe's neck ended in failure. "Like deer out on the highway, blinded by headlights. I'll aim my flashlight right into her eyes. When she freezes, you sneak up and lasso her."

Benjy clapped my shoulder. "Great idea, bro!"

Exchanging a shit-eating grin with him in the shadows, I assumed my approach, walking slowly up through the spongy meadow, my feet sinking down with every step. I could hear the cow's snorts 20 yards ahead of me. She'd reached the edge of the clearing and would not go beyond into the woods, like Benjy had told me. I aimed my flashlight up. Two glowing green eyes in the distance captured the flashlight's beam. Babe stood transfixed, like I had guessed she would. At her rear I saw Benjy sneak closer, rope in hand.

"Yes, bro," I growled to myself. "Get her!"

It seemed he'd finally roped the heifer, but just as he readied the lasso, his feet sank down into the earth with a loud sucking sound. The sudden noise shocked the cow. Babe bolted away out of his reach, kicking up a hail of mud. Benjy stumbled back, lost his footing, and landed with a muffled splash. I raced over to where he had fallen, only to almost join him flat on my ass in the muck.

"Son of a bitch!" he cussed loudly, his voice echoing over the mountain. "I almost had her!"

I extended a hand to help him up. Benjy took it. His bare fingers now felt cold and wet. "Bro, you're a mess," I said.

"Yeah, and freezing my fuckin' balls off for this bitch!" He jiggled the flashlight beam in Babe's imagined direction. "I can't just leave her, and there's no way she's gonna let me get close until daylight."

As much as I felt his anguish, I let out a chuckle. "Is this what people in these parts do for fun on a Friday night?"

Benjy's angry scowl softened. "Very funny."

"Seriously, bro," I persisted. "You can't blame her for being in heat. Happens to the best of us."

"I s'pose so," he smiled. With the next gust of cold wind I heard him shiver. "Shit, I'm cold," he chattered.

Looking 10 acres away toward the comforting lights of the house, I said, "You can't stay out here in this, all covered in mud. Come on—I built a fire. It's nice and warm inside. Think I saw some cans of soup in the kitchen cabinets, and I can put some fresh coffee on."

"But I'm a real mess—I'm covered in mud!"

Taking a heavy swallow, I started back up the meadow toward the house, my heart beating faster and faster. "There's a washer and dryer in the mudroom. That should take care of any mud."

Hands shaking, I spooned fresh-ground coffee into the filter and tried not to think about what it had been like to catch glimpses of Benjy as he'd stripped down in the mudroom, but I kept remembering. His old work boots had come off first, exposing the mud-soaked grime of his white socks. Ball cap, flannel shirt, and T-shirt had followed, then blue jeans. He'd popped the top button, exposing the brown curls of an untrimmed patch of man hair at the base of his washboard abs. I almost dropped the coffee filter thinking about what it had been like in the mudroom when I realized he wasn't wearing any underwear. At that moment I'd turned away to fetch him one of the big cotton blankets in the chest at the foot of the stairs—and in doing so had spied the most perfect square ass on any man I'd ever seen, an ass that was hard and frosted by the same colored fuzz that covered Benjy's face. In spite of my awe, we'd both laughed near the washing machine.

"You know how to use one of these things?" he'd joked.

"Naw, but how hard can it be?" The comment had fallen on deaf ears as I'd dumped his socks, jeans, and shirts into the soapy water. Truth was, I'd gotten half hard myself the moment I'd first met him. Now I was bone-stiff and shifting uncomfortably in my own blue jeans, wondering where my weekend—which had been meant to be a stress-buster—was leading.

The coffee dripped on, filling the kitchen with its rich aroma. I reached into the cabinet for two cups and passed the mirrored glass. My own reflection stopped me in place a second longer. At 31 I'd filled out perfectly—neat flattop, eyes that were a paler shade of blue than Benjy's, neat mustache. But I looked stressed, more than even I had realized until now.

"So this place belongs to a friend of yours?" I heard him ask. I tipped my eyes slightly away from my reflection and caught sight of Benjy, wrapped buck-assed naked in the blanket in front of the woodstove.

"Well, not really a friend. An acquaintance I helped get rich. I'm an investment planner in Boston." The coffee finished brewing. I poured.

"I don't never see anyone up here," said Benjy.

"That's 'cause this is his third house," I sighed. "He's been telling me to come up here for years. Finally I took him up on it. Been a hell of a stretch, all those problems with the foreign economies and shit. But, hey, I made it here. How do you take your java?"

"Straight up," he chuckled. As I turned around with the coffee cups in hand, I noticed Benjy flexing his bare toes in front of the fire like a contented cat. I tried not to stare, tried to look away from his long, hairy legs and big feet, the sparsely haired contours of his ripped chest; tried even harder not to wander down to the area between his legs, barely concealed beneath the corner of the blanket. At my appearance with the coffee, Benjy sat up. For an instant the blanket slipped open. I caught a flash of the meaty fullness of two fat nuts and the thick, soft tube of his cock resting against the shag of his patch before it did a logroll over his balls.

"Thanks," he said, taking the coffee cup.

I was already more hot than warm; a fresh line of sweat broke out on my forehead. I wiped at it with my arm. The pits of my T-shirt felt damp and unpleasant. I took a swig of coffee, but my heart was drumming so fast, I knew the last thing I needed was caffeine. "You doing better?" I yammered, trying to sound confident.

"Much," Benjy said. He settled back in the same big, comfortable chair I'd been in at the start of our roping adventure more than an hour earlier. He pulled the blanket back over him, but barely. With his chest and legs exposed, I was able to see how perfect his body was, from his long, flat toes up to those neat sideburns and the appeased look on his face. He drank all of his coffee, leaned forward to set the cup on the floor, and again the blanket slipped off him. I tipped my eyes at the fullness of his cock and balls. The rest of the room went out of focus. Just at that moment, when I was starting to question what was really developing here in the house high atop Wentworth Mountain, I heard the washing machine shut off. It let out a loud buzzing noise. I jumped up from my seat. "I'll throw your clothes in the dryer," I said.

No sooner had I done just that than I heard the soft, seductive patter of big bare feet on the mudroom's tiled floor. I looked up to see

Benjy hovering in the doorway, one hand scratching his balls beneath the blanket. "You need any help?"

"All set. They'll be dry in 60," I said, folding my arms, leaning my own gym-built ass against the washing machine. Benjy continued to hover at the door, hesitant, his presence and the tremor of something more filling the air with an undercurrent we both seemed to feel. He knew it. I knew it. The pressure built.

"Hey, bro," he eventually said. "I'd hate to get back into those clean things feeling so grimy, stinkin' so bad." He raised his right arm, bared the mossy patch of strangely sexy hair underneath, and aimed his nose into it. Right about the moment that I was going to ask him if he wanted to take a long, hot shower, Benjy smiled and asked, "Mind if I clean up first?"

The shower in the second-floor bathroom was a standup corner unit separate from the garden bathtub. I opened up the toiletries bag I'd dumped on the bathroom counter and fished out a bar of soap and some shampoo.

"There you go," I said. "Hot water, I think, is the one on the right."

In the breathless moment that followed, I did a half-turn toward the door but ended up going no further. Benjy's voice stopped me in my tracks.

"Ain't you gonna join me?"

I spun back to face him. "What?"

"You wanted to know what folks like me do up here for fun on a Friday night," he growled, a sexy smirk on his rugged, handsome face. "Why not come on in and I'll show you."

Even before he dropped the blanket, exposing his handsomeness fully, I eyed the fat spike of his cock sticking out through the flaps, now rock-hard at what I guessed to be a good seven inches.

"Fuck!" I sighed, nearly tripping over my own two feet in my haste to reach him. I yanked off my T-shirt with such force, I heard the stitching of one underarm rip. I quickly unbuttoned and unzipped my jeans and shoved them down together with my briefs in one push. That done, I went to my knees in front of Benjy as he grabbed the back of my head in one hand, the spear of his cock in the other.

Guiding it between my lips filled my mouth with the gamy, rugged taste of our night out on the mountain. The sweat surrounding his cock was pungent; I sucked him down, starved for him in a way I'd never thought would happen during my weekend of solitude at the mountain house.

Benjy moaned and pushed into my face, his heavy sac of bull nuts slapping my chin with each thrust. "Yeah, bro," he moaned. "Knew you were looking at my cock and balls." I mouthed a response around his dick. "And I'm glad. You're the best-looking dude I seen come up this mountain, ever!"

I looked up into Benjy's deep-blue eyes slitted half shut, the moan trapped in his throat keeping his mouth parted. He looked so handsome that his compliment about me sent a chill down my sweat-soaked spine. I gripped both of his hairy calves in my palms and traced my way up to the taut concrete of his ass cheeks. The hole between them was wet and hairy, and when he didn't stop me, I eased a finger into something so tight, I jokingly wondered to myself if he'd cut it off at the second knuckle.

"Fuck, yeah," Benjy grunted through clenched teeth. He pulled his cock out of my mouth and replaced it with his hairy nuts. Without waiting or being told to, I ran my nose, then my tongue, over the fur-covered bag of low-hangers. Like his cock, Benjy's low-hangers were heavy with the musk of an honest day's work. I lapped hungrily, sucked on his balls when licking wasn't enough. After that, to the surprise of us both, I withdrew my finger from his steaming asshole and licked my way between his legs toward it. The sour taste fueled me to probe deeper with my tongue until drunk on him.

I was face-deep in his ass when Benjy backed a step and hauled me up to my feet. Simultaneously he groped my hard-as-nails cock and smashed his mouth on top of mine, savoring—I could tell by his groans—the taste of his own maleness. Our tongues dug at each other's mouths. He pressed our cocks together. Some unaffected part of me wondered if he would reciprocate; I quickly found the answer after Benjy broke our lip lock and knelt down in front of me.

I had to steady myself on his strong shoulders. The incredible feel of his hot breath and wet mouth again sent the contours of the room spinning. Once I was sure I wouldn't pass out, I brushed a hand across one sideburn, then rubbed the other, my dick sliding in and out of the warm, unshaved lips between them.

"Benjy," I grunted, saying his name again as all the pent-up stress of the previous months unloaded to come rushing out of my cock in a geyser of hot white light.

Benjy came up behind me in the steamy mist. One hand gripped my waist as he entered. He braced the shower wall with the other and slowly pushed forward, his stubbled chin and cheek coming to a rest against my neck.

"Take it," he growled, demanded. My fuck hole, already well-soaped, resisted a moment longer before opening up to the condom-covered head of his cock. The scalding spray and incredible pressure on my guts shifted suddenly from painful to pleasurable.

The feel of him buried inside me, the gruff scratchiness of his crotch hair against my lower back, restored a playfulness inside me I'd thought long dead. Smiling, I leaned over and kissed him, and each time he pushed in I shoved back to meet his thrusts.

"Here it comes, bro," Benjy announced breathlessly. I barely heard his broken pledge over the streaming shower, but I'd felt it first—the quick fuck pumps growing quicker, the tightening of his nuts, which were no longer slapping against the bottom of my ass.

Benjy pushed in, howled, and blew. He'd shoot again later that night many times, as would I—but we lost track of loads, positions, and hours in the warmth of the house on the mountain.

The sun rose up through the pines. I watched Benjy dress as I pulled on my own clothes. "Time to rustle us some cattle," I joked, but he seemed torn as he donned the last of his things, his ball cap. Wordlessly he saluted me by running his strong, skilled fingers across the bill.

We found Babe down in the meadow, lazily chewing on the sod. Unlike the way she had reacted to us 12 hours before in the darkness, by daylight we were able to approach her without too much of a struggle. Benjy roped her. She resisted at first but finally gave in and clip-clopped after him. We started back toward the drive that would take them both down the hill and back to the duties of the dairy farm.

"You want to see the place?" he asked. There was a tremor in his voice. "It might be one of your last chances to."

Suddenly I understood what was bothering him, and I knew my decision to come to this place had been one of the smartest in my life. "Benjy, you ever think about investing? I mean, I could help you with that. In fact, I been thinking about it all night."

He seemed dumbfounded by the notion. "I wouldn't know how, where to begin."

"You wouldn't need to. You'd leave that to me." We paused on the drive and, in the silence of the next few seconds, exchanged a bottled look into each other's eyes. "Trust me," I smiled.

"I already do," Benjy nodded. "So, you wanna see the farm?"

"Sure, but give me 10 minutes first."

A dejected look replaced his smile, like my delay tactic was a Dear John or a brush-off. "Ten minutes, I swear," I promised.

As I watched him salute me again, his handsome smile conjuring so many images of the night before, I thought of all the things I could do for him and all that he could do for me in return.

Back at the house, I picked up the phone and dialed. On a Saturday morning, I knew the only thing I'd get was automated voice mail. I keyed in my supervisor's extension.

"Hi, Dave, it's Craig," I said. "Something's come up. I'm not gonna be in the office all next week, but I will be working on some new investments, from Wentworth…"

Assume the Position
Jay Starre

It was rough—four weeks of hell had just ended, although it was only for a weekend, then back we'd be at army training camp. I was sick of it and happy to get away for a couple of days. Thing was, I didn't know a soul in the godforsaken Midwestern state where our base was located.

"Want to go to Chicago? We can share a room." I heard a tentative voice asking.

I turned and confronted one of my fellow soldiers. Aaron Stacy stood there with an enthusiastic grin plastered all over his handsome face. The redheaded stud looked like an eager puppy. I didn't have the heart to say no. Later, I was very glad I had agreed.

We took the train and arrived in the evening, ready to hit the bars. The Windy City proved to be an alcoholic heaven: We were plastered before 11 P.M. We managed to find a seedy little hotel room that had only one small double bed. We had been sleeping in creaky bunks, so it looked like heaven.

I collapsed on the bed and gazed up at Aaron. He was standing there, uncertain, weaving on his feet, staring down at me with the weirdest expression on his face. "You don't mind us sleeping in the same bed?" he finally asked, his voice trembling.

I laughed. "You can sleep on the floor, soldier!" I barked out, mimicking our drill sergeant's gruff voice.

"Yessir!" Aaron snapped to attention and saluted, his body erect, although still weaving.

I looked at him and laughed again. His eyes were on the wall. What the hell was the matter with him? I had been joking. Then I happened to glance down and realized Aaron had a distinct bulge in the front of his khakis. I sat up and stared. He had a boner!

I looked back up at him with more interest. I had been spending every minute for the past month with other men, sweating, grunting, fighting, showering naked, sleeping in a crowded bunker. Men with hard bodies, with dicks and balls and asses. I was horny, I had to admit it. Now I was alone with this young stud, a short body thick with muscle, standing there at attention but drunk and vulnerable and with a big damn hard-on to boot. What was I to do?

"Get undressed, soldier! Snap to it, fucker!" My voice whipped out in the small room. I watched him, wondering if he would laugh it off or what. To my amazement, he obeyed with alacrity.

"Sir, yessir! All of my clothes, sir?" he snapped back. He was already tearing off his shirt.

"You can leave on your boots and tags!" I practically yelled. Why the hell I was yelling, I didn't know. I was drunk, but there was more to it. I had a lot of pent-up emotions boiling in me, and suddenly they were coming out.

Whatever Aaron was thinking, he was sure quick to strip. I watched him with keen interest. His naked chest was taut, two big pecs with no hair, two dark nipples that looked stiff and hard. His skin was alabaster-pale, smooth, and thick with muscle. He jumped around awkwardly as he stripped off his pants over his boots, but managed without falling, which was a near-miracle in his drunken state. Then he skinned down his army-green boxers and stood back to attention.

A big, hard dick stuck right out from his crotch. It was thick and fat, suiting his stocky body. A pair of plump nads hung down below that dick, nestled between two very hefty thighs. A patch of flaming-red hair surrounded the base of his hard pole; otherwise he didn't have so much as another hair on his smooth, fleshy body. He was expressionless as he stood there, although his entire body was trembling. His dick throbbed, jerking in time to the trembling of his limbs.

I took a deep breath to keep myself from shaking too. I moved around behind him in the small room, my own body only inches from his but not quite touching it. I shouted in his ear. "Assume the position!"

He snapped to, lifting up his arms and flexing them behind his neck, spreading his thick thighs and planting his booted feet wide apart. I almost laughed again—I had no idea of what I had meant for him to do, but what he did was just fine with me. I was wondering how far I could go with this bullshit—and smirking secretly behind Aaron's back as my mind raced ahead to a number of exciting scenarios.

But I had to catch my breath again as I surveyed the hunk standing before me. What a body! His broad shoulders bulged as he held up his crossed arms, the brawny biceps heavy with muscle. The V of his back descended toward a narrow waist, then curved back out in the swell of his ass cheeks. I stared down at them, round and full, so white and hairless they didn't look real. He had the most perfect skin I had ever seen. He was standing at attention, but he was shaking violently, and those two big butt mounds were quaking in erratic spasms that had me gasping with lust.

I wanted nothing more than to reach out and grab hold of those plump ass cheeks and squeeze and squeeze before pulling them apart and shoving something in the deep crevice between them—my fingers, my face, or my hard dick straining at the fly of my khakis.

"Assume the position!" I barked again, although I didn't know why the hell I did. I was drunk, but I was not quite drunk enough to grab Aaron's ass and do what I wanted to it. So I yelled instead.

What Aaron was drunk enough to do was another matter. My mouth actually fell open when he responded to my shouted order. He yelled back "Yessir!" and leaped forward. Jumping on top of the small bed, he landed on his hands and knees, pressing his head down into the mattress.

There he was splayed out on all fours, with his beautiful naked ass in the air, his face down, and his big ball sac dangling down between his hairless thighs. I guessed that was the position he assumed I meant.

What could I do? I stripped so fast I fell down. While he remained on all fours on the bed, his plump white ass quivering, I sprawled on the floor, ripping off my pants and shirt and underwear. I kept my eyes on that butt, getting a good look at the spread crack and a small crinkled opening peeking out between those white cheeks. I crawled forward when I had managed to get my clothes off and got up behind him, on my knees at the edge of the bed. His big ass was level with my face.

I had my eyeballs fastened on that puckered hole as I reached out, grasped one big butt cheek with each hand and dove into Aaron's crack. Right on target, my mouth connected with his ass slot, opening wide and smothering the hole with my lips and wet tongue.

"Sir, lick my ass, sir!" Aaron shouted out.

I had to stifle a hysterical burst of laughter. Aaron was really into this game! I was really into licking his smooth ass crack. There was only one thing on my mind at that moment—the silky smooth flesh that was burning my tongue and lips as I swiped and licked and tongued up and down that hairless crack. I slobbered on the puckered rim of his butt hole, jabbing my tongue at the opening, which quivered and convulsed in response. That sweet hole opened up to my tongue, and I was entering the tight confines beyond. I tasted male funk, inhaled musky soldier butt and crotch odor, and jabbed deeper with my tongue.

"Sir, please, sir, yessir, tongue my slot, get in there deep, sir!" Aaron was shouting out, although his voice was breaking and his breath was coming in gasps.

I spit all over his crack, moving one of my hands in to add it to my mouth. I slid a finger into his quivering anus alongside my tongue, jabbing past the first knuckle. He squealed, and his thighs splayed wider. "Sir!" he shouted. I rammed that finger as deep as I could, the slippery saliva I was gobbing all over his hole easing the entrance. His fuck hole was a tight channel, viselike around my digging finger. I worked it around, trying to stretch him out, but he remained tight as a drum. I came up for air, staring down at my finger buried up his butt hole, spit glistening all over his hairless crack.

His butt was up in the air, squirming around in circles as my finger frigged in and out of that tight little hole. His head was on his folded arms, his face turned to the side. I could see his expression, his mouth open and drool in the corners. His eyes screwed shut in concentration, beads of sweat on his forehead.

"I'm going to fuck your poor butt hole, soldier! You are going to have to open up that tight slot for my big, hard dick! Understand?" I barked out. I had no idea of what I was going to say beforehand. The words just came out.

"Sir, fuck my tight hole! Open me up with your big dick! I can take it, sir!" He replied, wiggling his plump white butt as my finger twisted deep in his guts.

"Assume the position, fuck boy!" I yelled out crazily. My finger up his clamping asshole was driving me nuts. It was incredibly hot and exciting—I was almost ready to shoot just from that alone.

I wondered what he would do this time. I found out. He squirmed around onto his back, reached down and clasped his legs behind the knees, then pulled them back to his chest. My finger remained up his chute all the while. He must have known what he was doing: His asshole opened up just a bit in that position, with his thighs pulled wide and his ass up in the air.

I stared down at that tempting target. I stood up, pulling my finger out of his clamping fuck channel. The small ring of muscle gaped open for a second, then clamped back down, drool oozing out of the tight lips. I spit back down on his crack while I massaged my hard pole and spit on it too. I pointed it down into his parted cheeks and shoved it up against that hot hole. The ass lips pulsed around my dick head.

I was gasping, the intensity of my own lust nearly too much. My dick looked huge next to that small slot. I am well over six feet tall, with long limbs and an equally long dick. The head of my rod was beet-red, contrasting sharply with the pale flesh of Aaron's hairless butt. The thing would never fit inside that tight channel.

"Sir, fuck my poor butt hole with your big dick! Stick it up me, sir!" Aaron grunted out, his face as red as my dick head.

Oh, well, what was I to do? I spit down on my dick and rubbed it into the head and his tight hole. I grasped the shaft with one hand, spread his cheeks with the other hand, and began to shove. Goddamn, it was so tight! But the spongy flesh began to stretch apart so that the tapered head began to go inside him.

"YES! SIR!" he shrieked. He shoved upward with his hips, impaling himself on the entire head of my dick.

"FUCK YOU, SOLDIER!" I shrieked back. The clamping vise around my dick head throbbed with painful force. I drove my hips forward and crammed half my dick inside Aaron's straining guts. I used both hands and pulled apart his ass cheeks. Then I shoved again, and my balls were nestled up against his spit-coated butt.

Aaron was whimpering, his face rolling from side to side, his mouth open and his eyes clamped shut. "Look at me, soldier!" I yelled.

He did. His eyes opened, the look of agony in them easy to read. "Open up that butt hole, soldier! Work that tight ass around my dick like you love it!" I ordered, my voice steely.

It worked. He looked up into my eyes, his soft green orbs melting as he began to writhe his hips up and down over my dick. I felt his tight channel caress my pole with its confining walls, and I held my dick still to let him get used to it. He began to loosen up.

I looked down, tearing my eyes from his. The tight ass lips were swollen and puckered around my shaft, stretched and straining as he worked his ass up and down. My dick went in and out like the steady pumping of a piston.

"That's it, soldier, work that tight ass over my big soldier dick!" I grunted.

"Yes sir, yes sir, yes sir!" he was moaning. I caught his eyes again, which seemed to help. He began to writhe around in circles, working his hole over my dick with quicker strokes. I looked down and saw his own dick was ramrod-hard on his belly, as red as mine. It was oozing a steady stream of precome. His fat balls were swollen huge, and I reached out and took hold of them, rolling them and squeezing them in my hands.

"You gotta unload these big fuckers, soldier! You gotta fuck yourself over my hard pole so hard that your poor nuts ain't got no choice but to juice themselves." I said, my voice lower, but the steel in it harsher as I rolled and squeezed his fat balls.

He groaned, his thighs quivering wider, his hips rising up into my hands and at the same time impaling his spit-slick ass channel over the entire length of my dick. He was huffing and grunting so loud, he couldn't reply.

"Soldier! Answer me!" I growled, squeezing his sac and jabbing at his hole with my dick.

He squealed. "Sir! Yessir! Make me unload my balls! Fuck the jizz out of me!"

I grinned. Then I let myself go crazy. With his big body sprawled out naked and wide open, his asshole snug around my dick, his balls in my hands, I gritted my teeth and went for it. "I'm gonna fuck your poor soldier butt hole to a squishy, slutty mash! I'm gonna fuck you till you come!" I shouted.

I pounded into him. He writhed and squirmed and mewled beneath me. I rammed my soldier pole in and out of his fuck cave, stretching it open with every violent thrust. He punctuated each stab with a shouted "Yessir!" His whole body went limp eventually, his previously snug butt hole gaping open as he lay there and took it. I squeezed and yanked on his nut sac with every shove.

It was more than I could take. Sweat flew off my face and ran down into my eyes. The mewling soldier beneath me was the victor as I couldn't hold back and felt my own balls roil, my guts clench, and my dick begin to spurt. I yanked my pistoning meat out of his spitty asshole and shot white cream all over his sweaty, pink butt cheeks.

"Sir! Come all over my butt!" Aaron shouted out. I was gasping, unable to reply as I looked up into his eyes. He was grinning, the fucker!

Then he shot his own load. His ass lifted up off the bed, his asshole clenched and convulsed, his balls pulled up tight against the base of his dick, and come spurted out of the purple head all over his white hairless belly. I collapsed on top of him, out of breath and suddenly remembering how drunk I was. His big, warm body felt terrific in my arms. He smelled like sweat and sex and come. I was shaking.

Then I looked into his eyes again. The green irises were sparkling. He was laughing. Then he grasped my head between his hands and shouted in my face.

"Assume the position!"

So I got fucked. What a weekend. Can't wait till next time.

Down the Hall
Pierce Lloyd

Being the only out student in a men's dormitory at a midsize private school isn't always easy. Being gay and attending a fairly conservative institution isn't always easy either.

When I began my senior year, I had been out to most of my friends for three years and to my family for two years. I had worked for the university every year since I began school but quit my job senior year to focus on my studies. I kept living in the dorms because it was significantly less expensive than renting an apartment.

I lived on the top floor of an all-male dorm. This became an asset to me because part of the research my professor and I were working on involved studying groups that share living spaces. We had received a sizable grant, and while Dr. Lawson had decided to conduct research in a nursing home, he asked me if I would help him to research a college dormitory. In addition to observing the students' socialization, my duties included checking on several students' well-being. As part of the study, twice a week I was required to go into each dorm room and ask all the students on my floor how their schoolwork was going, whether they were having any problems, etc. Then I had to fill out reports.

Unfortunately, as with most studies, there was a dilemma. I couldn't question any individuals without their permission, and few guys on the floor had any inclination to participate. It didn't help that, being older, quieter, and gay, I wasn't the most popular resident.

Then, after one unfortunate weekend of wild partying all over the building, circumstances worked out in my favor. A number of guys on the floor were written up for disciplinary measures—after being observed running through the building drunk and screaming. They were notified that they were in danger of being put on probation or even expelled from the dorm. The resident adviser offered them the chance to do community service to offset one of their disciplinary reports, and they all jumped at the opportunity.

He presented them with several options, including my project, and everyone chose to participate in the study. I guess answering questions twice a week beats picking up trash on fraternity row.

The first week went off without a hitch. I knocked on each door, reintroduced myself to the guys I had only met in passing, and filled out my reports. Most of the guys on the floor were on athletic scholarships. There were basketball players and tennis players and one or two hockey players. The rest were all thinking about pledging fraternities.

Then at about week 2 I noticed that something was up. Rumors began buzzing about my sexuality. Now, let me be up-front about this: I'm not a very political person. I come out to those I want to come out to. I don't worry about the rest. If someone asks me honestly, I'll be happy to tell him. But I don't make any big announcements. It's easier that way.

Anyway, I began noticing that the guys were watching me more closely. Maybe I'd left an issue of a national gay newspaper lying around when my door was open, but I'm sure I've been careful about where I keep the latest *Freshmen*. Maybe one of them had class with someone who knew me. Maybe they'd heard me through the walls the night I picked up a muscular stud at the gym.

None of my neighbors approached me specifically, but these guys weren't particularly mature. Most of them were just 18, and they'd brought with them the usual stereotypes and misconceptions that their high school buddies had instilled in them. Eventually the university experience would open most of their minds. It just takes awhile.

Every group of guys has a ringleader, and on our floor it was Gavin. He was a tennis player, tall and lean with dark hair, intense brown eyes, and a pathologically mischievous personality. Some of the guys hung on his every word, and the rest seemed to at least respect him. I soon got the impression that he'd never met a gay man and found the prospect not threatening but somehow hysterically funny. With Gavin in charge of the social climate of the floor, things began to take a turn for the bizarre.

It started one evening as I was doing my reports. As I approached the room that Gavin shared with his roommate, a shy blond swimmer named Patrick, I heard a voice say "He's coming!" and then the sound of giggling. I knocked at the door, which was slightly open, and heard a melodious voice say "Come in!"

The first thing I saw when I opened the door was Gavin, a big smile on his face, wearing only a pair of boxers—around his knees. His soft dick was big and circumcised.

"Hey, Steve. What's up?" he said. I glanced around the room and saw there were four other guys present, all standing around facing me, all with their underwear at half-mast. Gavin was the best-hung. Patrick had real blond pubic hair, and he was blushing bright-red. He looked pretty uncomfortable, but he was exposing himself just the same. All of the guys were pretty well-built, particularly Joey, who stood only about 5 foot 6 but had massive pecs and arms. He also had a pretty big ball sac, I noticed.

"Having some trouble getting dressed?" I asked.

"Gosh, it's just been a long day. I like to get back to my room and let it hang free," Gavin swung his big cock around.

I knew they were taunting me, but I was determined not to let it faze me. I wanted to prove that I was above this childishness, that it didn't bother me.

"Whatever makes you comfortable," I said. "It's your room." I forced myself to look at his eyes and nowhere else as I asked my list of questions. I moved on to the next boy, and the next. When I got to Patrick I heard Gavin say loudly, "Oops. I think I dropped your pencil. Better pick it up." I turned just in time to see Joey bending over, pointing his well-formed ass in my direction.

If I had been at all in doubt before, by now it was quite obvious that they were trying to get my goat. I quickly looked away and pointedly said, "You guys have a good night—whatever it is you do in here." When I shut the door behind me, I heard Joey and Gavin collapsing with laughter.

Soon the joke spread to the entire floor, and within two days the guys were naked nearly all of the time. They even walked down the hall naked, their tight bodies presumably meant to tease me and get some kind of a reaction. The resident adviser soon put a stop to the hallway nudity, since the hall was a public place. But all the guys started answering their doors in various states of undress—the shy ones stripping to their underwear and the bolder ones, like Gavin and his crowd, going buck naked. Soon most of the guys abandoned the use of shower curtains in the bathrooms, preferring to soap up their muscular frames in full view of the entire room.

Technically, it was sexual harassment. These young men were using their bodies to try to get a rise out of me. If I were a female, it would have been a clear-cut case. But I wasn't a female, and I guess that's what kept me from taking any kind of action against the guys. I may be gay, but I'm just as much man as anyone else, and I was determined to take it like a man.

Besides, although I hate to admit it, it's not often I get treated to such a smorgasbord of young male flesh. Practically every day I was confronted with beautiful bodies daring me to look at them.

I also began to suspect that the constant nudity was increasing the camaraderie on the floor 10-fold. Most first semesters were tense times, and it seemed like these young men were bonding like no other floor I'd seen. One day, I observed the only uncut guy on the floor, horse-hung Sven, giving a demonstration of his foreskin to four fascinated onlookers. He showed them how it retracted, and many of them were surprised to learn that his dick head was moist, not dry like theirs. In a way, the atmosphere was even educational. But the sexual tension for me was fierce and continued to be stepped up.

I knocked, as usual, on Gavin and Patrick's door. When I came in they were all completely nude, as was their custom now. I was asking Gavin about his week, looking directly at his eyes (my custom) when

I realized he had taken his cock in his hand and was stroking it. I tried not to look, but out of the corner of my eye I saw that it was growing under his touch. Joey, who could never control his laughter, began giggling, and when Gavin's attention was on Joey, I stole a glance at his prick.

Completely erect now, Gavin sported about eight inches of prime cock. I looked up to find Gavin meeting my gaze.

"Problems, Gavin?" I said dryly, trying to project the image that I was simply bemused by his efforts.

"I don't know what it is," he began. "I just have this...itch." He began stroking his dick faster, really jerking off now.

"Well, that's too bad," I said, moving to the next guy in the room. I tried to ignore the sounds of Gavin masturbating. The other boys smirked and pretended nothing was happening. When I finished talking to Patrick (who looked as shy as usual, although I allowed myself to notice that he had the most amazing abs I'd ever seen), I heard Gavin moaning.

"U-u-ungh...I think I'm gonna shoot a load!"

I looked over to see that Gavin's lying on his bed, spread-eagle, furiously spanking his cock.

"Anyone...here...want...to watch...me...come?" he grunted. In fact, we were all watching as he arched his back and shot spurt after spurt of creamy white semen onto his chest.

He sighed. "I feel much better now." Joey was laughing so hard he fell to the floor and kicked into the air, his nuts jiggling in my direction as he did so.

I excused myself and went to my room. Once there I pulled out my cock, which had been hard but hidden by my briefs during the whole encounter. I jerked off, the image of Gavin's orgasm burned into my brain.

Late that night there was a knock at the door. I threw on some shorts and answered it. There stood Patrick, clad only in a pair of boxers.

"Can I come in?" he asked. "I want to talk to you about something."

"Sure, come on in," I said, ushering him in. Fearing this could be another game, I left the door open.

"Can we please shut the door?" he asked. "I really want to talk to you in private." I let him shut the door.

"What's up?" I asked brightly.

"There are two things I wanted to tell you," Patrick said. "First is that I'm…I'm really sorry about what the guys are doing to you. I think it's stupid and mean, and I wish I had the guts to stand up to them and say something about it. But I don't know many people here, and I don't want to be the odd man out."

"Oh, it's no big deal. They'll get bored with it in time."

"No, it is to me. It feels wrong, and I'm sorry I've been a part of it."

"Well," I said, "I appreciate that, and I accept your apology. And the next time you greet me at the door with your cock hanging out, I'll try not to stare too hard."

He laughed at that. "So," I said, "what's the second thing?"

"The second thing I want to tell you…" His voice trailed off. He swallowed. "I want you. I've wanted you since I met you. I've never told anybody this, but I think I'm gay."

He was trembling. I reached out to put a hand on his shoulder reassuringly, but he threw his arms around me and embraced me.

My mind raced. On the one hand, he was attractive and I wanted very much to kiss him. On the other hand, it could still be part of an elaborate joke. On the one hand, I was four years older than he was. On the other hand, he was an adult with a mind of his own. On the one hand, his hand was rubbing my back as he buried his head in my chest. On the other hand…

Well, his other hand was working its way down into my boxers.

I gasped when he grabbed my cock with his right hand and began fondling it with a feather touch.

"I want you so much…" he said. I answered his unspoken question by kissing him deeply.

I came up for air and joked, "Now, this isn't just another game, is it?" In response Patrick knelt on the floor and started kissing and licking my cock head.

I liked this game.

"I guess not," I said as I sat down on my bed. Patrick pulled off my shorts and continued giving my crotch a tongue bath.

I allowed him to do this for a while while I remained passive, then I stood him up and stripped off his boxers. His naked body was a sight I'd seen several times before, but the seven-inch erection he was sporting was a new touch. We lay on my bed in a sixty-nine position, and I slurped greedily at his hard-on.

I pried apart his ass cheeks and located his tight hole with my fingers. I massaged and stroked it until it relaxed a little. I wet a finger with saliva and poked it inside, just up to the first knuckle. Patrick gasped at the sensation.

"Do you want me to stop?" I asked.

"No," he said, "Don't even think about stopping."

More confident now, I slipped more of my finger into his virgin butt. When the whole finger was in, I inserted another one and probed around inside his ass. I kept sucking his cock. He paused in his oral ministrations to moan.

"I'm gonna come," he said. No sooner were the words out of his mouth than he was shooting a hot load of semen at the back of my throat.

I was more aroused than I had ever been. I was thinking of things I wanted to do with Patrick that I would never before have allowed myself to think.

He lay motionless on the bed as I fished a tube of my favorite lubricant out of the nightstand. I squirted some into his butt and he giggled.

"That feels funny," he said.

"I'll make it feel all right," I said. "Roll over."

Obediently he rolled over onto his stomach. I put a pillow under his crotch so that his ass was sticking up in the air. With two fingers I eased his hole open again and spread the lube around inside him.

When he was good and greasy I straddled his butt. "I've never done this before," he said. "Be gentle."

I was surprised at the ease with which his hole opened up for me as I slid my cock head into him. Then, just as I slipped the first inch and a half of my erection past it, his ass ring clamped shut around my manhood. Slowly I massaged it into relaxation and eased the rest of myself into him.

His virgin ass took all of me in and then gripped my dick like a vise as I pumped it rhythmically into him.

I took a long look at Patrick, his tight little body strewn out on the bed for my pleasure, his back arched and his ass raised to greet me as he moaned into my pillow. I turned around to see his toes curling up from the sensations I was drilling into him.

I leaned forward as I fucked him faster. I breathed in the sweat and shampoo smell of his hair as I shot my load deep into him.

I withdrew and collapsed next to him on the bed. He put his arms around me and pulled me in tight.

Later that night he sneaked off to his own room. We were fuck buddies for the rest of the year.

The sexually charged, naked atmosphere on the floor never did completely go away. The guys just got so used to it, they kept it up. And more than a few of them caught on to the fact that they weren't just teasing me, but they were teasing each other. If you were to walk through the hall late at night, at many doors you would hear beds creaking, a youthful voice moaning in pleasure or the distinctive sound of balls slapping against an ass.

And my door was no different.

Hurricane Brass
R.W. Clinger

I've radioed for help to the mainland (26 miles away), and help—presumably—will be on its way within moments. I am trapped on Caldon Island, a private and tiny slip of land in the Atlantic off the coast of Miami that my dearest, rich, and queer friend, Mathew Kind, owns. A hurricane approaches (112 miles away, Category 5, moving about 9 miles an hour), and I must be saved or I will drown alone and horny!

"Mathew? Mathew?" I calmly say the name into the radio; it's the second time I've radioed for help. "Mathew…I know you probably have a cock up your ass or in your mouth, but could you get me help out here?"

A scratchy reply sounds from the radio, but before I can decipher it out, the radio dies.

Ferocious winds lift up from the lip of the shore and blow toward the wobbling windows and me. The steady, impulsive tempest drives me to think I will never lap up the juicy salt of another man's sweat in my short life. Never will there be another cock to tease! Another nipple ring to brush fingers against! Another bicep to press lips to. And never…Dear Queer Jesus, get me out of this storm!…will there be a hulking man between my legs, lapping up white hot come from my stiff inner thighs, begging for more and more me, calling me King, or Master, or even Hurricane!

I am a prisoner within the island house, with its expensive niceness. My partners are a stiff rod and hard nipples that need to be pulled and bitten, my only wish of island wishes. I dread the approaching storm and the tyrannical windy rain outside. I hear a voice coming from the radio on the floor, rush to it, pick up the mechanical device, and hear a strong, masculine voice that utters with sincerity and bravery, "I'm coming..."

I've heard this phrase many times before, perhaps uncountable times, usually from my boyfriends on hot summer days or (preferably) nights in July or August when I press my cock into their mouths and needy, begging asses. But this voice sounds rather unreal, perhaps even heated and devouring—heavy with a sense of erotic masculinity, testosterone-packed, willed to put me in my place—and forces my cock to twitch with deep-seeded need and survival tips in my chinos shorts.

I pick up the radio transmitter and say quite quickly, "Who's there?"

"Brass" is the only thing I hear, which confuses me, but makes me hard and harder, horny to the point of question, and the radio goes dead again immediately.

There is vodka (my favorite) to drink, and I take advantage of it. I pour one for myself and one for my rescuing hero—if he ever comes. I stare out into the storm and wait...wait...wait...not believing I will survive.

Something happens that is completely unbelievable, though. Hurricane or no hurricane, I think I am dreaming, but I know I'm not. I see through the rain someone approaching the island house by boat. In the distance the hero rides waves like fag lovers moving on a water bed...to and fro, up and down. The boat connects to shore, and a stranger jumps out and approaches the house running, dressed in nothing more than a pair of wet camo-green shorts that are plastered to his moving, gliding body. His big shoulders, Howie Long–shaped chest, almost black crew cut, cocoa-cream colored good looks, and thighs that are the size of palm trunks greet me with awe and new, precome-filled excitement. The stranger taps on the glass window of the front door as I place my martini down on a marble table. He looks delicious and thirsty, wet and glistening, tight and smooth, perfectly edible; a treat before a storm—how marvelous!

I walk over with ease and peer at his naked chest, his tight, green shorts, his massive and dark nipples that are the size of oysters. Dreamy and violet-colored eyes stare at me as the stranger taps on the glass. I see a Marines tattoo on one shoulder, then a tiny splotch of wet and glistening black hair that stretches from the center of his solid, rippling, and well-built abs down into tight meat-packed shorts. Immediately, having relief flush over me (as well as blood to my strong, hard cock), I quickly open the door and say with a pompous and ludicrous smile, perhaps even in a semidrunken manner, "Where the fuck have you been? I could be killed out here."

He eyes my golden-boy niceness up and down. He sees that I am dry and perhaps envies me—a power I have over him almost instantly. Mr. Macho marine man, with his Latino-colored skin, looks at the outline of my 10-inch cock and says with a Spanish accent, "My name is Brass...Mathew sent me."

I want to see if he is real or if I am too drunk, or if the queer gods in Pink Heaven have blessed me with such a firm stud's kindness. I touch his bicep with a overblown, perhaps careless manner, and introduce myself, "I'm Owen Snare...Mathew's friend...Do you have the canny ability to get us out of this mess?" His bicep is everything that I'm intended for. It is silky, smooth, and hard under my grasp. It can lift me and half a dozen blond, modellike men with chiseled chins and perfect icy-blond hair, if in need.

Brass's eyes keep a steady, intoxicating gaze on my solid outlined package. He—unknowingly—licks his plump, red lips and reaches down to his own cock, readjusting a nice-size package (that I easily estimate at eight soft inches) and says with direct authority, "I brought a boat for you. Someone's got to save your ass."

"Who's going to do that?" I count his six-pack. I am not afraid of him—I have had bigger game. Forward me touches his tattoo, rolls a finger over Earth and anchor and rope. I find the strip of black hair on his chest then and run two fingers up and down it, willed to get the shit beat of me or fucked, whichever comes first. Brass stands still, doesn't move, becomes hard in front of me with my touching, my clever and devious, horny fingers. He is soaked and slippery with Atlantic storm covering his body, salty and grinning with ease in front of me, and quiet. The hulking man's eyes drift up to my hand-some, debonair, and flawless face. I'm the most attractive man he has ever seen. I'm model-sweet. Every muscle in place. Every eyelash bat-ting for him. Every tooth twinkling with a sense of keen brilliance. I'm his wet dream come true, his bathroom magazine–brazen boy, everything that a military man has always wanted but is too afraid to scoop up. Yes, Brass has wanted something like me for months to slip his teeth and lips into (and something else too?), for a cutie man like me to come around and be held, nibbled on, and possibly cured by his Earth, anchor, and rope.

I run my finger along his green-cotton covered cock that goes from eight soft inches to nine hard inches and then a surprising 10...but doesn't stop there (no, sir!), flying into 11 polelike inches that could knock a building down, take an island out, strap a man like me between his legs and blow, blow, blow me away like a fucking hurri-cane. The top of his marine meat pops out of the rim of his green shorts and peaks with an island hello. It is purple and devilish, cut and horny, lined with muscles, and needs a greeting, which I most certainly share.

I snatch a hold of hardening, muscled USA meat on Bulky Guy and briskly yell in the whipping wind by the opened door, "Marine, I asked you a question! Who's going to save me from this island?"

He's turned-on by my grasp and replies, "You're going to die out here if I don't take you back."

I hassle him. The wind whips through my blond hair and over my white cotton shirt, separating the material from my chest, exposing one of my hard and bronze nipples. I have him right where I want him, I believe, because he drools over my boy-toy chest, because he needs a man who is bossy and bitchy and...he needs someone to fin-ger his tattoo, his chest, and his hardening, anchorlike rod.

He pulls away, though, and this pisses me off. Brass sees the radio on the floor and lunges after it, breaks the sexual concentration and devotion between us. His hand is twice the size of the radio. Massive sausage-sized fingers press buttons on the radio, and he speaks into it, "Base 1? Base 1...Brass here?"

No one answers. We are trapped together on the island. Blondie with Hurricane Brass—intended niceness. "There's no one there, Brass. Just you and me," I say. The words sound like sugar on my tongue. The words are what he wants to hear, but he won't ever mention them to his bar friends or the guys that hang out with him in the gym, pumping weights. He looks up at me with concern, both hands on the radio now, wind pushing him closer to me, drawing us together, attempting to seal or glue us into one meat slab of queer newness.

"Fuck that, Brass...we got better things to do than to worry about the mainland." I knock the radio out of his hand, and it flies to the floor with a loud crack that sounds like lightning or bones breaking. Fierce and tempestuous wind cranks louder, brushes over our bodies, through our hair, and over rippled muscles. I ask him, "What's your plan of action, since the radio is dead?"

Brass doesn't have time to answer me, though. What becomes of the moment is a scene out of some action flick with Jean-Claude Van Damme versus hottie Howie Long. Hard-bodied muscle-head Brass knocks both of us down by the pushing wind that flushes inside the house. He rushes toward me because he has lost his balance, causing both of us to fall to the floor. His hands spread and press against my hard, rippling body as we fall, practically cupped together. Brass has his head pressed into my cock region, which is nothing more than a slippery, southern, and heated equator where his mouth meets outlined, needed poker.

I say to him, "You don't waste any time on your plans, do you?"

My legs are spread, and he looks up between them, grins in his Latino, lust-driven manner. His violet eyes twinkle with a sense of blond need and emphatic desire. His shoulders glisten with a warm, sweaty kind of perspiration that can drive a fag lover into hysterics, make a pompous stud (like me) believe that he is Mr. World. I imagine his lip bleeding for some reason, which is a major turn-on as I feel him graze my hard, thumping island shaft with an opened, tongue-splintering mouth.

In his Spanish accent Brass says, "We can't fuck around...We have to get off this island."

But I don't listen to him. I sit up slightly, take the adventure in, peel out of my shirt, and then reach out for the back of his military-cut head and press his mouth over my chinos-covered, marine-needy shaft and command him, "I'm in charge of this operation, man. You'll do what I say."

"But the hurricane is coming." He looks up at me with those infatuating twinkles in his eyes. He is harmless and surprised at my needs. He is meaty and bold and begins to move away, but I press his head against my thick and stiff rod.

"We've got plenty of time to spare. Check the air pressure while you're down there."

Brass gurgles something under my weighty hands about not wanting to taste me, about not wanting to lap up some of my creamy new precome that has seeped out of the tippy top of my Owen rod for him to sweeten up his wet, day-saving mouth.

"Do your job, Marine. Don't waste my time. The sooner we get this over with, the sooner we can get off this island." I instruct the massive man over me, pushing his head into the V-shaped area of my spread legs.

He moves lips over outlined chinos. He makes my meaty friend in my pants more firm, makes it bulge with a growing passion and need to spurt sea juice up and over on my chiseled, nicely designed, rippled chest.

"Practice makes perfect on these expeditions," I whisper, as thunder roars overhead, as the hurricane heading toward Miami creeps closer and closer to the perfect hidden island in the Atlantic, destined to cause damage and uproar. As I lay with his tongue massaging hard chinos, I imagine sipping or licking martini liquid off his erect chest, sucking his seashell-size nipples. I imagine choking to death with his massive, atomic rod in my mouth, gagging me.

"Sirrr..." Brass gurgles under my working and moving hands, slobbering on my chinos and hidden cock. "Sir...I can't breathe." I hear him croak in his sober and saving voice. He is drowning over me, sucking dry cock and expensive fabric. Brass gurgles things I can't hear correctly, words that sound like a foreign language or indistinguishable phrases of terror or exhaustion, as if he has water in his mouth.

"Can't get enough, can you? Is the weather too bad down there for you?" I ask in a most pompously delivered manner. I am turned-on by his digging and probing and chanting over me. Of course, he is stronger than me and can pull off at any time, but Master Man down between my sweaty, throbbing, and delighted legs is intoxicated by my rushed and thunderous smells, by my threatening cock and chinos, sucking on whatever he can find, probing and digging with tongue, enjoying the windy, stranded moment on Mathew's island…just the two of us causing a fleshy tempest of our own.

Brass doesn't answer me. Brass pulls chinos down, and my rod slaps against his face. He sucks on the head of 10-inch me, cuddling my freshly shaved balls with one hand, rolling fingers over scrotum sac, teasing me.

I lay on Mathew's floor, arch my back, allow Hurricane Brass to cup his tongue over my pumped weather vane as hard rain splinters the abode's roof, as Mathew's hired-marine gurgles between my legs; laps up Owen cock into his slender mouth, pressing genuine, dark tongue against slick veins and pulsating man pole, allowing me to whisper nothing more than "Marooned."

Brass comes up for air, but I press his head down to finish his job. He laps more and more, making me harder and harder, causing me to believe that with my swelled dick both of us could float to safety off the island, through the torrid waves of the ocean, and into each other's arms on dry land.

I pump his raging, working mouth. I buck Owen stem into his throat and chant in a whimsical, devilish manner, "This is a storm you won't forget," as he toys with my pressure-packed left nipple, pulling at it with his free hand, twisting the flesh with manly presumptions that cause fluttering brilliance to shift to and fro behind my dreaming eyelids.

He's pissed, though. Brass has had enough of my direction, my sinister greediness. He pulls off my precome-leaking, marine-needy tool, his chest rising and falling, thunder raking over the island, nipples hard and pointed, and, exasperated, says, "This is a job that needs some secret maneuvers for survival."

And indeed it does.

I am determined to not give into his petty challenge, laughing as he first slips out of his camo shorts and slaps his hard 11-inch Latino cock against my juicy driver. He says something quick like, "It's time you let me do my job and keep your mouth shut."

Briskly turning him on, feeling both of his hands on my cock and balls, caressing my fresh, Caribbeanlike skin, I add, "Mathew doesn't pay you to talk. Mathew pays you for action and your physical power and—"

Brass breaks off my words quickly, "And action and power is what you're going to get."

A marine is taught to be prepared. A hired Marine is always prepared. He has a condom in his shorts, rips it open, slips it onto his 11 inches of throbbing, pumped niceness, and spreads my legs as if he were breaking me into two directions, east and west. Brass looks down at me, smiles in a delectable and charming manner (perhaps sharing a survival tip with me), and whispers, "Ready, Snare?"

I don't have time to answer. Brass has his fingers twisting my pecs as he pushes his glistening body part into mine, moaning, pressing eight inches into me, nine, 10, and giving that last inch a thrust that could seal the deal between him, Mathew, and myself with man glue.

He pumps everything he has into me as thunder roars, as rain and wind captures the island. He pulls at my neck and nipples with utter deliciousness, rubs my abs with pointed fingers, presses his cock into me, breaking me, pulls out, presses in again. It feels as if I'm a tight harbor and he's docking his boat-size cock into me. He whispers things in Spanish above me, slaps my hips, spreads my legs, and stares at me with his violet-eyed greed and necessity.

As the door behind him bangs on its hinges, I moan, "Brass…" I am powerless under his weight. He arches my back and pulls me over him, promotes his cock to slip deeper and deeper into my torso, spreading me away from the mainland and island, washing me with his sweat, dripping beads of sea water that choke me as they fall into the farthest reaches of my opened and awestruck mouth.

"Services rendered," he groans above me, all 6 foot 2 of Latino meat punching me with island passion, with what I will whisper into Mathew's ear later over new martinis, "Brass bliss."

Snatching onto my cock with his right hand, Brass begins to jolt my meat beast up and down, saying, "Time for a change of winds, Owen." He presses his long and strong fingers into my rod, pushes a drop of come to the tippy top of the erect slab, which prompts him to finger it even more, and allows the single drop to fall to my chest in a foreshadowing event of warmness.

I buck my hips, unable to keep an Owen storm under control. I can't help myself by his massive, slicked, and pulsating beauty above me. As I rock in his hand, he bucks inside me, pushing all 11 inches deeper and deeper into me, touching his dark and dangling balls to mine. Brass thrusts hard, both with hips and hands, allowing me to send warning signals with my moans like the wind outside, signaling that I am inevitably going to explode all over him.

I hear the familiar phrase again…"I'm coming"…as he jolts forward with his hips, pulls back, keeping his hands moving on my own stiff piece of brass, quickly pulls out of me, withdraws the condom off his oarlike rod, tosses it to the side…and we flush come over each other as if it is now raining inside the island abode like outside.

White spew flushes over my chest from his seeping, dripping, spitting cock head. Brass moves one of his hands up and down on my rod as his other hand generously rotates on his own slab of stormy meat. Man goo splashes our rippling-ab torsos. A sticky storm of jism flushes over our bodies with ease, both of our hips raging like the storm's motion outside, each of us gasping as our breath rises and falls, allowing our creamy stud spurts to decorate our skin with tropical coconut-colored beauty.

"Saved," he grunts with a glowing smile, smoothing his hot and furious come over my abs up to my chin, and fingers it into my mouth, teasing me, completing our stranded moment together.

Minutes later we grab our shorts and nothing more, willed to escape the island. Our hips touch as we exit the house and step out into the beating hurricane, allowing the seawater to wash man come from our supine bodies. Before running to the boat that will steer us to safety and dry land, Brass lifts me with his hulking, massive arms, draws my pecs to his lips, my nipples, and then my lips. My new boyfriend shoves his tongue down the sliver of my throat, eventually pulls it out, and informs me, "Hurricanes always make me horny."

I don't object.

The 10-inch Fix
Lance Rush

The warm night seems to percolate, waiting for something, or someone, hot to blow upon. It's my 25th birthday, so Kyle and I slip on our leather jackets and set out to get our dicks wet. We amble along neon streets, high on anticipation, shooting gazes at faded crotches with cock-starved eyes.

"Mmm! Big-prick alert!" Kyle warns. "Hot body. But shit! Bet he's packing a goddamn sock! Fuckin' false advertiser! Where have all the big dicks gone?" he protests, with an ironic chuckle.

He's fishing for a compliment. Before we were roommates, Kyle used to be a stripper, and to his mind, this makes him a minor celebrity. Truth is, he was the shit, for like 15 minutes. Doesn't matter. He's 5 foot 10, 175 pounds, with a patented bad boy's face and wavy brown hair. He could get by on his tanned, well-buffed body alone. But if that wasn't enough, he swings a big natural dick. It's cut, thick, with an unusually large head (to match its owner), and Kyle's a firm nine-inch believer that something so big and pretty should not be kept in his pants.

Walking beside him, he garners men's attention with his surly, street-tough looks and slow, syncopated bop. Me? I'm taller, darker, a quiet, less showy type. But this night my cock's breathing with a fire to fuck.

"Damn this! Let's grab a cab," Kyle suggests. He stands cornerside, holding his prick. Barely raises a brawny arm before one stops. In the backseat he starts fucking with me. He did that shit often, trying to get a rise out of me. His hand crawls up my thigh in a strong, confident grip. He knows in his balls that he can have me for the taking. His eyes pierce through the dark and he asks, "Why so tense? Loosen up, dude! The night is young, we're both hung, and it's your birthday!"

That slow, wandering hand settles on my lifting dick, rubbing and caressing it until the fucker's stone-rigid. I glance forward, the driver's ignoring us. Maybe it's the wild exhibitionist in Kyle that makes him so bold—he unzips me right there in the fucking cab! Ah! Shit! A wicked swipe of his tongue has me forgetting we're even in a freaking taxi! Mmm! I'm being taken down, inch by throbbing inch, drowning in his hot, rushing mouth! Yes! Both my fucking heads are spinning!

He wrestles with his cock until a nine-inch spike pokes hard and high from his lap. I latch on to his steely rod as he gobbles me down in loud cock swallows! I'm pulsing in spittle as I flog his long shiny dick. His mouth drags me down his slick gullet until my balls pulse at the pucker of his lips. Shit! There's a real fearlessness in his sucking! From his rearview mirror the cabbie watches us. Kyle doesn't give a fuck! Not even the jolt of potholes slow his ravenous suck. Smooth tongue and slobber peruse and polish every throbbing cock vein. I grab a shock of frantic hair and ride, driving his reckless face. He pulls away, shadowed in rushing city light, his full lips wet, and appraises it by whispering, "Decent dick, Lance. You just need to exercise it more," then going back to the bone. Groping my balls, he laps my drumming shaft. *Oh!* His tongue and my quick sliding hand are willful conspirators, boiling up come to the surface of our pricks! Yes! I feel a rush as he's spraying a gummy slime through my fist! I moan so low, I pray that fucking cabbie can't hear me.

My breaths are ragged gasps, and I'm nearing that orgasmic edge. With a quickness I push Kyle away and shoot in wild thrusts to the floor and vinyl seats, breathing like a long-distance runner. Cream keeps shooting, oozing forth, as Kyle keeps jacking, whacking my jittery dick! Whew!

We'd hardly tucked our gooey cocks away before we'd reached our destination: The Mirage. Notorious for exotic street trade, it's a denim, leather, come-as-you-are bar. 10 minutes later, we'd checked our clothes down to jocks and Timberlands. My eyes swept the room of sweaty dancing torsos until my radar goes off. I see him, standing feet away, alone, hot. *Hello.* I'm in deep, deep lust with the face, the physique of a tall black man. My eyes molest the lean brown sweep of him.

He's Harlem handsome: Toasted-almond skin. Direct eyes, real intense. A trendy little goatee. A sly, almost dangerous smile. He's got a mop of militant hair fighting between an afro and loose dreads. He stands 6 foot 3, maybe 200 cut, crunched and chiseled pounds. His outstretched supporter abounds—a thick, unseen chocolate treat. His strong black thighs are full and flexing. I check the ass. It's a tight, deep-brown, jutting mold. And he and it look so fuckable.

"Mmm! Yum! Bet he's not packing a fuckin' sock!" Kyle says, nudging me right into the man!

"This place is a zoo tonight. Way too crowded!" this hot stranger bellows.

"What? What did you say, man?" I yell.

"It's too TIGHT!" he screams.

"Yeah! Sure is!" I holler. But my mind is yelling *It's tight, all right. So is that body, those nipples, that big, pushing dick mound. Screw a freaking birthday cake! Just break me off a slab of that!*

The club song "Finally" begins to pump. Kyle and I hit the crowded floor and move like two horny men, on fire with rhythm and sex. Through driving beats we dance and dance until we're gleaming from the heat of a primal sweat. A few of Kyle's fans muscle through the crowd and start rubbing him—rubbing his legs, his naked ass, and he's in his element, clearly loving it. Suddenly that tall, handsome black brother who'd stolen my eye catches me by my waist! I spin around and there he is, pumping, grinding me hotter under my jock! Hello! It's too fucking *loud* to talk, to think of anything other than sex. Our bodies speak the same language. I realize, he's got That Thing. It defies description, but when a man has *it*, in droves, sparks fly. This night, invisible sparks seemed to fly off his skin, his smile. On a dance floor they turn into slow fires, and I'm drawn to his every licking flame. All this fire and smoke commands my fullest attention.

"I'm Tommy. Tommy King," he yells. "So…what are you into?"

"YOU!" I howl.

He grins. Ah! Yes! This Thomas King dude definitely has that *thing*. In the middle of a nasty groove he grabs my neck, pulls my face to his. We stare and breathe, and then, we kiss. Ah! Long and hot, daring and wet. Man! My fast heart becomes a bass line, pumping, thumping! He clutches my ass, pushes that hot writhing body against mine. All I feel is joint! A big, hard wall of meat flexing under a damp jock—and it's growing bigger, harder! I plant long, sucking kisses all across the taut brown scope of him. I lacquer his neck, his sweat-glazed shoulders. I lick his dense, wiry pits; spin and nibble on his dime-size man tits. I glide down each hard abdominal disc and slowly orbit his navel! Oh! His skin's like cocoa butter—and I just can't get enough!

"You wanna fuck around some?" he boldly asks. He's not shy. I like that!

My cock and I answer, "HELL YEAH!"

The wide intrusion of his prick shifts against mine. Then he steps back, looks around, and slowly peels down that jock. *Motherfuck!* Dick. Big, Thick, Elongated Black Dick takes my fucking breath as its hostäge! From my view of his basket I knew he packed some serious inches. I'd expected a big, firm, Harlem-bred boner, but damn! A fucking dick this imposing should be called "Richard"! Must be at least 10 inches of uncut, cock-strong meat, projecting straight as an arrow, willing me to do something! But there's so much, I don't know where to start!

"Suck me off, if you can!" he's challenging me, smack-dab in the middle of the dance floor. I'm hypnotized by its deep, dark, pulsating shaft, its doorknob head. He whips out a gold packet and slides a condom along his erecting monument. Then in a New York second he grabs my chin and feeds its steaming tip to my lips. I open wide enough to enclose his broad crown as it pushes through in a succulent stab! The shaft's smooth but heavy with vibration. Further down, fucker gets hot! He bucks, and I'm lapping vast meat, making perverse sounds to the beat of the music. Men dance around us as I suck on a fucking cock that tests the limits of my throat, my jaw! He pushes, and I'm gagging on neon-and-spit-drenched dick! I pull back, still determined to possess it.

Clutching big swinging balls, I led him into my motion. "Oh! That's fantastic!" he screams above the crowd. He clasps his thighs to my jerking neck, starts shaking in a kinkier dance than the rest. "Ease up, man," he pants. "Damn! Sure like dick, don't you? Let's go check out the backroom."

Our pricks stab a path through the mayhem. The backroom's packed. The high odor of cock and ass is everywhere. Every corner's filled with men moaning, men groaning, men writhing in near darkness. Somewhere in that mix Kyle's fucking, sucking someone. I glance at Tommy's body. It's a taut, ripped, heaving machine. But my eyes kept clinging to his long, dark dick—how, even limp, it hung and played drums along his mid thigh. No way he and his dick will fit in this room.

"Wait up. I used to tend bar here. There's another floor upstairs. Follow me," he says.

He leads me up a flight of winding stairs and into a smaller room. It's got a glass DJ's booth. Inside there's an old turntable, a soundboard, a swivel chair, and a gang of disco albums. A mess of spent condoms wrappers litter the floor. Tommy drops that jock. He flops to the chair, broad cock battling up his belly. He stares at me, like… like…my asshole's in for the time of its little brown life.

"Now, I want you to sit on this big fucking dick and ride it!" he bullies in this new take-charge voice. "And I don't want you squealing like some first-time faggot, either!" What up with the tough-guy attitude?! Who was he now, Bogart? But his pole's enormous, and he damn well knows it! It looms like a spear: long, thick, flawless in mold. Its freaking width threatens to break the safe he's sliding along its hub. Fucker juts straight up and wavers!

Those eyes howl *Come on!* Standing before him, my bone oozing, I lower down on his waiting prong, slowly absorbing its mighty flesh! Ah! *O-o-oh!* Slowly it bores through me, aching and hot with unexpected heat! A *mad pain* boils in me! As it jabs, Tommy flashes the grin of man with a massive dick, proud of the pain it inflicts. He lets that stout fucker marinate in the stew of my ass. I strain, clutching tight to his flex. Then, he pushes. *Ah! Aww! Oh! Shit!*

I feel something rip, tear in my core, and I shiver! When he lunges deeper, feels like a freaking torpedo's being launched up my asshole! Awww! I grunt against the steady slicing of his brutal pipe as he sets this intense and blazing fuck rhythm, sending that dick deeper up the bud of my gripping anus. Shit! My nipples prick him, digging into the swell of his panting chest.

"Like it, baby?" he asks with a plunge. "Want more?" he taunts, his tongue rattling in my ear. That wet tongue darts my torso. He wiggles, jamming his dick deeper. His hands sail down my belly. Yes! He's fucking me and whipping my rod with wicked-hard strokes! I'm rising up and down this big, ass-battering cock. The pain of 10 expansive inches slowly dissolves into pleasure.

"So...uh, what's your name, again?" he asks, in mid–banging thrust.

"Aw! Ah! L-L-Lance," I jabbered.

"I knew you liked me, Lance. I could tell," he sighs, lips going down slowly on me. Oh! Yes! He's fucking and purring in my pubic hair like a fine Persian cat! As he strokes my rod I feel its jism tearing down my thigh. My dick's a hard, unruly fucker propelling into the air, inches from his lips. He gazes at its plum knob dripping in juice, and he huffs, between deep slamming thrusts, "Motherfucking dick looks like it's about to bust! Get up. I think I want some of that!"

He "thinks" he wants me to fuck him? Hell! I'm so violently erect, I'm ready for anything! As I leave the stab of his invading prick, I wince painfully in its bloated absence. Thomas stands, hard cock shooting vertically up his belly. Sizable balls dangle from a pitch-black thicket. He turns, massaging the copper slopes of a perfect ass. I can't resist the urge to jab a digit up his chute. There's space to spare, and so I stab him with two. Oh! Man! He gapes that pretty brown hole wide, wider, until I'm mesmerized by its spiral. His hips rotate in slow figure eights. Every etched muscle in his thighs, his ass, trembles as he cries out, "I want you to fuck me!" Then he sighs, tightening his hole until it snatches my finger in its clutch!

He bends over the mixing board, tempting me with mounds of chocolate spice. I'm so excited, I can barely rubber my cock in my rush to fuck that meaty ass. My prick juices. I crouch in a low squat as he parts those gorgeous pear-shaped globes. I enter him with a cock-strong urgency, pushing through his beckoning asshole in one sound—thrust! Ah! Shit! A warm vise hugs and grips, cradling every fraction of my dick! Already it's raping me of my load, pulling me deeper in its heat. It's milking my balls, my breath! I'm wondering, *What kind of ass am I fucking here?*

Pulling back and aiming deep, I thrust, but he catches me in his mounds. Sweat beads on us, hot. "Fuck me!" I want to hit it slow, but he wants to be fucked fast, faster. I pump his demanding pucker hole as it expands like some elastic spit ring along my jolting dick. In and out, harder, quicker I'm thrusting, ramming through that gripping groove with every fucking inch I've got!

"Come on! Fuck that ass!" he insists, clamping down on me. But the ass intensity's too much! Every nerve of my cock helmet pulses! These nuts are choking the base of my thrusting shaft!

"Fuck! Damn it! Fuck it like a man! Shit! Throw it to me! Give me all that dick!" he yells. But I'm slipping into my own come nirvana! I grab Tommy's rigid dick and piston it in my fist. A charge of come vibrates through it. This seismic sensation sets me off! Spurts of jism rip through his dick. He comes in explosive, gushing rapid-fires, one after the next. Fisting his hot slimy meat, I detonate with a fury, blasting in gobs of white cock lava! He spasms, and I'm shaking fiercely as my come explodes in whipping sprays to the rubber up his ass! For a few humid moments we can't move.

"Man! That was…just…just…HOT DAMN! You're a…real…wild one, Lance!" he pants.

"Dude. We're…wild…together!!" I puff. "Too fuckin' hot…for…words. Just think…I almost didn't come out…tonight," I huff, staring at his 10-inch fix, a dick that launched an instant crush!

"But you had to, Lance. You deserve to bust a nut. I mean, it *is* your birthday, right?" he asks.

"Yeah. But, wait! How the hell did you know that?"

"Kyle. We used to club-hop back in the day. Even stripped at the same place. Hey! You look surprised. But it was his idea to come here, right? See, he wanted to sure you'd have a good time, and...well, he thought we'd dig each other. I guess he was right, huh? Happy birthday, man. Don't be mad! Shit! I consider tonight a gift for both of us," he smiles.

Damn that Kyle! I don't know whether I should be pissed or happy. But looking at Tommy's big, come-dripping cock, well, my asshole and I settle for the latter. We head back to that main room, that writhing lake of fire, filled with hot sweaty men.

We meet up with a sly, grinning Kyle. The devious fucker nasty-dances up to us, grabs our jocks, gives them a squeeze, and asks, "Hey! Was it fun draining these damn things? They sure FEEL content. Happy birthday, Lance. You can thank me later," he laughs, in a roar above the pumping music.

And we all danced ourselves, electric. By 5 A.M., as the three of us left the joint, we were washed in sweat, sporting damn near 30 inches of rigid-hard dick and ready to fuck again!

Straight Up
Hal Reeves

Why is it that small towns seem even smaller on hot summer days? Is it because everybody's at home in front of the air conditioner, leaving the streets deserted? Or because all the rubes have taken off for some theme park or camping site? And why is it that I always seem to get stuck between sales assignments in some asshole town where there's nothing to do but drink?

Fortunately, the town I was stuck in that day at least had a main street and a bar, though they called it a saloon. It was one of those dark wood-paneled places that smelled of beer and stale cigarettes, an odor I find agreeable and comforting.

At first I had to adjust my eyes to the dimness of the cavernous, empty room, but soon my sun-induced blindness left, and I could see the standard jukebox, pool table, assorted round tables bolted to the floor, and long mahogany bar. The place was empty, and for a moment I didn't even see the bartender. But within a few seconds he came out from the back carrying a case of whiskey, which he slammed down behind the bar. He was young and beefy, built kind of like a wrestler, which was probably the favorite sport in this nowhere hamlet.

"Directions or a drink?" he asked, rubbing the top of the bar with a damp cloth.

"Drink. Gin and tonic."

I watched him pour the liquor, kind of fascinated by his looks. Although he was young and handsome, his thick hair was so blond, it was almost white. Equally blond were his bushy eyebrows and mustache. It seemed like he should have had blue eyes, but they were brown. He looked kind of like a fantasy stud out of a science fiction movie. I must have been staring too long, because he suddenly said, "Was there something else you wanted?"

"No," I stammered, uncomfortable about being caught staring.

"Because it's a little early for pretzels or salted nuts," he said, smiling and looking at his watch.

"Yeah, I know. I finished my work early. Didn't feel like going back to the hotel. There's not much to do in this town, is there?"

"There's nothing to do in this town, buddy. We don't even have a cathouse any more. Paula took off for Chicago."

"Was she the madam?"

"Madam? Shit, she was the only pussy in town the past few years. Said she couldn't make a living on a few farmers and some horny high school kids."

"Yeah, well, things are tough all over," I said sarcastically. "This place is pretty quiet."

"During the week it's empty. But I make up for it on the weekends. Gets pretty wild in here," he said, putting his elbows toward me to rub his shoulders. I could see that his armpit hair, which stuck out from the sleeveless T-shirt, was also platinum-blond.

The room seemed a little steamy to me, or maybe it was just seeing his muscular arms and the definition of his big tits in the white T-shirt. "Maybe I should have a cold beer," I said. "Might be a better cooler on a day like this."

The bartender brought the beer, and when he placed it in front of me, he laughed.

"What's so funny?" I asked.

"I was just thinking about a guy who came in here last year. Summer day. Hotter than this. And my cooler wasn't working, so the beer was warm. And the place was empty, like now. And even before he orders a beer he's got an attitude. You know. Like, this is a shit town and he can't wait till the train leaves. And, you know, kind of talks to me like I'm his servant."

So far the humor of this story was eluding me, but I enjoyed watching the bartender talk and looking at his beautiful lips and even white teeth.

"Anyway," he continued, "he takes one gulp of the beer and nearly spits it out, saying, 'This beer tastes like piss.' "

I imagined I would now hear about the fight that ensued and how this handsome, heroic bartender tossed the guy out on his ass, but I continued to feign interest.

"Anyway, I was getting real tired of this guy's crap, and I had had a couple of brews myself, so I grab a stein and whip out my cock and piss into it. Then I slam it down on the bar and say, 'You got it wrong, mister. This tastes like piss,' figuring he'll get up and leave."

"And did he?" I ask, realizing his story has taken an interesting turn.

"No. He just looks at me with my dick still hanging out and smiles. Then you know what he does? Picks up the mug, gives me a big smile and says 'I'll drink to that,' and—swear to God—starts to take a swig of my piss."

"You're kidding. He drank your piss?"

"Nah. Once I saw he was willing to do that, I offered him something better."

"What? Chivas Regal?"

"Better than that," the bartender said, hesitating as if he were testing me before he told me any more of the story. But he didn't say anything, just started wiping the already clean bar and shifting ashtrays. I looked at his muscular arms, and when he turned away to put the gin bottle back on the shelf, I stared at his hard, round ass encased in the dark-blue denim of his jeans. When I looked up I could see him looking at me in the mirror as if he knew what I was staring at. I smiled and pursued the story. "Come on, tell me. What did you give this guy that was better than your piss?"

He turned around and looked in my eyes, his lips curled up in a cruel smile. "I gave him the opportunity to suck on my dick—go right to the source, so to speak. I could tell that was what he wanted. So after I let him chew on it for about half an hour, I gave him a pint of fresh cream."

I picked up the beer bottle but could feel it shaking in my hand, so I put it back down. The bartender was still looking at me, as if waiting for a comment. "Do you think that's what I want?" I finally stuttered.

"Don't know what you want. I know what I want," he said, reaching under the bar for a cigarette and lighter. When he took the first drag he blew the smoke my way, and I could feel his hot breath in the smoke.

"What do you want?" I asked.

"I want you to come around here and give me a blow job," he said, taking another drag, "and if you get tired of doing that, you can kiss my ass."

"What if somebody comes in?"

"Not a chance," he said. "Besides, this bar is tall and deep. You can keep a lot of things under a bar like this. Cartons. Supplies. Little things like coasters. And big things, like this." When he said this he stood back against the far wall, and I could see he had already pulled out his cock and was holding it in his hand. It wasn't fully hard yet, but was massive even in its semiflaccid state. It was uncut, and the foreskin was halfway back on the huge knob. The odd thing was, as hot as it made me, I was also wondering why this guy was stuck in this crummy bar (and town) when he had the kind of show-piece that could make him a fortune. But I wasn't about to debate the point, since I was practically salivating at the thought of sucking his dick.

So I moved around to the back of the bar.

When I came around he handed me a towel, which I put on the floor to protect the knees of my suit. Then I knelt down and started to service him. Once I was down on the floor, my nostrils were filled with the combined odors of the damp wooden planks, the stench of spilled beer, and best of all, the scent of sweaty balls and a slightly gamy foreskin. I had to open my mouth really wide to take his crown; it had been a long time since I'd felt any difficulty with a guy's shaft, but this one required maneuvering. I must have been doing it right, because the bartender kept pumping his meat slowly into my mouth, murmuring his approval with the right sighs and groans. Then I felt his hand on the back of my neck. "Slow down," he said. "I've got a customer."

I took my mouth off him, but he grabbed my head and pushed his cock back in. I tried to be as still as possible while still chewing on his joint.

"Give me somethin' light, Ed," I heard a deep voice say. At least now I knew whose sweaty cock was in my mouth.

"Sure, right away," Ed said, moving only slightly to open an ice bin nearby and reach for a glass. When he poured he said, "I haven't seen you in here for a while."

"No. I was in the country with the wife and kids. Had to get away from this fucking town for a while."

"Um. Pretty dull after the Fourth."

"After the Fourth? Hell, it's pretty dull any time. Since Paula left I can't even get a decent blow job."

"What about some of those hot little high school girls?" Ed said, pushing his cock deeper into my mouth.

"No way. I would never fool around with jailbait. Especially in my position. You crazy, Ed?"

"Well, you're not supposed to be drinking on the job either."

"There's nothing happening out there. Besides, who's to say I can't come in for a ginger ale. After all, cops get thirsty too."

Now I was nervous. I was giving a blow job right in front of a cop. All he had to do was lean over the bar to see me down on my knees. If Ed was nervous, his prick didn't show it. It was rock-hard and dripping with precome every few seconds. He even reached down to pull it out of my mouth and push my head into his blond bush and huge, sweaty nuts. As soon as I tasted them, I didn't give a shit anymore and began to find it erotic that a cop was within a foot of me.

"You look different today, Ed. Kind of nervous. Everything OK?"

"Sure. Fine. Just the heat. Makes me kind of restless, I guess."

"Doesn't make me restless," the cop said. "Makes me horny."

"Yeah, I know. But in a town like this, what can you do?" Ed said sympathetically, and just as he did he shot a load in my mouth. I could feel his whole body tense, and my fucking knees were aching. But this reward was worth it: a thick wad of warm come, sweet and bitter at the same time. A gusher that tasted like cornstarch splashing against my tongue. I tried to gulp it down without making a sound, and listened carefully to see if Ed would groan or sigh, but he didn't. He was so fucking cool, he was asking how the fishing was at some local watering hole.

I stayed down on the floor minutes after I was able to tongue off the last sweet drop of come, and Ed's huge tool slowly went from rock-hard to falling-down heavy. I stared at it, despite the fact that my eyes were stinging from my own sweat. The lower it hung, the more the foreskin closed up over the hood, and when it had totally closed I licked at the wrinkled skin, reluctant to stop sucking.

"Well, I had better get moving," the cop said. I could hear the squeaking of the stool as he got up and his heavy footsteps walking away from the bar. I waited a few minutes before getting up. My shirt was soaked with sweat. Ed was smiling.

"Good job," he said. "Even better than that other guy."

"Sorry I couldn't get around to your ass," I half apologized.

"You leaving town today? Or could you stay over? I got a cabin just outside of town."

"Let me think about it," I said, anxious to take a piss and splash some cold water on my face. "I'll give you my answer after I use the john."

My own cock was hurting like hell as I staggered toward the john, and I could feel the dampness of precome on my shorts. I figured this asshole wasn't about to help me out, so I'd have to whack off in the urinal. On the other hand, I could take him up on his invitation and save my juice for later.

The john was as dimly lit as the rest of the place. I could hardly see my way to the single urinal on the wall. But as soon as I pulled my stiff rod out of my pants, I realized I wasn't alone. I heard his voice before I saw him.

"One down, one to go," he said.

I turned around and saw the tall, dark-haired cop leaning against the wall. He was still wearing his tan-colored police hat and mirrored sunglasses. His shirt, also tan, fit snugly around his muscled chest, and there were damp spots at both armpits. If his pants were equally tight, I had no way of knowing, because they were down around the tops of his leather boots along with his light-blue boxer shorts. And while his cock wasn't a museum piece, it was still an impressive package, with its thick blue veins and big pink crown. He was one of those studs who has a really thick bush of hair around his nuts, which is a super turn-on to me. The funny thing is, he was still holding a bottle of beer, which meant Ed must have known he was in here.

"You like beer?" he asked, giving me a kind of sadistic smile.

"Yes, sir," I said, figuring it's always best to be polite to the arms of the law.

He tipped the bottle and poured some of the beer into the palm of his hand, then wiped his balls with it. "Help yourself, fella."

I willingly licked the beer off his nuts, then went down on his cock. He took my head away just long enough to give me a swig from the bottle, then put my head back where it belonged. His body smelled of beer, sweat, and Aqua Velva, which was probably some concession to his wife's sense of delicacy.

When I reached behind to grab his ass, I was impressed with how big and round and hairy it was—the kind you had to pry open if you wanted a taste, which I did.

He must have sensed that, because he turned around and opened it himself, as if he didn't have the patience to wait for me to sniff and tease. I took his lead and went straight for his asshole, which was moist with sweat and smelled of leather, probably from a car seat or a motorcycle saddle. Whatever I was doing, he loved it, and he kept grinding his butt into my face—as if I could get my tongue any deeper into his bowels.

"Strip," he commanded, and I obeyed, glad to get out of my sweat-soaked suit but reluctant to drape it over the cruddy-looking trash can in the room. When I was naked, he had me lean over the urinal. I could feel the coolness of the porcelain as I stared down at the light-yellow water, which had a dissolving cigarette in it. I could feel him spit on my ass, then slide the beer bottle against my crack.

"Beautiful. Beautiful," he was murmuring, obviously in appreciation of a butt that some guys had offered to pay for. Then I could feel his meat against my asshole, his arms around my waist, and his face against the back of my neck. "Here you go, buddy," he said, his sexy beer breath against my face.

Then I could feel the quick thrust as the son of a bitch gave me the full rod without any kind of caution. He didn't care if he ripped my ass apart, and I didn't either. I could tell this was a guy who mostly fucked women, because he was one-two-three; with a loud groan he shot his load up my butt and he was out and over at the sink washing his dick off. I didn't give a damn what he thought now, so I just stood there admiring his gorgeous cop butt and whacking off. He just studied his own handsome face in the mirror as if I were invisible, even when I finally came and shot my load across the room, just missing his muscular leg. While he tucked his shirt back into his pants, tightened his belt, and adjusted his hat, I stood there like an idiot, stark naked and breathing heavily from two tiring workouts.

When he was ready to leave, he put on his best chamber-of-commerce smile and said, "Our town doesn't have much to offer, but it's a good place to live, and the people here are kind of peace-loving, which makes my job easier. There's not a lot of excitement, as you probably guessed when you arrived, but every now and then a stranger like you comes, and we do what we can to make him feel welcome. Now, if you're planning to spend the night, maybe I'll see you again. Maybe we could all meet at Ed's place. My wife, she has choir on Tuesday nights, and I'm sure Ed and me and some of the boys could show a good-looking guy like you the kind of hospitality you're not likely to see in too many places."

Then he strode to the door, looking me up and down one final time. "On the other hand, if you're leaving town today, have yourself a good trip, you hear? And be sure to come and see us again sometime."

By the time I finished dressing in that dirty little men's room, I had pretty much made up my mind to stay the night. Before I left, I could hear country music outside the door. When I stepped outside, I was surprised to see there were several men in the bar.

I figured Ed would have a big grin on his face when I stepped outside, but he was so busy talking to some young guy at the bar, he didn't even look my way.

One guy did, though—a handsome guy with thick auburn hair and a trim beard. He gave me a smile and a wink. "You want a game of pool?" he asked, holding a cue in his hand.

"Not right now," I answered, "I've got to get back to my hotel to make some phone calls. Maybe I'll see you later."

When I suggested this possibility, he looked into my eyes intently and started to chalk up his cue. As he chalked it with one hand, he made a jerking-off motion on the stick with the other. "Count on it," he said.

Just as I was leaving, I could see the guy that Ed was talking to walk around behind the bar. He had a nice-looking, kind of naïve face, I thought. But then I only saw it for a few seconds before he knelt down out of sight.

Memento
Les Richards

His warmth covers me, is all through me. Hands moving across skin, fingers tugging hair. We move together on sheets in darkness. His voice husky, hoarse. Whispering love words, fuck words, into my ears. A tongue duels with mine, probes mouth, explores teeth. I open eyes, and I'm like born just this minute. No memory of anything. Except music in the club. Garbage.

Crows. Blowfish. Dancing silhouettes beneath colored lights; occasional flashes of faces when we moved toward a bright bar and its long mirror, recognized guys perched on stools.

An illuminated clock was like a moon rising at the far end of the bar, hands reaching toward 2 A.M. We moved feet faster, panicky at the idea of sleeping alone. Not tonight, not Friday night, with its promise of a string of pleasures until Monday. Changed partners, sometimes lips meeting, hands roving, caressing, dancing from one side of the floor to the other.

And he was facing me again. His hands and mine clasping and unclasping. His dry; mine moist with anticipation. We were breathing into each other's faces, Opium like a sweet cloud around him. Black hair glossy beneath pinpoints of light. Beck blasted from speakers, his lyrics lost. But who cared about lyrics, messages, with hot bliss somewhere beyond in the night.

He's on his knees, straddling me, teeth nipping one nipple then the other, and I writhe with painful ecstasy. He's a shadow against the rectangle of a window. Faceless. No idea of where we are, who drove, or when we left the bar.

I was feeling almost virtuous that Friday morning while I dripped coffee in the kitchen, filled Jessica's bowl with cat food. Feeling optimistic, muscles tuned, ready to jump into the ring again after a 10-day period of getting past Gordy. He walked out to his car on a rainy night, carrying his final suitcase, pounded on the door a few minutes later, and threw his key to the apartment across my shoulder. There wasn't a sign or relic of his living and sleeping with me for almost three months. He even took the cock ring he gave me for my birthday.

I sat at the kitchen counter, drinking coffee, keeping an eye on my watch, thinking anyone could get through Friday. That's something Steve said. There weren't many days when he didn't walk through my thoughts. I seldom saw Lily anymore because of him. "I never realized," she said to me the Sunday afternoon she dropped by my apartment.

He'd slept overnight with me. We stayed in bed reading Sunday papers, chewing bagels, drinking orange juice, playing. His cock never tired. He was a gusher; if he was inside me, I felt the warm spurt of it. He was in the shower when I answered a knock at the door. Lily brushed past me in her usual energetic way, saw I was still in a robe and nothing more, and was saying I must really be recuperating from something heavy last night when Steve passed the bedroom door from the shower. Not even a towel. He hadn't heard the knock. He reappeared in the bedroom door, his angular face flushed— the first time I'd seen him embarrassed—a pair of jeans pulled on and zipped. Lily's full red lips held a smile, blue eyes blinked but showed no judgment.

She'd stopped by on the way to a brunch to see if I cared to go. She segued into the party she'd done last night with her current man. By that time Steve was dressed, his brown hair brushed with my brush, and standing at the apartment door, thanking me for putting him up overnight. It sounded so lame.

"See you Tuesday night?" he asked Lily.

She nodded, said not to be late. Steve had known Lily longer than I. When Lily and I briefly slept together, she'd confided that I didn't have competition from Steve. "I've never felt as close to another man," she said over breakfast in her house. "No sexual tension." I thought I wouldn't mind some sexual tension with Steve. That was last year: I was 23, a Goucher graduate hired for computer stuff with a small corporation in Baltimore, and still a gay virgin.

He's a better lover than a dancer. Not as light on his feet as he is heavy on passion. Surroundings familiar now. We're in my bed. Windows, rectangles of night sky, icy tree limbs reflecting glints of light from streetlamps, the familiar texture of sheets I've laundered, and a twisted comforter at the foot of the bed. "Did you drive me home?" I whisper. Faint concern about my car. I can't remember scratch. Don't really care while my hands explore the sweet curve of his butt; wonder if it's white against a tanned body. Can't recall if we ever exchanged names. Just nonstop dancing. "Sshh, sshh" is all I hear, and he's still above me, his lips brushing my forehead, my mouth, my neck; and his hands are slowly parting my legs.

I became a stalker after Lily introduced me to Steve. Something quick and sensual in his first glance. Shaggy brown hair, a sort of oriental curve to pale-blue eyes, a compact body soft in the right places. I turned up wherever I thought he might be. He was somewhere in his 30s, sold real estate, acted in little theater, took his two Springers for obedience classes, made no bones about preferring beer to wine. He'd suddenly lighted a match to what I'd felt about other men. During our first time, after he'd pushed deep inside me, I told him I loved him. Maybe because we'd been toking. It was a curious, queasy, carnal feeling. But I could read his eyes, almost hear the word *naïve* through my head. He put up with me for a while, until I saw him kissing a boyish guy good-bye in the vestibule of his house. I never saw him again, although Lily would mention him now and then. Sometimes I would sit with Jessica purring beside me, realize I didn't possess a single token—not a T-shirt or one of his white cotton handkerchiefs, nothing—of the times I'd fucked with him, slept with him, eaten, dressed, and showered with him.

"I don't understand," I told Kyle, a guy I'd met barhopping with Steve.

"What's to understand?" Kyle shrugged narrow shoulders, eyed me hopefully. He seemed as sure about things as the totals on the cash register he punched in a supermarket.

"Come on back to my place." I did for one night, a Saturday, and he seemed enthusiastic as he let me into the living room of the house he was buying near the waterfront in Fells Point. He initiated me to being on top. Insisted we use condoms he thought were safest. He came with a gasp, I shot inside him, and he said hot tops were few and popular. He tilted his head when I kissed him before leaving Sunday afternoon. "Well, we've done it," he said. "So we can be friends now."

I'm suffused with the throb of him inside me. Filled with him from my scalp, to tips of toes and fingers, stomach, chest, somewhere behind my heart. Steady, sometimes fast, sometimes slow, to pace a pulse along arteries, almost blocks breath in my throat. Darkness is a mask across his face. I remember crisp black hair, navy eyes, the ache of wanting him while we danced in the bar. Air rasps in and out of his mouth. My hands grip his butt, pull him tight against me. We're both sweating. My erection probes his belly. Until gray and black shapes revolve around us—thinking I was in love with Burt was like trying to walk across a stretch of quicksand.

"Who's the stud redhead?" Kyle asked one night in a bar.

"Burt Starrett. He's works a construction job."

"Construction?" Kyle fluttered eyelids. "I'll bet you're bottom these days."

Not necessarily. Burt believed in do and do alike. As long as we shared. Everything. Sometimes he even stood in the bathroom door and watched me piss. He insisted I give him a rundown of each day of the week we weren't together. Nobody'd ever seemed to care before, and I felt flattered at first. His body was lean and hard from manual labor, even though he was a foreman now. Curly red hair framed a farm-boy face with brown eyes you couldn't predict. They went from soft to hard like a light bulb is switched on and off. "Why you always fuckin' watching me? Wonder why I came to that bar? Think you're better than I am, with your diploma?" Eyes hard. Then soft. "It doesn't matter. We're in love."

He threw that word around a lot. At 28 he sounded like an authority on love.

"You're different. You need love. Like me. Some of these fags just want to do it. When we fuck, we're like one." The brown eyes rebuked me. "Don't grin. You know what I mean." That night I was staying in his house; he wanted me to give up my apartment, move in with him. But I was confused about him, maybe about love. He brought a Gap bag out of a closet, emptied it across the bed. Blue jeans and white shirts, like his. He insisted we dress alike when going to bars, just about everywhere. I felt like a mannequin. Guys eyed us like we were queers from the '60s or something. He planned every hour of Saturdays and Sundays for us. He didn't like my place. Jessica disappeared under furniture if he noticed her. One Friday night I phoned him and said I wasn't feeling well, would see him next week. I needed to think. I felt like one of those French Foreign Legion guys in a Turner Classic Movie. They're surrounded in an oasis, hiding inside a crumbling little fort, waiting.

He walked into the out-of-the-way bar where I was drinking with Kyle. He sat down on the stool next to me. Glared at us. I felt Kyle stiffen beside me. Burt's mouth pulled a smile, set like wax. "Just one question," he said, leaning into us. "Have you two been to bed together?"

Kyle put down his mug and said: "Before you came along." Burt dropped some change into the jukebox and, when the selections were finished, he said we were going home. Before I stepped outside I looked back at Kyle, still seated on a stool at the bar, his face white.

Back at his house Burt fucked me like he was drilling for oil. I'd be black-and-blue. I began to feel I should protect myself. But he stopped. Still kneeling astride me, staring down into my face, sweating, breathing hard; a lamp was on, and I could look into glazed brown eyes and the wax smile. "We've got to prove how much we're one." He slid off the bed, pulled me into the bathroom. The bright light paled our skins. He pushed me down to the side of the tub. Told me what we were going to do.

"No," I said. "I don't do the shower stuff. Whatever the fuck they call it." I stood up, and he grabbed my shoulder, threw me against a tiled wall. His hand curled into a chunky fist. I ducked too late, slumped onto a clothes hamper. Managed to stand, swung my own fists.

"Shit," he said, "I don't fight queers." He turned his back, walked into the hall. "Get the fuck out! Now!" He disappeared somewhere into his house while I tugged on clothes and left, hurrying along the dark sidewalk to my car. My jaw ached like a nail was driven into it. I thought it was probably like the hurt after an operation. Cutting, to remove something even more painful.

Next morning I woke—last night hanging like dark clouds in the distance—rolled over onto my stomach, and slept past 1 o'clock Saturday afternoon. Later that day, Jessica following me around, I realized there wasn't a trace of Burt in my apartment. Not like the shaving things, bottle of Eternity, and those jeans and white shirts I'd kept at his place. I gazed into the bathroom mirror at purple bruises along my jaw, neck, arms and shoulders. Even my butt sore. Something told me it wasn't the first time he'd beat up on a lover. Was his opinion of himself so low that his possessive routine with a guy, almost inside his skin, was maybe his way of hoping for some kind of blending to make him feel better about himself? I thought about it during the next few days while I took vacation time and played recluse in the apartment until I looked like myself again.

I open my eyes. I've been out of it. He's still here, we're in a spoon position, his cock limp along my ass, his arms folded across my chest, his whiskey breath across my ear. No trace of Opium; he smells richly human. I reach up and fold a hand around one of his. The bedside alarm glows 4:15. He mumbles something in his sleep. I drift off.

"Christ!" Kyle exclaimed when he came by to see how I was. "Burt looked luscious. But I kept thinking of some Mafia goon when he was around. Why'd you put up with it?"

Neck muscles complained when I shook my head. "I don't understand love with guys. It's just a word." We were sitting on the sofa. Kyle's fingers stroking my wrist. "I read somewhere that the rich are different. I think gay men are different. Shit, I never ran into all this weird crap with girls. Maybe you had to bargain some for bedtime. But they usually were glad to have you around."

"You haven't been out a year," Kyle said. "You'll find somebody. We'll all find somebody, sooner or later. Too bad it wasn't us. Maybe you're too eager." Then he told me about Lily. "She's getting married, I hear. Some hunk who's straight. I guess it's time. She might've turned into a fag hag."

It was like he'd thrown a grenade. With all her men, Lily'd found someone to stay home with. I was nursing a stiff jaw and feeling out of the loop for my latest effort. Nobody else was whining. Kyle accepted a string of overnights as the way things were.

So the next weekend I was out with Kyle and bounced from Burt to Gordy. As different as denim from khaki. He was two years older, blue-eyed, and he shrugged and grinned when called a 'dirty blond.' We danced most of the night, and I was careful, drank beer instead of bourbon. We made love—he wanted my cock inside him right away—and slept that night in his apartment. Smaller than mine and meticulously neat. We ate lunch in a place in Canton, and he told me he was a teacher, junior high, woodworking, electrical shop. He didn't explain about breaking his lease but moved into my larger place the following week. He repaired frayed wires on lamps, loosened doors that stuck, and brought in enough rubberized tile to redo the kitchen floor. Jessica watched him for a couple days, and she ended up stretching out along the back of the sofa while we sat there watching television or fooling around. I was exclusively top. Didn't mind in the least. But ironic, I thought, because he was the handyman and I was a computer nerd.

"Why'd you wait so long to come out?" he asked one night in bed. "I was doing it when I was a teen."

"I wouldn't have minded. It was my family. Perverted they called it. Don't get me wrong. My folks were good to me, gave me an education. I was busy with girls by 17. Liked it. But I kept thinking about men. My fantasizing was with men." Then Lily introduced me to Steve, and the walls came tumbling down. "I guess you might say I'm bi. But I'll never go back." It sounded so final. But I knew it was true.

Two months and two weeks after I met Gordy, his college roommate drove down from Boston for a visit. Sean wore a crew cut, was muscular, and his bass voice and laugh were singular among my friends. We stayed in, cooked supper, Sean mixed martinis, and the former roommates reminisced, mostly about guys they'd shared. Gordy told me in the kitchen, "You'll like him. He's been watching you." I gulped bourbon, finished another. Didn't want to be a wet blanket. Try it, you'll like it. Some refrain from an old commercial. I kept repeating it to myself as Sean unzipped my fly, undressed me. Before long Gordy was watching him suck me off. Lay back and enjoy it. I did and reached a jolting climax. Sean growled approval. Then I lay there while Sean's ass moved up and down as he fucked Gordy. A bleak feeling flowed through me. And before Sean got busy the next morning I hurried along to the shower, and he was pumping Gordy when I came back to the bedroom.

He's inside me again. A gentle, pulsing thrust. Waves of pleasure. My cock stands up like a totem pole, and I feel a painful rush through my testes and splash over his belly and chest. He lowers himself onto my stomach and slides up and down, rubbing the gluey stuff between us. "Wonderful," he whispers. "You're adorable." He deep-kisses my mouth. We are locked together in thick darkness, and I fade again, escaping the first twinges of a headache.

"He didn't use a condom on you," I said to Gordy after Sean left.

"You're talking about Sean!" Gordy accused. "We did this all through college."

Jesus Christ! I'd tried to be careful. I'd only heard of guys who'd died. I didn't know any after such a short time out. I bought the sturdy condoms Kyle preferred. I dreamed of Gordy losing weight, looking haggard. During the next two weeks life and spontaneity seeped out of things for us. We argued. Until the Friday night when he stormed out, threw the key across my shoulder.

I come to in bright daylight, hands of the alarm clock pointing to 10:15. I don't need to turn my head to know he's gone. Finally, I sit up, close eyes against dizziness and a curdling in my gut. I look at the emptiness beside me. We've wrecked sheets, pulled one corner loose, mashed pillows. I smile at the idea of his having slept with me, fucked me, closed his mouth around me. Startling looks, navy eyes, silky black hair, bristly jaws. Or was it bourbon, blowing it beyond reality? Suppose he phones me. I don't know his name.

I swallow two aspirin, suck on a Coke. A warm shower soothes me. Fill Jessica's bowls with food and water. She stares at me as if I've had all the fun. I begin to look around the place. Everything's in order. As if a phantom made love to me all night instead of a sinewy, gentle guy. A robe hangs around me. I flush condoms. Strip sheets. Look for bikini briefs beneath the bed but see only dust the vacuum missed. New black bikinis. First time out. Kyle was with me when I bought them at Macy's. A finger of guilt points. I can't believe it. I walk from room to room, scuffs scraping bare floors. Find my jeans on the living room rug, wallet undisturbed in the back pocket. Crazy!

I drip coffee, sit waiting for it, remembering stories my friends tell about taking guys home from bars, parks, streets. Jewelry, watches, money. Bikinis? After two cups of coffee I punch in Kyle's number. We check in after nights out. Maybe wanting to brag.

"Is that you?" He sounds amazed, as if he'd watched all night. Wonders how I'm together enough to call him. "Didn't think I'd hear from you. Unless to tell me off. I mean, you were in bad shape. He stopped dancing with you. Asked me if you'd get home OK."

I sink down onto a kitchen stool, gaze out a window at a slice of Inner Harbor visible from my place. Feel like I caught the wrong plane. What's to say?

"Some guy. Nobody I've ever seen," Kyle says. "But he was acting concerned. You hugged him. Waved at me. And I guess you saw Will and me leave."

A downer name for such a beauty. I wonder if he lived up to it. Some day I'll ask Kyle.

"I'm going back to sleep," I tell Kyle.

"He must've been fun. I'm glad."

I hang up. Rest elbows on the counter, cup chin in hands, close eyes. Noon light is painful. Want to shut things out. Steve would say I'm losing control. Careless. But I don't think I'll ever forget this one. No face to go by. Tender passion. Something sensual about stealing my underwear. Does he sniff it? Does he...no, don't think. I walk through the apartment. Not a sign of him, anybody. None of them ever leaves anything. But my lover last night took something away with him. Something of mine.

The Astonished Flesh
Scott D. Pomfret

You know who you are. What kind of person. You are a top. Each time you hold the Conversation with a man who in one short moment will become a lover, you try to touch on sexual history, and Status, and expectations, and the use of protection. But you are also always sure to announce in a voice utterly without compromise: I am a top.

You say it hard, defiant, as if it were a title taken from the Burke's book of peerage, a title both honorary and hereditary. I am a top. Brooking no argument, no opposition, no penetration. No nonsense.

Some of them say, But have you ever…

You say, roughly, This isn't a negotiation, but a bottom line, so shut up and bend over and open that flowered hole. I need only a second to lube and glove and an hour to pound away, and in the end, trust me, we'll both be happy, friend. Completely satiated.

You say this because you've always been a top. You've been at this game a long time. You know your appetites. You know your body. You've given a hundred lessons in what excites you, where should be touched, where should be let alone, what drives you crazy. You are a stickler for control.

Sure, when you were younger you gave a couple of tries at the other. But you concluded the plumbing had too many twists and turns and kinks, that you were a little narrow-gauged, and that anatomy was destiny, and no amount of persuasion was going to change that, and you never admitted it might have something to do with fear.

So you're a top. That's your story and you stick to it. You go about your business, you beat your chest, you fuck men, you throw away the used condom after asking—politely, insinuatingly, indulgently, even patronizingly—where he would like you to deposit it. And does he have a towel you could use to clean up?

And then there's Eric. You meet him at a dinner party, an obvious set-up. Karen, the quintessential vindictive fag hag, has long been threatening to find someone to put you in your place. She is tired of your being right and of her losing arguments. She is tired that you are prettier than she is. She says, I've got just the man for you, don't you disappoint me.

You vow to disappoint her. And she gives you a knowing smile.

He comes in late, and hurried, and has a drink in his hand before he's out of his coat, and he's already deep in the conversation before he has even said hello. A heather-gray cashmere mock turtle clings to his chest. His finger and thumb are thickened by elegant silver rings. From time to time in the heat of argument he rubs the careless stubble on his chin. He's full of bluster and punditry and opinions. He has just come from some do-good cause in some downtown UU church basement, and he pontificates endlessly about world hunger and feeding the poor. Eric browbeats the party into sullen agreement.

He drives you crazy. Even if he'd been Quasimodo, you'd have taken him home, just to put a little something in his mouth. A ball of socks. Or something. Just to get him to shut the fuck up.

But Eric is no Quasimodo. He's a rooster, a peacock. He's broad-faced, with strong jawbones that might have been ugly if they had betrayed the least asymmetry. He has a George Clooney haircut he swears he had before George Clooney was popular. His shoulders are slightly rounded, his neck slightly thick, but he carries himself like a lean man. Like a predator.

You don't know what it's like to be hungry, he insists. He contemptuously points out the comforts of Karen's dining room. He talks like a man who has overcome obstacles, a tough childhood, and has secrets a softer boy could not even imagine.

The problem with hunger, he says, is you can philosophize about it as much as you want, and you can say it will never happen here, or to me, and you can say it's their own damn fault and you can talk about the good of the economy and the flaccid welfare state that creates flaccid welfare wills in the working poor, but when the appetite calls, big brown eyes, gaping mouth, swollen belly, sunken eyes, how can you expect to turn it down?

Eric quickly figures out why he's there, at the party. All the while he talks, his eyes hold another conversation with you. They follow you around, even when you're prating to others in an opposite corner, even when you leave for the kitchen. He stands back to the wall, arms crossed on his chest, his feet spread like there's so much in his crotch, he's got to make room. His gaze is physical, intrusive, irritating.

You finally have to acknowledge it, to neutralize it. Stare frankly back from close range. You both know where this night is headed. Karen is not going to be disappointed.

As the party breaks up you take him home, offer him a nightcap. It's a game of cat-and-mouse: To see who will move first, kiss first, undress whom first, kneel first, who will take the first sweet bite of asshole. It seems like forever that he prowls around your apartment, drink clutched in the strong hand, never quite turning his back on you but cataloguing everything about the way you live. Your cock is aching.

But there's no mouse in the room. Only two goddamn lions. Two tops. Two street fighters circling one another, slightly crouched, watching your backs. Your brain is saying: *I'm going to put this guy beneath me. I'm going to hammer away at him until he whimpers.*

When you embrace, you bang chests like a couple of hoops stars. His hands are callused, small, and tight as a grip of death. His calluses are old and permanent and crusted with dirt. These hard hands find your hands, and they are eloquent in the denunciation of your softness. *Rich boy,* they whisper over your palms. Your face flushes. Rich boy.

You set your jaw. You'll show him "rich boy."

You get aggressive. You pull his cashmere up and over his head. For a moment his hands are raised and bound in it, and the collar is a crown around his forehead. Your eyes meet, he struggles away, the sweater falls, and his hard nipples give you a short-lived advantage. His belt loosens. His pants fall. He swats your hands and fingers away from his ass as if they were flies and he a Southern belle on a picnic. You have a hundred hands, it seems like, and your fingertips stink of ass. His butt's a loaf of bread you want to drive your thumbs into and tear open to let the hot, fresh-baked steam escape.

You part again, as if there is an invisible referee making you play by the rules. His chest is heaving; he seems surprised by your resistance; this is not a battle that's lost or won yet; this is not a rape; color has spread across his skin; you've already inflicted a bruise on the neck, another on the collarbone, your own wounds are undetectable so far, all buried in the heat of skin. His belly's a soft pout above his tented boxers. His hips are leaner than you expected, and it seems his cock is the only thing holding the cloth up.

You have the Conversation. You say, Come into the bedroom. You show him the drawer beneath the bed that has every condom known to man, and jars and tubes and lotions of every assortment.

Pick your poison, you say. You think: *In a moment, I am going to be deep inside this guy.* Your own confidence makes you harder still. You have one thought, one desire, one hunger. Life is simple.

The Conversation throws Eric off at first, because you give him the standard I-am-a-top speech. He looks knowing, then skeptical, then says, So it's just oral and nothing more?

He stares at the condom display with distaste and adds, I know I should get in the habit, but I don't swallow...

And you say, Let's get in the habit, starting tonight. What's your pleasure: We got strawberry, kiwi, lime?

The choice or the offer weirdly embarrasses Eric, and you think: *Victory.* Advantage for the good guys. You are going to subdue this butch son of a bitch, this guy who it pisses you off to be attracted to.

You're close again, now on the bed in boxers, straining against one another. You mash lips, but Eric's not one for kissing. That's just wasted breath, lost energy, that's what you do after sex, before you sleep. If at all. For an athletic guy like Eric, kissing's the equivalent of a post-coital cigarette.

You are at a crossroads, a standstill, and you begin thinking that this might not work out. The thought terrifies you. Confidence leaves you. You want this guy bad, you want to prove something to him, you can't bear this empty bed. You compromise, you think now: *I don't have to fuck him—just get him turned belly-down and slide it along his crack till I come on the base of his spine. Get him to make a narrow space out of his closed legs. Get on top of him. Reach around from behind. Reach under and between the legs, feel the shaft of him, past the hanging nuts, stroke from beneath so that he's forced to raise his butt, make it available.* And that lordosis would be enough to count as a win.

Though you'd love to fuck him to prove the point.

You laugh out loud. But it gets less funny; he doesn't laugh with you. And he's got 30 pounds on you, he's a tough guy; he makes the use of that viselike grip—not forcing you, not that. But persuading you, breaking you slowly like a wild horse. Wearing you out. You feel yourself moving toward the bottom, inexorably, inevitably.

To avoid it, you break his rhythm; you think: *Suck him off, maybe, take the starch out of him.* Your lips drop down his barrel chest, his overround but rock-hard belly. You wriggle down beneath him and breathe your hottest breaths. You're a dragon; his cock twitches; his balls move like a swallowing throat; a dribble shows on his tip, which reminds you to reach for the foil, shuck it like a skin of summer corn, and let your mouth follow it down over the shaft.

You wait for him to death-grip the back of your neck and jam you down over him before you're ready, until you choke. You think Eric's the kind that would get off on that. You know his kind, who give head like a garbage disposal.

And that's how you lose. You lose to kindness. When the callused fingertips touch you, they skim the skin of your nape. They scratch sideways, ever so gently, as your head goes up and down. There is a layer of air between them and your skin, a layer of electricity, that shivers down your spine and seems to get lost somewhere down there, at the base of your own spine, in the place you swear is dead, which you swear is a one-way street, where you swear you have no appetites.

Eric's is a gentleness you could never get with a weak man or a soft man; scritch, scritch, scritch. A cat's scratching at the door that wakes you from sleep, makes your hair stand on end, an ominous suggestion, a subtle seduction with a hint of something dangerous that might slip in. Something so startlingly intimate, you cannot resist.

You like him better than you have all day. You glance up at him; his eyes are closed. You are jealous of his closed eyes. You are thankful for his thick cock.

Then he stops you, takes his cock from your mouth. You feel deprived, disappointed, a baby without his bottle. But Eric gives you hardly a moment to think about it. He presses your shoulder, presses you over and down. His weight pins you and presses the breath out of you. He lies full-length on top of you, breath in your ear. He flattens your buttocks, and his cock jams between your legs, touches your scrotum beneath.

You are frozen. There is a quick moment when your body pretends it does not know what is happening. Your mind races inside, gerbil on a spinning wheel. What has happened to your resistance, your strength, your pride? They all seem beside the point. They're all luxuries. They're sidelights to the insistent growing, gnawing hunger his gentle fingers have awakened. No matter how you deny it, it is there: It takes over everything, it infects your thinking, your actions, your desires, it makes you do things you never thought yourself capable of doing. Trade in your mother, trade in your principles. It is the deepest kind of hunger.

Here's the truth of the matter: You don't lose by submitting. You lose by wanting to submit. And you want it. Now. To your astonishment. You stare at the white wall in front of you. You clutch at the flannel sheets. You want it. You want it bad. You shift a little to make it easier, and that is all the permission Eric needs.

He becomes all businesslike motion. His hand drives your lower back. In the drawer he finds a tube of something he likes and lubes up his still-gloved cock. Then, ever so carefully, he slides it in. First a little, just the tip, making room, a pig looking for truffles—pump pump pump. Then a lot. A whole lot.

You gasp; you can't find the proper label for what you're feeling. Pain? Pleasure? The strokes get long. Your belly crooks with sudden fear that he might hurt you, somewhere deep inside where you can't see, might not even know, until it was too late. And the fear excites you. *Jesus,* you think—*who is this guy?* And you're talking about yourself, not Eric. You're talking about this body you're in, this penetrated body that can't possibly be you, but only on loan for the day or an hour.

You think, *I am a top, I should fight this.* You think, *He's taking something from me.* You think, *How much longer can he go on?*

As if in answer, Eric dismounts. He grabs your ankle and turns you over like he's opening a familiar door. Letting himself in, making himself comfortable. You yourself have done it a hundred times to others, but it is shiny and new to you. You crane for a look; you live in terror of what's behind that door, what it means, like a kid in a dream who can't leave well enough alone.

You are on your back, legs slightly spread, slightly bent. Eric is rock-hard, there's a trickle of sweat on his belly. His face is cool, eyes sparkling, but no hint of triumph, only wet hunger. His gaze takes you in, embarrasses you, enters you first, so you have to look away, ashamed at your subjection, your want. You pull back your own thighs to make room. Eric fingers your ass, positions himself, plunges it in.

You are filled with suddenness, with disbelief. It is your bedroom, sure, your own bed, but it is entirely unfamiliar, a strange, exotic, foreign place: The flannel sheets are as thick and luxuriant as a Persian rug; the wall seems coated with a bright new paint, the few hanging prints all seem to depict fresh and different scenes, they seem to doubt who you are. And the furniture seems now to have been chosen by a complete stranger a long time ago. You realize: I have been living in deprivation.

Eric—you think that was his name, wasn't it? Eric? You don't know. Your mind is a sieve, you have forgotten everything, everything but your ass and his body, his cock inside you.

You find your ankles around his ears. You feel disposable, convenient, creased along the folds. His thrusts bang your head on the back-board—boom boom boom. The neighbors will complain, you don't care, your belly jiggles, you are owned, you are taken. His hands grip your hips, the muscle of your thigh. He grunts, he sweats. There's a lot of hip on him; a muscly butt pile-drives it home.

And you are not just a hole in the wall in this unfamiliar new room. You are active. Your ass is prehensile. Your ass is voracious. It's a stranger come alive with stories to tell and appetites to fill and a life all its own. It reaches out to take Eric in, invites him deeper. You feel punished, elated, a warm spread of pleasure in your crotch. A circle of heat. A great swallow.

Your own erection, your own orgasm seems beside the point. And then it is all the point, the only point, and you reach for yourself, and you think, *Oh, my God, he's not going to make me come this way,* but even before you can finish thinking, your mouth opens, he bites you, your teeth clash, and the hot jizz is on your belly, and those first drops trigger you to spasm again and again, and for the briefest moment you think you might come forever.

He bends you, leans on you, until your ankles are now around your ears, and he kisses you on the mouth between your own ankles. His tongue is like a lion licking its young: bowling them over with its abrasive strength, tousling your head like you were a kid. Something aggressively, abusively affectionate about it, the best kind of love.

You look up into his face, astonished, thinking, *Why this guy? Why Eric?* You've been with smaller guys it would have been easier to take in. You've been with prettier men.

Your belly is full of him. Full of your own pleasure. Your back cracks. Your body gives a little thrill. A circle of heat radiates from where he enters you. He is faster and harder, and you wonder why your body does not simply break apart. Very briefly, almost without stopping his stroke, he smears more lube from the tube to make sure the condom doesn't melt from the friction, you guess desperately, or maybe your own insides have just burst. The cool jelly is counter-point, but in a moment it is hot and fired as the rest of you. And somehow bursting seems like a good thing, a promise, an ultimate joy. You wish you could be entered all over. By now you welcome his gaze. His sweat drips, you think the drops will be a relief, but each one is like acid, makes your skin jump, ripple—a fiendishly designed water torture from some Asian jungle. You swear you are wearing someone else's skin.

He cries out as he finishes. There is something triumphant in it.

But you have won too, even though Eric does not know.

He stays in you, you squeeze him, he grows small. There's a little electric-eel jump of life in him, but then that is gone too, and he exits with a soft pop.

He unfolds you. Returns you to a certain stature. Spreads your limbs, thanks you; he is almost breathless. He doesn't need to ask what to do with the spent condom.

You are completely speechless. You can hardly look at him. Your ass is tender, you probe it with a finger. He says, I didn't hurt you, did I?

You snap, No!

But you are not sure, and you want to be hurt like that again. Soon. Now.

After he goes, you are tender, you touch. Your ass is almost proud now, and as astonished as you are. You are a different person than who you were. You have different hungers, different needs, another mouth to fill.

Private Rico's Salute
M. Christian

Sergeant Walchek was pissed. "YOU MOTHERFUCKIN', COCKSUCKIN' SCREWUPS!!!" That was accurate: He didn't scream (one exclamation point), bellow (two exclamation points), he roared—barracks' windows rattling in their frames, toilet water rippling, tiles bouncing off the walls—(at least, probably more, exclamation points).

"YOU FUCKIN', FUCKIN', FUCKIN'…(he seemed to search through his vast profanity vocabulary for just the right word)…ASSHOLES!!!!"

The whole unit stood around the latrine, heads hung in shame. As far as they'd been concerned, it hadn't been that bad a day. Fuck, 10 miles in full kit, half that through a thunderstorm as only Georgia had thunderstorms. So what if Sgt. Robinson's unit had passed them, plowing through the sucking mud to get back to the barracks first—it wasn't like it really fuckin' mattered, especially after 10 miles.

But it had obviously mattered to Sgt. Walchek. His stocky body seethed and tensed with fury till it seemed he'd either explode into bone-and-skin shrapnel or burst into a hurricane of fists and teeth. Instead, he just climbed up on the urinal trough—and pissed on them.

"CAN'T YOU DO ANYTHING FUCKIN' RIGHT?" Tiles clattered to the floor; a window slipped out of its frame, letting in a gust of cold air. "YOU ASSHOLES!!!" His piss steamed in the suddenly cool room, splattering against the face of Private Hernandez, stinging the eyes of Pvt. Blake. His big, hard dick was like a righteous fire hose, calling down the venom of a wrathful USMC god.

"YOU CALL YOURSELVES MEN??!!" And compared to the

Sergeant's now throbbingly hard meat, that was hard to do. "YOU'RE FUCKIN' DICKLESS WONDERS!!!" Massive, bobbing with his hammering pulse, his cock seemed to point out the flaccid failures of the entire unit—an accusing, dotted-with-pearlescent-pre-come finger of fury. "FUCKING PANSIES!!!"

It was Pvt. Blake who really started it all. Blake was cocky, the whole unit knew it…personally. Not all of them had taken it, but all of them had sucked it at once time or the other. Blake was also a cocksure asshole, and despite how big and tasty his meat was, they sure as hell wasn't gonna follow him into combat—the latrine, yeah, but he thought too much with his dick and not enough with his head. "FUCK YOU, SARGE!" he tried to yell back—but, face it, Blake's dick might have been almost as big as the Sarge's, but it was a big "almost." An inch can mean dick—unless it was in measuring a cock. "I AIN'T FUCKING DICKLESS!" His own was also hard, throbbing with his own pissed-off anger.

"PUT THAT GODDAMNED PINKIE AWAY, GOD-DAMN IT!" the sarge bellowed back with laughter, "OR DO SOME-THING WITH IT!"

It was going to be that kind of night, Rico thought, feeling his own hard cock through his jock as Blake grabbed hold of Pvt. Schwartz and deftly shoved a thumb up his asshole. Knowing now that he was tight and ready, Blake's massive cock smacked where his thumb has tasted—balls slapping against the pale man's tight thighs, sending a ripple through his muscular ass.

Seeing Rico's wistful smile as Blake slammed his cock in and out of Schwartz's puckered asshole, the Sarge singled him out: "AND YOU, RICO—YOU'RE THE FUCKING WORST!!! A COM-PLETE FUCKUP, A MOTHERFUCKIN' PIECE OF SHIT."

"Fuck you, sir" slipped out of Rico's lips, half a whisper as he started at Sgt. Walchek's massive dick bobbing just a few feet away from it. Yeah, Rico was pissed off—he'd done his fucking best at whatever he'd done—but seeing Sgt. Walchek's cock just took all the fight out of him. He felt his asshole twitch in anticipation and his mouth grow hungry for the taste of his meat.

"I CAN'T HEAR YOU!!!" screamed Sgt. Walchek, jumping down off the trough, beads of lingering piss splattering across the faces of the grunts nearby. "GODDAMN IT, RICO, CAN'T YOU EVEN FUCKIN' YELL RIGHT?"

Cock or no cock, that got the beefy Private. Looking up from Sgt. Walchek's massive cock, he stared straight into 30 eyeballs fractured by bright-red blood vessels. "FUCK YOU!!" It wasn't a scream and certainly wasn't a bellow, but the yell was pretty much the best Rico could do with the lingering thought of Sgt. Walchek's cock still in the back of his mind. "FUCK YOU, SIR!!!"

"RIGHT, SHITHEAD—LIKE YOU COULD EVEN DO THAT RIGHT!!!" Sgt. Walchek screamed back, hot spittle landing on Rico's face like grease from a range. "WELL, PRIVATE—DO YOU THINK YOU COULD DO THAT RIGHT?"

Walchek's hand snapped out and grabbed Rico's cock with the force of a hysterical vise. Startled at the force and speed of Walchek's hand, Rico shrieked and tried to drop down to one knee—but the Sergeant's grip was too strong, too relentless: when Rico went down he found himself hanging by his dick in Sgt. Walchek's hand.

'A FUCKUP, THAT'S WHAT YOU ARE, RICO—NOTHING BUT A FUCKUP. ALL YOU ASSHOLES ARE BAD, BUT THIS PIECE OF SHIT IS THE WORST!!!"

Sgt. Walchek's grip tightened even further on Rico's cock. The whole world boiled down to just those two elements. No longer was he in a barrack's latrine on a Marines base in Georgia. No longer was he in a room where a dozen burly marines were busy sucking, fucking, and jacking each other off. No, the world was his screaming dick in Sgt. Walchek's hand.

That and Sgt. Walchek's pounding yell in his ears: "YOU CAN'T DO SHIT, RICO—CAN'T DO SHIT!!!" Then Sgt. Walchek twisted his grip, and whatever determination he'd had to try staying on his feet vanished: gritty, piss-reeking tile slapped into Rico's ass...with Sgt. Walchek's pale baseball bat of a cock bobbing just inches from his face.

Somehow Rico was able to think in that situation. He knew—in a flesh—what Walchek held against him.

That's why he knew—then and there—that he had to prove himself to the Sergeant. He had to do whatever it took. So, facing Walchek's throbbing cock, he did what he had to do—he opened his mouth and hungrily swallowed Sgt. Walchek's dick.

It was a good dick…nah, let's be fair—it was a *great* dick. As far as cocks went, it was tremendous…hell, it was excellent even for a baseball bat. With hungry determination Rico opened wide and meticulously eased the Sgt.'s cock down his throat. One inch, two, three—more. One after another till Sgt. Walchek's pubic hairs were tickling his nose and the big sergeant's balls were happily slapping against his chin.

Not surprisingly, Walchek's grip on Rico's cock faded from an iron clasp to a simple handshake—until it faded altogether as the huge sergeant moaned, deep and brassy, and rocked back on his heels. As he moaned and started to fuck Rico's hungry face, Rico put a strong hand on his sergeant's tight, burly ass and yanked him forward, plunging his thick sword even deeper down his throat.

All around them the latrine was a symphony of orgasmic sounds as the company performed its own form of close-order face fucking, asshole-fucking, jerking drill. The sounds stoked Rico's fire until he felt that his own cock—still tightly enmeshed in his jockstrap—was going to burst like a firework.

Someone, against all those fuckin' horny sounds and his sergeant's cock deep down his maw, Rico remembered what he had to do.

Slowly, ponderously, like shoving a tank uphill, he started to push Sgt. Walchek backward. Opening his eyes for a quick sending, he looked up to see the huge man's eyes slammed close, his mouth working like he was chewing gum—or thinking of another man's dick in his own hungry mouth. Distantly, Rico became aware that Walchek had tumbled backward against one of the other grunts (who was doing his own grunting into the pursed asshole of Pvt. Snyder). In a quick flurry of muscular limbs, the grunt grabbed hold of their rapturous sergeant and helped ease him down onto the piss-soaked tile floor.

Rico followed Walchek down—never once letting his lips leave his throbbing, trembling member. As Walchek descended, Rico inched forward, keeping him hard and wet in his starving mouth and throat.

Then he was down—on that piss-slick floor, Sgt. Walchek's legs swung wide as Rico slowly moved along his body, until he was snuggled nestled with his chin in his furry walnut balls and his cock still in his sucking, sucking, sucking mouth. There—right where Rico wanted him.

Rico sucked—he sucked like he was the only fag in the world and Sgt. Walchek's was the only cock. He sucked it like he did everything: with all his might and will. He might not be the best soldier, the best grunt, and he sure as shit didn't (at least to Sgt. Walchek) know how to fucking salute, but he did know how to suck cock—and Sgt. Walchek got all of his masterful ability and determination.

He played the big man like a virtuoso with a mouth on a fine instrument: As he felt Walchek start to come—the bitter salt of his precome ringing in Rico's mouth—he changed technique (more tongue, less tongue, more lips, less lips, more teeth, less teeth) until Sgt. Walchek, groaning like a madman, descended away from spurting in Rico's mouth.

All perfect military strategy—all a diversion. One finger at first, but then two—then three, all of them slipping into the sergeant's hungry asshole. As he sucked, Rico slowly started to fuck: three fingers became four, four…stayed four for a long time, a slow feeling-out of the territory.

Then, with a shuddering moan, four became five, and Rico was at the door. At five, Rico felt around Sgt. Walchek's asshole, familiarizing himself with the hot, tight, warm territory—feeling out the point of his prostrate, the inner doors. Five slipped in, swallowed just as hungrily, as Rico still sucked and sucked his pulsing cock—feeling Sgt. Walchek's hot come sliding up, moment by moment into Rico's starving mouth.

With his mouth working away on his dick and his hand deep within Sgt. Walchek, Rico worked him—played him, masterfully fisted and sucked him.

He could tell—by the deep instincts within him, Rico knew: It was almost time, just about the moment. Skillfully, with inching patience, he moved his hand slowly, slowly, until he had a pummeling fist, a bone-and-skin jackhammer pounding away into Sgt. Walchek's tight asshole.

Then it *was* time—come jetted into Rico's mouth, Sgt. Walchek's come contracting down around Rico's hammering fist like an anaconda swallowing and digesting its prey. Then Sgt. Walchek's heavy, hot come filled Rico's mouth with its salty bitterness, a divine glory of come.

Then it really was time, as the come slowly faded into a dull ecstasy—Rico let Walchek's semisoftening cock slap onto the sergeant's greasy, sweaty belly—and methodically crawled up his long, so-hard body. Then he was up to Walchek's still-panting mouth, he pissed him—just once—and said, very softly, "So how was that salute, sergeant?"

And Walchek, still high and blissful from the come, smiled, opened his eyes just enough, and said: "Damned fine salutin', soldier. Damned fine salutin'. "

The Act
Dale Chase

I didn't get the part. Never mind how long I'd known the director or how many times he'd fucked me in the past, he gave the role to someone else, and I had to wonder if Derek Fall was really a better actor or just a better fuck. Watching him prowl the stage only complicated things. Every time I looked at him, a battle started inside me: jealous fury squared off against overwhelming desire.

The part was the best thing to come along in years, and every young actor in San Francisco auditioned. Six of us were called back to the ancient Lindsay Theatre for a second reading, and it was then that I knew I was in trouble. Not only did Fall's reading match my own, I got hard watching him. Winning a lesser part was little consolation, and I found rehearsals of the four-man, two-act play more difficult than anticipated—because in addition to mastering my supporting role, I had to balance envy and lust, which caused me more than once to forget my lines and endure an embarrassing silence that Fall seemed to relish. At those moments I could feel his smirk, even though his gorgeous James Dean face never betrayed a thing.

After a week's rehearsal I was clearly undone, and writer-director Abel Groff, gay theater patriarch, called me on it. "If you're in some kind of snit at not playing the lead, please get over it, because you are not doing justice to the part you've been given, not at all. Don't you see, Brian is trapped by his feelings, he's tangled without hope, he's suffering! All I'm getting from you is distraction."

I couldn't respond.

"All right," Abel sighed, "just work on it, will you? You're a fine actor, Carl, and you'll do a wonderful job if you'll let yourself get into the role." He studied me then as only a man whose dick had been up my ass could do. "You probably just need a good fuck," he added, glancing at his watch. "I'd do you myself if I didn't have an appointment." And then he was gone.

I remained in the cramped communal dressing room long after the theater was dark. Fall's image clung to me. He'd made a production of changing from jeans to tight black slacks, enjoying, I was certain, my unease around his exposed cock. He'd revealed it slowly, sizable shaft lingering in the mirror, and I'd feasted on the sight: long, thick, and half hard. My asshole had clenched involuntarily, my own dick stirring.

Anyone else I would have already approached, but Fall had a way of daring me to make a move while threatening me if I did, all of it accomplished in a charged and brutal silence. I hated the way he hoarded his words, saving everything for the stage, and the way he toyed with me like some defenseless prey.

His looks, of course, drove me wild. Never mind how cold the blue eyes, they bore into me like a rigid cock. His blond hair and exquisitely cut features—he was James Dean incarnate—seemed almost crafted, and yet his presence was truly animal, so base and raw that I was continually unsettled. Abel was right, I did need a good fuck. And I knew from whom.

Things were no less difficult onstage. Every time I was put up against Fall, it was my erection prodding, never mind Brian, my poor tormented character. I passed that first week in bittersweet misery, and Fall knew it and played me accordingly. We existed in a state of near perpetual arousal, and at night I devoured anonymous cocks to exhaustion. By next day's rehearsal, however, I was desperate all over again. And then, after Abel's admonishment, when I decided to forgo everything for a quiet night, an unattended asshole and lone jerk-off, the door opened, and I looked up into the mirror and saw Derek Fall in all his glory.

He approached me as if it was scripted, and while I hated his arrogance, I stood for him, pulled down my jeans, and presented the ass he had owned from day one.

"Pussy boy," he growled, as he shoved his cock into me. He said it again as he began a vicious stroke, and I responded as I knew he wanted. "Your pussy boy," I said, riding his dick and crazy with heat because I knew how the scene would play, because it was a scene, Abel Groff's scene, although onstage the sex was simulated, clothed in shadow. Now it was alive, and as Derek Fall rammed his sizable dick up my ass, I knew we were playing our respective parts, but, of course, didn't care. I had what I wanted, I was getting my fuck, and as I writhed on that magnificent tool, all that mattered was that cock up this ass, never mind if the ass was Brian's or mine.

Fall didn't utter a word during the entire act and, outside of the rhythmic slap of flesh, the room remained silent. I longed to cry out but didn't, taking his hose to the root and still wanting more. I couldn't get enough of him now that he was inside me; it felt like a cobra sliding up into my bowels, and my asshole pulsed in exquisite delight as it swallowed what seemed a mile of cock. Other than hands on my hips and dick up my ass, Fall gave me nothing, and once he'd pumped his cream into me in a massive gusher, he simply withdrew. His exit was as abrupt as his entrance, and I remained bent over the dressing table as I heard the door close.

He didn't seem to care that I too had delivered a massive load, milky puddle validation that we had indeed shared the act. My hand was still on my cock, as if it needed consolation, and my asshole throbbed in recollection. I stood up slowly and stared at the door, knowing it was Fall who had fucked me but having the eerie feeling the encounter had been with his character, that Jake Cavett's prick had been the one up my ass.

"No, no!" Abel Groff screamed the next morning during rehearsal. "I told you how to play it. Can't you follow simple directions?" He was onstage in seconds, shoving me aside to show me Brian's move toward Jake. When he turned to me after the demonstration, I offered nothing, and this enraged him further. "Well?" he shouted.

"Yes," I managed, glancing at Fall, who leaned against the sofa back, erection prominent inside his jeans. Approaching him was agony, my own need overwhelming poor Brian's. I didn't care about scenes or characters or any of it anymore. I just wanted to pull out Fall's dick and climb on.

I managed to get through rehearsal but suffered a near-collapse at day's end and again remained behind in the dressing room. I half expected Fall to come in for a repeat—he knew it a given—but heard instead fading chatter and the clicks and groans of a theater shutting down for the night. For a while I considered quitting the play—an eager understudy could step in—but knew I'd go on, unable to resist Fall's promise. Exhausted, I finally forced myself out the door.

A single light illuminated the stage, and I paused in its meager stripe to remind myself I was an actor in a play and would perform before hundreds of people. It was, after all, an act; I should simply get on with it. I had gathered a bit of calm when I heard footsteps in the wings. Derek Fall stepped from the shadows and strode toward me, and I thought of Brian, who lusted after Jake so pathetically— and yet I dropped my pants and waited.

Fall freed his cock, and as I stared at the magnificent pole I wondered if it ever went soft. The head was blue-purple and swollen with need, precome oozing in stringy gobs. He backed me to the sofa, and I eased down and raised my legs, offering him the only thing he wanted. I watched his face darken as he slid his piston up my alley, and when he began pumping it was with a jackhammer fury that sent shock waves of pleasure through me.

As he fucked me I wanted more than anything to pull away his clothes and confront the animal who took me with such authority. I wanted everything of his—lips, tongue, nipples, balls—but for now took what was offered, the pile-driving cock that tore into my ass.

My dick stood tall, and I wrapped a hand around it and jerked madly as Fall's prick drove deep into my rectum. He never let up, hammering my ass with his fat bone, searing my chute until my gut began to churn. I searched his face for some kind of reaction, some bit of pleasure, but he remained expressionless even as he slammed into me, balls banging my ass. I could tell his load was rising only by his urgency, frantic now, cock wild and untamed, insatiable and pumping furiously. My own prick was on fire and ready to let go, but still I kept watching his face. I wanted to see him at that most vulnerable moment; I wanted something of his besides another pint of cream, a grimace or groan or squeal, a man instead of an animal.

When Fall finally came it was another gusher, as if he hadn't gotten off in weeks, but still he didn't react up top. I'd never seen a dick so disconnected, all that fury trapped inside his meat as if it had a life of its own. My own cream spurted in reply, arcing up onto my shirt in answer to his own long climax. Never before had so much juice sprayed out of my cock, but even after I was empty my balls felt heavy, ready for another go. Only then did I begin to realize the enormity of my need for Derek Fall.

As before, once he'd gotten his fuck he abandoned me. I kept my legs up long after I heard the outer door slam, its echo like a cell door closing. My flaming hole faced empty seats, but I saw instead an imaginary audience who, I decided, were entitled to a better finale. I squeezed and stroked my softening prick, come gathered at the slit; I cupped my balls and pulled at my bag; I slid a finger into my dripping pucker and played in the fresh come; I let the audience linger where Jake Cavett had been.

"Oh, Christ," Abel Groff said when I ran into him that night at a club we both frequented. "He's fucking you, isn't he."

I nodded.

Abel sighed, shook his head, then reconsidered. "Maybe it's not a bad idea. Maybe…tell me, has he used any of Jake's lines?"

"No," I lied.

"But you're his Brian."

Was I? Brian was ineffectual, weak, so incredibly needy. Anyone could fuck Brian. "I don't think so," I told Abel. "It feels very…me."

Abel eyed me. "You're a good little pussy," he mused, "and maybe for the good of the play, if Jake is fucking Brian, then we've got a bit of reality, don't we? What more could a director ask?"

Abel refused to fuck me that night, even when I presented myself to him in the men's room at 2 A.M. He was at the urinal, dick in hand, and I went limp when he turned me down. "For the good of the play," he said, adding quickly, "I know, I know, it's unheard of,

Abel Groff begging off, but I want it pure, don't you see? Jake and Brian and nothing else. You've got his come up your ass and that's purity." He zipped up and patted my shoulder. "Go home," he said softly. "Let Brian sleep."

It was an awful night, passed in dreams as frustrating for their lack of clarity as for their paltry payoff. At one point I lay in the dark clutching my dick, trying to figure out if it had been Brian or me, deciding finally it didn't make any difference.

Fall and I had a culmination scene late in the second act that was to be the focus of the following morning's rehearsal. So far we'd skated through it; Abel concentrating on earlier bits, leading us up to it much as Jake led Brian. It wasn't the play's climax, however—sex in that context would have been cliché even for Abel Groff. No, the climax was Jake's suicide just before the curtain fell.

Now Fall and I were alone onstage. The rest of the cast had been called for afternoon, and we had just a few crew members. The old Lindsay had never seemed more cavernous. Even though it was just a rehearsal, I'd dabbed makeup over dark circles that shadowed my eyes. My entrance was calculated and determined; I wasn't Brian, and I wanted them to know it. I was Carl, and it was all an act.

Partway through Abel's instruction, I tuned him out because he didn't matter anymore. Derek Fall—Jake Cavett?—was in charge, and he and I knew it, possibly even Abel knew it, although no director is ever going to admit a loss of control. My dick began to fill in anticipation of Fall's body against mine, and I glanced down to see the all-too-familiar bulge at his crotch.

The scene was Jake's ultimate acquiescence to Brian's advances, which had for most of the play been limited to mutual hand jobs and cock sucking—all shadowed, all simulated. Now Brian was to be granted his wish. Jake would, with all his rage pooled inside his balls, fuck him full-on. This required the usual bit of nudity, and Abel reminded us yet again what we didn't need to hear but what he obviously enjoyed saying: "Remember, you can get it out, you just can't put it in."

Part of Abel's success had been controversy over the "getting it out" that was such an integral part of his plays. Audiences could always count on at least one or two cocks making an appearance, and this had brought attempts to shut down every one of his productions, but San Francisco's liberal majority had prevailed, and exposed cocks had been allowed to stay. The new play, however, went a step further, and word was already out that an erection would be visible in the second act. Talk was heavy; Derek Fall's prick was going to be famous.

Abel insisted we take it all the way during rehearsal, which meant Fall had to produce a stiff prick. All I had to do was bare my ass, but the foreplay, that long arduous scene in which Brian pleads for his sexual life, was so emotionally demanding that by the time Cavett presented his cock I was as battered as Brian.

The entire second act took place in Jake Cavett's bedroom, much of it his raging soliloquy on love and loss. Bottle and glass stood empty on the dresser, bedclothes were tangled, and Jake had retreated to an overstuffed chair and opened his jeans. He had a hand down inside, working his cock, eyes closed as if this was the only solace. At this point I made my entrance.

It didn't matter that Fall had fucked me. I was Brian now, and Jake Cavett was going to do it because we were onstage and had an audience, however limited. There was something extra in slipping inside someone else for a sexual act, in playing a part, but this time I knew it was different, and as much as I tried to be Brian, to assume his need instead of my own, I played the scene for myself. When it was time for Jake to push Brian over the arm of a chair and enter him, to present the much anticipated and highly visible erection for all to see and for me to receive, I felt myself open to him, asshole begging even as he slid his rigid prick between my legs in a masterful simulation.

The fuck was real, never mind theater. As we writhed for Abel and the few others present, I squeezed my thighs together and took him, massive dick working me with a steady thrust. His meat skated my balls as it plowed blindly forward, and I wanted more than anything to grab my dick and jerk off but, of course, that wasn't in the script. I had to take him without any visible response other than gratitude, and take him I did, thighs slippery with his precome, asshole pulsing with the mere proximity of that swollen sausage.

Jake cries out "Pussy boy" as he gives it to Brian. He has succumbed at last to love and its attendant pain; he rails against it all, professes love and hate as one, swears, then comes. The audience could not see his cream spurting between my legs, or my own seconds later. I had not touched myself. Derek Fall's heat and the raw pleasure of his skin against mine had been enough to send me over.

Cavett's disintegration begins at this point. His dick is still up Brian's ass when he starts to come apart and lashes out in his own brand of cruel self-preservation, closing with, "You're just a fuck, Brian. A good one, but that's all you'll ever be."

"Wonderful!" Abel Groff shouted. "Let's stop there."

Fall's dick was softening, and I let it slide from between my legs. My heart was pounding, and I heard an awful rush in my ears. I managed to pull up my jeans and gather enough strength to face our director, but when Abel saw me, he knew I was in trouble. "Let's take a break, shall we?" he said. "Ten minutes."

We both watched Fall hurry away, then Abel put his hand on my shoulder. "It's fabulous, you know. The energy between you is absolutely electric; it plays all the way to the balcony. Opening night, there won't be a limp dick in the house. The theater will reek of come."

"Abel…"

"I know, but it's what we want, Carl. Anguish, pain, passion, two men unable to connect except with cock and ass."

"It's exhausting," I said.

"I would imagine. We'll work on the dialogue next." He looked into my eyes. "And remember who you are. He's rejecting Brian, not Carl."

We picked up exactly where we'd left off: Brian enduring Jake's wrath because he'd stirred him above the belt as well as below. It was devastating for Brian, and the scene ended in shouts, broken glass, and slammed doors. We ran through it so many times, I began to lose myself, and Abel called it a day when I finally broke into tears.

Derek Fall didn't fuck me again until opening night. As the play was finely tuned I gradually came unglued, managing to keep Brian alive while Carl went under. I continually sought out fresh cock but found myself accepting only James Dean types, surly blonds who invariably disappointed, never mind how big a sausage they crammed up my ass or how beautiful the owner. I finally had to admit I was hopeless about Fall and, worse, that it was probably a one-way street.

The dressing room was frantic opening night—too many well-wishers and hangers-on. Fall had kept his distance but managed to stand half naked long enough to catch me looking at his prick. Once he'd accomplished that, he gave it a long artful stroke, put on his costume—torn jeans and T-shirt—and left.

It was a packed house, and where I usually enjoyed exhilaration I now felt anxiety. My hands shook, I snapped at assistants, and I pushed one fellow actor so far, he stormed out after a single departing comment: "Get fucked, Brian."

I was alone in the dressing room when Abel came in. Seeing my distress, he said, "You'll do fine. Let Brian have his night, OK?" He kissed my cheek and left, not waiting for comment.

"Five minutes," someone called outside the door.

When I walked onstage I had no idea who I was. Brian and Carl had finally become one, and I felt hundreds of eyes watching this hybrid creature who played the part for real, who said the lines and hit the marks and lived the agony Abel Groff had scripted. By the end of act one I had nothing left. I ran outside and stood in the alley, taking deep breaths, trying to regain some bit of balance for what lay ahead. I halfway wanted Abel to come out and console me, but he didn't. I think he knew we were beyond that.

When act 2 began, I watched Jake Cavett's raging soliloquy from the wings, fighting what I knew was fast becoming a truth. Tears were in my eyes when I made my entrance.

Brian's move toward Jake was calculated, almost coy, but as his failure became apparent, as Jake sat unblinking, hand inside his jeans, Brian grew desperate and began to plead, offering unconditional love in addition to his body. When Fall stood and pushed me toward the chair, I dropped my pants, baring the ass I so wanted him to have.

He came up behind me, erection brushing my crack, and then instead of sliding between my legs he pushed into my asshole in one long, glorious stroke.

I didn't care there was an audience. I wriggled back onto his cock and clenched my muscle because I wanted him to know I was there, Carl not Brian, and he responded with a full-on fuck, one I'm sure Abel thought the ultimate mastery of sexual simulation. And never mind Fall had gone in before. This was a whole new game, and as I felt that long prick shoving in and out of my channel, I hoped desperately that what had happened to me was happening to Fall as well, that Jake had been pushed aside and now, onstage, before hundreds of eager faces—and who knows how many stiff pricks—he might at last be himself.

Thanks to creative lighting and carefully planned angles, the audience could not see what has happening to me. Confident they were watching a simulation, they enjoyed an innocent thrill while I received the prick of a lifetime. Their presence made the entire act so incredibly public that my swollen cock began to throb and I unloaded into the chair while Jake raged behind me, driving his dick into me with renewed fury. I took it all, letting his angry words flow past as that snake of his plowed my channel, and when he came I squeezed for all I was worth, sucking dick with my ass to quench an unbearable thirst.

The rest of the scene—Jake's retreat, denial, shouts, the hurled bottle—was just that, a scene. I let Brian endure it and at the appointed moment made my exit. Standing in the wings, I had only a minute's respite before the finale began, Jake's suicide. I forced myself to watch him down the pills and liquor; I felt an awful dread even as his come dripped from my ass.

The lights dimmed as Jake fell to the bed, then everything went dark, and when they slowly came back up to an eerie shadow, they found me onstage. I felt for a pulse and let out a cry; I had no trouble with the requisite tears.

Jake Cavett was on his side, curled slightly, eyes closed. I climbed in beside him and took him into my arms, kissed his cheek, and placed my hand over his crotch to knead the lifeless prick. Not a single sound, barely my own breathing, then a slow fade to darkness. When the curtain fell, it took the audience a moment to react. Stunned silence, then applause.

I was grateful Fall didn't leap from my arms. He lay still and let me prod his dick until others rushed onstage to pull us up, hug us, congratulate us. I didn't want to let go but rose to take my bows with the rest of the cast, then just the two of us side-by-side, and finally Fall alone to thunderous applause. From the wings I joined in.

Abel had arranged a party at a friend's penthouse, and after an hour of backstage crowds and champagne I was finally alone. Before leaving, Abel made me promise I'd be along soon. "You're sure you're all right?"

"Fine," I told him. When he raised a brow I added, "OK, not so fine, but I survived."

"You were wonderful, Carl." He patted my shoulder and left.

I needed to change but managed only to take off my makeup. Time was what I wanted now, room to absorb what had happened, to sort out performance from…performance. I wandered out onstage in a confused sort of elation, reminding myself the man had fucked me in front of 500 people. I flopped onto the bed and burrowed into the covers. Fall's scent was there, and I closed my eyes and inhaled deeply.

"Carl."

He'd crept in like a cat and stood leaning against the headboard, beautiful in the half-light. I rolled onto my back and opened my arms. When he slid on top of me, I felt no bulge at his crotch and none of that awful tension he usually carried. He seemed to have uncoiled, as if the play had solved him, and yet I still wasn't sure just who I had here.

There was no urgency now. Fall simply hung on for a few minutes, burying his face in my neck while I ran my hands up under his shirt and kneaded his back. He was lean and smooth, taut as an animal, and I explored every inch, gradually working down into his jeans. I squeezed his ass and he groaned softly, then pulled back and began to strip. I lay paralyzed at the sight of him, skin tawny-gold, cock quiet, flaccid yet still so formidable, something that belonged on a lion, not a man. His chest was hairless, well-defined, nipples ripe; his stomach had a stripe of hair that splayed out into a golden bush engulfing the cock I coveted. Just looking at the whole of him sent me into a frenzy, and I reached out and took his sizable prick into my mouth.

He eased back onto the bed and lay beside me as I swallowed all I could of him, tongue inching down his shaft, squeezing and sucking until he began to fill. As he stiffened I licked him to the root, then pulled back and fixed on his knob until I could feel him oozing juice, and I raised up off him to finger his dripping slit and stroke this magnificent meat. And I realized only then what he was giving me, that this was the first time he hadn't arrived fully primed.

When he began to pull at my crotch, I stopped working his cock long enough to shed my clothes, then slid back down to him but in reverse, my dick in his face, his in mine. We took each other then and lay sucking pricks onstage, bare as newborns and playing to that imaginary audience.

I wanted it to last forever, my hand cradling his heavy balls as I sucked his fat knob and licked that long, sweet shaft. Everything was in slow motion now, the feast of a lifetime, and as much as I wanted to shoot my wad I wanted more to keep eating, to suck my way to infinity or die trying.

Fall's prick finally began to grow hot inside my mouth, jamming into my throat with a thrust that told me an eruption was imminent. My own load was churning as well, and I began to push into him, to fuck that beautiful mouth I had never so much as kissed. Fall was moaning and slurping, lapping at me as I jammed into him while I took his massive meat deep inside my throat, sucking it until it began to squirt. Seconds later my own explosion hit, and we lay feeding off each other, hands squeezing ass as we swallowed gobs of cream in the ultimate exchange.

Even after we were spent, we didn't let go. I buried my face in his balls, inhaling his musky scent while he ran his fingers through my dark bush. He was so incredibly gentle, I had to remind myself it really was Derek Fall's dick in my face. And then he slid a finger into my crack and further, into my pucker, probing lightly, as if he hadn't been there before, then pulling out to gather spit and sliding back in. I knew then, as he finger-fucked me, that we would go on to Abel's party and later, behind a locked bathroom door or on a remote terrace corner, he would fuck me. Derek Fall would fuck me.

All Big and Shit
R.J. March

Iwanted to fuck his brains out, I wanted to fuck him blind, but I was worried about the Canadians. I am always worrying about the Canadians. Who doesn't around here? This is fucking Buffalo, dude.

I gave Jeff a lift because he said he'd be late if I didn't, and I didn't want him to be late for his first day on the job. He'd just gotten hooked up at Shoes R Us. I've had a job for a while at U R Cool. We sold T-shirts with Farrah Fawcett pictures on them, and Skechers, and Fubu jeans. It was a good place to work because you got a 40% discount and there wasn't anything to do but fold the Farrah Fawcett T-shirts and ask people if they wanted to buy "some socks to go with that outfit" or a "really cool hemp necklace."

Jeff looked like the guy in Third Eye Blind. I think it's that guy, the one that sings. Or maybe it's the Better Than Ezra guy. I can't remember. I only know that I saw Jeff in his boxers once and sprouted myself some mighty wood and had to cover it with my dad's golf-club towel, which seemed kind of appropriate at the time.

So, I like guys, but I don't like to talk about it, you know? I don't go around saying I'm gay or anything, because I'm really not too sure about that right now anyway, and my mom thinks I should make sure before I march in any gay pride parade. I think she's offering some good advice, but there's something about Jeff that would make me march down the middle of my hometown in my mom's bra and panties if I knew I was marching toward Jeff with his Abercrombie boxers around his ankles, ass flying high like any proud rainbow fucking flag, ready for some major plowing.

I've got a fattie, a cock like a third fucking arm, which would make a great name for a band, I'm thinking. Once me and this guy, Bryan—said he was the district manager of one of our biggest competitors—We Be Phat, we were fucking around in the store after hours. He'd been on my shit all day, telling me he was going to get me my own store and shit, and he liked the way my hair looked because I had the tips bleached, and wanting to know how much I benched—like 210 at the time, by the way, and practically 250 now. He hung out after 9 because he said he wanted to compare our closing procedures to the ones at his stores, and I was like whatever, you know? The lights went out and he had me back in the office, his hands all over me. "You look so tense," he said, massaging my pecs, dropping down to my crotch, where I'd sprung a leak, if you know what I mean, and I'm saying, "Tense? You don't know tense." And he starts undoing my jeans and digging around in my boxers, getting my man in two hands and bringing it out into the open.

"At last" was all he said.

Jeff played with the radio and then he played with the end of his shirt. He had to wear this completely gay shirt that said YO! SHOES R US! which I thought was totally offensive but there's marketing for you, and I was thinking of majoring in that next semester at Buff. U., and then I could get a job—uh, nowhere, you know what I mean? He looked better in a wife-beater, because then you could see his Superman tat and the hand-sampled heart he'd drawn himself in sixth grade, long before I'd ever met him. He dug at himself, getting a good handful of his crotch and squeezing it hard, grinding the heel of his hand into himself, making even me wince and thinking he might have had crabs or something—scabies—whatever. I watched the road because my car wasn't exactly insured, but whatever he was doing or trying to kill down there got my attention. I got a bone myself that stuck up against the steering wheel and made my driving skills strictly retarded. *Shouldn't have worn the warm-ups without some protection* was what I was thinking, looking forward to the next turn I was going to make, my dick head wedged nicely.

Jeff said, "Dude, I am so not into this. Wouldn't it be cool if you could just keep on going? Why don't we drive to California—I hear everyone is cooler out there."

"Who told you that?" I asked.

"Some dude from L.A."

That district manager was from California. I liked thinking about him. I hadn't done anything since him and was feeling kind of backed up, which is why I nearly got off on the steering wheel, seeing Jeff scratch himself. I liked thinking about Bryan and Jeff together, what they might do. I liked thinking about Jeff bending himself over for this guy who wasn't much older than us and letting him fuck him. I was thinking that Jeff could, like, lean over a chair or something and completely open his ass for this guy, who was hot, really, a fucking sketchy hottie, all tall and black-haired like some Homme Vogue—French for *Hottie*—model, his hair always getting into his eyes and his buzzed little goatee itching all the time, making him look thoughtful yet completely fuckable, which he was.

When he opened my jeans and pulled out my pole, he looked a little pale, a little beyond happy. He held me with both hands and said, staring at my cock's single eye, "At last." Considering the dime-size opening of my piss slot, I was about to consider this guy a bit gone. I never knew anyone to praise the beast so highly. It was a daunting piece—so said my history professor—a dick to fear, according to some of the other guys. It was an ass-stretcher, a mouth-wrecker. I'd come to think of hand jobs as the only way I would ever get off, hadn't met a girl or guy willing to actually insert it. I've heard it all when it comes to my dick, but never "At last."

The next thing he said was: "We need some lube," his voice strangled. He flicked my dick head with his finger and I nearly came— lube? I was finally going to get some. I watched him undress, undoing his Gucci belt for him, unknotting his Hermes tie. He was too cool for this shithole store, but that didn't make much difference to me. He let his pants drop, and I eyeballed his hairy thighs and wanted to feel them against mine, and I stepped toward him.

Jeff said, "I need some Gatorade—I think I'm dehydrated." I stopped at 7-Eleven and stared at his ass as he walked into the store.

That was one thing I hadn't ever seen, his bare butt, but it was something I was very interested in, like it was a hobby, something of a pursuit. In jeans it was a sweet bubble. Naked—who knew? Smooth cheeks? Fuzz-covered? It was a crapshoot, this second-guessing, but crap I wouldn't mind shooting, if you know what I mean.

"Get me something not—you know," I yelled out through the window.

"Canadian?" he called back.

Exactly, I thought.

The DM didn't really have hair that got into his eyes or a little goatee, and he'd have never made the pages of any fashion mag. He was actually kind of balding and a little on the fat side. And his clothes were all from, like, the Polo outlet. It didn't matter to me, though, because he was married and had two kids and used to play football in college. All of that was like some sort of aphrodisiac for me. I was the one that pawed him from the start, letting him know from minute one that he could do whatever he wanted to me, that I was his for the taking. He was crazy about my cock, though, cock-crazy like you wouldn't believe, throwing himself on it, first his mouth and then his ass. He was fired up and wanted to be tore up—wasn't like the old lady was going to notice or anything, he said to me. He took off his tasseled Cole Haans. "Do me a favor," he said, holding out a shoe for me. "Smell this and tell me what you think."

I took the shoe and took a big whiff. My cock dripped like a honeycomb. "I think you fucking stink," I said, and he said "Damn straight," smiling hard and punching my arm.

He started sucking my knob. It's a big old red thing, like a tomato hanging from a fucking thick-ass vine. He made some gurgling noises, some choking noises, some more gurgling noises. I saw him whip his own out: a nice-looking piece of meat, very pink, very straight, very long, rising up out of a thick patch of reddish hair. He swung it around like a bullwhip, and it sprayed out a golden thread of leakage that marked up his Ralph Lauren chinos. He got his mouth close to my halfway mark, a bulge in a vein that pretty much marked the 4.5 inches of dick, with that much to go to get to the base. He handled my nads hard, like a man, and I stayed quiet, enjoying the soft slip of his tongue, the firm grip of his lips. He tugged on my prick for a while, banging his nose into my bush, his fingers moving up toward my butt hole.

The one time I saw Jeff in his boxers, in his room at his parents' house before he got kicked out for selling acid to his cousins, I was drawn to the swinging bob of his cock as he walked across the room, fresh from a shower and in pursuit of something to put on, probably to cover that swinging bob, that juicy hang. He had a nice body, his stomach all boxed up with muscle, his tits not big like mine, but there, enough to want to put your mouth on them. He wasn't into bulk, wasn't bulky himself, no interest in fat hard tits or big wagging quads, but boasting some sweet ass cheeks and knuckle-biting thighs—sweet things, those thighs, fucking sweet.

We were listening to Ben Folds, getting ready to go see *Armageddon.* I had a secret bone for Ben Affleck because I figured he had a secret bone for Matt Damon but forgot about it, seeing Jeff in his shorts. He put his hands inside them as if I wasn't there. "Dude," he said, running his hands through his perfect fucking hair, "What am I going to wear?"

He came back to the car with a bottle of water for me and a can of Canada Dry—his idea of a joke. "Don't even," I said, not letting him into the car with the ginger ale. "Just get it the fuck out of here." He took it to a garbage can, holding it like a grenade or a turd.

"Dude," he said. "You are totally fixated on this Canadian thing. What is up with that?" He looked at me like I was fucking Winona Ryder, and I felt like a complete asshole, but what was I going to say? How could I explain myself?

"Fuck, man," I said, putting my face in my hands, feeling like Johnny Depp for a minute. "I don't even fucking know," which was about as close to the truth as I cared to go.

He had such sweet-colored hair, kind of blond, kind of not. Like how I wanted my own hair to look but couldn't, not really, anyway. I wanted to touch his hair, to put my nose into it, to smell him and lick his scalp and his neck and all the rest of him. All the fucking rest of him. He was narrow but thick, a guy with meat on his bones. He knew that Post Office was a game his parents used to play, an excuse to make out. He said to me once, "Dude, you ever hear of Post Office?" I shook my head, and he said, "It's like this excuse to make out. You go to the post office to get your letter, and the post office is like someone's bedroom, and the letter is SWAKed, man, sealed with a kiss? You never heard of that?"

"Never ever," I said, but I would have like to have. I would have liked to play Post Office with Jeff.

One of the things about Jeff that bothered me was that he had no idea about my cock, none that I knew of, anyway. Like I said, not everyone said "At last" like my dick was a fire hydrant in the middle of a desert.

But all Jeff could say about it at this point was "What about it?" because he hadn't seen it. Now, Bryan, he's still talking about it, catching me online, calling me up every once in a while for some pretty hot phone. I can still see his squirming, hairy ass, blond fuzzy cheeks, grinding and chewing, eating up my fat cock slowly, taking the whole thing slowly the way a boa swallows up an armadillo. I was thinking then that he was going to take all of me into him that way. I leaned back in the chair I was sitting on, this dilapidated office chair from like the 40s or something, and watched his ass drop lower and lower, and more of me disappeared, ready to be sucked up into his ass like some sort of reverse baby. He had his shirt off by then, and I was playing with the hairs on his back, which I always thought would gross me out but found a little more than kind of sexy, like I was thinking, *This is a guy, man, a fucking guy.*

"I feel like I'm trying to fit someone's knee up my ass," he said over his shoulder, and I saw beads of sweat on his forehead and across his scalp, clinging to the sparse little hairs there like dew. "You are fucking big, babe," he said, and later, when I was fucking him, the two of us standing and him holding on to a wall because I was whaling on his ass, he kept calling me Big Man, Big Man, like, "Come on, Big Man, fuck my ass, yeah, fuck it, Big Man."

"Tell me about your wife," I said, my voice all hoarse and shit, and he started telling me about her tits and how often he fucked her and how she gave the best head, and I started getting dizzy and my cock felt dizzy too, and I grabbed his titties, these huge fucking red nips— fucking *cherries,* dude—and I started slamming him, and he said, "Give it to me, Big Man, give it to me." And I did.

He let me squirt off into him, his big shoulders heaving under me, and when I was done, shaking like a weasel, laying all sweaty across his big back, he shook me off and uncorked himself—the noise we made was fucking gross, I'll tell you—and told me to get down on my knees. I opened my mouth, ready for him, and he blasted my face. It wasn't excessive, though—just enough to get me off again, hosing his ankles with a meager yet admirable amount of what I call the reserves.

We were outside of the mall, and Jeff's shift started in like 20 min- utes. He said to me, turning in his seat, bringing one leg up and put- ting his chin on his knee, "This is so fucking stupid."

I asked what, and he said, "Everything, man, everything."

I was wondering if he was scared because he sounded kind of scared. He looked out at the parking lot. Security drove by, making me feel safe. It was some fucked-up-looking dude who looked like he was looking for his Siamese twin, and I started thinking about win- ter, because what the fuck did this guy do in the snow without his Siamese twin? Jeff leaned back in his seat, throwing his head back. He made a noise that sounded like AHHH.

"What's up?" I said, because he was scaring me and I didn't feel safe anymore.

"I can't say," he said, looking at me with these eyes that, like, ripped my heart out, they looked so sad and wet. I wanted to reach out and grab him and hold him and I wanted to tongue-kiss him until we both died and the dichotomy was so strong that I just sat there like a fucking mushroom.

"Who killed Kenny this time?" I asked.

"Not funny," he answered.

I decided to be bold for a change. I put my hand on the back of the seat in the general vicinity of his shoulder, close enough to be *around* him, and I asked him, all sincere and shit, "Dude, are you all right?"

He played with the scuffed hem of his stovepipes and whispered something I couldn't hear.

"What was that?" I asked.

"Never mind," he said quietly again, but this time I heard him. He licked the knee of his pants. I felt my thighs through my warm-ups, loving the feel of the nylon, thinking about running into the sporting goods store for another pair, these pants were so sexy. My dick rested against my belly, hot and fucking engorged, which was a pretty decent description as far as I was concerned.

"Will you pick me up after work?" he asked me, and I said, "Sure, no problem." And he got out of my car, not really closing the door. He looked like a kid going to the principal's office. He disappeared behind a Jeep Wagoneer and was gone.

I'll tell you about this Canadian thing. When I was a kid I had this dream that the U.S. was going to be invaded by Canada, and it was so fucking real that I woke up screaming. And every winter afterward, when the lake froze up, I'd think about that dream and how easy it would be for them to just walk across the ice and take over the whole fucking country, all these Canucks telling us what to do and making us pay more for cigarettes, changing the way we talked and shit. It's stupid, but it stayed with me. And then one day my dad had this job selling fruit juices and he crossed the border and I never saw him again, and now he's like some Canadian or something. It's like they grabbed him and washed his brain so that he forgot about us, me and my mom. Once I was drinking a beer and found out it was a Labatt's and I spit it out—that's how much I hate the Canadians.

Stupid, huh?

I waited for him at 9:30. He came out the doors with all the other mall workers, looking fried. "I ate dinner at Chik-fil-A," he said, an explanation.

I headed for home, and we almost got there, but he stopped me. "I've got to piss," he said.

"We're almost there," I told him, looking at him, wondering if he really wanted me to stop.

"Dude," he said. "Don't make me wet myself."

I pulled over—what else could I do?—and he stepped off to the side of the road and started pissing. I found a song we liked on the radio and turned it up, mostly to drown out the sound of him pissing, which had given me another bone, making me feel simple and a little like Pavlov's dog, something I learned about my one semester at Buff. U. He turned around when he was finished and put himself away, and I saw everything—his fucking cock, a drip of pee, his darker-than-his-head pubes, the slow zip of his stoves, and a trail of sparks from his fly.

When he got back into the car he moved in close to me, closer than he needed to, and I was wondering what was up with that when he told me he had to talk.

"Go ahead, dude," I said, fingering the keys in the ignition, not intending to go anywhere until he said so.

"Maybe we could go to your place," he said, because he was living at home again and felt kind of wussed-out as a result.

"Sure," I said. "Whatever."

At my place he flopped down on the couch, and I ran around throwing shit here and there, trying to look like half the pig I really was. Like, anything that was food and moldy went right in the trash, and the dirty clothes went into the coat closet, and the porn magazines—not many!—were all bundled up like old newspapers and thrown behind the bedroom door. I put on Rufus Wainwright on the CD player, followed by the new Luscious Jackson, and tried to chill but couldn't. Jeff was looking at the toes of his Skechers and making me nervous, looking all Party-of-Fived out.

"What's up," I said, wanting to put my arm around him again, as if I'd actually done it before. "Do you want to lie down?"

"What?" he said, looking at me as though I'd asked to eat his liver. And he was lying down already.

"I don't know," I said. I didn't. It was Jeff, here in my living room, in some kind of emotional turmoil. I fed on it and turned it into my own. Jeff with the perfect hair, the cute body, the best ass.

"This music," he said, making a face.

"You don't like it?"

"I want to die," he said.

"I can change it," I said back. "But I don't have any Foreigner, dude."

"This guy is totally Canadian, you know."

I went pale, feeling it. I could have fainted.

"No way," I said. "Don't fuck with me."

"I swear to God," Jeff said. "I have a friend at Discs 4 U. He fucking told me."

"Not true, not true."

"And one of the girls in Hole."

"Shut up," I said. "I can't hear you anymore." I put my hands over my ears.

He wiggled his fingers, some dumb kind of sign language I didn't get, and he said something I didn't hear, so I said What? and he said, "I said I fucking love you."

"Shut the fuck up," I said.

"Whatever," he said, getting up.

"Where are you going?" I asked.

"Home, dude, I'm walking home."

"Why?"

He turned around. "I guess because you haven't asked me to stay."

It was weird because it was Jeff, but he let me undress him, and I got a hard-on that, like, oozed my pants. He didn't want any lights on, but I got him to let me at least light a candle I had from the Bath and Body Works, a gift from an ex-girlfriend. His skin was beautiful, his shoulders so pretty. I kissed them feeling kind of stupid but what the fuck, and I saw myself as a total Chester, all close and touchy, gross, the kind of friend you don't want to find yourself alone with.

"We could take a bath," Jeff said.

"Yeah," I said. "Sure."

He still had his boxers on, but I could see he had a boner too. He walked to the bathroom, and I followed him, flicking on the switch.

"No lights," he said, so I ran back for the candle that smelled like my fucking grandmother and reminded me of a girl I never wanted to see again.

I just want to jump ahead here because what I liked best about the whole thing—even though he, like, completely changed his mind the next day—was the way, when it was over and we were dripping onto sheets that smelled a little too much of me, if you know what I mean, the best fucking thing was the way that Jeff put his arms around me, holding my head to his chest, where I listened to the bass beat of his heart, the fill and empty of his lungs, and the little squeaks and gurgles your stomach makes after you eat something at Chik-fil-A.

I filled the bath, squirting in some shampoo for bubbles, and Jeff got himself out of his boxers, and I saw his hard-on for the first time. It was white and beautiful, banana-curved, a righteous sword. His balls dangled low, dark-skinned, almost red in the light of the candle. He stepped into the sudsy water and laughed. "It's fucking hot, dude," he said. "You trying to cook us?"

I still had my clothes on, all of them, although I was desperate to be naked. He squatted slowly in the foam until he could tolerate the heat. I just stood there watching him. He was like something out of a fucking movie, naked like that and beautiful the way he was always beautiful, and I felt like such a fag and I didn't even care, first of all because he said "I love you" first.

I took off my shirt, Jeff staring at me. I felt like a stripper but completely self-conscious. I ran my hand over my pecs because I couldn't help it, wanting to feel how full they felt and to touch my nipples, which always gave me a little rush anyway. "You're big and shit," Jeff said, and I said, "Yeah."

"It's cool, though," he said, playing with the candle. I played with the waistband of my warm-ups—that's all there was left. Jeff was completely engrossed with trying to burn himself and dripping hot wax into the water. I reached into my pants and tugged my woody, letting him know that I was totally hung and wicked-hard, but he was too busy making the bath bubbles disappear.

"Dude," I said, turning sideways casually, wanting him to get the full effect before I set the beast free, changing things forever between us. "Are you into this or what?" I guess I sounded kind of annoyed, because he dropped the candle into the bath. "Shit!" he said. "Fucking clocked my nuts, man."

I played with the cords that tightened my pants, thinking this was fucked-up, feeling as though my dick was going to burn through the nylon that covered it. I saw him glance at it, once, twice, the third time he started staring and his mouth went open, but he didn't say anything. It was time—I had his attention. I took off my pants, turning away from him, showing my bare ass first, giving him back. When I turned around again, the breath left him. "Dude," he said airlessly. I stepped toward him, the big stick wagging him. I knelt on the tub's edge, the heavy, sappy head dipping at his face. He looked around it at me. "Fucking amazing," he said.

"I guess," I said, shrugging. I'd seen bigger, actually, and more than once—once, up on Skyline Drive, this guy jacking off in his car, fucking whacking his dick against the steering wheel and making the horn blow, and then Donny Hays, this Indian kid I worked with at U R Cool before he got caught blowing a security guard in the public toilets.

What I had going for me was thickness and a huge fucking knob. I gripped the base and swung the hose around a little until I started pulling on my pubes, which kind of hurt. His mouth was close, and it was open, but he wasn't doing anything with it. He played with himself underwater. "Awesome dick, man," he said, sounding all sincere.

"You want me to come in?" I asked. I bobbed myself in front of him, feeling buzzed and juicy, ready for anything.

Jeff shrugged his shoulders.

"What do you feel like doing?" I said, and he shrugged again, staring at my prick.

"Lick it," I told him, dropping my voice, making it sound—I hoped—sexy. "Lick my dick, dude," I said.

I was shocked when I saw his tongue, more shocked when I felt it. It was hot like a flame, swirling into the fat piss slit, then dragging around the head. He turned his head and had my balls in his mouth and sucked them hard, making me feel queasy and real turned-on. He took his wet hands out the tub and grabbed my hips, holding them hard, and he got the head of me into his mouth, tongue dancing wild.

What the fuck, I was thinking, *what the fucking fuck!* Everything was normal one minute—as normal as things get with me—and then this shit happens. It was too much like a dream, too unreal, too good to be true. I started thinking about all those times I was laid up with an aching boner because he let his pants drop low on his ass, or reached up under his shirt to play with the feathery hairs there, or grabbed my tit and pinched the hell out of it just for the hell of it, or pissed right next to me like I wasn't there at all. And here he was now, struggling with my swollen knob, two-fisting it, giving me the chills and sweats all at once.

He rose up out of the tub all shiny and wet, suds dripping off him the way I wanted to, and he let my dick swing from his mouth. "Ever get fucked?" he wanted to know.

"Only once," I said, a painful confession and a lie too. I'd gotten rammed a few times, up on Skyline on those afternoons I had off, guys with pickups and dirty fingernails and little bent dicks wanting to pop my cherry—as if.

"Let me see it," he said, and I turned around and bent over for him. I put my hands on my cheeks and spread them for him, giving him an excellent view of my pink hole, knowing this because of the breeze he blew over it.

He licked me there—now that was a first, for real—and wiggled his tongue into the wrinkled opening, which he replaced with his finger. He grabbed my balls through my legs and started sucking on them at the same time, and I was ready to die because what else was there, man, what else?

When he slapped his own pointy pecker head against my pucker, I opened up big-time, leaning back against him and trying to get him inside me fast. I wanted all of him in me, as much as I could get, and he put his hands on my shoulders and slid in slow until I could feel his hips against my ass and his dick end somewhere in my guts. "How is it?" I wanted to know.

"You tell me," he said.

"Excellent?"

"Fucking right," he said, shoving in, his body taking over mine like I never imagined. His hands went all over my chest, squeezing my tits until they hurt and fucking me harder all the while. He roamed over my abs until he got hold of my big cock, taking it with both hands again and pulling on it, thumbing the sticky head, causing some serious leakage.

"You leak as much as I come," he said, laughing, and I banged my ass against him.

"Easy," he whispered. "Easy easy easy." But I didn't want it easy. I fucked myself on his bone, grooving on the fiery slide it made up into my asshole, digging his wild balls bucking against my own wet skin bag sticking between my legs. I reached behind me and took one of his pale nips into an easy pinch, tugging on it and making him moan. "Oh, fuck," he said, warning me, and I steadied myself, ready for whatever he was about to give up.

"Dude," he said. "I'm going to—"

"Whatever, man, whatever."

"It's cool?" he asked, missing a beat, and I helped him pick it up, sliding my butt down his shiny pole. "Fuck," he breathed, and started ripping me apart, shredding my ass with power thrusts, gripping my dick like it was what kept him alive, and I felt myself jell, ass cheeks puffing, cock cream flying out of his fists.

Like I said, he held me later on in my bed, doing it all over again—this time by hand, which was cool too—and I had my head against his chest and it was like fucking beautiful, just fucking beautiful.

And like I said, he changed his fucking mind the next day, waking up straight again and totally not into guys. We stayed friends for a while, but it was fucking strange, you know, having had his dick up my ass. It was kind of hard looking at him and not dropping a wasted load into my shorts.

I went to the lake one day and looked across it. You couldn't see Canada, and that kind of made me feel better. I knew I was going to find someone I liked as much as Jeff, it was just going to take some time. Meanwhile, the new guy at U R Cool was giving me some dirty vibes and staring at my crotch, like, every time we closed, so who knows.

About the Authors

Derek Adams is the author of a popular series of erotic novels featuring intrepid detective Miles Diamond. He has also penned over 100 short stories, which, he insists, are ongoing chapters in his autobiography. He lives near Seattle and keeps in shape by working out whenever he can find a man willing to do a few push-ups with him.

Trevor J. Callahan Jr.'s fiction has appeared in numerous magazines and anthologies. He lives and writes in southern New England.

Dale Chase started out writing for motorcycle magazines, then switched to erotica, which he says is a much better ride. His work has appeared in *Men, Freshmen, In Touch,* and *Indulge* magazines as well as in volumes 2 and 3 of the *Friction* anthologies. One of his stories has been acquired by an independent filmmaker and should reach the screen next year. Chase lives near San Francisco and is at work on a novel.

M. Christian's stories have appeared in more than 100 magazines and anthologies. He is the coeditor of *Rough Stuff: Tales of Gay Men, Sex, and Power,* and author of the recently published book *Dirty Words.* He also writes several online columns.

R.W. Clinger lives in Pittsburgh, where he works as an administrative manager and part-time private investigator. He spends his evenings and free time with his life partner and his writing. His short stories have appeared in *Blackmale, Indulge, In Touch, Locker Room Tales, Friction 2,* and *Friction 3.* His first novel, *The Last Pile of Leaves,* will be released later this year.

Wendy Fries publishes erotica with startling regularity, writes software reviews, and is working on three books of speculative fiction: *Sorcerer's Apprentice, A Brew Uncommon,* and *Wicked Game.* Wendy is still valiantly attempting to write an erotic story in which jellybeans play an important part.

Greg Herren has been writing since he could hold a pencil. Raised in a religion so repressive that it "makes a Baptist service look like a circuit party," he was finally able to free himself from the brainwashing so that he could write. His work has appeared in *Genre, Lavender, IMPACT News, Southern Voice, Houston Voice, The Washington Blade, Men, Frontiers,* the anthology *Men for All Seasons,* and also in the upcoming anthology *Rebel Yell 2.* His first novel, *Murder in the Rue Dauphine,* will be published by Alyson in the fall of 2001.

The Hitman is the author of *Hardball* and has penned over 500 short stories and articles for magazines and anthologies. He has also written episodes of the TV series *Star Trek, Voyager.*

Victor Ho resides in San Francisco with his partner, Chris Yen. They have just completed a novel and two restored houses together.

Aaron Krach is a writer and artist living in New York City. His work has appeared in a variety of publications, from *Inches* to *In Style* and just about everything in between. He is the Mediawatch columnist for *A&U* magazine, the gay sexual culture columnist for ThePosition.com, and a film critic for *Lgny* and *HX* magazines. His short films, "Eulogy," "Diary-AH," and "TSTHEN," have screened at experimental festivals in New York and Brazil.

Pierce Lloyd lives in Southern California, where he has too little time and too much fun. He began writing erotica in college because it beat studying for tests.

R.J. March is the author of *Looking for Trouble.* His work has appeared in *The James White Review, The Mississippi Review, Men,* and *Freshman* as well as numerous anthologies, included all volumes of the *Friction* series.

Roddy Martin's work has appeared in volumes 1 and 3 of *Friction, Best Gay Erotica 1998, Advocate Classifieds, Freshmen, In Touch, Indulge, Blackmale,* and in magazines for teens and children.

Alan Mills's writing has been featured in *In Touch, Indulge,* and *Blackmale* as well as numerous anthologies, including *Skinflicks, Casting Couch Confessions,* and volumes 2 and 3 of *Friction.*

Promoting sodomy everywhere he goes, **Scott D. Pomfret** is a writer and attorney in Boston. In the former capacity, he writes erotic fiction, short stories, and articles on gay issues. His work has appeared in the *Tampa Review, Fiction International, The Long Story, Indulge,* and other publications. In the latter capacity, Pomfret is a defender of gay rights and is currently cocounsel on a constitutional challenge to Massachusetts sodomy laws.

Les Richards is a pseudonym for a mystery writer who lives on the edge of a Maryland woods with his cat, Jim. His mystery novels have been published in the United States and in Europe. His short stories have won two government grants. He says his gay stories are a welcome change of pace. His erotic stories have appeared in *In Touch* and *Indulge.* His ambition: to write the great American gay mystery novel.

Lance Rush's short fiction has appeared in *Bear, Inches, Blackmale, Guys, Indulge, Hombres Latinos, Honcho, Mandate, and Torso* as well as several anthologies. He is currently finishing his first novel.

Dominic Santi is a former technical editor turned rogue whose erotic stories appear in volumes 2 and 3 of *Friction*, *Best Gay Erotica 2000*, *Best Bisexual Erotica 2000*, and dozens of other smutty anthologies and magazines. Santi recently edited (with Debra Hyde) the politically incorrect anthology *Strange Bedfellows* and (along with mjc) the electronic book "Y2Kinky: Erotica for the New Millennium."

Dave Shaw is a human-resources and adult-education professional whose fiction works have been published in various gay erotic magazines and anthologies.

Jett Simpson is a resident of San Francisco. His erotic short stories have been published in *Playguy*, *In Touch*, *Mandate*, *Advocate Men*, and *Advocate Freshmen*. The story included in this anthology was inspired by a friend from Silicon Valley whose computer plays host to a variety of 21st-century men. Jett is currently working on a new story.

After growing up in California, **Jay Starre** moved to British Columbia at the age of 20. He worked in the fitness field for some time before becoming a full-time writer. He has written for a variety of gay magazines, including *Honcho*, *Inches*, *Indulge*, *Blueboy*, *Bunkhouse*, *Bear*, and others. This year he has stories in half a dozen gay anthologies.

Bob Vickery (www.bobvickery.com) is a regular contributor to various magazines, and has two anthologies of stories: *Cock Tales* and *Skin Deep*. He also has stories in numerous other anthologies, including *Best Gay Erotica 2001*; *Best American Erotica*, *1997* and *2000*, *Friction* (volumes 1, 2, and 3), and *Queer Dharma*. A motion picture, *Love, Lust and Repetition,* based in part on his writings, is currently being made by independent filmmaker Edgar Bravo.

Sean Wolfe lives in Denver, where he works for a nonprofit organization. His work has appeared in various magazines and anthologies, including volume 3 of *Friction*.

About the Magazines

Blackmale ("Side Effect"): For subscription information, write to *Blackmale* at 13122 Saticoy St., North Hollywood, CA 91605, call (800) 637-0101.

Firsthand ("The Guy From the Circle-X"): For subscription information contact Firsthand Limited at 310 Cedar Lane, Teaneck, NJ 07666.

Freshmen ("Holding the Ladder," "Down the Hall," "All Big and Shit," "On the Dotted Line," "Plaza Del Sol," "Family Affair"): For subscription information call (800) 757-7069.

Honcho ("Assume the Position"): For subscription information contact Jiffy Fulfillment at P.O. Box 1102, Cranford, NJ 07016 or at 462 Broadway, fourth floor, New York, NY 10013.

Inches ("Wild on the River," "The 10-inch Fix"): For subscription information contact Jiffy Fulfillment at P.O. Box 1102, Cranford, NJ 07016, or at 462 Broadway, fourth floor, New York, NY 10013.

Indulge ("Hurricane Brass," "In Love and War," "The Foreman and the Grunt," "The Astonished Flesh," "Constantine's Cats"): For subscription information write to *Indulge* at 13122 Saticoy St., North Hollywood, CA 91605, or call (800) 637-0101.

In Touch ("Little Leather Boy," "Hot Prudes," "Memento," "Vietnam Siesta"): For subscription information, write to *In Touch* at 13122 Saticoy Street, North Hollywood, CA 91605 or call (800) 637-0101.

Mandate ("Scandinavian Sex Education"): For subscription information contact Jiffy Fulfillment at P.O. Box 1102, Cranford, NJ 07016, or at 462 Broadway, fourth floor, New York, NY 10013.

Men ("Immersion," "The Act," "Adam On," "Hard," Straight Up," "Roped and Steered," "Headlock"): For subscription information call (800) 757-7069.

www.trustmag.com ("Private Rico's Salute"): For subscription information contact PMB #523, P.O. Box 410990, San Francisco, CA 94141 or visit their Web site.